Praise for The Dragon's C.L.A.W.

"This book is a masterful collection of spies, intrigue, and the ever present government bureaucracy churning too slowly and at cross-purposes with both offensive weapons and efforts at peace. Yes, it is a work of fiction (especially the "science") but, as in reality, the spy hunters find spies, real and imagined: the bean counters care only about the numbers; and, the scientists either see their weapons as protecting against the "Other" or maintaining peace. Read this book to find out how it all plays out. You won't put it down until the final page."

Nancy Hollander, internationally recognized criminal defense lawyer who has represented scientists accused of spying and peaceniks accused of getting in the way.

"Dr. Yonas worked as a leading scientist for many years in a major national laboratory and in Washington and has maintained a reputation for brilliance and integrity. He now tries his hand at a spy thriller, and the results are captivating. He has mixed his deep knowledge of particle beam physics with geopolitics, and his insider experiences make many of the plot and dialogue details quite convincing. Yonas' suggestion of collaborations between Mexican drug cartels and Chinese government/industry involvement is not quite invented out of whole cloth—this plot element may stay with us for a while, both in literature and also in the newspapers."

Anthony Fainberg, research physicist, defense consultant, and author

"Gerry Yonas introduces current day science concepts in a realistic manner into his plot along with characters who are credible based on my experience working in the national laboratories. The book is fast paced and easily readable by all audiences. While this is science fiction, the science involved in the plot makes one ponder what other ideas are out there for development into either good or evil applications, like the Manhattan Project quandary in WWII over nuclear energy for weapons or electricity. I thoroughly enjoyed reading this book and highly recommend it to sci fi aficio   alike."

D   os National Laboratory
Direc

Other Books by Dr. Gerold Yonas

Death Rays and Delusions

Project Z Novels
The Dragon's C.L.A.W.
The Dragon's Brain

THE DRAGON'S BRAIN

BRAIN

A Project Z Novel

Dr. Gerold Yonas

Artemesia
Publishing

ISBN: 978-1-951122-95-9 (paperback)
ISBN: 978-1-951122-00-6 (ebook)
LCCN: 2024941356

Artemesia Publishing
9 Mockingbird Hill Rd
Tijeras, New Mexico 87059
www.apbooks.net
info@artemesiapublishing.com

PROLOGUE

ALEK SPRAY STARTED HIS EVENING by detonating a miniature nuclear weapon in a Las Vegas casino. Now things were getting worse.

Sweeping the unconscious woman into his arms, he took off running across the rooftop toward the helicopter. Her midnight-blue beaded evening gown dragged through the mounds of snow built up on the roof's surface. The wind whipped her blonde curls across Alek's eyes, competing with the blowing snow to block his vision. Despite these obstacles, he hurtled forward, carrying her through the snowstorm, 25 stories above the Las Vegas Strip.

This is a job for an action hero, not a physicist, Alek thought.

Swirling snow swept from the helicopter's rotor blades, cutting the visibility to nearly zero. Alek reached his destination, boosting the unconscious woman into the helicopter with the help of the man inside. The two exchanged a few words, shouting over the noise of the rotor blades. Then Alek spotted the red-haired woman emerging from the door of the hotel. He ran back across the slippery rooftop to grab a stack of laptops from her. Together, they made their way to the helicopter, struggling against the buffeting wind and the stinging cold.

Alek strained to see in the almost total whiteout. His heart pounded and, despite the freezing temperatures, he found himself bathed in sweat. His feet slid on the icy rooftop, and he almost lost his balance. *Get a grip; you've got to get her to a hospital*, he told himself as he clutched the laptops to his chest.

They had nearly reached the helicopter when three men burst out of the door onto the rooftop, guns drawn. As a bullet zipped past his head, Alek felt grateful for the blinding storm thwarting the shooter's efforts. He remembered how, not that long ago, he had been happy. He had found someone he loved and was ready to make a plan for the rest of his life. How quickly everything had changed.

Alek and the redhead shoved the laptops into the helicopter. Another shot whizzed past him, and the redhead turned and fired back.

"Get in here!" Alek shouted, grabbing her shoulder. "Shut the door. Come on, let's go."

As the pilot struggled to lift off in the storm, Alek remembered the words of his boss, Harold Percy, the distinguished older man who was now shouting instructions at the helicopter pilot.

Percy had told him, "Technology is a knife. A knife can butter your bread or slit your throat. Our job is just to build the knife."

The physicist shook his head at the memory as he reached out to stroke the unconscious woman's cheek. Would things have turned out differently if he had never built the knife?

PART ONE

Chapter 1
Moving Forward

DR. ALEK SPRAY GRIPPED THE steering wheel of his Ford Focus tightly as he ascended the winding road that led to the town of Los Alamos, New Mexico. He felt a rush of adrenaline as he glanced to his right at the Jemez Mountains, glowing pink from the rays of the setting sun. *The trip to Washington, D.C. was successful*, Alek thought, *but nothing beats the feeling of coming home.*

After crossing the river, the highway snaked its way up the mountain, narrowing to one lane carved into the soaring orange cliff. On the other side of the car, the ground fell away, offering a sweeping view of the Rio Grande Valley framed by the Jemez and Sangre de Cristo Mountains. The tiny car's motor strained as the elevation rose to more than 7,000 feet above sea level. *You've got this*, Alek urged the car, thinking that his loyal Ford might be reaching the end of its lifetime. "You've made it up this hill plenty of times," he murmured, pushing the gas pedal down.

Taking a risk, Alek raised his eyes from the winding road to drink in the scenery. The mountains loomed purple, silhouetted against the pink and orange streaks of sunset creeping across the deep blue sky. No matter how many times he had made this drive up the hill, it always took his breath away.

Ahead, Alek could see the series of mesas where the town of Los Alamos perched. High on a set of cliffs, isolated, and surrounded by mountains, Los Alamos represented both an ingenious and an unlikely place to house the most technologically advanced scientific laboratory in the world. Was J. Robert Oppenheimer crazy or brilliant when he chose this remote location to build the world's first atomic bomb? When Alek first moved to the town and began working at Los Alamos National Laboratory, he might have answered "crazy," but the place had grown on him.

Alek chuckled to himself as he reached the top of the mountain and rolled into the small city, past the sign that read, "Los Alamos: Where Discoveries Are Made." He certainly had made some discoveries in Los Alamos. He'd discovered he could finally move on from his divorce and could find solace in his work after the death of his daughter. Los Alamos was the place where he had made both scientific and personal breakthroughs. He had even discovered a woman who... *No*, Alek stopped himself. He couldn't think about Gabi now. He wondered if he should have called her. As far as he knew, she was still working in Albuquerque. But when his plane landed in Albuquerque, he didn't call Gabi. Instead, he went directly to the long-term parking lot, collected his car, and headed north, blasting the eighties channel on SiriusXM to chase away any "what if" thoughts.

As Alek drove into Los Alamos, he was not surprised to find the streets mostly empty. The city emptied out each night when the workday ended, and thousands of lab employees headed down the hill. Alek supposed he should consider himself fortunate to have found somewhere to live in Los Alamos. So many people he knew commuted to Santa Fe, about 45 minutes away, or even farther to the outskirts of Albuquerque. Finding a place up on the Pajarito Plateau was considered a feat. Alek's aptly named apartment complex, Arroyo Vista, which sounded exotic unless you knew it translated to "ditch view," was new by Los Alamos standards, built in the '70s. He parked the car and grabbed his suitcase, surveying the sagging building. *Home sweet home.* Actually, Alek had to admit to himself that his real home was the lab. The apartment represented a place to sleep and store his stuff—that was about it. And speaking of sleep, he'd better get some. Tomorrow would be a busy day.

* * *

The next morning, Alek strode into the lab director's

office without knocking. Fortunately, Lab Director Harold Percy was accustomed to this sort of interruption—especially from Alek. Percy had given his senior researcher the nickname "smart Alek" because of his sarcasm and penchant for "dad jokes," but Percy had come to acknowledge that Alek was legitimately smart.

Nearly single-handedly, Alek had created a public-private partnership to fund a massive alternative energy project. Even as the director of Los Alamos National Laboratory, Percy had never seen such innovation and progress. Alek, and his Project Z, were about to change the world.

"Yes?" Percy murmured, straightening a silver cufflink. Unlike many of the lab employees who chose jeans or rumpled khakis for their daily outfits, Percy paid close attention to his appearance. He felt that as the first African American director of one of the U.S. Department of Energy's national laboratories, he had an image to uphold. Percy's cufflinks and his well-polished Oxford shoes stood out in a workplace where most people dressed like they were moments away from going camping. His clothes always looked freshly pressed—never wrinkled or mussed—despite long days of political wrangling in Washington or lengthy travel between DOE sites. Even as he neared his sixties, Percy's brow remained equally unwrinkled—at least until he raised an eyebrow at Alek's unceremonious entrance. "How was D.C?" he asked.

"Salvador Gutierrez is a force of nature," Alek said. "He's already recruited several other investors from private industry, and, with his connections, I anticipate many more."

Percy nodded. "We certainly are fortunate that Gabi's old high school buddy turned out to be a tech entrepreneur with more money and influence than Elon Musk."

"Honestly, I didn't want to like the guy," Alek admitted. "It turns out he's brilliant but really down-to-earth."

"And he and Gabi used to be an item?" Percy asked. "Why'd they break up?"

Alek scoffed, making a face. "Sal and Gabi were never together. They may have gone on a couple of dates in high school, but Sal isn't interested in women."

"Ah, no wonder you aren't jealous," Percy exclaimed. "She's still available."

"Shut up," muttered Alek, looking down to cover the flush spreading up his face. "I'm focused on science, not dating. Let's talk about Project Z."

Trying not to smile, Percy leaned forward, attempting to look businesslike. He thought of Alek like a son he never had, and he wanted the best for him, but he also knew better than to try to bring up his personal life. "So, we've brought Lawrence Livermore Lab on board along with Sandia Labs and Los Alamos," Percy said. "I have a phone call with the Secretary of Energy tomorrow. Now that we've brought in the private investors, I think we'll have her full support."

Alek smiled. "It won't be long till we have the funds to start building the Project Z facility. My dream of creating an unlimited supply of clean, affordable energy will finally come true."

Alek perched on the edge of Percy's desk and the older man couldn't help but notice the lanky physicist's well-worn jeans and HOKA trail-runner sneakers. Did Alek look the part to create a national energy consortium? Of course not, thought the lab director, but Alek was the brain behind the technology that made it possible—a groundbreaking use of Low Energy Nuclear Reaction, or LENR, to generate power. That power could mean the difference between life and death in third world countries. It could end pollution and put a halt to global warming. Transformational was an understatement.

Ironically, the technology behind the LENR had been funded and developed with the goal of creating a lethal space weapon. Alek, a dedicated peacenik, had built a device that could have multiple weapons applications—heck, both the Chinese government and a Mexican drug cartel had nearly killed Alek in their efforts to obtain this technology. But Alek wasn't interested in weapons, he wanted to save the world.

"Sal's reeling in the big money, and we have cooperation from the DOE and all three national labs," Percy said. "There's one more person we need to get on board."

"Who?" asked Alek. "Sal knows everyone in big tech and he's recruiting all the top investors."

Percy stood up, fiddling with one of his cufflinks. "The Chinese government," he replied. "I think we need to work with General Wu."

* * *

In Washington, D.C.'s exclusive Cosmos Club, Sal Gutierrez, the self-made billionaire inventor and newest member of the Project Z team, was enjoying drinks with a handful of private investors. Sal felt certain that his financial backing, not to mention his marketing expertise, would pave the way for developing the innovative LENR technology. The next step would be finding a way to convert the power that the LENR generated into a commercial energy source. This would take research, political savvy and, of course, large amounts of money. Sal could leverage all three, and the people gathered around that Cosmos Club table could play a significant role in this success.

Housed in a historic mansion in Dupont Circle, the Cosmos Club had been a private social club and a Washington institution since its inception in 1878. Known as a gathering place for the intellectual glitterati of the town, the club had counted three presidents, a dozen Supreme Court justices, and 36 Nobel Prize winners among its members over the years. Dark paneled walls, antique oriental rugs, and crystal chandeliers provided the backdrop as Gutierrez wrapped up his pitch.

From the furnishings to the standard menu of prime rib and Yorkshire pudding to the aging wait staff, the Cosmos Club emanated the feel of old money: distinguished, stuffy, and sedate. But several of the men and women joining Gutierrez that evening represented a new breed. Gathered around the mahogany table enjoying their after-dinner bourbon were two leading investment bankers, the head of the U.S. Defense Advanced Research Projects Agency, a CEO from a venture capital firm, and a handful of wealthy young entrepreneurs who had achieved considerable success in tech-based inventions. From clever software applications to timesaving devices, their inventions had yielded the entrepreneurs considerable income. Now, Gutierrez's plan would make them more.

"*Mis amigos*, now is the time to make the world safe, secure, and prosperous," Gutierrez said. "Many of the problems facing the world can be solved with a single invention, the ultimate source of energy. We call our work 'Project Z.' Led by a team from Los Alamos National Laboratory, we are developing a revolutionary device that will generate clean, affordable, unlimited energy. Today, I am offering you the chance to play a part in helping fund this project and deploy this revolutionary technology across the country." The handsome 35-year-old billionaire leaned back in the plush chair and adjusted the collar of his Brunello Cucinelli suit jacket. He waited for his companions to take the bait.

Natasha Simon was the first of the prospective investors at the table to speak. Russian by birth but raised in Israel, the chemist had recently emigrated to the United States to create a high-tech start-up focused on neurofeedback technology. Simon had wiry red hair, an angular face, and a reputation for not wasting time with polite small talk.

"Cut to the chase. We're not getting any younger. How does it work?" Simon had made enemies of many male scientists and inventors because of her no-nonsense nature. Some men called her "aggressive," others called her "pushy," or even "a bitch." Gutierrez, on the other hand, appreciated Simon's blunt attitude and was looking forward to working with her.

"I'm glad you asked," he replied. "Two major breakthroughs have changed the once discredited claim of cold fusion into one of the most exciting inventions of the century. The first was a reaction trigger, invented by Dr. Sunli Hidalgo. The secret is a high current relativistic electron beam super focused onto the trigger, which causes the instant transmutation of ordinary materials into entirely different elements with a tremendous release of energy—"

Carl Herbert, the owner of IonTech, one of the country's premier manufacturers of linear accelerator technology, interrupted brusquely. "How much energy?"

Gutierrez picked up a nearly empty water glass from the table. "This amount of material could provide fuel for a multi-megawatt power plant—the same as 20 tons of coal. The device uses a Low Energy Nuclear Reaction to create an enormous amount of electrical energy from a tiny amount of fuel."

Simon smiled, exchanging a glance with the computer software developer by her side, as Gutierrez continued. "The second invention, created by Dr. Alek Spray, a physicist at Los Alamos National Laboratory, is the high gain invention that keeps the energy going. It's like a furnace as long as you keep feeding in fuel."

Menlo Scoville, the CEO at Cleveland Ventures, one of the country's most prominent investment firms, leaned forward, his curiosity growing. "So, explain to me exactly what you want to build here. What will our money help you create?"

"Excellent question," Gutierrez replied. "We want to build a prototype of a Low Energy Nuclear Reactor using an electron beam accelerator to trigger the reaction. If we can demonstrate this system's ability to generate radiated electromagnetic energy, we can then develop a method to capture that energy in a direct converter to supply the energy grid. If that works, we can miniaturize the system and deploy it safely with minimal expense."

"What about nuclear waste?" Herbert asked sharply. "There's no radioactive waste? There's no danger?"

Gutierrez shook his head. "No radioactive waste and no pollution. The only byproduct is a harmless transmutation sludge."

"Yes!" Simon shouted, leaping to her feet. "I knew it!"

"This uh... sludge excites you?" Scoville asked, raising an eyebrow.

In response, Simon began to pace back and forth beside the table, talking almost to herself. "What you are describing is nuclear transmutation, which creates byproducts—usually neodymium and praseodymium. They are rare earth metals... and rare earth metals are the key to powering the magnets used in electric motors. If you can produce clean, affordable energy and make rare earth metals in the process, you have a gold mine on your hands. Actually, a platinum mine, no, even better, a neodymium mine."

Scoville pulled his cell phone out of his pocket and googled the word "neodymium." "Neodymium is the strongest permanent magnet material yet discovered," he read aloud. "It's mostly mined in China and it's very rare."

"Yeah, that's why they call it a rare earth metal," Simon said with unconcealed sarcasm. "The price of neodymium has increased 100 percent this past year due to the demand for permanent magnets for electric vehicle batteries. This is what I call a win-win."

Gutierrez smiled. "Exactly. We will make a profit both on the Project Z devices and their byproducts." He looked around the table, locking eyes with each prospective investor. "I'm offering you the chance to get in on the ground floor on an invention that will outshine history's greatest pioneers in technology—Edison, Westinghouse, Bell... If we do this right and protect our interests, we will all be successful. If you want to go ahead and are willing to take on a sizable interest, my lawyers will come by with papers to sign."

* * *

Gabriella Stebbens hurled herself down onto the queen-sized bed in frustration. Max raised his head and gave her a baleful glance, clearly irritated that she had disturbed his sleep.

Gabi grabbed the squishy chin of her brown-and-white-spotted rescue pit bull. "Don't give me that look, Max," she said. "I'm the one who pays the rent here." The dog wagged his tail and rolled onto his back for a belly rub, clearly unconcerned about rent, or any of the other matters on Gabi's mind.

"I wish I could be half as relaxed as you," Gabi told Max, pulling her hair out of the elastic band. Released from the professional pulled-back look that she preferred for work, the long blonde curls sprung free and careless. Gabi often joked that her hair had a mind of its own and did whatever it wanted. But could she do whatever she wanted? She pulled her cell phone out of her pocket, her finger hovering over the message button. *Should I text*

Alek? Would he even want to talk to me?

On the one hand, Gabi knew she should keep her relationship with Alek strictly professional. After all, she had only met him because she had been assigned to Los Alamos National Laboratory as part of an FBI investigation of possible espionage. When two of Alek's employees stole his physics research and experiments, he'd landed in the center of the operation. So, she couldn't help but get to know him as she figured out what was going on.

As for what was going on... Who would have guessed that Chinese spies were working with funding from a Mexican drug cartel to create the ultimate weapon? Up until recently, Gabi thought that kind of thing only happened in cheesy technothrillers. The investigation had taken her from Los Alamos to Washington, D.C. to the forests of Mexico, wrapping up in an underground facility in China where she and Alek narrowly escaped being struck by a beam from a massive collective laser accelerator called the Dragon's CLAW. Fortunately, instead of hitting her or Alek, the beam pulse practically vaporized the cartel leader, El Verdugo. Both he—and a large part of the investigation—simply went poof.

Gabi sat up on the bed, grabbing a pillow and remembering that day in the subterranean laboratory. Alek had pretty much saved her life. El Verdugo had been funding the Chinese scientists' work in exchange for what he hoped would be his own personal lethal beam weapon. But the day he was killed, the two scientists who had worked for Alek at Los Alamos also vanished. Turns out the two had been working with both the Chinese and the cartel.

Where did Will and Joe Ramos go and does it even matter? No, thought Gabi, *that doesn't matter.* The only question that really mattered was whether she should call Alek.

Gabi reached for her phone and then pulled her hand back. *Maybe he's just not that into you*, she thought to herself. She sighed and planted a kiss on the sleeping dog's wet nose.

* * *

Will Ramos walked into the hidden warehouse tucked in the forest outside of Monterrey, Mexico. He couldn't believe he was back here again.

The dilapidated building had once been the Cincoleta Cartel's primary fentanyl manufacturing facility, but Will and his twin brother, Joe, had converted the warehouse to a laboratory where they worked on the LENR technology. Using the formulas and data stolen from Los Alamos, along with what they had learned working for Alek Spray, Will and Joe had made some significant breakthroughs toward developing the ultimate beam weapon. Now, they were back at the factory to work on another LENR device.

Will flipped on the lights and began straightening the scattered equipment strewn across the long workbench in the center of the large room. *Of course, there have been many setbacks,* thought Will. *Es lo que es.*

First, they had accidentally vaporized their rental house in Altavaca, New Mexico. *Some experiments just work a little too well*, Will thought with a wry chuckle. Then, they came out here to Mexico and were on the verge of perfecting the technology when they got word that the Policia Federal Ministerial, basically the Mexican version of America's FBI, was onto them. They'd had to clear out and head to China, where they'd built the large accelerator known as the Dragon's CLAW.

Everything had been going fine in Beijing until Alek Spray and his friends showed up. Once again, it was time to get going. This time back to Mexico to start over again.

Joe hadn't been much help, but that was typical. People said that Will and Joe were identical, but those people were only looking at the surface. *I've always been the smart one*, Will thought. Now that Juan Velásquez, known as El Verdugo, The Executioner, was dead, Will was having to push Joe again. His brother was content to sit back and sell their services as "technical consultants" or something equally demeaning to other cartel heads to get by, but Will knew that they (well, mostly he) could do so much more with what they knew. It was time to create new professional opportunities. He needed to follow through with the next step of his plan.

Will grabbed a broom and began sweeping the floor

of the dusty building. The dust mocked him, rising into the air and settling on new surfaces—a never ending task. There was still so much to do. While the brothers were in China, the Policia Federal Ministerial had confiscated every piece of equipment in the warehouse. Before he could execute his new plan, Will was having to rebuild the lab.

He looked around the warehouse. Velásquez was gone, but that opened the way for a successor. Soon, thought Will, soon I will have the power to step into the spot the drug lord left behind.

Chapter 2
Uneasy Alliances

HAROLD PERCY OPENED THE ENCRYPTED email from the lab's chief security officer and found it contained no surprises. General Wu and his underground Chinese military group, the Chinese People's Consortium, were continuing to collect intelligence from the lab using a tiny, short-distance information transmitter embedded in Percy's executive assistant's computer. The device appeared to be designed to transmit large amounts of coded information in only seconds, thereby avoiding detection. Following the security guidance of the lab's chief of security, Amanda Berger Aragon, Percy had left the device alone and had employed a counterterrorism approach by sending staged information; but so far there had been no indication that the Chinese were even monitoring the transmitter. *What is the retired Chinese general up to? What is he trying to accomplish? Is he up to no good or just playing with me?*

Percy wished he knew the extent of the information Wu had collected from his eyes and ears inside Los Alamos. The evidence of Chinese People's Consortium and Ministry of State Security spies was indisputable, but what were their plans? Wu didn't strike Percy as entirely loyal to his own country or even to the CPC, the clandestine group he allegedly led. In fact, Percy suspected Wu's goal was to line his pockets. Then again, most spies were opportunistic and motivated by greed.

Plus, although no one could prove it, Percy was certain that Wu had somehow been profiting from his connection to Juan Velásquez. With Velásquez dead, the retired Chinese general surely needed to find new ways to divert funds into his personal coffers—which gave Percy leverage. The lab director preferred to keep the general in plain sight. But getting Alek, Sunli, and Chang to agree to work with the Chinese would be a challenge. With that in mind, Percy invited his colleagues to the conference room to make his pitch.

True to form, Percy waited until the others had assembled around the conference room table before joining them. He stood at the door unnoticed, observing the three for a moment.

Peter Chang and Sunli Hidalgo were deep in the midst of an animated conversation. Brushing her hair away from her face, Sunli reached for a notebook and pointed to the page. Chang smiled and leaned in closer. Percy had endorsed Chang's application for American citizenship and had welcomed him to Los Alamos, but science probably wasn't the whole reason behind Chang's decision to leave China. Watching Chang and Sunli, Percy wondered if Sunli knew the power of her cool, understated elegance. As if she had heard his thoughts, the scientist crossed her legs, revealing another inch of thigh beneath the edge of her slim, charcoal gray skirt. *Yep, she knows*, Percy thought.

Then Percy turned his attention to Alek, who was sitting at the other end of the table, his head buried in a stack of papers. Oblivious to everything else going on in the room, Alek ran a hand through his brown hair and sighed in frustration. Percy cleared his throat loudly and the three scientists looked up in unison, suddenly noticing him standing in the doorway.

"Thanks for taking this meeting. I know all of you are quite busy working on Project Z, but I believe this is a matter of some importance," Percy said, taking a seat at the head of the table. "I have a proposal that will address numerous issues we are currently confronting with this project."

Percy paused for dramatic effect and then dropped the bombshell. "I want to pursue a collaborative, binational agreement with China to help fund and build Project Z."

Noting the angry expressions on Sunli and Alek's faces, the lab director held up a hand. "Now hear me out before you say anything. Joining with China on energy research could dispel the concerns many U.S. citizens still have about their government. Working together to create unlimited energy for the entire globe would be the ultimate demonstration of peace."

Chang nodded. "Despite the recent nonproliferation arms agreement, people still view China as the enemy," he said. "Bringing America's former enemy into the project would show the world that the two countries can work together to benefit mankind."

Percy smiled. "I'm glad you see it that way. And there's an added benefit—the Chinese have money to spend on the project," the lab director said. "I'm sure General Wu can help us funnel some of that funding to our lab."

"Wu?" Sunli exclaimed, rising to her feet. "Surely you don't intend for us to work with the leader of a rogue group of retired Chinese generals. You know how closely tied he is to China's Ministry of State Security? That's the Chinese government's secret police. Haven't you heard the old adage about not inviting a fox into a henhouse?" Sunli stopped to catch her breath. She shuddered. "Plus, I cannot stand that man."

Chang rose and put a hand on Sunli's shoulder. "After everything that happened, she shouldn't have to work with Wu," he said, glaring at Percy. Sunli sniffed, calming slightly, but fury lingered in her eyes.

"I don't trust the General," said Alek. "How do you know he won't betray us and simply pass our research along to the Chinese?"

Percy wondered if he should tell Alek about the transmitter found inside the lab. Not that Chinese spies were unprecedented... or unexpected. Nevertheless, Alek was somewhat of a Boy Scout: honest, truthful, and expecting the same from everyone else. Percy wasn't surprised to see Alek resisting the idea of collaborating with the Chinese general. He would need lots of reassurance before agreeing to allow Wu into his lab.

"China's leaders called on Wu to participate in key negotiations with the United States. He is already part of this. We will have more leverage and control if we can bring him into the fold." Percy stood, signaling his intention to wrap up the meeting. "Plus, with Wu on board, China will contribute more money to the project."

"Percy, Sal has recruited numerous investors," Alek said, his voice rising in anger. "Sal is bringing in a ton of money. Funding isn't an issue."

Percy smiled. "Funding is always an issue. Someday when you're a lab director, you'll understand."

* * *

Will was grateful he still had the loyalty of some of his old cartel contacts. The *lugartenientes* provided him and Joe with an old pickup truck so they could travel back and forth to the nearby city of Monterrey to purchase equipment and supplies. Their former associates also supplied updates on the chaos within the cartel that had followed Velásquez's death. Will felt reassured that he had made the right decision to leave China when they did. Learning about El Verdugo's fate cemented the need to extort funds from U.S. officials. Will wanted big money. He needed it. He deserved it.

"Here's the plan," Will told Joe. "We just call that *pendejo* Harold Percy and tell him that, unless we receive a transfer of $100 million into an offshore account, we will start setting off Dragon's CLAW weapons in the U.S."

"*Estupido*," Joe exclaimed. "We have the parts to build only one weapon. *Uno*," Joe held up one finger. "Plus, I'm not even sure that will work."

"It doesn't have to work, *sabelotodo.* I'm sure Percy will fall for our threat." Will turned away from Joe in disgust.

"I'm not being a smartass. I think you're underestimating Percy. He won't automatically give in."

"Think about it, *tu tonto*," Will replied. "Percy knows we have mastered the LENR technology. He also knows that the gadget can create an electromagnetic pulse that will destroy all the computers that control the power systems in all of the country." Will clapped his hands together gleefully. "*¿Puedes imaginártelo?* We can just threaten to shut everything down. Think about all those freezers filled with rotting food, all the water supplies cut off, and all the transportation gone. We can threaten to stop everything unless he hands over the money."

Joe shook his head. "No lo se," he murmured. "You want to blackmail the U.S. government?"

"Yes," Will exclaimed. "Percy will waste no time calling in the higher ups in Washington. U.S. leaders tend to do whatever they can to prevent terrorism, and $100 million is a small price to pay to protect American lives. We can even text Percy a photo of the device to drive home the danger. The scarier and more possible the attack seems, the sooner we can get our hands on the government pay off."

Brimming with confidence, Will picked up the phone to explain the situation to Percy, grateful that he had the foresight to save Percy's direct cell and office phone numbers, so he didn't have to fight his way through the battalion of secretaries guarding the boss.

Percy's initial response was cool. "My long-lost scientist, how lovely to hear from you," the lab director said with unconcealed sarcasm. As Will presented his demands, Percy's voice turned from bemused to disdainful. Instead of quivering in fear and agreeing to Will's demands, the lab director laughed coldly. "You and Joe don't have the technology, the ability, or the *cojones* to detonate a low energy nuclear device," Percy scoffed.

"You know we do," Will spluttered. "Don't force me to make a decision that America will regret."

"Regret... that's something I bet you and Joe know a lot about," Percy replied calmly. "Do you regret squandering the education and opportunities you once had? Do you regret collaborating with criminals who viewed you merely as collateral? Do you regret making this call?"

Percy's voice was steely. "Drop this now and I'll refrain from contacting the authorities. We'll just consider this a little joke... because that's what you are, Will Ramos. A joke." With that, Percy hung up the phone.

Joe watched his brother on the phone, his expression changing from hopeful to beaten. Then, suddenly, Will threw the phone to the ground and slammed his fist into a nearby workbench, splintering the wooden top and leaving his hand bloody. He winced, trying not to acknowledge the pain.

"Will?" Joe said tentatively. "*¿Hermano?*"

Will stormed out of the warehouse with Joe following. How could Percy doubt them? Didn't the lab director realize he was dealing with ruthless terrorists who had access to unprecedented weapons technology? Why would Percy disrespect their conviction and skills?

Percy can't treat me like this, Will fumed. *I have a compact LENR device and the technology to trigger it. I'll show Percy we mean business. All I have to do is get the American's attention. Then Percy will pay.*

"Uh, Will," Joe said tentatively, "I have an idea that maybe could help convince Percy."

"What is it, Joe? I'm kinda busy right now trying to figure things out."

"So, you want to scare Percy, right? To convince him we have dangerous technology, and he needs to do what we say."

"Yes, Joe," Will sneered. "I'm glad you were listening."

Ignoring his brother's sarcasm, Joe plunged ahead. "So, I have an idea. Most of the nuclear power stations are still vulnerable to a short range EMP attack since their cooling water control and transmission systems are located outside. An attack on a nuclear power station would disrupt the operation and cause panic because everybody thinks about a meltdown and then all hell would break loose."

"So?" asked Will.

"So, let's set off the device at a nuclear reactor. Show Percy and everyone else in the world what we can do."

* * *

Brushing a speck of lint from his dark green dress uniform that he wore despite his retirement, General Liu Wu stood to greet Harold Percy. Known both for his short temper and his vanity, the nearly 70-year-old former Chinese general frequently wore his military uniform with its gold striped cuff insignia. Percy had never understood the reasoning behind the uniform. Perhaps Wu felt the shoulder epaulets for rank and multiple service decorations reinforced his position as the leader of the Chinese People's Consortium. Maybe he wanted everyone to know that, despite his alleged retirement, he was still the leader of the CPC.

Percy held out a hand to greet the general. Ignoring the gesture, Wu sat down, signaling to the waitress across the room.

Wu had not appeared surprised when Percy called with an invitation to talk, which confirmed the lab director's suspicions that Chinese spies were deeply embedded in Los Alamos. Information leaks remained alive and well. For decades, the Chinese Ministry of State Security—China's intelligence, security, and secret police agency—had hidden operatives embedded at Los Alamos. Everyone at the lab was aware of this. No matter how hard Percy and the lab security staff worked to protect vital classified information, espionage continued. Spies had targeted Los Alamos since the Manhattan Project. Some things never change.

The general suggested that they meet in Las Vegas to talk. Percy knew that General Wu hadn't meant Las Vegas, New Mexico, the small city on the eastern edge of the Sangre de Cristo Mountains about 100 miles from Los Alamos, but the "real" Las Vegas in Nevada. Wu apparently owned a small casino just off the strip, called the Lucky Dragon Hotel and Casino.

Now Percy sat across from the one-time general in the casino's Shanghai Lounge, a dark room with stereotypical Chinese decor. He admired the beauty of the Asian waitress who brought him his Tsingtao, a popular brand of Chinese beer. Wu had ordered Baijiu, a distilled grain sorghum alcohol as popular in China as vodka was in Russia. Gulping the drink down, he ordered the waitress to bring him another and keep them coming.

"I'm assuming that you are here to tell me about Project Z," General Wu said as he downed another glass of the Baijiu the moment the waitress set it down.

Percy quickly got to the point and explained Project Z. It took him 10 minutes, during which time Wu actually ignored the next glass of Baijiu delivered. As the lab director had hoped, Wu was intrigued.

"And Dr. Spray is the head of Project Z?" Wu asked.

"Yes. He's putting together a team to develop the technology. We even have a guy you may know, who came from China's Advanced Energy Lab, on the research team," Percy said. "A simulations physicist named Peter Chang. He recently moved to New Mexico with his girlfriend, and we recruited him for the project."

Wu coughed and looked distressed, but quickly regained his composure. "Peter Chang... yes, he worked for us. Left rather abruptly if I recall. Do you happen to know his... ummm... his... girlfriend?"

"Oh yes, I forgot that you might know her. Dr. Sunli Hidalgo worked with us before she went to China to care for an ailing family member. Her father or mother or grandmother... someone was sick. Anyhow, she decided to bring this sick relative to the states, and Chang chose to come with her." Percy noticed that Wu had turned pale and was shaking his head slightly.

"Are you okay?" Percy asked. Wu looked confused so Percy continued with his explanation.

"You'd remember Dr. Hidalgo if you saw her. She's a small woman with black hair—attractive. She's kind of cold though, not at all friendly, but a brilliant scientist."

Wu took a swallow of his Baijiu and nodded with recognition. "Yes, I think I remember her. I believe she also did some work at China's Advanced Energy Lab. I'm glad to see two Chinese scientists are part of the Project Z team."

Despite his positive words, Wu fidgeted with his napkin, pulled his cell phone from his pocket, and scrolled through a few pages, and then finished the glass of Baijiu, prompting the hovering waitress to bring another.

Percy decided to get to the point. "I'm sure I'm not telling you anything you don't already know. Rumor has it you have people keeping tabs on our operation. Care to tell me what's going on?"

Wu smiled. "Surely, Dr. Percy, you know my eyes and ears are everywhere. I can't afford to miss any... uh... opportunities. Plus, when it comes to espionage, I'm the least of your worries. You and I, Percy, we're two of a kind."

"Exactly," replied Percy. "Let's both admit we have no secrets. I'm certain that with your encouragement,

China's leaders will make a sizable monetary contribution to Project Z."

"Perhaps," said the general. "Would you and your colleagues be interested in building this facility in China? We have several key locations and the infrastructure established for a massive underground accelerator just like the prototype machine you proposed."

"We have a location in mind here in the states," Percy said, shifting uncomfortably on the black lacquered chair.

"Oh, you do? Tell me about it."

"I'm not at liberty to discuss the location right now," replied Percy, wondering if Wu's espionage tactics had already revealed how the Project Z team was struggling to find a place.

The Chinese general stood. "Percy, I believe you have the technology and the ability to build this prototype, but without the right location, it's no better than a scientist's wet dream." Picking another imaginary piece of lint off his uniform, Wu extended his hand. "I will consider discussing this opportunity with my colleagues in China. Call me when you find a place to build Project Z."

* * *

Alek slipped into the corner booth of his favorite Los Alamos diner, the Friggin Bar. The nondescript establishment, named after its first owner, Joe Friggin, had been serving lab employees since the 1950s. Despite its cracked red Naugahyde booths, notoriously bad service, and suspiciously sticky tables, the Friggin Bar was still the best place in town to grab a cold beer and a green chile cheeseburger and catch up on the latest gossip from the town and the lab—both of which were so intertwined that they had become one and the same.

Peter Chang, Alek's friend from grad school, and now his coworker, had already ordered. Alek smiled to see the cheeseburger and bottle of Dos Equis waiting for him. But Chang's expression seemed serious. Alek felt a twinge of worry. Has something gone wrong with Chang's work on Project Z?

"I need to talk to you about something important," Chang said, leaning forward. Alek thought back to when he first met Chang in an advanced theoretical physics class at Princeton. Chang had focused all his time and energy on his studies, which had earned him few friends, but had impressed his professors. Chang had a rare talent for converting theoretical equations into computational physics. When he returned to China, he used that skill to generate simulations and 3D models for weapons research at the Advanced Energy Lab in Beijing.

Alek glanced around the diner. "Remember, no classified conversations here."

"No, of course not," replied Chang, shaking his head. "It's not about the project... Well, it kinda is... It's about Sunli."

Alek raised an eyebrow. *What is this about?* Sunli Hidalgo, his team member on Project Z, had made significant contributions to their recent breakthroughs. She had first researched Low Energy Nuclear Reaction theories under Mexico's famous physics professor, Dr. Roberto Rodriguez. Then she'd been kidnapped by the Cincoleta Cartel and forced to work with the Chinese to develop LENR weapons applications. One of the people she'd worked with in the secret Chinese lab was Peter Chang—who helped engineer Sunli's escape.

"Uh, you kinda rescued Sunli from China. She wouldn't even be back here working on our team if it weren't for you," said Alek. "Please tell me you don't regret getting her out."

Chang burst into laughter. "Regret it? I don't regret it one bit. Alek, here's the thing, I think I'm in love with her." Alek coughed, choking on his swallow of beer. Sunli was certainly beautiful, in a polished though aloof way. Her petite frame was perfectly proportioned. Her tailored skirt suits complemented and accentuated her looks. Practically everything about Sunli attracted admirers, but she never returned that interest or even acknowledged it. Raised by a strict Chinese mother and a father with a traditional Mexican patriarchal viewpoint, Sunli fit no stereotypes. Alek had hired her for his team at the lab a few years ago, and she had proven to be the most driven scientist he had ever worked with—which said volumes considering the caliber of the researchers at Los Alamos.

But... love? Alek had never known Sunli to date, to show interest in another person, or even to have a non-science related conversation. *Now Chang says he loves her? Good luck.*

"Umm, that's great I, um, guess," stammered Alek. "So, did you ask her out?"

"No. I, uh, should I?"

Alek took a big bite of his cheeseburger to avoid answering and then made a face. He put down the burger and lifted the bun. *Onions! It figures. First Chang falls in love and now onions,* he thought with a chuckle as he picked the offending purple and white slivers off the patty.

Chang leaned across the table, his face earnest. "Seriously, should I ask her out?"

Alek laughed ruefully and said, "I'm hardly one to give romantic advice. I've been divorced almost as long as I was married, and I haven't been on a date in..." He thought for a minute. *How long has it been since I've been on a date? Did going on that picnic with Gabi count?* He shook his head. "I haven't been on a date since before my ex-wife was my wife. I think I'd take it slow if I were you. We have a lot of work to do, and you guys will be working together. You don't want things to get... well... awkward, y'know."

"That's fair," Chang said with a nod. "I figured you'd tell me to just be patient and see what happens. I think that's why I wanted to talk to you—I knew you'd tell me to take it slow. After all, you and Gabi..." Chang broke off and shrugged.

"What about me and Gabi? There's nothing between me and Gabi," Alek spluttered. "I mean we are professional colleagues, friends... but of a work sort."

"Sure, keep telling yourself that," said Chang as he reached for the ticket. "I've got lunch covered today. Thanks for the advice but... well, here's something I've been thinking about that you should really consider. You don't meet very many people in life who make you feel the way... the way Sunli makes me feel. And you can only wait so long. Anyhow, good talk. I'll see you back at the lab."

Alek watched Chang walk out the door into the bright New Mexico sunlight, his black hair silhouetted against the turquoise sky. *Can I follow Chang's advice? Do I even deserve to be happy?* Alek decided to do the only thing he could do to deal with those questions—he headed back to work.

Chapter 3
The Best Laid Plans

WILL HAD SLOWLY WARMED TO Joe's idea of using the LENR device to wipe out all the electrical systems in a nuclear power plant. The scarier the attack seemed, the sooner they would get their hands on the government pay off. *We'll show Percy we mean business*, Will thought to himself.

Joe had chosen the location for deploying their creation. The Laguna Verde Nuclear Power Plant sat on the coast of the Gulf of Mexico in Alto Lucero, Veracruz, Mexico, about a 13-hour drive from Monterrey. The only nuclear power plant in Mexico, Laguna Verde had four reactors and was owned by Mexico's national electric power company. Over the years, Mexico's news outlets had criticized Laguna Verde for having insufficient security, which Joe felt would work to their advantage. "In and out and no one gets hurt," he told Will.

Joe explained that since it provided nearly a third of the country's electrical power, Laguna Verde represented an essential part of Mexican infrastructure. Disabling the power plant would plunge much of the country into darkness for weeks, maybe months. Plus, attacking a nuclear power plant added to the overall drama. *Maybe too much drama*, Will thought.

"Will there be some sort of core meltdown or radiation leak?" Will asked as Joe leaned over the lab table making the final adjustments on his gadget.

"No, it's just an electrical disruptor," Joe replied. "Not dangerous at all."

"Have you ever heard about the nuclear accidents at Chernobyl or Fukushima? When a nuclear power plant loses electrical power, it can't cool the reactors. That could lead to a meltdown that releases a ton of radiation into the air."

"Those accidents were both a long time ago," Joe muttered without looking up.

"What's that got to do with anything?"

"A lot, *pendejo*, a lot." Joe sighed impatiently. "Those accidents you claim to know so much about led to the installation of safeguards that prevent meltdown and ensure containment if there's an electrical failure. It's all about showing the threat of what we can do and scaring the public so that the government will act."

"What do you know? I don't remember you paying much attention during grad school. If it weren't for my help, you never would have graduated."

Joe slowly set down the screwdriver he had been holding and turned to face his twin brother. Fury seethed in his eyes.

"If it weren't for you, *mi querido hermano*, I never would have even been in graduate school. I never would have ended up working for the cartel."

"Amigo, cálmate, hombre," Will said, raising a hand. He had never seen his brother so angry. "Think of all the money we've made so far... and all the money we can make now. We started with nothing and soon we'll be running the Cincoleta Cartel."

"Becoming a criminal armed with a nuclear weapon was never my goal in life," Joe sneered. "Estoy seguro de que nunca fue el plan de nuestra madre para nosotros."

"Never Mamá's plan for our life? How dare you say that? Even in la escuela primaria, we helped Mamá pay bills by running errands for the cartel. If it weren't for the cartel, Mamá would never have gotten her house." Throwing his arms in the air, Will stomped out of the warehouse. Joe just didn't understand.

Will remembered how innocent it all had seemed when it started. They would pick up packages a couple of times a week, make a few deliveries, and always get paid in cash. Their mother had been thrilled by the extra money, although she always warned them, "*No haga nada peligrosa*... Don't do anything dangerous." Then she would hug them tightly and thank them for their help.

When the boys started high school, they began meeting once a week with one of the tenientes. They never learned his last name. Instead, they just called the lieutenant by the name "Miguel." While Miguel may not have been his real name, he was the first real male figure in the brothers' lives, and they both welcomed the fatherly attention he gave them. Miguel asked about their grades, encouraged them to study hard in school, and recognized their value by giving them increasingly dangerous tasks. Will remembered having to warn Joe to be careful never to unwrap the packages of fentanyl they delivered. The boys quickly learned how to duck for cover during a shootout and how to smuggle weapons into a prison when pretending to visit a man they called Papa. Will loved the words of praise that the cartel leaders offered almost as much as he loved the wads of cash he would bring home.

When the boys finished high school, Miguel made them both an offer. He would pay for them to attend la universidad. Will had excelled in school, but Joe's grades were mediocre. Nevertheless, both soon found themselves enrolled at el Instituto Tecnológico y de Estudios Superiores de Monterrey, or Monterrey Tech—a prestigious, private university in Monterrey, Mexico. There was just one catch, they had to devote themselves to studying the sciences, particularly physics, and complete at least one high-level operation for the cartel every month. Joe didn't want to go, but Will insisted. "Where else would we get this opportunity to attend college and have spending money in our pockets for a little fun on the side?"

Those were the days, thought Will. The days before things got so serious... Before they met El Verdugo and started to understand his plan.

And now, Will realized, *now we're the ones with the nuclear weapon. Joe says it won't be dangerous, but what does he know? What do either of us know?* Will had thought threatening Percy would be enough and clearly he'd been wrong about that.

* * *

After a couple of days in Las Vegas, Percy was relieved to return to the quiet of Los Alamos. He drank in the cool mountain air of northern New Mexico, a welcome relief after the blistering Vegas heat. He was anxious for an update on Alek's research and eager to share the news about his meeting with General Wu.

That afternoon, Percy and Alek decided to trade the lab's stuffy offices and conference rooms for a stroll through downtown Los Alamos. As they passed historic buildings, once the homes of some of the world-famous scientists who had worked on the Manhattan Project, Alek suddenly stopped walking. "Here we are in the town that gave birth to nuclear warfare," he said. "I can't help but wonder if someday our research will change the legacy of the lab."

The two men turned down the historic Bathtub Row, named after the only nine houses in the town during World War II that had full bathrooms with bathtubs. Housing in Los Alamos was a little less primitive now than it was in the '40s. At least most people had bathtubs. Percy paused in front of a house once owned by Nobel-Prize winning physicist Hans Bethe. "Give me a full report," he said.

Alek brought Percy up to speed on the team. The group included scientists from the U.S. national labs and some private technology companies, one a large aerospace company that had fallen on hard times after the cancellation of their intercontinental ballistic missile program due to the U.S./China nonproliferation treaty. Design work was well underway. "Sal is a godsend. He's keeping the investors informed and the money flowing. He's brought in several industry experts—I can't tell you their names here, but I'll fill you in when we're back at the lab behind the fence. All in all, it's a great group. A dream team."

"Dream team, huh?" Percy chuckled. "So, what has this dream team accomplished so far?"

"We've calculated a direct energy conversion method using the particles from the reaction to use magnetohydrodynamics, a process of a conducting fluid moving through a magnetic field to produce an electric current as a first energy production stage in the process. In the second stage, the particles will become trapped in chambers directly producing electricity to deliver to the grid."

"Excellent," Percy replied. "Now I think we must get serious about moving forward. And that means bringing the Chinese government on board."

Alek resumed walking, his eyes on the Bathtub Row Brewing Co-op, a popular taproom a little farther down the street. "You're dead set on working with Wu? He's going to have to do something to earn my trust, and Sunli certainly seemed opposed to having him on our team."

"What if he's willing to undergo a polygraph test?" asked Percy. "We can use technology to ensure he intends to cooperate fully and is not simply in this for his own gain."

Alek nodded, considering the options. "Yes, an interview with a lie detector machine would make me more inclined to trust him. I mean, if he's willing to do that."

"Of course he will be," Percy replied, secretly relieved that Alek didn't appear to be aware of the unreliable nature of polygraphs. With the right training, anyone could convince the machine they were telling the truth. That's why polygraphs weren't allowed in court cases, but what Alek didn't know wouldn't hurt him. "So, it's agreed then," Percy said, clapping Alek on the back. "I'll get a commitment from Wu and Chinese leadership, and you just have to convince Sunli to go along with the plan."

Alek scoffed. "That won't be easy."

Changing the subject, Percy gestured to the brew pub. "Let's get a drink and you can tell me more about the project."

Alek looked grateful to dive back into technical topics. "Our analysis shows that once the reaction is triggered, the device can extract electricity directly rather than having to go through the inefficient process of converting heat to steam to spinning turbines to electricity," Alek reported. "We are even thinking about recycling the reacted fuel to minimize waste."

Alek held the door open for his boss. The brewery wasn't busy, and they grabbed a table in the corner.

"The entire concept is incredibly efficient, clean, and cost effective. I am certain we'll be able to create the ultimate source of electricity for the world," Alek continued.

Percy signaled the waitress and ordered two glasses of the brewery's Hoppenheimer stout—a beer brewed in honor of Oppenheimer's legacy. The brewery, called the Tub by locals, had a slogan that Los Alamos was "a drinking town with a science problem." Most of the time, that slogan rang true.

"The only hurdle left is finding a place to build the first Project Z facility," Alek said. "It isn't going to be easy to find the right setting."

Percy drummed his fingers on the table impatiently. "What kind of location are you thinking of?"

"The site will require a massive, partially buried and EMP-shielded facility at a remote location. We'll need an enormous excavation to ensure safety protocols can be met, just in case things go wrong."

"Hmm," Percy muttered, then smiled as he saw the waitress approaching with their drinks.

Percy didn't want his chief scientist to worry, but he did have some concerns about the cost of constructing the kind of facility that Alek had in mind. Building a site that could meet these requirements seemed impossible. Finding a location where they could dig an underground tunnel of such an enormous size was only the first issue. Then, they needed to come up with the money to excavate and construct the facility. They needed a solution soon.

* * *

Joe stepped back and took a long, hard look at their completed creation. *How could something that small have taken so many hours to build?* It didn't look like much—a barrel shaped metal container, covered in wires and connectors. At the heart of the machine was the dense plasma focus that Joe had modified to produce a focused electron beam that would trigger the Low Energy Nuclear Reaction and release a powerful electromagnetic pulse.

Joe knew they should test the gadget, but they didn't have a properly shielded facility for carrying out EMP experiments. The last thing they wanted to do was wipe out their electrical power in the warehouse and disable their truck, or, even worse, alert the authorities to what they were doing. When they first started working on this technology, they'd been able to carry out some small tests, but... Joe laughed ruefully. Then there was the experiment that basically vaporized their house in Altavaca, New Mexico. *This device shouldn't have that kind of impact—at least, if I built it right, it should only affect the electrical grid—but it is very powerful. What if I miscalculated? It's too big of a risk,* Joe mused.

He made the sign of the cross and reached for his mother's set of rosary beads that he always carried in his pocket. *At least Mamá didn't live to see her hijos become criminals. It would have broken her heart.*

At first, being friends with the cartel had been fun, even when that involved going to college. Although Joe had never liked homework or studying, he remembered how much he had enjoyed *la universidad*. With some spending money from Miguel and a little bit of freedom, he had found himself a girlfriend. He and Adriana were even talking about getting married. Joe was starting to dream about finding a research job at the university, buying a house, and raising some kids with Adriana. But no, that was not going to happen. On graduation day, Miguel showed up with new instructions and forged American citizenship papers. He and Will were going to continue their education by going to graduate school at the University of New Mexico—whether they wanted to or not.

Will of course was excited and had handled all the arrangements with Miguel. Joe had no choice. He was just a piece of collateral—along for the ride. One night as they prepared for the move, Joe decided to speak up to Miguel and tell him he wasn't going. The next day, Miguel brought his boss with him, Juan Velásquez, the drug lord known as El Verdugo, the Executioner.

Velásquez was short and stocky, but he radiated a sense of power, emphasized by the heavily armed bodyguards who were always by his side. The cartel leader smiled at Joe, withdrew his knife, and caressed the blade lovingly, all while advising the brothers that he knew where their mother and little sister lived. That, more than the handful of cash and the promise of future payouts, was more than enough for Joe to agree to enroll at UNM.

UNM was nothing like *el Instituto Tecnológico y de*

Estudios Superiores de Monterrey. Once again, Miguel had provided their accommodations, but, instead of a dorm room, the brothers shared a small stucco house on Albuquerque's Carlisle Boulevard. The roof leaked, bugs crawled in and out through the cracks in the stucco, and homeless people threw trash and empty beer cans into their front yard. Inside the house, they had twin beds, a worn-out couch, and a couple of card tables. On the plus side, the internet worked, there was always money for beer, and no one noticed when they threw their own empty beer cans in the front yard. Slowly, the brothers began plowing through their PhDs in nuclear engineering. When the classes got too hard, a call to Miguel ensured they had the resources to cheat.

After about a year, Adriana got tired of waiting and married a local boy with a good job, but for Will and Joe there was no time for dating. The classes were challenging, especially for Joe, who had never been strong academically, though he had the innate ability to build things and did well in some engineering areas. Although Joe didn't like graduate school, the worst part of those three years was waiting to find out what Miguel was planning. One week before graduation, the brothers were surprised by a knock at the door.

"Miguel, *qué sorpresa*," Will exclaimed. Glancing nervously at the black Mercedes parked in front of their house, he ushered the cartel leader into their dingy living room. Miguel's tailored suit and shiny shoes looked entirely out of place amid their secondhand decorations, pizza boxes, and textbooks. Without a word, he took a seat in a rickety chair and began making two stacks of $100 bills on the card table.

"*¿Qué es esto?*" Will asked, his eyes riveted on the money. Joe trembled slightly, knowing, given the amount of money on the table, he wasn't going to like what was coming next.

Chapter 4
A Blast from the Past

ALEK WAS PACING BACK AND forth in his boss' conference room, frustration etched across his face. "We can't find a location that meets our criteria. It must be a large underground facility so we can ensure EMP shielding. It must be in a remote area with access to qualified personnel. It must be somewhere the public will welcome the project and not throw up political roadblocks. It just doesn't exist."

Percy threw up his hands in exasperation. "Surely, we can find somewhere to build this thing. Have you checked with the Nevada National Security Site? It covers nearly 1,400 square miles. I bet somewhere out there in the desert they can find somewhere to build you a lab."

"Yeah, it's a big desert," said Alek. "They may have the room there, but the cost of excavating and building the infrastructure... Percy, we have money, but not that much."

Percy patted the younger man on the back. "Listen, why don't you spend some time out there and figure out what sort of space they have available? It's an amazing place—particularly for anyone who works in the nuclear weapons industry." Trying to ignore the bitter look Alek shot at him over the mention of weapons, Percy continued. "Have you ever taken a tour of the historic Nevada testing sites?"

Alek sighed. "No, visiting former nuclear weapons detonation locations wasn't a highlight of my childhood. I guess that was part of yours?"

Percy chuckled. "Not exactly part of my childhood, but it is a little like an eerie Disneyland for people in our business. You should check it out. In fact, this is an order. Spend some time at the Nevada National Security Site.

Take the historic tour and scout out some of the new testing areas. Maybe you can find the perfect place."

"Percy, I hardly have the time right now for sightseeing, much less nuclear security sightseeing. There's work to be done." But Percy had already lost interest in the conversation and was focused on his computer. "We should ask Wu to get the Chinese government to send a representative along with you. Kind of a show of good faith and cooperation. Two countries working together to find the perfect place to build a binational lab."

"So now I get banished to Nevada and I have to babysit a potential Chinese spy?"

"Not a spy. Don't be ridiculous. Just a fellow scientist from a partner nation. It's a sign of... of collaboration. You should be grateful that I didn't ask you to take Wu with you instead. But... just in case, take Gabi with you for a little FBI protection. Plus, that's as close as you'll ever get to taking her on a date."

Percy laughed as he watched Alek's face redden. He held up a hand before his chief scientist could speak. "I mean it, Alek, I need you to do this. Contact our Nevada program manager and she'll set the whole thing up."

* * *

Will handed Joe a bottle of Carta Blanca, one of the first beers brewed in Monterrey. The small brewery had grown into a major corporation and had sparked an explosion of industry in the city nearly a century ago. "Soon we will be as famous and successful as Carta Blanca," Will declared, clinking his bottle against his brother's in a forced toast.

"Remember when Miguel told us we needed to land jobs at Los Alamos National Laboratory?" Joe asked. "I never thought they would hire us."

"Yeah, but we had the advantage because we had worked with Senor Rodriguez at Monterrey Tech," Will said. "We understood the theories behind cold fusion and the breakthroughs he had made."

During the interview with Alek Spray, Will had convinced Spray that, based on Rodriguez's theories, the key to the trigger was a super-focused electron beam. Will wanted to use their dense plasma focus device in a mode where they could attach a metal target to the top so that the generated beam would strike the target. What Will hadn't explained was the entire washing machine-sized device could be deployed as a tactical or even a space weapon. But that was what Miguel and Velásquez wanted, and they needed the resources, equipment, and funding behind Los Alamos to achieve that goal. Will planned to try out a systematic set of experiments at increasing power levels with a target material of copper, which was the material Professor Rodriguez had suggested in his publications. Alek gave the idea the thumbs up.

Alek set them up in an abandoned lab on the outskirts of the property and provided them with enough money for equipment. At first, the brothers followed the work of others and repeated their experiments over several months, first at 10,000 amperes and then increasing in five steps to 50,000 amperes, which was the limit of their small energy discharge.

The dense plasma focus consisted of high voltage capacitors, a discharge switch, and a small vacuum chamber with a target at the top. For a year, they conducted experiments at ever increasing levels of electron beam current, but they weren't making any progress. Miguel kept calling to say, "El Verdugo is tired of waiting." The pressure was getting intense.

Will remembered the day when Joe tried to convince him to give the whole thing up.

"*Hermano*, it's just not working," Joe said. "I hate Los Alamos and I hate belonging to the cartel. Yeah, they pay us well, but we don't have any time to enjoy the money and what will happen if we can't make this work?"

"That's why we have to make it work," Will told Joe. "You know that. Failure is not an option in the cartel."

Fortunately, the next week they had a breakthrough and decided to move the experiment to the basement of their house. Tests went well there—until they didn't. Technically, the experiment was a success, they just failed to modulate the power output. *Not every scientist can say they accidentally vaporized their house*, Will thought with a snort of laughter. Good thing it was a rental.

Then the move to Mexico, then China... They had been through a lot in their quest to perfect this technology, and they still might be struggling if the cartel leader hadn't kidnapped Sunli Hidalgo and convinced her to share her expertise. "Not that Hidalgo deserves the credit," Will pointed out. "She couldn't have done anything without our work."

Will grabbed Joe's empty beer bottle and popped the top on two new beers. "Think about all we've been through," Will told Joe. "We deserve the money and power.

"We've worked for it. We deserve it. Failure has never been an option for us."

* * *

Harry Reid International Airport in Las Vegas, Nevada assaulted all of Gabi's senses. Slot machines rang, neon signs blinked, and harried travelers dragged crying children toward the baggage kiosk. Everything seemed glaring, loud, and headache-inducing.

She had been surprised when Alek called and invited her to join him on the trip to Nevada. *Is this just business?* she wondered, trying to push away any hope that it meant something more. After several calls to FBI headquarters, Gabi had finally managed to rearrange her workload and was starting to get excited about the time away with Alek. Then he texted to explain that he was bringing a Chinese scientist. *Stupid, stupid, stupid,* Gabi told herself. *What made me jump to the conclusion this is anything more than work?*

Gabi tried to smile when she saw Alek approaching, wheeling his suitcase with one hand while steering their Chinese "guest" with the other. Wu had contacted the Chinese leaders and arranged for a scientific representative from their country to join the visit. *Oh great, it's a woman,* Gabi thought, trying to pretend she didn't feel a pang of jealousy.

Mei Huang's purple-streaked pixie haircut and large round glasses did nothing to enhance the sense that she was a serious scientist, despite Wu's assertion that she held a PhD. Mei held a Kleenex to her nose and sniffled and sneezed while apologizing profusely. *She's probably going to give us all COVID,* Gabi thought, deciding not to offer her hand for a handshake when Alek awkwardly introduced the young woman.

"Mei doesn't speak much English," he explained.

"Come on, Mei," Alek told Mei, who stood staring transfixed at the crowd pouring through the airport, a liquid stream of raucous humanity on a desperate quest for a good time.

Gabi herded Alek and Mei out the door and into the taxi line, where the brutal Las Vegas sun beat down on them. She grimaced. *Can this get any worse?* Gabi slipped off her cardigan, tying it around her waist, wishing she wasn't wearing a fitted tank top. She couldn't help but notice Alek averting his eyes, while Mei continued to look around like some kind of bobble-head toy.

"Why are so many people taking taxis?" groaned Alek. "No one takes taxis anymore."

"Because it's Vegas," replied Gabi, twisting her hair up into a ponytail, and wiping away the beads of sweat on her upper lip. The heat felt like a heavy weight bearing down on them.

"Three." Gabi held up three fingers as the cab pulled up. She practically pushed Mei through the cab door. Alek helped the driver with the bags and then squeezed in beside Gabi. The taxi smelled of cigarette smoke and regret. In other words, thought Gabi, it smells like Vegas.

And to think I was imagining a romantic dinner for two in one of Vegas' fanciest restaurants, Gabi chided herself as they arrived at the hotel and she peeled herself off the sweaty vinyl cab seat. "We have an early start tomorrow, so I'm going to order room service and get a good night's sleep."

Gabi said a silent thank you to the J.W. Marriott Hotel for accepting the government rate for such a lovely resort room. The hotel room was bigger than most of the apartments she had rented. Heck, the hotel bathroom was larger than her entire apartment. The king size bed... it was large and empty as well. At last, she slipped into a dreamless sleep.

* * *

The Nevada National Security Site was located outside of Las Vegas in an area chosen in 1951 for its remoteness. Alek, Gabi, and Mei met their tour guide, a scientist named Tim Paisner, at 6:30 a.m. in front of their hotel. They boarded the small private bus that would transport them to the site.

Gabi stared out the window as the bus progressed down the highway, leaving civilization behind. She clutched her Starbucks cup tightly, willing the venti triple sugar-free vanilla latte to do its work.

Despite the proximity to the crowded Las Vegas Strip, the land extending in every direction was barren—void of houses, stores, or other signs of civilization. Brown, rock-studded mountains climbed from the sandy desert, looking oddly like prehistoric beasts gazing down upon the Joshua trees dotting the land below.

After about an hour of driving through the desolate hills, the bus turned onto Mercury Highway and pulled up to the main gate of the Nevada National Security Site. Warning signs on either side of the road announced, "Restricted Area," "Radiological Hazards," and "Obey All Posted Signs." Two armed soldiers, in full camo, entered the bus and asked for their IDs.

"We'll have to collect your cell phones now too," said Tim. "You know, because of the cameras. Although we are visiting historical sites today, a lot of top-secret work goes on out here. Plus, we're right next to Area 51," he added with a wink.

Reluctantly, Gabi placed her phone in the plastic sack Tim held out to her. This only compounded the sense of isolation. Here we are in the middle of nowhere and we can't even make a phone call or send a text.

"Anyone have any other mobile devices or anything with Bluetooth? Smart watches, Fitbits, iPads, air pods, location trackers, thumb drives? Hand them over now— we can't be too careful." Tim smiled, but his tone sounded serious. At the Nevada National Security Site, security was—literally—its middle name.

IDs checked and badges issued, the bus resumed its journey with Tim as the narrator offering up the play-by-play of everything they drove past. "The Nevada National

Security Site was formerly the Nevada Test Site and before that the Nevada Proving Grounds," Tim explained. "This was the home of 928 nuclear device tests. Today there are no full-scale nuclear tests conducted here, but the site is still used for nuclear weapons-related development and research, and it stands as a sort of museum documenting the beginning of the atomic age. Today, we will visit a number of these nuclear testing sites."

As the bus rolled through the property, Tim instructed them to pay attention since he would be pointing out important historical sites.

"The first tests conducted here were atmospheric, or above ground tests, carried out in the 1950s in response to growing fear of Soviet attack," Tim said, gesturing to a few rows of weathered wooden benches standing in the desert. "This is where invited observers and members of the press would sit to watch the detonations."

"They just sat there while the bombs went off above them?" Mei asked incredulously, stifling a sneeze.

Gabi leaned over and whispered to Alek, "See, she does speak English." He shrugged.

"They wore special goggles to protect their eyes from the flash," Tim explained. "Those who didn't have goggles were told to face away from the blast and cover their eyes with their hands, but the reflection from the pale ground was so bright that most could see the bones in their hands."

Mei shivered. "That hardly seems safe."

"Harold Agnew, the third director of Los Alamos, once said that every political leader should have to witness an above ground detonation while dressed in only their underwear so they could feel the heat," Tim explained as the bus moved on past the former viewing area.

"Our next location is about 10 minutes away," Tim said. "Get ready. You're going to love this part."

Gabi glanced over at Alek. He looked pale as he stared out the bus window. Swinging into the seat beside him, Gabi touched his arm. "Are you okay?" she asked, without waiting for the answer. "Detonating nuclear weapons while people sat and watched... it's hard to imagine," she continued. "And the fact that we're so close to a major metropolitan area. It really does seem insane."

Alek finally turned away from the window, looking almost surprised to see Gabi there beside him. "The thing is, a lot of people think the United States should go back to full scale nuclear weapons testing," he said. "They say it's the best way to find out whether the weapons that we're building actually work."

"But is it safe?"

"There were definitely questions and concerns about radioactive fallout, and then all atmospheric testing was banned in 1963. That's when we turned to underground testing. A lot of the computer simulations and data we rely on today was derived from those tests."

"But we stopped those too?" asked Gabi.

"Yes, in 1992, the United States voluntarily joined with Russia, the United Kingdom, and France in a test moratorium. Then President Bill Clinton signed the Comprehensive Nuclear-Test-Ban Treaty in 1996, though the Senate has never ratified the treaty. According to documentation, the nation stands prepared to resume testing if needed at any time."

"So, what do you think? Do you think we should resume testing?"

Alek's eyes returned to the window as the bus rolled through the desert. "Here's the thing, the concept of deterrence only works if your adversaries believe your weapons are credible. Our enemies must think that a first strike could lead to retaliation and then to mutually assured destruction. Nuclear weapons are too dangerous to use... so that's how we use them. We use them to deter war."

Gabi sniffed. "Yeah, I've heard people say that deterrence means we use nuclear weapons every day."

"Well, we haven't had a world war in more than 80 years. It's a delicate balance, especially in today's multidomain threat environment. It's much more about psychology than fire power, but we have to be certain our deterrent will work."

"So how do we know? How do we prove the weapons we build can do what they're supposed to do?"

Alek sighed. "The labs are doing subcritical experiments now—tests with small amounts of nuclear material that don't create a self-sustaining nuclear explosion. Those are happening right here, underground here in Nevada, right now. That should be enough to assure the validity of the weapons. Politicians have tried for decades to eliminate nuclear weapons, but somehow deterrence is still the best strategy we've got."

"Does it make you feel..." Gabi hesitated. "Does it concern you that your research may help develop new, more lethal weapons?"

"Yes and no," Alek replied. "You can't stop the pace of science, research, and knowledge. I see science as the pursuit of the truth. Unfortunately, it's part of human nature that people use that knowledge to build nastier, more lethal weapons. You know, it's like Percy says, science is a knife."

"A knife?"

"It's all in how you use it. A knife can butter your toast in the morning, or a knife can slit your enemy's throat."

"How sharp is your butter knife? Maybe we should skip breakfast tomorrow?" Gabi said with a chuckle, then added, "Yeah, I see what you mean."

Alek grabbed her hand with sudden intensity. "I wish we could build a world without nuclear weapons. You don't know how much I wish that. But for now, all we can do is hope for wise leadership and stay prepared."

The two held their gaze for several minutes before realizing the bus had stopped.

"Everyone off the bus," Tim said. "We get to go four wheeling. It's time for the Crater Crawl."

* * *

Will and Joe Ramos set out for Laguna Verde in their un-airconditioned pickup with the device sitting under a tarp in the truck bed. It was a long drive from Monterrey. They were leaving in the late afternoon, planning to arrive at the nuclear power plant just before sunrise so they could deploy the device while it was still dark. The two were driving across Mexico to commit an act of terrorism. What could go wrong?

Apparently, their truck. It had proven more unreliable

than they expected and had already suffered several mechanical delays on their route. They had been able to make the necessary repairs themselves but had lost several hours. Now the old truck rattled along the highway in the night with Will blasting music on his phone, trying to stay awake by singing along in Spanish. Despite the racket, Joe managed to doze.

He woke up with a start when Will abruptly pulled the truck to a stop on the side of the road. "Another problem with this stupid truck?" Joe asked.

"No. *Es los federales*," Will hissed in a whisper as two Mexican officers approached the truck. "Be cool."

Dressed in black fatigues and carrying AR-15s, the officers ambled up to the vehicle slowly. "*¿A dónde vas esta noche?*" one officer asked. The other added, "Where are you headed?" just in case the truck's occupants didn't speak Spanish.

"Uh... a business trip," said Will nervously as the other officer began wandering toward the back of the truck.

"*¿Que es esto?*" the man asked, gesturing toward the tarp covered object in the truck bed. Slowly he began lifting the tarp.

"It's a... uh... distiller," hollered Joe. "We... we make tequila."

"*Si, vamos a Guadalajara a comprar agave*," Will added quickly.

"Oh, you're going to Guadalajara to buy agave to make tequila?" said the officer. "You aren't going the right way."

"We have to drop off a bottle first... for... uh... testing," Will stammered. He reached under the seat and pulled out the bottle of Don Julio tequila he had brought along. "See?"

The officer raised an eyebrow. "Really? That's a Don Julio bottle."

"Oh, we just used the bottle because ours are still in manufacturing, isn't that right, Joe?" Will said.

Joe nodded eagerly and chimed in, "Here, taste it. You'll see it's much better than Don Julio."

The officer took a swig, nodded, and handed the bottle to his companion. "*Si, eso es mejor*. In fact, I really prefer that to Don Julio." He took another drink, savoring the taste, then handed the bottle back to Joe. "Even so, you do need a permit to transport this sort of equipment..."

"Ah," Will replied. "Perhaps in place of a permit you will accept... *este?*" He held out a $100 American bill. The officer looked away. Will pulled a second $100 from his wallet and pressed the money into the officer's hand.

"*Muy bien,*" said the officer. "Safe travels. *Ten cuidado.*" The men began to walk away, but then one turned back suddenly.

"By the way, that delicious tequila, so much better than Don Julio, I'll have to buy some when it hits the market. What's its name?"

Will looked down at the bottle of Don Julio and then smiled at the officer. "We call it... *Garra de Dragón.*"

* * *

Tim explained the next part of the Nevada National Security Site technical orientation tour. "Many of the underground nuclear tests involved drilling a vertical hole into the ground and then detonating the device inside the hole to contain the release of any dangerous gasses or radiation. These tests created subsidence craters that varied in size due to the depth of the burial of the devices. Some explosions threw giant boulders of granite into the air, others created massive collapsed craters following the underground explosions. We're going to go see some of those craters, but we'll have to take this truck to tackle four-wheel drive territory. The roads are a little rough."

In the rugged pickup, they set out across the site, which Tim pointed out was larger than the state of Rhode Island. Miles and miles of nothing to see but Joshua trees, chamisa plants, tumbleweed, and sagebrush stretching across the desert, framed by the mountains, with cloudless blue skies above.

The drive was rough. The dirt roads didn't look like they'd been maintained since testing ended in 1992. Blasts had heaved rocks onto the roadways and severed the land with fissures. The passengers shouted to hear each other as the truck trundled across the lunar landscape, up and down hills winding through the endless desert.

Finally exiting the vehicle, they hiked up a hill along a

steep trail. Giant basalt boulders, black with sharp edges, lined the path where they were thrown by a long-ago test blast. Topping the ridge, they looked down into a deep crater.

Tim returned to tour guide mode. "This is Schooner Crater. Created in 1968, the approximately 30 kiloton blast formed a hole 260 meters wide and 64 meters deep, roughly two football fields long and two football fields across. Because of the resemblance to the moon's surface, NASA used this crater to train astronauts to practice moon landings."

Tim gestured at the ground. "Do you see the shiny black things on the ground that look like pieces of glass? Those are rocks fused into glass by the heat of the blast. You can pick them up if you put rubber gloves on, but we'll have to check you with a Geiger counter before we leave."

"It's still radioactive?" Mei asked.

"Yep. It's been nearly 60 years since the test, but some contamination remains."

Mei sneezed then took a pair of rubber gloves from Tim, put them on, and grabbed some of the rocks. She pitched them into the crater. The sound of the falling rocks echoed eerily across the empty desert. Gabi noticed that Mei was smiling as if enjoying a private joke.

"Back in the day we used to throw old tires into this crater and make the new guys go get them," Tim said.

The next stop was a massive, smooth beige hole in the ground. The group gathered on a steel viewing platform stretched precariously over the crater. They gazed across the 1,280 by 320-foot cavity, awestruck by its size. "The Sedan Crater is the largest man-made crater on Earth. It was created in 1962 by a 104-kiloton thermonuclear explosion," explained Tim. "It's listed on the National Registry of Historic Places and is the most visited spot on the Nevada Nuclear Security Site."

"It looks a lot different than the last one," Gabi said.

"That detonation took place in dense rock, while this was formed in soft alluvium, soil made of loose clay and sand. See how the sand is falling into the bottom of the crater? The sides are constantly slipping. It has actually gotten shallower as the years have gone by."

"I bet you didn't make the new guys retrieve old tires from this one," Gabi said.

Tim shook his head. "Nope. Just look at the sides of it. If someone fell down there, they'd never be able to climb back up."

Tim gestured to the truck. "Okay, load up. We're headed to the control point, where all the data from the experiments is received and processed."

"*Is* received?" asked Mei. "Don't you mean *was*? You said full scale nuclear tests haven't been conducted since the early nineties."

"That's true, but we still use the control point to aggregate data from the new experiments that scientists are carrying out. All the information flows into the control point for storage and analysis," Tim said. "Of course, during the height of nuclear testing, it was a much busier place. The whole site was back then."

Fifteen minutes later, they reached a large building perched on top of what appeared to be a man-made hill. Tim punched in a code to enter the building and led them into a large room where computer screens lined the walls.

"This is where the technicians and scientists sit during the experiments," Tim said.

"Is there a bathroom here?" Mei asked timidly.

"Down the hall and to your right," Tim answered. "It's unisex."

Gabi looked around the dimly lit room filled with computer monitors and high-tech devices. The cement floor was dusty, and the uninsulated building was built of steel and rattled slightly with every gust of wind. The contrast between primitive and state-of-the-art struck Gabi as glaringly incongruent. Nothing about the site was what she had expected.

Tim droned on and Gabi found her attention wandering. She glanced over her shoulder. Mei had been gone for several minutes. Had she gotten lost? "Guys, I'm going to find Mei and visit the bathroom," she said. Alek nodded absentmindedly.

Gabi turned and headed down the hallway that Tim had indicated. On the left she saw a doorway marked, "Restricted. Top Secret Access Only." Then she heard a familiar sneeze.

The door wasn't locked. Slowly and quietly, Gabi pushed it open. Mei was hunched over a bank of computers. Her round glasses sat on the counter beside her. Unaware she was being watched, the Chinese woman removed a USB drive from one computer and inserted another. Gabi stifled a gasp.

"Mei, what are you doing?" Gabi said firmly and loudly. Startled, Mei grabbed the thumb drive from the computer, shoved it into her pocket, and ran out a door on the other side of the room. Without a moment's thought, Gabi chased after her, shouting, "Spy! Spy! Call the Security Police Force," at the top of her lungs.

Moving fast, Mei slammed through a side door, exiting the building and sprinting across the driveway with Gabi right behind her. The two raced toward where two trucks were parked, motors still running to keep the AC going. Mei jumped into one and gunned the motor, sending a spray of rocks and gravel flying toward Gabi, who quickly swung into the second truck and gave chase. Alek and Tim ran out of the building and stood in the driveway, mouths agape.

The trucks careened down the winding dirt road, whipping around corners and flying over rocks. A few times Gabi watched Mei's truck teeter on a turn. It seemed like she was about to lose control and flip, but then she recovered, balancing for just a moment on only two wheels. *Is this really happening?* Gabi thought.

In the distance, Gabi saw the approaching jeeps of the Security Police Force. *Thank God,* she thought. *I'm not even armed.* Farther down the road, a contingent of jeeps had positioned itself to block Mei's path. *This will be over soon.*

Spotting the officers, Mei swerved off the road and headed into the pockmarked field, dodging the craters. Sighing, Gabi followed. She couldn't let Mei, or those USB drives, out of her sight. Mei's truck bounced over boulders and whipped from side to side to avoid the largest obstacles. Gabi blinked as the dust from the truck wheels blurred her vision and filled the air with a choking haze. Then she heard a loud pop and saw Mei's truck veer to the side and jolt to a stop. Her front tire had blown. *Game's over*, Gabi thought, watching the small woman climb out of her truck. Gabi also exited her vehicle and called out, "Okay, it's over. I'll take you in." But instead of surrendering, Mei started running toward Sedan crater. Startled, Gabi followed on foot.

Gabi's sneakered feet sank in the soft sand as she chased Mei onto the viewing platform. Mei ran to the edge of the platform that hung out over the edge of the crater and dipped behind the protective rail. She reached into her pocket. Gabi hoped she wasn't reaching for a gun.

Mei withdrew a small box and held it up. "This is a satellite transmitter," she shouted. "Don't come any closer or I will use it to send the data on these USB drives directly to China!"

"Mei," Gabi said, "you can't get away with this." She edged closer and climbed over the railing. "Just hand those drives over to me." Gabi took a step toward Mei when, without warning, the Chinese woman dove over the edge.

Gabi lunged forward and grabbed Mei's foot. Despite Mei's small size, the momentum was too much for Gabi. They tumbled over the edge.

Chapter 5
Matters of Life and Death

WILL AND JOE RAMOS ARRIVED at their destination just before noon, spotting Laguna Verde's distinctive red buildings silhouetted against the blue sky. The power plant's rectangular concrete structures perched on the edge of the Mexico's gulf coast, with the lush mountains of Northern Veracruz behind them. Despite arriving several hours later than they had planned, Will was happy to see that the area was peaceful. The streets near the plant were not too crowded. Maybe everyone was taking *la siesta*.

Will and Joe sat in the dilapidated pickup truck and looked down the hill at the power plant. The noon sun gave it a bleached appearance. Will squinted to see if he could spot any vehicles moving. All seemed quiet.

"See, I told you there would be no security in this spot," Joe said.

Will nodded. "I wish we were here this morning like we planned."

"It doesn't matter. They are not patrolling the fence." Joe sounded excited, impatient to get the device placed.

"Right at this moment, I guess," Will muttered as he put the truck in gear. He drove slowly, eyes looking for a security vehicle or any guards that might sound the alarm. Luck seemed to be on their side. He pulled off the service road close to the fence. He and Joe got out. As Will exited the truck and opened the tailgate to begin unloading the device. He squinted at the Laguna Verde power plant.

"*¿Eso es un reactor nuclear? ¿Estás seguro?*" Will asked his younger-by-one-minute nearly identical twin brother. "It just looks like a building. Where's the cooling towers? Y'know, like in the movies."

"*¿No confías en mí, hermano mayor?*" Joe replied with a grin. "You should trust me. I paid attention in grad school. When they're built on the coast, nuclear power plants use seawater for cooling. *¿Ahora quien es el idiota?*"

Will turned away with a grimace. He was used to being the brains behind their dynamic duo. He couldn't get used to Joe being in charge.

They positioned the device near the security fence closest to the largest reactor. Will worried that a security guard would step outside to smoke a cigarette or stretch his legs. Did they have cameras? Did they look in this direction? Nothing happened as they finished positioning the device. They got back into the truck and drove east from the power plant.

"We need to get as far away as possible before triggering the weapon to minimize our exposure to the electromagnetic pulse that will follow the detonation," Joe explained. The pulse could be sizable, and they didn't want to risk it frying the ignition system on the truck.

Giddy with exhaustion and excitement, both men were already thinking about the extortion money. Their optimism was premature.

As Laguna Verde shrunk in the rearview mirror, Will pulled the truck to a stop a few miles away from the reactor fence where they had positioned the device. They got out and opened the truck tailgate, then sat in the bed of the truck, as if getting ready to watch a firework display.

"Now, all we have to do is push the button on the remote to detonate the explosive generator that provides power for the weapon," Joe said. "That will create the electromagnetic pulse and short out the reactor's cooling water control and transmission systems for a little bit. It won't take them long to get it back up and running, but it will scare the public. This should convince the higher-ups in D.C. to take us seriously. They'll pay the $100 million we asked for just to stop us from deploying another device."

Will handed the remote control to trigger the weapon to his brother. "*Después de todo, tú lo construiste.* After all, you built it," he said.

Will looked away and took a deep breath, enjoying the salty humid air of the coast. He liked the tropical climate—so different from the dry air of New Mexico. He also didn't want Joe to see how impressed he was by this plan. "How will we know if it worked?" Will asked finally.

"See those lights on the edges of the buildings?" Joe said. He pointed to several lights that were visible even in the daylight. "When the lights go out, that means the EMP has shorted out the electricity. That'll be our cue to hit the road."

"So, let's do it, *pinche*," Will said impatiently.

"*¡Vamos!*" Joe replied. He pressed the detonation button and stood back, waiting for the lights on the power plant to wink out.

The brothers stood frozen, staring, waiting for something... anything... to happen.

Will started to turn to his brother to tell him that he'd messed something up. Nothing was happening.

And then it happened.

The denotation emitted a powerful EMP, creating an enormous, blinding flash of light erupting from the transformer station beside the reactors, outshining the noon sun. Joe and Will squinted as the white light filled the sky. Then they jumped up and down, celebrating. Their Dragon's C.L.A.W. had worked! *Now Percy will take us seriously,* Will thought.

The brothers stood in the truck bed, unable to tear their eyes from the scene. Will was hoping to see the plant's employees coming out of the buildings, wondering who had turned off the lights. He laughed at his own joke. Instead, he saw steam rising from the roof of one of the buildings, then a white mushroom cloud erupted from the red and white Laguna Verde buildings and spread out over the ocean. Then Will noticed flames erupt from the facility as smoke began billowing up, traveling along the transformer lines.

"Why is there fire?" Will asked. "I thought you said it was safe. That there were fail-safes for the reactor."

"I don't know, *hermano*," Joe responded. He was too surprised by what he was seeing to think straight.

What neither Will nor Joe knew was that the EMP had knocked out the reactor's electronic control system as well as the backup emergency diesel generators. That might not have been too much of a danger as relief valves should have activated, however those valves were also affected by the EMP. Without power, the reactor cooling system began to fail, causing pressure to build as steam surged into the relief valves overwhelming all of the plant's failsafe systems. Within moments, a fitting exploded, a cooling line shattered, and a huge cloud of steam had been released into the sky.

"*¡Dios mío!*" Will exclaimed as the transformer towers on the boundary of the plant began exploding one by one, shaking the ground beneath them. The brothers reflexively ducked as something within the plant exploded, throwing giant pieces of twisted metal into the air, with jagged chunks careening down onto the beach.

"Umm, Will," Joe whispered in a trembling voice. "Will, this wasn't what I expected."

"Who cares, it worked, didn't it?" Will exclaimed, his thoughts already getting past the problem and thinking about how this would work to their advantage. This amount of destruction from a single weapon would surely get Percy's attention. He'd know that Will Ramos had the *cajones* and was someone to be taken seriously. To be respected. "Now all we have to do is contact Percy and wait to collect our money. It's time to celebrate."

Will pulled the bottle of Don Julio tequila from beneath the front seat of the truck and offered it to his brother. It was time to drink a toast to their future wealth. Standing beside the ancient truck in a desolate field watching the billowing steam clouds, the brothers whooped and shouted and drank to their success.

* * *

As Will and Joe celebrated, lost in their delusion of coming riches, they did not realize that death waited above them.

Ten thousand feet above the coast, a MQ-9 Reaper drone was just coming on station. After a tip from the lab director at Los Alamos, the National Security Agency had been monitoring Will and Joe Ramos to see if they would make good on their threat. NSA officials had confirmed the threat through signal intelligence, and when they realized that the Ramos brothers had left the warehouse, they prepared to act.

Unfortunately, it had taken time to convince their Mexican counterparts of the threat, and then even more time to get approval from the Mexican government to allow the U.S. military to fly one of their predator drones in Mexican airspace. The NSA agent in charge still wasn't sure they hadn't broken a few treaties already. *Oh well*, he said to himself. *We're about to break another one.*

The Reaper pilot noted the spike in energy created by the EMP as it detonated. They were too late to prevent the attack. *Well, that's someone else's problem now*, the pilot thought.

"Possible target, three clicks east of the plant," the pilot said. He pointed to a truck on the monitor he was watching. The NSA agent leaned down. They could see two men cavorting next to the pickup, clearly excited by what they had just witnessed.

"Requesting authorization," the pilot said.

"Those are our terrorists," the NSA agent said. "You're authorized to engage."

The pilot nodded and swung the Reaper around. The laser guidance system activated and painted the truck. In a few seconds, the Hellfire missile was on its way.

Will glanced up, alerted by the noise, but had no time to react as the Hellfire slammed into the bed of the dilapidated pickup and exploded in a massive ball of flame.

* * *

"Well, we'll never be even now," Gabi told Alek. They were sitting on the tailgate of the ambulance parked beside Sedan crater watching the rescue effort, which was rapidly turning into a recovery effort instead.

Alek shook his head. "There's no way she could have survived being buried in all that sand." He turned to Gabi and brushed a strand of hair off her forehead. "What do you mean by, 'We'll never be even?'"

"That's the second time you've saved my life. I'm never gonna catch up," she said. Alek laughed, remembering how he had rescued Gabi from the drug lord last year in the Dragon's CLAW accelerator tunnel in China.

"Oh, I wouldn't bet on that," he said, slipping an arm around her shoulders. "I'm sure you will save my life soon. Anyhow, all I did was help you up onto the platform. I bet you could have climbed up by yourself."

"I don't think so. My arm was about to give out. It's a good thing you got there in time." The two gazed at the crater where rescue crews were attaching a long rope ladder to a crane. "I wonder if they'll even find her," Gabi said. "If she had stayed still instead of trying to climb up the side she might have made it. Can you imagine being buried alive under all that sand?"

"I don't want to imagine that," Alek said with a shiver. "Mei definitely had me fooled."

Alek turned, seeing Tim walking toward him, gesturing and shouting, "You have a phone call."

"Percy, I'm sure," Alek said, holding out a hand to help Gabi up. The two followed Tim to the truck, and he drove them back to the control point building, where a waiting security police officer handed Alek an antiquated but secure landline phone.

Naturally, Percy was on the other end of the line.

"So, here's what happened," said Alek.

"You already know?" Percy asked.

"Know? I was there. I am there. I mean here."

"In Mexico? I thought you were in Nevada. I called you in Nevada."

"Wait," said Alek. "What are you talking about?"

Percy filled Alek in on the explosion at Laguna Verde and the NSA strike on the Ramos brothers. Alek was more focused on the explosion at the power plant than the deaths of his two former employees.

"That had to be an LENR device. They stole our technology and built an EMP weapon," Alek exclaimed. "How are the Mexican officials explaining this explosion to the public? Has the damage been contained?"

"The plant is shut down, and officials in Mexico are blaming the explosion on safety violations. It should take them about a month to restore the electricity and get the plant running again. I guess the Mexican government would rather throw the power plant operators under the bus than admit their security guards couldn't even spot a terrorist attack. There wasn't any contamination, just a small amount of radioactive steam released, so it's not that big of a deal," added Percy. "Except that we finally located Will and Joe."

"It is a big deal!" Alek shouted. "They built an EMP weapon using my technology. You told me to build the knife and now Will and Joe have stabbed me with it."

"Alek, I think you are taking this a bit more personally than is healthy. It's not really news that the LENR technology can be converted into a weapon. Look on the bright side, the two people who knew how to do that are gone. Now, what was it you wanted to tell me?"

Alek sighed and launched into the explanation of what happened with Mei. Twenty minutes later, he returned to the lobby of the building where Gabi was waiting. Another 20 minutes passed as he filled her in on the fate of Will and Joe.

Alek sighed. "This whole trip has been a complete boondoggle—a gigantic waste of time."

"Why was it so important to Percy for you to do this tour?" Gabi asked.

"Oh, you know Percy—always trying to teach me a lesson. I think he wanted me to recognize and appreciate the role nuclear weapons and weapons testing play in keeping the country safe. It's not like I don't get it. It's just that I'm more focused on trying to find a place to build the prototype for Project Z."

Gabi looked out the window at the Nevada desert, the rows of Joshua trees standing like silent sentries monitoring the rescue crews. "Didn't you say scientists were doing underground testing out here somewhere? Maybe there's a former testing location that would work."

Alek followed her gaze off into the distance. "Yep, this place is so remote and so large. There's got to be somewhere," he said. "It's time to ditch the history lesson and look for a site."

"What are the requirements?"

"What we need is a huge hollow cavity like the Chinese had for their accelerator in Beijing... something underground or tunneled into the side of a mountain to provide electromagnetic shielding... something away from any public interference or possibility for contamination."

Alek waved a hand at Tim, who was still their assigned tour guide despite everything that had happened.

"Take me to your tunnels, Tim," Alek called out. "We need a big place to do big things."

Chapter 6
Yucca Mountain

THE SETTING SUN SENT THE shadows of the Joshua trees stretching out across the sand. "I think we've seen every underground facility and tunnel they've built here since 1950," Gabi groaned.

Alek nodded. They had traveled 1,000 feet below the surface of the desert to a series of underground laboratories that would have been perfect. Unfortunately, the entire two-mile-long tunnel network was already spoken for—an experiment underway in every space.

They rode a train several miles deep into a mountain where scientists had once detonated nuclear weapons. It would have been perfect, but now the tunnel was being used for nonproliferation and radiation monitoring tests.

They hiked up a hill to visit a site that would have housed the last full scale nuclear test before the testing moratorium. Alek deemed it too small and too shallow, even though the remaining cabling and diagnostic equipment could have helped speed up the build process. "We're just going to have to build something brand new," Alek muttered, his shoulders slumped as he sat down hard in the pickup truck. Gabi climbed into the back seat.

"You know there's one more place I think you should check out," Tim said as he started the ignition. "Of course, it isn't exactly in the Nevada National Security Site. It's more Nevada National Security Site Adjacent." Tim pointed to a mountain range in the distance, purple against the darkening sky.

Alek raised an eyebrow in confusion and then understanding spread across his face. He pounded on the dashboard, whooping gleefully. "Tim, you did it! You solved the problem. Why didn't I think of it! Yucca Mountain—it's the ideal spot."

* * *

The next day, back in Los Alamos at the lab, Alek practically bounded across the parking lot with Gabi trailing behind him. "So, explain to me exactly why this place is so ideal?" Gabi asked, speeding up her pace to catch up.

"Well, it's already been tunneled out, for one thing," Alek said. "The tunnel is eight kilometers long and about eight meters wide. It's got a lot of alcoves and side tunnels, they call them drifts, in it as well."

"Why was it built?"

"It was supposed to be a repository for the country's nuclear waste," Alek said, swiping his badge to enter the building. "Congress authorized it back in 1987, but there was a lot of political and environmental opposition, plus safety concerns about hauling nuclear waste across the country."

"Wait, don't we haul nuclear waste across the U.S. now?" Gabi asked. They entered the elevator and Alek hit the button for the top floor of the building, where the lab director's office suite was.

Alek shook his head. "Not high-level nuclear waste. Low-level waste—mostly used gloves and tools contaminated by transuranic radiation—are stored at the Waste Isolation Pilot Plant near Carlsbad, New Mexico, but high-level waste is kept at the reactor sites where it's generated. Meanwhile, Yucca Mountain has been abandoned for more than a decade. A $19 billion hole in the desert ideally located 90 miles north of Las Vegas."

"Ideal for Project Z," Gabi said.

Alek waved to Percy's assistant and pushed open the office door without knocking. "We found a site!" he exclaimed.

Percy held up his hand and gestured to the phone. He scribbled, "Wu is on speaker," on the notepad his desk. Sunli, seated in an armchair near Percy, scowled at the phone.

"Unfortunate, the thing that happened with that young lady," Wu's voice echoed tinnily from the phone speaker. "The People's Liberation Army recommended her for this collaborative visit. It serves them right for try-ing to deceive my dear friends."

"Yes, that was definitely a tragic miscalculation," Percy said. "Seems that her body couldn't be recovered."

"Pity," Wu said. "Mei Huang was a promising young scientist. Now, she'll always be part of the United States National Registry of Historic Sites."

Percy coughed. "So, it appears we've found a location for Project Z," he said, changing the subject abruptly and making eye-contact with Alek, who held both thumbs up enthusiastically. "I'll be in touch with more details soon."

"Excellent," Wu replied. "I look forward to learning more."

Percy hung up the phone, and both Sunli and Alek began shouting.

"You're not going to force me to work with General Wu."

"Yucca Mountain is the perfect location."

"That man is misogynistic and manipulative."

"I can't believe we never thought of it."

"Wu can't be trusted."

"I can't wait to get started."

"Peter and I will leave the project if we have to work with Wu."

"Who do I need to contact at DOE to get the ball rolling?"

Percy stood up. "Hang on, hang on, one at a time here. Alek, take a seat. Sunli, take a breath. Gabi, nice to see you."

The lab director waited for a moment, savoring the silence, and then he sat back down behind his polished oak desk.

Percy turned to Alek. "That's great news. I knew we would find the right location. I will contact the necessary people at DOE. Now, we may need help from Sal to provide some leverage with the local politicians and business community. I suspect as a casino-owner, Wu has some pull with the, shall we say less-above-board businesspeople in the area. He can be an asset there."

Sunli sprang from her seat. "I told you I can't work with Wu, and his mafia connections are certainly not a justification for collaboration. If Wu's in, I'm out."

"Well, that's your choice," Percy replied. "We'd hate to lose a key member of our team over something so trivial. Perhaps when you gain more experience working in the national nuclear security enterprise, you will understand why politics trumps science every time."

* * *

As the pilot announced that the plane had begun its descent into Las Vegas, Sunli stifled a sigh and gritted her teeth, replaying the past 24 hours in her mind. *Harold Percy is certainly a worthy opponent*, she thought. And, in the end, Percy had gotten his way. Sunli had stormed out of Percy's office straight to Peter Chang's, and, while Chang didn't convince her to abandon her ideals, he certainly helped her remember how much she had put into the project and her commitment to its success. Plus, Chang had promised to run interference between her and Wu. Chang's devotion was sweet... and quite useful, she thought with a sniff. *I guess I'll keep him around.*

So, reluctantly, Sunli had returned to Percy's office and agreed to the plan to collaborate with Wu. "Keep your friends close and your enemies closer," she told Percy. Before she knew it, Percy had arranged for her to accompany him and Wu on a tour of the proposed site.

At Percy's urging, Sunli had chosen what her boss called "a less conservative outfit" for the visit. She was wearing a short black pencil skirt, crimson silk blouse, and high heels. She knew Percy hoped her presence would help convince Wu to agree to their proposal. Basically, she was bait.

Although she didn't appreciate being used, Sunli appreciated Percy's manipulative tactics. As Sun Tzu had written, "The supreme art of war is to subdue the enemy without fighting." *I prefer to destroy Wu rather than subdue him*, thought Sunli. The Chinese general deserved to suffer for the way he had treated her and her mother. If she could find a way to hurt him, she would.

Wu had suggested they meet at his penthouse in Vegas for a drink so they could travel together to Yucca Mountain. The penthouse was located above the Lucky

Dragon, which Wu had bought years ago as a money laundering scheme.

Wu opened the door of his suite and ushered them into an expensively furnished room with floor to ceiling windows looking out over the fountains at the Bellagio. The retired general handed them both glasses of Baijiu and refilled his own glass.

"Let us drink to the idea of a binational public/private corporation," Wu exclaimed, downing his Baijiu and reaching for the bottle. "Tell me about this *ideal* location you have found."

Percy launched into the history of the Yucca Mountain facility, but Wu seemed more focused on Sunli than anything else. He reached over to refill Percy's glass, and they drank a toast to "profitable new beginnings," as he scooted closer to Sunli on the elegant white leather couch.

Sunli politely declined a refill—and noticed Percy surreptitiously pour most of his drink into a nearby potted plant when the general turned his head. Given the amount of alcohol in the beverage, Sunli guessed this would be a death sentence for the philodendron. She was relieved, however, that Percy was making an attempt to stay sober.

To distract Wu, she asked about the large blue and white vase sitting in a teak curio cabinet by the couch.

"I'm so glad you asked," Wu replied. "This is a genuine imperial Ming vase. I paid $5 million for it, and it's one of my prized possessions." Wu smiled and moved a little closer. Sunli struggled to conceal her revulsion. "I can see you and I share impeccable taste," he said.

Finally, the awkward cocktail hour ended, and the three piled into a large black SUV for the drive to the facility, which sat on the edge of the Nevada National Security Site. Wu took swigs from his pocket flask while Percy explained how much analysis had already been conducted regarding the long-term safety of the Yucca Mountain location.

As Percy talked, Wu kept his blurry eyes focused on Sunli. She feared his confidence was rising along with his blood alcohol level. *Does he really think I'd simply forgive him for holding me captive in Beijing?*

Wu scooted closer to Sunli on the SUV's bench seat until his leg touched her bare thigh, revealed despite her efforts to tug down her short skirt. She glanced at Percy, who appeared to be oblivious to Wu's inappropriate behavior. Sunli struggled to hide the revulsion and impatience she was feeling. She reminded herself of the end goal, even as she wondered when the endless drive through the desert would end.

At last, the SUV reached a guarded security gate and Percy flashed his Los Alamos badge to enter. Wu gasped when he saw the enormous opening in the side of the sand-colored rocky ridge rising thousands of feet above the desert floor. The volcanic rock housed a long tunnel drilled decades earlier but never used. Percy led the way to a golf cart parked near the entrance. Sunli was dismayed to realize she would have to share an even smaller space with Wu in the golf cart as they traveled into the mountain. She willed Percy to drive fast as he piloted the cart alongside the abandoned train tracks leading into the distance. Much like the underground facility in Beijing, white fluorescent lights lined the tunnel and pipes and conduits stretched along the sides into the darkness.

"This tunnel is five miles long and could easily hold the reactor and the power generation equipment with practically no cooling systems," Percy pointed out. "Naturally we will need to modernize and upgrade; the facility has been shuttered for decades, but we think it is ideal for our purposes."

Parking the cart, Percy got out and began walking ahead of Wu and Sunli, describing the future home of Project Z and its potential. Wu strolled behind Sunli. She glanced back, feeling Wu's eyes on her, and he sped up his pace to reach her, grabbing her arm. Checking to ensure Percy was too far away to hear them, Wu pulled Sunli close and whispered in her ear.

"Percy doesn't realize how willing you were to help Velásquez—how quickly you agreed to contribute to our work. What if he knew we never had to force you? What would he think if he knew his top scientist had agreed to join the enemy just because she was obsessed with seeing her scientific theories actually work?" Wu hissed.

Sunli wrenched her arm out of his grip, but he reached out and grabbed her again.

"You and Percy need me to convince my government to support this project. The question is…" Wu leaned close to Sunli, exhaling his alcohol-laden breath inches from her face. "*Nǐ huì wèi wǒ zuò shénme*… what will you do for me?"

"The answer is nothing," Percy interrupted with a gruff shout. He had apparently noticed Wu's behavior and now strode rapidly down the tunnel toward them. "Wu, this negotiation is between us. Leave Sunli alone."

"Oh, so now you are her noble knight offering protection?" asked Wu. "As we say in China, *ni ren pa yu, huang yan pa li*—over time, lies will eventually be laid bare."

Sunli scrambled away from the two men as fast as she could in her heels. She leaned against the rocky wall of the tunnel, trying to catch her breath.

"Share the money, share the research, share the woman," Wu bellowed at Percy, slurring his words slightly. "You think we need you, or China?" Percy asked, teeth clenched, barely containing his fury. "We can secure the funding from other sources. We have reached out to China in the spirit of international cooperation, but we can easily ask Indonesia, or Japan, or India." Wu's eyes widened at the implied threat. Each of those countries would be happy to participate and get a leg up on China. "It would be a shame if I had to call the head of China's Science Directorate and tell them we were cancelling the project because you couldn't keep your dick in your pants. Would you really hurt your own chances at increasing your own wealth over a woman?"

Enraged and clearly drunk, Wu launched a punch at Percy who skillfully blocked his arm, throwing the general to the ground. The two men stared at each other in silence. Sunli watched the standoff, wondering which of the two was the most stubborn. Finally, Wu rose from the ground, brushing the dust from his expensive suit.

"Let's head back to Vegas," Wu said, appearing to have fully regained his composure.

He didn't even acknowledge Sunli. It was as if the past 15 minutes had never occurred.

Yonas

"Seriously, we need to head back to the SUV," the general commanded. "I need to get to Beijing as soon as possible. We have a binational laboratory to start."

Chapter 7
Live On the Scene

SAL GUTIERREZ EXTENDED HIS HAND to Alek. Despite the dust swirling in the Nevada desert wind, the billionaire wore a bespoke suit, his spotless $4,000 Loro Piana Summer Walk loafers his only nod to "dressing casually" to tour the Yucca Mountain site.

He gestured to the older man beside him. "Alek, this is Albert Godones, from CRS Industries. Al's team will be to knock out the task of installing all the service roads and utilities and setting up living quarters onsite for the staff."

Al reached out to shake Alek's hand. "You made the right choice with your project lead here," Godones told Alek. "I've known Sal several years and his projects are always on-schedule and under budget."

"Yes, he's been a lifesaver—both at bringing in private investors and keeping everything organized and running smoothly," said Alek. "We will never regret choosing Sal as project lead."

Alek knew Sal was more than just a project leader. The self-made billionaire had connections everywhere. Whether he was charming an influential congressman, winning over a CEO from a legacy energy industry, or crafting an agreement with the head of the board of the world's largest asset management company, Gutierrez had exceeded all of Alek's expectations. Plus, the man was honest, funny, and sincere. Although the media often described Gutierrez as the next Elon Musk, Alek often pointed out the significant differences between the per-sonalities of the two billionaire tech entrepreneurs.

"Stop singing my praises and let's see that tunnel," Sal said. "We need to convert an abandoned hole in a moun-tain to a modern laboratory, so we'd better get to work."

* * *

Less than a month later, hundreds of workers swarmed the site, building roads, installing fiber and cables, and converting the central one-mile-long section of the dusty, dark, and cold tunnel into a working lab facility, with a side tunnel housing the computer controls for all the operations.

As the construction process moved forward, both Sal and Alek visited the site periodically, with Sal still headquartered in D.C. handling investors and politicians, and Alek guiding the project from Los Alamos. Throughout the demanding construction period, Alek's only constant was his daily runs in the New Mexico mountains, his sole release after stressful days.

At the end of each workday, when the sinking sun sent purple and pink streaks across the sky, Alek would leave the lab and head to the Pajarito Mountain Ski Area trail for his nightly jog. As his feet pounded the rocky path through the Jemez Mountains, he would feel some of his stress lifting.

While he ran, Alek thought about his former friends and colleagues Ron Digali and Candale Gregory, both of whom died in mysterious circumstances related to Project Z. He desperately needed their insight and expertise for the project's development. More importantly, he missed their friendship and support. Although Alek found he could bounce ideas off Sunli and Chang, they kept to themselves, never socializing with their colleagues outside of work hours. His other co-worker, Tom Lowe was busy with his family—two young children and a third on the way—and Sal Gutierrez maintained an impenetrable wall between his professional and his private life. Percy spent much of his time in Washington, shaking hands and talking up the project to politicians, while never missing the chance to mention the need for additional funding for his lab.

Alek ran several miles each night before returning to his lonely Los Alamos apartment, which somehow felt emptier than ever before. Soon he would move to Nevada and make his temporary home in one of the staff housing trailers near Yucca Mountain, but for now, it was back to the dingy off-white walls and lumpy beige couch.

From what Alek had gathered from their brief text conversations, Gabi was busy working a methamphetamine case in Albuquerque with the FBI's Violent Crimes Task Force. Although they were close enough to see each other in person, neither Gabi nor Alek suggested taking that step. Some evenings, they would exchange text messages, sharing memes and witty banter, but rarely venturing into the area of real feelings or fears. Alek found it ironic that now, at the peak of his career, he had never felt lonelier.

As the days passed, Alek found his thoughts wandering toward the past, returning to the accident that had claimed his young daughter's life. Everything would be different if it had never happened. He would still have a family, his life unshadowed by the constant feelings of shame and guilt. Then again, without the accident, would there have even been the breakthroughs that led to Project Z? Some days, the guilt, sadness, and loneliness seemed to be his driving force. What would it be like if things were different? Would he always be alone?

More than once, Alek stopped himself from picking up the phone to call Gabi and suggest they meet in Santa Fe. He would remember that he didn't deserve to be happy. If he had been paying attention to his daughter instead of obsessing about work that day... Alek told himself that he deserved to be lonely. He forced himself to focus on his work.

So, Alek worked. He worked from early in the morning to late every night. Although he wished he could turn to Digali, Alek had approached the pulsed power experts at Sandia Labs, who devised an ultra-high voltage pulsed trigger for the LENR reaction built upon the prototype Sunli had developed in China. Rather than try to optimize the trigger as would be needed for a compact space weapon, they decided to start the reaction in a small volume of fuel. Even if the ignitor were millions of volts instead of the much lower level that Digali had suspected, the reaction could spread to an adjacent fuel in the chain reaction that they called the high gain.

Drawing upon Sunli's theories, Chang's simulations,

and building on the lessons learned in the Advanced Energy Lab in Beijing, the project made progress. Sunli had discovered the mathematical physics theory of the trigger, and Alek had developed a way to channel the electromagnetic pulse that the trigger created to achieve a high gain reaction. There was no way to rigorously calculate every aspect of the experiment, even with Chang running simulations using the national lab's supercomputers. Instead, the scientists over-designed the triggering parameters to deal with this complex process, but they also assumed they would achieve a large output of energy. They moved forward with a scaled-up facility that could easily become a working power reactor if the high gain energy output was achieved.

As the site preparations continued, Sal Gutierrez hired IonTech to design and manufacture the accelerator used as the trigger, the ignition chamber, the energy flow channel, and the direct EMP converter, which would provide external energy storage. Alek decided that they only needed to run the nearly 100-megawatt energy generation for a few minutes to prove the principle of a future reactor, and the output could be transmitted along power cables to a storage unit outside the tunnel. With every passing day, they were getting closer to their goal of creating an endless source of clean, affordable energy. Sometimes Alek felt overwhelmed with disbelief that it was actually happening.

"Pinch me," he texted Gabi.

"I can't—I'm not there. Pinch yourself," she texted back.

A month later, the staff trailers were in place and Alek relocated his handful of belongings to Nevada. The single-wide trailer was a step up from his Los Alamos apartment. Although it had wheels, at least it was new.

Sandwiched between Death Valley, the Nellis Air Force Bombing and Gunnery Range, and the Duckwater Shoshone Tribe reservation, the Yucca Mountain facility sat on desolate, windswept land. Barren hills formed of volcanic rock undulated across the plains leading to the mountain ridge housing the facility. With no trees or other vegetation to stop it, the wind whipped across the desert, spreading a fine layer of gritty volcanic rock dust over everything inside and outside of the trailers. At times, Alek wondered if he had moved to another planet. Each night when he finally wrapped up work about 11 p.m., he sat outside his trailer in a lawn chair. Even after living in New Mexico, he had never seen so many stars.

Characterized by unreliable cell phone service, extreme temperatures, and limited access to health care, the Yucca Mountain site was far from a resort destination. The nearest city of any significant size was Pahrump, which was where Alek went for groceries and where some of the site construction crew went to patronize the legal prostitution establishments. Many of the construction workers actually lived in Pahrump or a smaller, nearby town called Amargosa Valley. While these locals welcomed the good jobs and high pay that came with the project, they were suspicious of the scientists and often muttered under their breath about the potential of dangerous radioactive materials contaminating their land. Alek had heard that the Western Shoshone Tribe was planning to hold a protest march on Mother's Day to highlight the danger Project Z posed to Mother Earth. The decades of distrust between the U.S. government and the nearby Indian tribes were evident in every encounter. No matter how much he tried, Alek couldn't convince the tribe members that Project Z in no way resembled the long-debated plan to store high-level radioactive waste on their ancestral land.

Despite the opposition from the Native Americans and some of the local residents, Project Z had already captured the hearts of the majority of the American public, thanks to Sal's frequent media interviews. Handsome and well-spoken, Sal had managed to hit every popular podcast and his name had been trending on YouTube for weeks. With Sal and Percy singing Project Z's praises, politicians had embraced the dream of unlimited, clean, cheap energy that could dramatically improve so many aspects of life. The media pundits embraced the concept of the LENR and quickly broke it down and simplified it for their viewers. On TV and social media, Project Z was hailed as the solution to many of society's problems. Even

Alek thought some of the claims and positive speculation were unrealistically optimistic, but he kept those thoughts to himself.

As Project Z's likelihood of success grew, President Thornton's scientific advisor decided it was time for a photo opportunity. Dale Croft, the bowtie clad, former Stanford professor who once discounted Alek's work, now sang Alek's praises. Croft was eager to stage a news event featuring politicians touring the Yucca Mountain facility while reporters streaming live video shared it with the world.

Alek had his misgivings about Croft's plan. "I don't trust reporters," he texted Gabi late one night.

"Most of them are just trying to do their jobs," she texted back. "Don't be so paranoid. If it makes you feel better, I'll come out to Nevada for the photo op to give you some moral support."

"Really?" Alek tapped out on his phone, feeling a jolt of excitement. "You'd come here?"

"Why not?" Gabi texted back. "It's about time I actually see this thing you're working so hard on. Plus, it's possible I also might want to see you."

Alek put down the phone, smiling, and repeated her text to himself. "It's possible I also might want to see you."

* * *

The day of the news conference, media trucks filled the rudimentary dirt parking lot closest to the Yucca Mountain site entrance. Well-dressed young reporters armed with hair spray and cell phones ordered tripod-toting videographers to capture footage from every angle. A handful of newspaper journalists, representing the few printed papers left in the nation, gathered by the site entrance smoking cigarettes and grumbling. Online correspondents stumbled across the uneven, rocky ground without looking up from their phones as they live streamed the buildup to the event.

Alek, Sunli, Chang, and Gutierrez were ready. Percy was traveling with the presidential delegation. Gabi hadn't arrived yet, but she had texted Alek to let him know that her plane had landed in Las Vegas, and she was on her way. Alek was also expecting some representatives of the Chinese government to be there, possibly even General Wu who was rumored to still be staying nearby in Las Vegas. The thought of dealing with the unpredictable Chinese general in the presence of live video news crews made Alek's stomach clench into a hard knot.

The construction crews had built a small stage in front of the entrance to the facility. Thornton would address the crowd, then Alek and Sunli would make some brief remarks about the project and take questions from reporters. Then, with cameras rolling, the old and new members of the Percy Study team would give President Thornton and his entourage a tour of Project Z. Teenagers from the Pahrump High School band stood waiting by the stage with their instruments, ready to launch into a well-practiced rendition of "Hail to the Chief" as soon as the president arrived.

Two police cars with lights flashing led a line of black Chevy Suburbans into the parking area. Alek knew that behind the dark tinted windows were President Thornton, Senators Plumkin and Braxton, Dale Croft, Harold Percy and all the various spokespeople, assistants, and Secret Service agents who traveled with the president. Following behind the motorcade, Alek spotted a nondescript rental car, a white Toyota Camry, with Gabi behind the wheel. He hoped she saw him look in her direction and smile.

Thornton headed to the stage, flanked by large men in black suits who made no effort to conceal they were Secret Service. The band began their performance, working hard to overcome the fact that several of their instruments were slightly out of tune after several hours spent waiting in the hot Nevada sun.

Alek allowed himself to feel a small thrill of excitement. This would be when the public learned about what they had created—a safe, clean, unlimited energy source that would change every aspect of the world. Alek knew he could never make up for the past, could never redeem himself, but at least he finally had one thing to contribute, something positive to help mankind.

But as Alek approached the presidential delegation,

ready to shake hands and welcome their visitors, he gasped. Wedged among the presidential delegation was Bob Bradley, *The New York Times* science writer who had accused Alek of using technology derived from alien spacecraft to build the LENR system. Alek thought Bradley had dropped his extraterrestrial conspiracy theories after the Capitol Hill anthrax scare. His presence at Yucca Mountain suggested otherwise.

What could be worse than Bradley? He spotted General Wu, decked out in his dress uniform, standing to the left of the stage, swaying slightly as if he had already had too much to drink. The ex-general had been respectful and somewhat helpful with the project so far, but Alek still didn't trust him. Before Alek could worry about Wu, he realized that President Thornton had already stepped up to the microphone and was addressing the crowd.

Alek struggled to process what Thornton was saying. The audience seemed to be enjoying the message, periodically cheering and bursting into applause as Thornton stressed the need for the United States to achieve energy independence, end global warming, and put a stop to poverty and inequity throughout the world. Project Z offered the solution to global problems, and America's future (along with four more years of Thornton's leadership) was finally in our grasp.

Sunli grabbed Alek by the arm and the two of them stepped onstage as the Pahrump High School band played "God Bless America." The noonday sun beat down upon them, causing Alek to squint out at the audience. He tried unsuccessfully to locate Gabi in the crowd.

Sunli, polished and poised as always, didn't appear to be feeling any ill effects from the rising temperatures in the Nevada desert. Her tailored black suit and cobalt silk blouse contrasted nicely with the desert hues of their Yucca Mountain backdrop. Her shiny black hair, twisted into an elegant chignon, suggested sophistication and practicality. The temperature had passed 100 degrees, but Sunli stayed calm and collected. Yes, she was a brilliant scientist, but she certainly was not an awkward nerd.

Alek was happy to play the nerd role. Sunli would discuss the long-range plans for clean, affordable, unlimited energy using Project Z, and he would address the technical questions about the facility and the device. They had it all planned out.

But they hadn't planned on Bradley and Wu. As Sunli concluded her remarks and Alek moved toward the microphone, Bradley stepped forward, brandishing his reporter's notebook and shouting. "Dr. Spray, can you confirm that you have built the Project Z system from an alien spacecraft that you have hidden in this tunnel, and you are reverse engineering extraterrestrial technology so your lab can develop an entirely new space weapon?"

Ignoring Bradley's outburst, Alek tried to gather his thoughts, but then Wu stepped onto the platform and grabbed the mic. The retired general weaved slightly, paused to gain his balance, and began speaking with slightly slurred words that suggested he'd had more than a few drinks before going onstage.

"Project Z is a binational project," Wu said. "It represents a collaboration of China and the United States working together to provide a global solution to our energy crisis. A successful union of two countries committed to solving the most pressing problems of mankind."

Alek and Sunli exchanged panicked glances, trying to figure out how to resume control of the news conference. Meanwhile, Bradley wasn't giving up.

"Why would the U.S. government spend $19 billion dollars on this proposed nuclear waste disposal facility and never open it?" Bradley shouted as Thornton's press secretary and several Secret Service agents headed toward him. Other officers surrounded the stage.

"It's clear that Yucca Mountain has always served as a secret hiding place for alien spacecraft and now Dr. Alek Spray is using this alien technology to create his revolutionary Project Z," Bradley bellowed. "Why do you think we are out here in the Nevada desert so close to Area 51? It's not a coincidence. Inside this tunnel is an extraterrestrial spacecraft that our government is using to create a potentially deadly device."

The Secret Service agents encircled Bradley and escorted him through the murmuring crowd away from the stage. Alek recovered enough to announce they would now begin the closed tour of the facility for the presidential delegation.

"We will rejoin the press corps and provide additional opportunities for questions after the facility tour," said Alek. "Only journalists with proper identification and clearance for the tour may join us," he said, looking around to make sure the Secret Service had dealt with Bradley. "But we will be available for all of the press immediately following the tour."

Assisted by the Secret Service, Alek ushered Thornton and his entourage off the stage and into the Yucca Mountain tunnel. "I'm excited to show you our LENR technology," Alek told the President. "Best of all, everything you will see in this tunnel has been created by Earthlings. One hundred percent alien free."

Chapter 8
A Romantic Interlude

HOURS LATER, ALEK AND GABI sat in the lawn chairs in front of Alek's trailer, the shadow of Yucca Mountain looming behind them, watching the sunset paint the desert with streaks of gold, orange, and red. Gabi raised her Dos Equis in a mock toast while the sun melted into the gilded horizon, and the evening's first stars appeared in the clear sky above.

Alek responded by clinking his beer bottle against hers. "To Project Z and incredible sunsets," Gabi exclaimed.

"Here's what's really crazy," said Alek. "This sunset thing... I hear rumors that it happens every night."

Gabi smiled. "I'm sorry I arrived late today. Traffic was a bitch," she added with a laugh.

"I was afraid that you weren't coming," Alek admitted. "I spent more time looking for you than preparing what to say. You know, the remarks I didn't get to give thanks to Bradley."

"That was quite a news conference," Gabi said.

"Yeah, things got pretty exciting," Alek replied, chuckling. "I wasn't prepared to deal with Bradley and Wu."

"You did fine," said Gabi. "Seriously though, did everything go okay once you got into the tunnel?"

"It was great. Thornton and the senators were impressed, the news coverage was overwhelmingly positive, and Croft was so happy I thought he would wet his pants."

"Are you happy?"

"I am now," Alek said. "I'm always happy when I'm with you."

With the sun gone, the air temperature had dropped,

and the sky had taken on a periwinkle hue streaked with scarlet. Gabi pulled her sweater around her shoulders. "I'm glad I'm here too."

Alek looked at the woman sitting in the rickety lawn chair beside him. The twilight bathed her in an ethereal glow. Was Gabi finally here beside him in the Nevada desert? Was he hallucinating?

Gabi leaned forward. "So, tell me the truth."

"Yes," said Alek nervously, wondering what she was about to ask.

"What's the deal with the aliens? Are scientists really hiding extraterrestrial spacecraft at Area 51?"

"If I told you, I'd have to kill you," Alek replied with a wink. "Actually, I've never been to Area 51."

"Well, we should go." Gabi jumped up and grabbed Alek's hand. "I hear it's nearby. Let's go on an adventure."

The two climbed into Alek's Toyota 4Runner, which had replaced the Ford Focus when he relocated to Nevada. They headed down the desolate road leading to State Route 375, also known as the "Extraterrestrial Highway." As dusk turned to darkness, they drove in comfortable silence through the desert, a full moon tinting their route a silvery blue.

"I think it's about a 40-minute drive," Alek said.

Gabi focused on the road ahead through the eerie, empty landscape. "So, what was it like being married?" she asked. "Sometimes I think a tube of toothpaste lasts longer than most of my relationships. You actually did the whole commitment thing."

"Julie and me... I guess we got married 'cause it seemed like the thing to do," he said, sighing. "It didn't take long for us to start quarreling about little things. She didn't like how much time I spent at the lab, my taste in music, the way I always forgot to hang up my damp bath towel. The best part of our relationship was Maggie, but even from the beginning I didn't do anything right. I didn't hold the baby right or fix the bottles correctly. I always felt like Julie was judging me, criticizing me, finding things she wanted to change. That's what I like about talking to you—there's no judgment," he said.

"There's no judgment because I'm not married to

you," replied Gabi. "According to my friends who are married, the judgment comes with the wedding rings."

Another mile passed through the silvery desert. Alek thought about the tipping point in his marriage—the real reason he and Julie were no longer together. Was his daughter's death the event that finally severed the ties between him and Julie? Or had their bond been broken long before?

"Maggie was only two, and, in many ways, I think we were just staying together 'cause of her. Even if the... if the accident hadn't happened, I don't know how much longer we would have made it."

Alek trailed off, reliving the moment he had found his daughter's lifeless body in the swimming pool. "Still, Julie blames me, and I blame myself. If I had been watching Maggie like I should have instead of working..."

Gabi placed her hand on Alek's thigh. "It was an accident," she said. They drove in silence for several more minutes, each lost in their thoughts.

Finally, Alek asked, "You never talk about your past relationships. What's the deal?"

Gabi looked away. "Work has always been the problem. No one understands what it's like to work in law enforcement and investigation... except other FBI agents, and, trust me, those relationships never succeed."

Alek said nothing, keeping his eyes on the road. Other than the occasional cactus, the barren desert stretched ahead for miles, an undulating plateau of silver and black.

"I think... I think I've never felt like anyone really 'got' me," Gabi said. "You know what I mean?"

"I used to," said Alek. "I kinda feel like someone 'gets' me now."

"That's it!" Gabi shouted. "That's it. Stop the car. It's Area 51."

Alek pulled the 4Runner over and parked in front of a high fence topped with barbed wire. Gabi jumped out and began taking photos with her iPhone. A red and white sign announced, "Restricted area. Photography is prohibited. Use of deadly force is authorized."

Alek pointed at the sign. "Am I going to have to use deadly force to restrict your photography?" he asked, grabbing Gabi's arm.

"This is Area 51 where mythical secrets are hidden," said Gabi. She looked at Alek and raised an eyebrow. "We've journeyed to the edge of the mystery together. Coincidence or fate?"

Alek looked Gabi in the eye. They were all alone in the desert under the moonlight on the edge of a mysterious government installment.

"This is definitely not a coincidence," he said, drawing her into his arms.

* * *

When Alek woke up in the Little A'Le'Inn motel in Rachel, Nevada on the Extraterrestrial Highway, Gabi was lying in the bed beside him, her blonde curls fanned across the pillow.

"Hey," said Gabi, opening her eyes slowly and smiling.

"Hey," Alek replied as he ran a finger along the creamy skin of her inner forearm. "Was that an alien abduction?"

"Who exactly are you calling an alien?" Gabi asked.

"Well, you may not be an alien," replied Alek, "but last night sure was out of this world."

Gabi propped herself up on one elbow, looking around the hotel room. "Hmph, the décor is kinda under-whelming. I expected at least a bedspread with spaceships on it."

"I don't know about you, but I think convenience was the deciding factor in this location. It's the only motel close to Area 51."

Gabi ran her fingers through Alek's hair. "Yeah, I think we were in a hurry. A few space aliens and some curtains from 1985 can't scare us."

"I didn't even look around last night," Alek laughed, wrapping an arm around her. "I suppose it's too cheesy to say I only had eyes for you, but that's true," he added, while Gabi ducked her head to hide a blush. Alek looked around the shabby hotel room. "It is pretty awful. But I'd much rather see your beautiful face when I wake up than little green men."

Alek squinted at the sunshine peeking through the hideous curtains. "Despite the lumpy mattress, I think we slept pretty late." He reached for his cell phone to check the time.

"We did get a workout last night," Gabi said with a giggle. Then she noticed the look on Alek's face. "What is it?"

Alek shook his head. "It's… uh… it's nothing. Just some texts from Percy about a supply chain hangup. Procurement delays on some parts. I'm, uh, gonna jump in the shower, and then maybe we can grab a bite to eat."

Twenty minutes later, Gabi declared the showerhead suboptimal. "Last night was so magnificent that I hope we return soon, regardless of the crummy shower," she said, reaching for Alek's hand as they walked to the motel's attached restaurant. Gabi laced her fingers through his and tried not to notice as he pulled his phone from his pocket and began scrolling through texts.

The Little A'Le'Inn motel was basically the only business in Rachel, Nevada, a town of about 50 people that rarely had visitors. In 2019, a Facebook post urging people to storm Area 51 had brought thousands of people to Rachel and had sparked a half-hearted music festival called Alienstock. Since then, the town had enjoyed relative calm. The restaurant served basic American fare, no men-from-Mars specials. Over a breakfast of eggs, bacon, and biscuits, Gabi tried to make conversation, while Alek texted Sal and Percy and then left for 15 minutes because he had to "make some calls."

"My flight leaves early this afternoon from Vegas," Gabi said when Alek returned. "I'm headed back to Mexico to follow up on the meth trafficking case. Honestly, the cartel has been in shambles ever since Velásquez died. You made it too easy," she laughed.

Alek mopped up the last bit of his poached egg with his biscuit. He and Gabi had discovered they both liked their eggs slightly runny, topped with Tabasco sauce.

"Yeah, I've got to get to work too. The big test is less than a month away."

They both looked at their empty plates until the silence became awkward. "So, I'll get the check and we can get you back to your rental car," he said.

"Yeah," she replied, gathering her curls into a ponytail. "I guess it's time to head out."

Forty minutes later, Alek pulled up at the trailer where Gabi had left her rental car. "I'd get your bags, but I guess you never unpacked," he said with a forced chuckle as they stood beside her rental in the hot Nevada sun. He reached out and took her hands. "Gabi, I'll be honest, I'm not really sure what happens next."

Gabi could hear Alek's phone buzzing in his pocket. She leaned in and kissed him on the cheek.

"So, if we can get these procurement issues worked out, we're going to test Project Z in about a month," Alek said finally. "Maybe you can come down for the excitement?"

Gabi smiled as she slipped into her car to head back to Las Vegas. "I wouldn't miss it for the world."

Chapter 9
Flipping the Switch

AS THE HARSH SUMMER SUN rose over the barren desert ridge of Yucca Mountain, construction of the Project Z facility was in full swing. Alek and his team had sacrificed sleep to keep the project on target. No one had a moment of free time and most of the staff spent their days deep in the tunnel where the cool air and darkness contrasted with the baking brightness outdoors.

Alek carried out component experiments, while Chang and Sunli conducted ongoing simulation studies. Gutierrez took care of the business side of the project and dealt with the investors, while Percy stayed busy keeping the politicians happy and informed and making sure the government money was flowing. The lab director reassured Alek that the project had the United States President's full support.

Thornton's tour and the news conference had sparked worldwide interest in Project Z—and had raised some controversy. Bradley posted a series of columns on his personal website criticizing the project and ranting about collusion with aliens. When the reporter began appearing on the morning network news programs making increasingly ludicrous allegations, *The New York Times* finally had enough and let him go.

Alek knew Bradley had little credibility aside from his dedicated group of conspiracy theorists who spent their days posting hateful rants on social media. Even so, Alek found it hard to avoid reading the bizarre stories and the even stranger comments and arguments posted online.

Project Z also sparked renewed interest in Area 51 and had brought a steady stream of UFO enthusiasts to the region. Alek joked that the marketing team that put

Roswell, New Mexico on the map by publicizing Roswell's alien connections appeared to have relocated to Yucca Mountain. Business of all kinds was booming in nearby Pahrump and the Little A'Le'Inn motel in Rachel was booked solid for the next six months. Not that Alek had time to get away to the motel, although he often thought about what it would be like to return there with Gabi. Unfortunately, since the news conference, both of them had been busy, some days not even having time to exchange more than a few texts. When they did talk on the phone, their conversations were shy and awkward, not at all like the time they had spent at the edge of Area 51 in the Nevada desert under the silvery moonlight or the night at the motel that followed.

General Wu continued to insert himself where he was neither needed nor wanted, wandering through the facility unexpectedly at odd times of the day and night, always with his pocket flask in hand. He had become a constant presence, always asking questions, taking notes, but contributing nothing to the work. Alek had started referring to the general as "the necessary evil." Everyone grudgingly tolerated his presence and tried to ignore the interruptions he caused.

Wu often made a point of visiting the lab where Sunli and Chang were working, spending hours muttering in Chinese and watching Sunli's every move. Chang didn't appear pleased by the presence of the retired general, but Sunli made an effort to keep Wu happy. Sunli could stay calm and control Wu's volatile behavior.

Sunli had moved her belongings into Chang's trailer, and neither of them had made any attempt to hide their relationship from their colleagues. "Sunli's mother keeps asking when we're getting married," Chang told Alek, adding, "I think I'm going to start shopping for a ring."

Finally, the day arrived when theory plus simulations plus engineering came together, leading to Project Z's first full operational test. Gutierrez had closed the site to all but a handful of approved visitors. Not even the press would be invited to watch when they turned on the device for the first time. Alek had texted Gabi the date of the experiment and added her to the visitor list, but she hadn't said whether she would be able to make it. Alek already felt so stressed that he wondered if he would be better off if she didn't come. On the other hand, he desperately wanted to see her, and he felt she needed to be there.

Inside the control room, Alek, Tom Lowe—one of the founding members of the Percy Study team that started Project Z—and the other scientists and technicians were ready. This was the moment that would prove whether the theory, simulations, and engineering were correct.

Everyone's eyes shone with excitement, their faces illuminated by the blue light from six computer screens displaying every aspect of the Project Z system. Large banks of computers lined one wall of the room, ready to analyze every aspect of the process. Meanwhile, from the Pentagon to Beijing, remote observers hovered in front of computer terminals ready to collect data and feed it back to the control room in real time. As the Project Z technical staff monitored the output and readings, Alek prepared to throw the switch and engage the device.

To prevent distractions, Sunli, Chang, Percy, Gutierrez, and Wu were watching from the adjacent observation room, separated from the control room by thick panes of glass. Gabi slipped into the room at the last minute, and she and Sunli exchanged hugs.

"It's so exciting," Gabi whispered. "I wish I had a better grasp of how the whole thing works."

Chang leaned forward, eager to explain. "The process begins by channeling a small amount of fuel, called the primary, and then transmitting the electromagnetic radiation into the adjacent fuel supply, the secondary. The fuel is a thin sheet of nickel that surrounds the output from the primary and is continuously fed into the reaction chamber. The resulting continuous reaction produces transmutation products and channels more electromagnetic radiation along with a high current electron beam. The electromagnetic radiation and electron beam are directly converted using magnetohydrodynamics and electrostatics into an electric power output at a level of 100 times the input power, namely a power level of hundreds of megawatts."

Gabi nodded, trying to hide the fact that she had

stopped listening shortly after Chang began to talk. Percy put his hand on her shoulder. "Let me explain how it works, Gabi," he said. "You plug it in."

Gabi snickered and Sunli held up a finger indicating that they were getting close. A timer on the wall was counting down the last few seconds. Outside the observation room, in the rest of the facility, an electronic voice could be heard counting down the final seconds.

As the timer reached zero, Alek whispered to himself, "This is for you, Maggie."

Everyone in the observation room held their breath, and he threw the switch.

Nothing happened.

Alek stared at the computer screens in disbelief.

"*Wǒ lēi gè qù! Zhè shì húchě!*" Wu shouted so loudly that Alek could hear him in the control room.

Sunli turned to Wu. "I'm sure it's a minor issue. Try to calm down," she told the general.

Chang hurried to the control room and began inspecting records and readouts as Lowe and the other scientists scanned the settings on the control board. Wu crept into the control room, hovering in the background.

Alek began barking instructions at Lowe, who turned and held up his hand, "Look, man, we'll figure this out. Just give me a minute." Alek spun away and slammed his fist into the wall. He ran out the door and headed down the tunnel, his face twisted in frustration.

From inside the observation room, Gabi watched Alek's anguish, his frenzied search for answers. She watched as he punched the wall in anger and ran out of the control room. Gabi debated whether she should give him space or go after him. After a moment, she followed the sound of Alek's footsteps in the underground tunnel.

Alek strode rapidly down the dimly lit tunnel, traveling deep into Yucca Mountain. Gabi ran after him, shouting his name, but he didn't respond. Finally, breathless from the chase, she caught up to him and grabbed him by the arm.

"Alek, it's going to be okay. You'll get it working," she said.

Alek wrenched out of her grasp. "It's not okay. Nothing is." He turned away from her, leaning his forehead against the rocky side of the tunnel. "I have to do this. I have to. You don't understand."

Gabi slipped her arm around him, and they slid to the ground, backs against the rocky wall of the tunnel.

"It was... It was my fault," Alek said in a whisper. "My beautiful baby girl... If I hadn't been so careless, so preoccupied with work... so irresponsible. It's no wonder Julie could never forgive me. I can't forgive myself." Alek took a ragged breath, trying to pull himself together.

She gently wiped away his tears. "Alek, it was an accident. It wasn't your fault."

"No, it is," Alek choked out, trying to explain. "That's why the LENR became so important to me. That's why something good has to come from this. There must be a reason. It has to work."

"Alek, it will work," said Gabi. "Remember, we're taking a leap of faith... together."

Gabi gently brushed her lips across Alek's cheek as he buried his hands in her blonde curls. Forehead to forehead, their breathing synchronized. Both raised their heads, locking eyes.

"Alek, I have to tell you something," she said.

"I know," he replied. "Me too."

Suddenly they heard running feet pounding on the concrete floor of the tunnel. From somewhere down the corridor, they heard Lowe shouting, "Alek, Alek, where are you? I figured it out!"

Lowe rounded the curve, sprinting toward them. "Alek, one of the software sequences was off so the converter systems hadn't been activated," Lowe exclaimed, gasping for breath. "I fixed it. It's okay. Come back to the control room. We have to reset everything to test it."

Lowe held out his hands and helped Alek and Gabi to their feet. His face shone with uncontainable excitement. "Alek, this is it. Project Z is going to work."

* * *

This time, when Alek engaged the switch, the computer screens showed power increasing. Beneath them, the ground started to rumble, then the green light indicating full power came on. The scientists and technicians held their breath. Gabi crossed her fingers. Wu sipped from his flask of Baijiu. Chang mumbled a prayer in Chinese. Sunli grabbed his hand.

The power light stayed on for two full minutes, then the vibration ceased, and the control room fell silent as the machine completed its first successful run. The overhead monitor displayed the ignition, the energy transfer to high gain, and the conversion of the output to electricity generation—a 100 percent power output.

The room erupted in shouts of joy.

Project Z, the ultimate source of clean, affordable, unlimited power, was finally a success.

PART TWO
Two Years Later

Chapter 10
Golden Days

ALEK SPRAY TOOK A DEEP breath, inhaling the sweet smell of pine trees as he jogged down the Pajarito Mountain Ski Area trail. His feet pounded the rocky ground, and the late fall sun warmed his shoulders, bathing the path ahead with clear, bright light. The mountain air had always been clean and sharp, but recently everything seemed to shimmer with a new vibrancy. Any trace of air pollution that had once marred the vast sky above these New Mexico mountains had all but vanished since the Project Z technology started replacing pollution-generating fossil fuels.

As the sun sank in the sky, casting streaks of pink across the Jemez Forest, Alek reached the trailhead, eager to grab a bottle of water from the back of his new electric-powered Toyota 4Runner. While he missed the sound of the engine, it had been an easy switch to make. The new truck even had full self-driving functions, but Alek usually preferred to be in control.

Taking off his glasses, Alek toweled the sweat from his face and then jumped in the 4Runner to head back to Los Alamos. The run had been great, but he had dinner plans.

Gabi Stebbens was waiting on the portal of Alek's adobe casita when he pulled into the gravel driveway a few minutes later. She sat on a wooden turquoise bench while Max, her white and brown spotted pit bull mix, rested his large head on her lap. Both the woman and dog rose when Alek arrived, Max wiggling from snout to tail in anticipation of greeting his friend.

After Alek bent down and gave the ecstatic dog some affection, he turned to the woman waiting on his porch, the setting sun illuminating her blonde curls in a fiery halo. Alek Spray—the nerdy Los Alamos physicist, the inventor of the revolutionary Project Z device, the divorced scientist who had spent years alone punishing himself for his past mistakes—couldn't believe his good luck.

After a shower and a change of clothes, Alek and Gabi headed for the nearby town of Española, where the legendary restaurant El Paragua had served northern New Mexican cuisine since 1966. Alek had always joked that dressing for dinner in New Mexico meant changing into your good jeans, so that was his choice along with a University of New Mexico sweatshirt. Gabi wore jeans as well, and a long-sleeved navy thermal. As an FBI agent, she could master many different looks, but her off-the-clock choice was always casual and relaxed.

Alek's dark brown hair was still drying from his shower and dusk was approaching when they arrived at the restaurant. The sky lit up in an explosion of fiery red, orange, and purple, bathing the underside of the cumulus clouds in color as the sun put on its best and final show of the day.

Walking into the courtyard in front of the restaurant, Alek and Gabi were greeted by the smell of Hatch green chiles roasting in a rotating screen drum over a firepit on the patio. "I'm thinking we should order something with green chile," Gabi murmured as the tangy odor wafted through the air.

Soon they were seated inside the cozy restaurant enjoying a meal of carne asada and each other's company. From the beginning of the meal with chips and salsa to the steaming sopapillas near the end, the two didn't stop talking, laughing, and eating.

"I love sopapillas, but we did leave Max alone in the house," said Alek. "I'm not as fond of sofa-pee-as, if you know what I mean."

"He'll be a good dog," replied Gabi. "Believe me, I warned him that if he wants to visit, he has to behave. Max and I wouldn't do a thing to mess up your beautiful new home or your lovely new leather sofa. Your casita is wonderful. I can't believe you lived in that horrible apartment for so long."

"Well, don't forget the trailer at Yucca Mountain," laughed Alek. "Of course, we did have some fun there. Remember the night after the first test..."

Both fell silent for a moment, thinking about the Project Z device's first successful test at Yucca Mountain in Nevada and the celebration that followed. Project Z could change the world. It had already changed Alek Spray.

Alek smiled and reached across the table for Gabi's hand, slightly sticky from the honey. "I'm glad you're here," he said.

"Not as glad as I am," Gabi replied.

* * *

Harold Percy had agreed to meet Salvador Gutierrez for a drink at the prestigious River Inn Hotel in Georgetown, a boutique establishment frequented by the fashionable people of Washington, D.C. Percy had just wrapped up a series of meetings with the Secretary of Energy, and he wanted to let Sal know Secretary Diana Dehoyos had nothing but compliments for the Project Z team.

When he arrived, Percy found the bar pleasantly dark with flickering candles and low-hanging pendant lights— a soothing environment after a long day of meetings. Sal was already there, chatting with a man Percy couldn't quite place. Was that the Chair of the Cleveland Ventures investment firm or a senator? The man looked vaguely familiar in the way many wealthy white men in their sixties looked.

Percy slid into a booth and ordered a whisky neat, watching Gutierrez. As an openly gay Hispanic man who had crossed the border illegally and grew up undocumented in New Mexico, Sal certainly didn't fit the D.C. stereotype, but he had never let that stop him. Wealthy, influential people clamored to spend time in the presence of the self-made billionaire whose high-tech inventions had changed the world.

At last, Sal headed toward the booth, the gray-haired man he'd been chatting with followed.

"Harold, you know Senator Mitchell from New Hampshire, don't you?"

"Of course," Percy said, standing and extending a hand to the senator. "So nice to see you again, uh…"

"John," the senator supplied.

"So, we're wrapping up the installations in the Southwest, right?" Percy asked as Gutierrez and Mitchell sat down and signaled to the waitress. Gutierrez ordered a Coke, and the senator requested a gin and tonic.

"I hear New Mexico, Nevada, Arizona, Colorado, and Utah are all installed and operational," Percy said. "Are we ready to head into Texas?"

"Absolutely," Sal replied, adjusting the cuff of his hand-tailored Alfred Dunhill suit. "I will admit it's been more challenging to convince the Texas coal and gas CEOs, but they've finally realized what happens to dinosaurs. They've decided that partnership sounds better than extinction, so they're embracing Project Z."

Percy put down his glass. "I've got to hand it to you, Sal," he said. "I never thought you could do so much, so fast. Two years ago, when you told me you planned to build terrafactories in New Mexico to produce all the components for the Project Z power plants… well, I honestly thought you were crazy. Giant factories on 50,000 acres of land with robotic assembly lines… I never thought you'd find enough people to build the factories, much less assemble the parts."

Gutierrez leaned back and chuckled. "I knew there were tens of thousands of skilled migrants seeking work, and thanks to our investors we pay significantly more than other employers. Plus," he said with a wink at the senator, "the legislation that streamlined permits, simplified regulations, and added tax breaks didn't hurt either. We got the job done."

"You're too humble," said Percy.

"I'm being honest. Every step of this process is easy."

"How so?" Mitchell asked.

Sal smiled. He clearly enjoyed explaining the Project Z process. "John, the only way we could deploy this technology so rapidly was to use what already existed. We have installed Project Z reactors at every power plant in the Southwest—regardless of its previous energy production output. Nuclear, gas, solar, wind... we use the existing infrastructure and build onto that, taking advantage of their connection to the grid."

"How long does it take to set up and connect the LENR machines?" Mitchell asked.

"Once the components are built, and it's time to set up each new Project Z plant, three 18-wheelers drive into a legacy power plant complex and connect to existing structures," Sal explained. "The time from delivery to implementation is less than a month. After a Project Z plant has been up and running for about three months, successfully supplying power and producing rare earth metals, we shut down the legacy power generation sources and render them safe."

"Producing rare earth metals as waste products of transmutation... that's genius," Mitchell said.

"That's just science," Sal laughed. "So many parts of our high-tech lifestyles depend on these metals, and both the United States and China were facing shortages. Investors love being able to stop the climate crisis and profit from the sale of the rare earth byproducts. It's what we call a win-win."

Swirling the ice in his glass, Mitchell asked, "Are the installations going equally well in China?"

"Things in China aren't moving quite as quickly," said Percy. "They've managed to install several Project Z plants in the northern part of the country, but they don't have Sal."

Sal smiled. "These are truly the golden days here in America. Unlimited, clean, affordable energy is the transformational step that will resolve so many societal problems. Already we have seen a dramatic drop in carbon dioxide pollution. The dangerous climate change driven weather patterns are diminishing. Project Z is a solution we can share with the world."

* * *

General Liu Wu surveyed Beijing's latest installment of the Dragon's CLAW. He strode rapidly through the underground facility, followed by a handful of low level

Chinese military officials who scribbled notes on their iPads as he barked out orders and commands.

"Clean this area. Check those gauges," he commanded the anxious underlings who scrambled to fulfill his orders, not realizing that the former general's scientific knowledge was limited, and his power was merely for show.

The Americans called the devices "Project Z" after the partnership between their government and private industry that funded their construction, but Wu preferred the name that both the Chinese and the Americans had given this technology when it was first developed: the Dragon's CLAW. The acronym CLAW had once represented the name "Collective Laser Accelerator Weapon," but the technology developed to create a deadly weapon had been transformed into a benign, globally beneficial energy producing device.

"Don't forget. The weekly report is due in the morning," Wu reminded the staff as he wrapped up his inspection. He had stayed busy visiting all the Dragon's CLAW facilities and supervising the expansion of the project, which had achieved unprecedented success.

Naturally, Wu also made sure that a portion of the profits from every Chinese facility funneled into his vast personal savings, which he concealed among various money-laundering entities including the casino in Las Vegas, Nevada.

Wu prided himself on his ability to acquire whatever he wanted, but the one thing he still had not obtained was the affection of the woman he had admired for several years: Dr. Sunli Hidalgo. Her delicate stature, mixed Chinese and Mexican heritage, and brilliant mind left the general transfixed, almost speechless, in her presence. Nevertheless, he felt certain that eventually he could win Sunli away from the man she now called her husband, the computer simulation wizard, Peter Chang. Both Chang and Sunli were still working at Los Alamos National Laboratory in New Mexico, but Wu looked forward to the day he could bring Sunli back to Beijing and take her as his wife.

Perhaps that would require the death of Peter Chang,

but eventually Sunli would realize where she really belonged.

The golden days were coming. Wu just had to be patient and focus on his plan.

Chapter 11
Unwelcome Developments

SUNLI HAD LOCKED HERSELF IN the hotel bathroom. Peter Chang could hear her sobbing from behind the closed door.

"Sweetheart, please come out so we can talk about it. The ceremony starts in less than an hour." Chang paced back and forth in the lavish Swedish hotel room. The room's soothing pastel color scheme, high thread count white linens, and scenic views of the water had done little to calm its occupants. Sunli's crying continued to build in volume as Chang found himself reaching the end of his patience. He was a physicist not a counselor, and he had never been comfortable dealing with emotional problems. Plus, he and Sunli were still basically newlyweds. He'd never seen her act like this. Chang had no idea how to help his wife.

"Please come out so we can talk about it, okay?" Chang pleaded. Slowly, Sunli opened the bathroom door.

The normally composed scientist's face was red and puffy from crying, with streaks of mascara running down her cheeks. Her usually sleek black hair had fallen out of the once elegant chignon. In contrast to this disarray, Sunli wore a sophisticated, form-fitting, beaded black ball gown and high heels. She was dressed for a special occasion. This was the night Dr. Sunli Hidalgo would receive the Nobel Prize for her groundbreaking work on Project Z.

Chang sat Sunli down beside him on the king-sized bed and stroked her hair slowly as if he were trying to tame a wild animal. "Please tell me what's wrong."

"I don't know," Sunli said haltingly. "I should be happy. I should feel honored, but instead I feel hopeless. It feels like nothing matters now. Winning a Nobel Prize for my research has always been my goal, but now that I've achieved it, there's no reason to go on."

"Don't be ridiculous," said Chang. "You're just between projects. You need to appreciate this moment. Not everyone wins a Nobel Prize."

"Especially not people who really don't deserve it," Sunli muttered under her breath.

"What do you mean? Why do you say that?"

"You know as well as I do that Project Z would never have become a reality without Alek's groundbreaking work, not to mention the support you and Lowe provided. Even the Ramos brothers deserve some credit. I shouldn't be the only one honored tonight."

Chang wrapped his arms around Sunli. "Darling, you developed the theory of using a high current electron beam as the trigger. It was the crucial step that allowed us to create a predictable energy release."

Sunli looked at Chang sadly, tears still streaming down her face. "I was a part of the team. Alek nominated me and he persuaded the entire scientific community to support my nomination. He helped me achieve my lifetime dream, but now I just feel empty. There's no challenge... no motivation... nothing to look forward to."

"What about me?" asked Chang. "Our marriage? We could start a family. Don't you have hope for our future together? For the life we will build?"

Sunli didn't acknowledge his questions. She stood, dried her eyes, and wiped the smears of mascara from her cheeks, then grabbed a tube of dark red lipstick from the dresser and applied it carefully. Sunli's emotional breakdown had ended. She was back in control.

"We have to leave now, or we'll be late," she said in a calm, expressionless tone of voice. "It's not every day a person receives a Nobel Prize."

* * *

"I don't know why you can't close the cabinets," screamed Gabi from the kitchen.

Alek was sitting in the living room of his Los Alamos casita working on his laptop. He wondered if he should respond to Gabi or just ignore her. Lately, whenever she came to visit, it seemed as though she spent the entire weekend scolding him. He didn't hang up the bathroom towels after he showered. He needed to take the trash out more often. He bought the wrong things when he went to the grocery store.

Alek knew that Gabi was under a lot of stress from her job as an FBI agent. For the past few months, she had been working on shutting down a heroin trafficking operation in Northern New Mexico. Drug use was increasing across the state, and unemployment had risen in some areas as Project Z decreased jobs in the oil and gas industries. The availability of unlimited affordable power had left some people unemployed and others underemployed with little challenge or motivation. Across the Southwest, more and more people were using and selling drugs.

"Gabi, come sit down," said Alek. "Maybe we should talk."

"I don't have time to talk," Gabi replied, slamming the cabinets closed. "There's too much to do and all you ever do is sit on the couch and stare at your laptop. Maybe if you did just a few of the things I asked you to, I'd feel a little less tense."

Alek shook his head. What happened to the warm and positive woman he'd gone zip lining with through the Mexican jungle? The Gabi he used to know seemed to be gone.

"I'm going for a run," said Alek, looking out the window. Some light snow was falling, but it wasn't enough to stop him from enjoying a jog on the nearby mountain trail. Alek turned to Max lying on the living room floor beside him. "Do you want to come, Max?" he asked, reaching out a hand to pet Gabi's dog. In response, Max growled. *Even the dog is grumpy*, thought Alek as he headed out the front door.

* * *

Harold Percy was having trouble sleeping. The director of Los Alamos National Laboratory had always prided himself on his ability to get a good night's rest despite the gravity of the high-level national defense issues he dealt with. Lately, however, sleep had become... well... nothing but a dream.

His workdays dragged on endlessly. There was little to do and the crippling fatigue he was feeling exacerbated the problem. Percy couldn't remember a time with so few important projects and crucial research taking place at the lab. On the one hand, he had no energy, but on the other hand, there was nothing to do.

Percy wasn't used to doing nothing; he had never considered slowing down, even as he entered his sixties. Then again, he had never felt like this before.

He had tried exercising more, taking sleeping pills, even supplements from a health food store—which he had previously dismissed as a "hippy-dippy Santa Fe thing"—but the insomnia persisted. Along with the sleepiness, Percy found himself developing a sense of hopelessness. He couldn't sleep. He couldn't work. He felt overcome by feelings of despair.

His wife had gone to stay with her sister on the East Coast, so he found himself alone in the big empty house eating frozen dinners and binge-watching Netflix. Late one night he phoned Alek.

"So, you can't sleep either?" Percy said when Alek picked up the phone.

"Yeah, but I guess that's a good thing since you're calling me. What's up, boss?"

The two chatted for a while about their inability to sleep and the growing irritability that everyone they knew seemed to be experiencing lately. Alek told Percy that Gabi had taken her crabby pit bull back to Albuquerque, and admitted, for once, he wasn't terribly sad to see them leave.

"It's like some kind of strange grumpiness virus," said Alek. "Everyone is tired and depressed. Gabi and I keep fighting about the dumbest things. I used to be calm and easy going, but now everything gets on my nerves."

"I feel the same way," Percy replied. "What if it actually is some new kind of virus... maybe something that escaped from a secret weapons lab."

"But, after the global pandemic in 2020, all the world leaders agreed to outlaw biological weapons," said Alek. "Even though no one could prove that biological weapons were to blame."

"Oh yeah. It certainly wouldn't be like government officials to lie," Percy laughed. "You know, I'm going to look into this. Now that I'm not doing any sleeping, I have a lot of free time on my hands."

Percy hung up the phone abruptly, leaving Alek sitting alone on the couch in his dark house. Something had changed—both in his life and in Percy's—and the only thing he was certain of was that it was not a positive change.

Chapter 12
In Search of a Diagnosis

ALEK SAT AWKWARDLY ON THE paper-covered exam table as the doctor reviewed the results of his blood tests on his laptop. "Mmhmm. Hmmm. Mmmm."

"Yes?" Alek asked anxiously.

"Yep," said the doctor, looking over his glasses at Alek. "You are like all my other recent patients... perfectly fine."

"But my symptoms?" asked Alek.

"Your symptoms are the same as everyone's... anxiety, depression, fatigue, insomnia, irritability... and every test I run shows you all are in perfect health."

"Could it be some kind of virus?"

The doctor looked skeptical. "I guess it's possible, but there's no elevation of white blood cell count or any other indication of illness."

Just then they heard a crash from the waiting room and the sound of the receptionist shouting.

"Sir, stop throwing things. You have to pay your copay before you see the doctor. It's our policy!"

The doctor shook his head. "But something has definitely gotten into people lately, and it doesn't seem to be getting any better. In fact, I think it's getting worse."

Alek thanked the doctor and left the clinic, doing his best to avoid the police officers who were now escorting the angry patient out of the building. Was everyone going completely insane?

As he got in his car, his cell phone rang. It was Percy with the results of some inquiries he had made to the World Health Organization. The WHO had collected and studied blood samples from people who had reported similar problems—depression, insomnia, irritability, fatigue. After extensive study, they had found absolutely nothing interesting. The same symptoms were repeated over and over with no signs of any sort of disease.

"The majority of the reported cases are in the south-western parts of the United States, although there are some indications it's also happening in China," said Percy. "I still wonder if it is some kind of biological weapon the Chinese accidentally released."

Alek stopped himself from snapping at Percy over that comment. Everyone knew what had happened years ago when the United States government blamed the Chinese for releasing a deadly virus. A new accusation of biological warfare could leave the world teetering on the brink of World War III.

This strange malady was definitely affecting him. They had to figure something out.

* * *

It was the first meeting of the Percy Study team since the Project Z technology was implemented and, in keeping with tradition, it took place in the basement of Harold Percy's Los Alamos house. Percy lived close to the lab and occasionally called important meetings in the electromagnetically shielded room in the basement of his home, which was dug into the side of one of the canyons near the lab. In addition to Alek and Percy, Chang and Sunli had come over, Tom Lowe had flown in that day from Lawrence Livermore, and Gabi had driven up from Albuquerque.

Alek hadn't seen Sunli since the Nobel Prize award ceremony in Stockholm. Normally reserved but professional, she seemed rundown and listless. Chang, though slightly irritable, didn't seem overly affected by the mysterious malady. Alek and Gabi had talked through their issues and were working hard to be kind and patient with each other. Lowe, however, seemed moody, impatient, and ready to get to the root of the problem.

"I keep losing my temper," Lowe said. "I've been screaming at my wife and kids."

Chang turned on his iPad. "I used AI to map where the reports of increased irritability have been reported. You can see the highest number of incidents is in the southwestern part of the United States."

"I can't take much more," Lowe said. "I feel like I'm going crazy. I went to the doctor recently, and she said it's all in my head."

Chang put a hand on Lowe's shoulder and gestured at the iPad screen. "With this many reports, it can't be imaginary. But what if this sickness we're experiencing... what if it really is all in our heads?"

"What do you mean?" asked Gabi.

"What if this illness has something to do with the way our brains function? What if some kind of interference is changing the natural activity of our brains?"

"Wouldn't an illness like that show up on a medical test?" Gabi asked.

"Not necessarily," Chang replied. "Have you heard of Havana Syndrome?"

Alek nodded. "No one's ever really proven that's real, but there have been reports for decades."

"Oh yeah," said Gabi. "That strange neurological sickness that has affected CIA officers and diplomats in Cuba and Moscow. Some people say it's some kind of adversary attack."

"Some people say it might have been caused by weaponized microwaves," Alek said. "I read an intelligence study that reported the cause could have been electromagnetic energy attacking the central nervous system."

"Right," Lowe said. "Diplomats in Cuba had symptoms ranging from dizziness to anxiety to cognitive fog. Some said it was caused by directed pulsed radio frequency energy or sonic attacks. Similar neurological attacks occurred in 2019 and 2020 at the White House. No one ever pinpointed the cause, but many people theorized it was some kind of targeted attack. What if this is similar?"

Chang looked up from a report he was reading on his iPad. "Those so-called attacks started in 2016, but there haven't been any reported recently. In fact, none in at least three years," he said.

Percy stood. "We'll get the lab's counterintelligence team to investigate this. It could be Russia."

Chang pulled up the map on the iPad again. "But why

would Russia target the southwestern United States? Surely D.C. or New York City makes more sense."

Percy shook his head. "I don't know. But, if I wanted to weaken the United States by unleashing a debilitating illness that changes the way people think and function, I'd target a place where some of the country's most brilliant scientists are focused on the most crucial national security issues."

"In other words, Los Alamos National Laboratory," Alek said.

* * *

Following the team meeting, which ended with no resolution and the only plan being for Percy to meet with U.S. counterintelligence, Gabi and Alek headed to his casita in the 4Runner. "The best part of having this meeting on a Friday afternoon is that I could convince you to spend the weekend with me," Alek said.

Heavy blue-gray clouds loomed low on the horizon, and occasional streaks of lightning split the sky. "Is that lightning or an electrical attack by the Russians?" Gabi asked with a laugh, and then said, "I guess it's not funny."

"Maybe not your best joke ever," Alek said, "but kinda funny. We need to do some research on the electromagnetic environment in the area. We have to identify the existing EM energy in the background in order to figure out if we are experiencing some kind of external attack."

As they drove, Alek told Gabi what he had learned about Schumann resonance when he was in college.

"Schumann waves are a set of peaks in the extremely low frequency portion of the earth's electromagnetic spectrum. In many ways, the earth acts like a giant electrical circuit that traps standing waves of electricity between the surface of the planet and the ionosphere. Lightning and solar flares can increase the resonance."

"I've read about that," said Gabi. "Some new age people in Taos say that the Schumann resonance can affect human consciousness. I've also read that extremely low frequency waves may be the cause of the famous Taos Hum."

"I'm not sure about that," Alek said. "The Taos Hum is

probably something a bunch of hippies made up back in the '60s to get attention."

He turned onto the dirt road leading up to the casita as the clouds gave way and rain began to pelt the windshield. "Basically, the Schumann resonances are the resonant frequencies of the Earth's atmosphere, between the surface and the densest part of the ionosphere. They're named for the German physicist Winfried Otto Schumann. Although the frequencies fluctuate, Earth has a standard background frequency of 7.83 hertz."

They pulled up in front of the casita but didn't get out of the 4Runner. Gabi stared up through the truck's sunroof at the falling rain streaming through the ponderosa pines soaring above them. "Just in case you were wondering, I find all this science talk super sexy," she said, "but right now I'm more interested in going inside and fixing dinner than learning about Schumann resonance."

"Oh, that hurts... I mean hertz. H-E-R..."

"I get it," Gabi laughed, kissing Alek on the nose. "You're such a nerd." Hand in hand, the two ran through the rain.

Chapter 13
Examining the Options

EARLY THE NEXT MORNING, ALEK went to the lab, which was empty on a Saturday, to grab diagnostic equipment. The machine consisted of two horizontal magnetic inductive coils for measuring the north-south and east-west components of the magnetic field, and a vertical electric dipole antenna for measuring the vertical component of the electric field. A specialized receiver and an antenna were attached to the complex device.

When Gabi woke up, she found him in the front yard, setting up a test.

"Here, hold this." Alek handed Gabi his phone as he raised the antenna. He asked her to click on the app that connected the phone to the sensor system and hold the phone so he could see the display. Alek looked at the readout and gasped in shock. It read 42 hertz.

"That's ridiculously high," exclaimed Alek. "There shouldn't be anything sending out such a powerful high frequency signal. It must be an error. Like I said, the standard resonance frequency in the environment is 7.83 hertz."

Alek fell silent, lost in thought for a few moments, then returned to his instruments.

"What are you doing?" asked Gabi.

"I'm measuring the amplitude of the signal. The higher the amplitude, the stronger the signal."

As Alek tuned the instrument, he continued explaining. "The amplitude of the Schumann resonance magnetic field should be about 1 picotesla. It's a very weak signal." Alek looked at the readout on his iPhone in disbelief. "This can't be right. This says the amplitude of the wave is 164 microteslas. That's more than three times as high as the earth's magnetic field."

"I need more coffee," Gabi replied, and handed Alek back his phone.

Leaving Alek to his testing, she headed inside to retrieve coffee for both of them and her own phone. Sitting in her bathrobe on the front porch of the casita, she sipped the steaming coffee and scrolled through social media. "Hey, there's a post on Reddit from the Los Alamos High School physics teacher. She says that, in the past few months, she's measured a significant amount of electromagnetic energy that's disrupting students' experiments. Could that be the same thing we're seeing here?"

"Get dressed so we can go for a drive and take some readings," Alek said.

"Wow, a guy wants to take me on an exotic vacation," Gabi laughed. "How can I resist?"

A half hour later, they'd packed up the equipment and set out in the 4Runner. Every 15 minutes they stopped on the side of the road and repeated the measurements. The frequency stayed high at 42 hertz, but the amplitude dropped ever so slightly as they headed north.

They drove and measured and drove and measured and the reading stayed consistently at 42 hertz even after they crossed over the border into Colorado, but the amplitude continued dropping. The further north they drove, the closer the amplitude got to its expected range.

"Ummm... how far are we going to drive?" Gabi asked.

"Let's head back toward Farmington and take some measurements there. But first, how 'bout a pit stop?" Alek pulled into a convenience store parking lot for a snack before getting back on the road. In the store, he eyed the rotating rack of premade fried burritos and considered getting one, but then he spotted Gabi making a face.

"What? The Allsup's burrito is the ultimate road food. I'm so glad they expanded their locations."

"I'm pretty sure it's not even food," Gabi replied.

"The Allsup's burrito is the purest form of tangy, salty, high-fat, fried, mystery-meat-containing concoction that anyone has ever consumed while driving. When you squirt on that vinegary, red hot sauce you achieve the essence of the road trip in all of its glory."

Gabi laughed. "That can't be good for you... but it does sound kinda yummy. Get two." She looked at Alek and smiled. "You know, I'm starting to feel a little better. It's almost like, the further north we drive, the better my mood gets."

"Unfortunately, we need to start driving back the opposite direction," said Alek. "Kiss me quick while we're still getting along."

As they headed south to Farmington, the sun setting and the taste of the Allsup's vinegary hot sauce lingering, the tension and anxiety returned, filling the truck.

"Hey, that's the new Farmington Project Z Power Plant," Alek pointed out as they drove into town. He pulled over and gazed at the small building that housed the LENR equipment. "Isn't it gorgeous? Just a year ago, this city had massive coal and gas plants belching carbon into the air. Who would have thought we could make such a fast transition to clean, affordable energy for the entire area—including the Navajo Nation. Project Z has really changed people's lives."

"Since we're here, should we take a reading?" Gabi asked.

Alek nodded and began unloading and setting up the equipment. "Cross your fingers," he said. They both looked at the electronic display. "Forty-two hertz with an amplitude of 312 microteslas," Alek said with a sigh. "At least our findings are consistent."

"I guess," replied Gabi. "The problem is, what does it mean?"

* * *

On Monday, Alek explained his findings to Percy.

"How can an electromagnetic frequency make people sad and grouchy?" asked Percy, leaning back in his chair and propping his feet up on the desk. Alek glanced at his boss' polished loafers. As always, the 60-something-year-old lab director was dressed in a tailored suit, looking more like a business executive than the rumpled physicists he supervised. After many years in leadership at the national lab, Percy was more comfortable testifying before Congress than conducting experiments. His days as a scientist had passed.

"I still think it could be a virus," Percy mused. "If China has accidentally unleashed a new kind of bioterrorism... now that would make sense."

"I told you it isn't a virus," Alek said tersely. He could feel the frequency acting on him, making it difficult to stay calm and rational. "Remember there is a multilateral ban on any sort of biological weapons development."

"That doesn't mean China or Russia is abiding by that agreement," Percy snorted. "Don't be so naive."

"Listen to me, Percy." Alek struggled not to raise his voice. "This is a serious problem. We're talking about a public health issue. People have a right to know."

Percy placed a hand on Alek's shoulder. "Okay, calm down. Counterintelligence is looking into it. I'll discuss the situation with the president's scientific adviser. In the meantime, please don't talk about this with anyone. All you will do is start a panic. There's no reason to worry the public when we really have no idea what's going on."

Alek bit his lip and shoved his balled-up fists into his pockets. "I'll do some more research and investigation, but I honestly think this poses an extremely serious problem. If we don't contain it quickly, things will get worse."

"I'll book a flight to D.C. tomorrow," Percy replied. "You do more research. But remember, for now, let's keep things in perspective. A few grumpy people isn't a global pandemic."

* * *

When Alek left the lab a few hours later to head home, he discovered it was snowing. This was the earliest in the season he ever remembered seeing this much snow. The light jacket he had worn to work that morning didn't stop the biting wind that swept the snow across the walkways in writhing snakelike patterns. *It's only October*, he thought.

Gabi had returned to Albuquerque again, taking her dog with her. While he missed Gabi, Alek felt relieved they had left, and he was especially glad to see Max go. Lately, the dog seemed unusually jumpy and irritable, and Alek didn't want to be around an unstable animal. He had always loved pit bulls and pit mixes and had never agreed with proponents of breed restrictions, but lately, the once friendly, docile dog was acting snappy. *Rather like everyone else*, Alek thought.

Alek sent a quick text to Chang to see if the simulations expert was free to grab an after-work beer. Chang rarely went out with friends, preferring to spend time with Sunli, but Chang had recently made a few comments suggesting the honeymoon was over. Perhaps the mysterious malady was taking a toll on their relationship. Both Chang and Sunli were extremely private, and Alek felt reluctant to ask what was going on.

Chang was already sitting in a booth at the Friggin' Bar, nursing a Dos Equis. Although the physicist was nearing 40, his jet-black hair and lean physique suggested a man barely out of college, but today there was a certain heaviness to his limbs. *No doubt about it*, Alek thought, *Chang looks sad*.

Alek slid into the booth across from him, ordering a Dos Equis of his own from the young waitress. It had only been a few years since Alek had met Gabi when she was working undercover for the FBI as a waitress at this bar, but it seemed like a lifetime ago. So much had changed since then, including the quality of service at the Friggin Bar. Gabi had been a terrible waitress—even she would admit that. Even so, Alek wished she were there waiting tables, wearing red lipstick and spilling the drinks.

"Hey, how's it going?" Alek asked Chang.

"It's been better," Chang replied. "This sickness or whatever it is... it's really affecting Sunli. One minute she's crying, the next minute she's screaming at me. I don't know what to do."

Alek struggled to picture Sunli showing such strong emotions. The Nobel Prize winning scientist rarely displayed any feelings. She was always calm and contained.

"Gabi and I have had our share of fights lately too," said Alek. "This illness is making everyone short tempered and irrational."

"It sure is," Chang agreed. "Plus, I'm having a hard time feeling motivated lately. All I want to do is sleep, but then when I get in bed, I lie awake for hours worrying about everything."

"Listen, Gabi and I went for a drive on Saturday and took atmospheric frequency measurements. The readouts were off the charts—most at 42 hertz. On top of that, we measured the amplitude of the wave at 312 microteslas right next to the Project Z plant in Farmington. The amplitude got lower as we drove away from Farmington, but it never fell to what I'd call a normal reading," Alek said.

The waitress came by again, and the two men ordered another round and a couple of green chile cheeseburgers. The greasy burgers topped with Hatch green chile were the bar's specialty. In fact, Alek wasn't sure if they even served anything else.

In between bites, Alek said, "Percy thinks it's a bioterrorism weapon or a new virus from China, but he agreed to talk to Dale Croft, the president's scientific adviser. Not that I expect Croft will actually be any help."

"Nope," Chang agreed. "We have to figure out what's causing it and find a way to mitigate the effects. I need Sunli to get back to normal." He sighed deeply.

"The thing is, we're both much better with calculations and equipment than we are with understanding the human body," Alek said. "We may need to talk to some medical experts, maybe a neurologist, to learn more about how a frequency like this can impact the brain."

"I'll ask around and see if anyone knows someone doing research in this area," Chang replied. "The one thing that does make me feel better is knowing I'm not the only one going through this."

"That's for damn sure," agreed Alek. "Somehow it's comforting to know everyone feels like this."

Chapter 14
The Dragon's Brain

THE TECHNICIAN COWERED ON THE ground beside the Low Energy Nuclear Reactor, known in China as the Dragon's C.L.A.W., as General Wu berated him for failing to carry out his work as expected. Wu's eyes bulged and a stream of furious Mandarin, along with flecks of spit, flew from his mouth. Finished with his outburst, Wu dismissed the man, both from the underground chamber and from his job there. This would be the fifth technician he had fired in the past two weeks.

The staff knew to tiptoe around Wu and had always struggled to keep the general calm and happy, but lately these incidents were becoming more frequent. The general's irrational anger and hair-trigger temper put all the Dragon's C.L.A.W. employees on edge.

On top of that, many of the engineers and technicians working to install the devices throughout northern China seemed to be suffering from an illness that left them listless and depressed. Complaints of exhaustion, anxiety, and malaise were so common among his staff that Wu had even suspected they were suffering from some biological weapon... some kind of virus unleashed by the Americans as a form of retaliation for the outbreak that began in Wuhan in 2019. Medical tests, however, had ruled out that theory and had shown no evidence of disease.

Now Wu had learned that some of the technicians were spreading the rumor that the illness was somehow connected to their work. The chief engineer had asked for a meeting to explain that many of his staff members were planning to walk off their job sites until the illness could be investigated and they could receive adequate medical care.

"They say that the machine is hurting their heads," the engineer said. "They call the illness *Lóng de Dànǎo*, the 'Dragon's Brain.'"

"*Zhè shì huāngmiù de!* That's ridiculous!" Wu exclaimed. "The reactors can't harm them. Fire them all and hire replacements. And hurry. We must stay on schedule."

The engineer nodded. "What are you waiting for?" Wu bellowed. "Get out of here now."

Now, alone in the accelerator tunnel, Wu began pacing. His staff was unreliable. His projects were behind schedule. He had to get to the bottom of these complaints about *Lóng de Dànǎo*, the Dragon's Brain.

Similar plants were going up in America, particularly in the southwestern part of the country. Wu wondered if his Project Z colleagues in America might have any insight into his workers' complaints. Despite his distress, Wu smiled at the thought that now he had a reason to contact the scientists at Los Alamos. *Lóng de Dànǎo* was merely an excuse for his staff to shirk work, but he could use it to his advantage. Soon everything he dreamed of would be in the palm of his hand.

* * *

"Welcome to my playground." Natasha Simon greeted Sal Gutierrez, ushering him into her high-tech lab. The private facility, located in Arlington, Virginia, was usually off limits to visitors due to the sensitive nature of their research, but Simon had extended an unprecedented invitation to Gutierrez. She wanted him to understand, appreciate, and collaborate with her on her latest project.

Dressed in olive drab army pants and a white lab coat over a colorful Hawaiian shirt, the Israeli chemist looked more at home in the lab than she had at the Cosmos Club or at the various formal dinners and scientific conferences where Gutierrez encountered her in the past. Surrounded by complex machinery and bustling scientists carrying out mysterious research, Simon was in her element, presiding over a kingdom of specialized equipment, electronic readouts, and high-pitched beeps.

As they walked through the lab, Gutierrez stopped in

front of a handful of scientists who were fitting a strange looking, knob-covered hat onto a man's head.

"What are they doing?" he asked.

"That is a near-infrared spectroscopy headset that measures hemodynamic responses to neuroactivation," Simon explained. "It's completely painless, battery-powered, and lightweight."

Simon gestured to another test underway on the opposite side of the room. A woman with a device affixed to her forehead sat in front of a computer monitor, typing on a keyboard as a readout displayed her brain function on the screen beside her.

"Here, we are studying the use of magnetoencephalography to enhance cognition. We're trying to develop a battery-powered interface system that pairs an external transceiver with electromagnetic nanotransducers that are nonsurgically delivered to key neurons."

Gutierrez held up his hand, smiling. "Natasha, remember that I am a businessman, not a neurophysicist. You have to simplify these things for me."

"Somehow I doubt that," Simon responded. "But I brought you here today precisely because you are a businessman. I've found the partnership that we created with the Project Z project to be extremely beneficial, and I'm hoping you will agree to work with me on some other ventures as we move forward on this new research. In fact, Project Z has helped make all this possible," she concluded, gesturing toward the lab.

Tucking a stray piece of wiry red hair behind her ear, Simon led Gutierrez into her office where she perched cross-legged on the couch. Gutierrez took a seat in a nearby chair.

"I'm starting to get more of an idea for how you've been using the rare earth metals collected from the Project Z devices," he said. "I know that these metals are the key elements for making batteries and magnets, and you appear to be using numerous lithium-ion batteries and magnetic devices for the experiments you're conducting here in the lab."

Simon laughed. "You must admit it has been an effective collaboration. I provided the funding for you to start building your power plants in exchange for what is basically the waste product of your reactors."

Gutierrez smiled knowingly. "Well, I'd hardly describe neodymium, praseodymium, and other rare earth metals as waste products, even if they are the transmutation sludge byproduct of Project Z. But I'm extremely intrigued by your use of my so-called waste. I take it you are creating battery-powered magnets to alter brain waves?"

"Naturally," Simon replied. "Our studies have demonstrated that neural stimulation can entrain and modify brain waves in order to enhance the slow wave sleep that is vital to brain health and may prevent dementia. I also believe we can use electrical stimulation to treat neurological disorders, and we can create a closed loop feedback system to enhance cognition. I want to partner with you to develop this new technology. I've named it 'Brainaid.'"

Sitting on the couch with numerous stray red curls standing out from her loose topknot, Simon tapped her sneaker-clad foot in time with music that only she could hear.

Gutierrez considered her offer. The woman gave off a sense of barely contained energy with an edge of danger. She looked ready to spring into action at a moment's notice and, despite her friendly manner, Gutierrez thought that he'd never want to be on the bad side of the former Israel Defense Forces intelligence analyst. Natasha Simon was a force to be reckoned with.

As if she knew exactly what Gutierrez was thinking, Simon smiled warmly and said, "By the way, call me Nat."

"Call me Sal," Gutierrez responded. "And I hope soon you will also call me partner on this intriguing new project."

Chapter 15
Media Mania

IT'S ONLY A MATTER OF *time*, thought Alek. The New Mexico news media had picked up on the mysterious malady that Alek and the Percy Study team were investigating, and, with typical sensationalism, had blown the entire situation out of proportion. From the front page of the local paper, to the radio reports, to TV stations, the illness had become the big news story of the year. Although most of the attention was concentrated in the southwestern states, conspiracy theories had begun sweeping social media nationwide with speculation about everything from government mind control to alien invasions. Alek usually tried to avoid mindlessly wasting time online, but he found himself drawn to the increasing number of podcasts; YouTube videos; and X, Reddit, Instagram, and TikTok posts speculating about the illness. The outlandish theories continued to grow, and Alek continued to doom scroll.

Despite his frustration, he felt compelled to watch the 10 o'clock news on KRQE.

The news anchors sat smugly behind their desks, reporting on what they had started to call the "Southwest Syndrome." The male anchor, a handsome Hispanic man, looked appropriately concerned about the situation, while his co-anchor, a much younger Anglo woman with straight blonde hair, nodded in sympathy.

"Tonight, we'll bring you a live report from the county jail where officials are dealing with dangerous overcrowding after an unprecedented wave of violence sparked a dramatic increase in arrests," said the male anchor.

With exaggerated sincerity, the female anchor continued. "And we'll bring you team coverage of a mysterious illness sweeping New Mexico and show you how the outbreak is leading to massive disruptions across the state. But first, we have an exclusive interview with the director of the University of New Mexico medical school who will share the latest statistics and research on the outbreak."

Alek hit the mute button on his remote, silencing the television. He had thought he wanted to see the news coverage, but he couldn't take much more. For three straight days, the news media had been speculating about the cause of the increased violence, the malaise, the depression, and the sleeplessness plaguing citizens across New Mexico. The crime rate, and consequently the incarceration rate, were up, and so were suicides and hospitalizations for mental illness. *The only people who could possibly be happy about this situation must be the criminal defense lawyers*, Alek thought.

Clicking off the TV, Alek walked out the front door of his small adobe house located outside the Los Alamos city limits. He looked up at the carpet of stars overhead, enjoying the silence and the sharp cold air.

Pulling his phone from his pocket, he called Gabi. "What's up? Have you seen the news?"

"My God, everyone's gone crazy," Gabi said. "This heroin case I've been working on… apparently half of the dealers have shot each other, and the other half want to make a deal to rat out their former friends. I can't take much more. I'm counting on you and your scientific talent to fix this mess."

Alek didn't respond. Finally, Gabi broke the silence.

"Alek, what's going on? I think something's wrong with the connection. Should I hang up and call back?"

"No, it's not the phone," Alek said and fell silent again.

"Alek, what is it?"

"It's… it's this illness… Southwest Syndrome… the strange 42 hertz frequency. I think I know the cause."

"Alek, that's fabulous! Now we can do something about it! Thank God."

Gabi waited through another strained silence.

At last, Alek resumed speaking. "Here's the thing," he said. "I've done the calculations, consulted with several neurologists and psychologists, and examined all the evidence. I can't ignore something that's staring us right in the face."

"What?"

"The problem is Project Z."

"What? How?"

"It was right there all along. I didn't want to see it. Didn't want to admit that the breakthrough…" Alek stopped for a moment, choking back the beginning of a sob. "The breakthrough that cost my daughter's life… the thing I've worked on for so long… it's hurting people. The signals from the Low Energy Nuclear Reactions are creating these neurological issues. I'm to blame."

"Alek, no. No, it's not your fault. Project Z is the greatest technological breakthrough ever invented. This is just… just a glitch."

Once again, Gabi waited on the other end of the phone in silence. "Alek? Alek, talk to me. What are you thinking?"

Alek looked up at the black sky, the air so cold and dry that ice crystals floated like diamond dust beneath the thousands of bright pinpricks twinkling above. "To quote Robert Oppenheimer quoting the Bhagavad Gita," he said, "'Now I am become Death, the destroyer of worlds.'"

* * *

President Jack Thornton had expected his second term in office to be easy. He had sailed to reelection buoyed by the success of Project Z. Thornton anticipated that the history books would describe him as the groundbreaking leader who helped bring clean, affordable power to America and the world. Now, however, this strange illness threatened his legacy.

Thornton wasn't certain Southwest Syndrome was serious—in fact, he wasn't even sure it was real. The one thing he knew though, was that he had to get the situation resolved as soon as possible. That's why the president had given his full support to Senator Larry Plumkin, the Republican from Mississippi, who had demanded a hearing about the illness. Thornton welcomed the hearing. He believed the more evidence they could uncover, the faster they could eliminate the problem and calm public fears.

He was wrong.

Room 216 of the Hart Senate Office Building would be the site of testimony from the U.S. Surgeon General and the directors of the National Institute of Infectious Diseases, the National Institutes of Health, and the Centers for Disease Control and Prevention. Numerous patients who claimed they suffered from Southwest Syndrome were also scheduled to testify, and spectators and news reporters had packed the chamber in anticipation of an exciting afternoon of pseudoscientific claims and mystifying medical terminology. They would not be disappointed.

When the day of the hearing arrived, the senators from the intelligence committee sat on a raised dais facing the witness stand, with the United States Senate seal affixed behind them on the imposing white marble wall. Members of Congress and the public filled the seats in the large chamber, while a handful of people hovered in the back of the room. Elevated platforms for television cameras on the sides of the room ensured the media would have a good vantage point to capture closeups of both the witnesses and the listening senators.

As the moment for opening remarks grew closer, several more people crowded into the chamber, carrying signs and dressed in what appeared to be tinfoil hats. Photographers jostled each other to get the best shot. One of the newcomers wore an entire suit crafted of aluminum foil and held up a sign reading, "Beware the Alien Epidemic." The camera lenses swung in his direction as he entered, accompanied by the clicking of digital shutters.

Senator Plumkin, the chair of the committee, kicked off the proceedings with opening remarks summarizing the limited government findings regarding Southwest Syndrome and then called on Dr. Maduabuchi Ekpo from the Centers for Disease Control and Prevention to take the witness stand. As Ekpo launched into an explanation of the tests and research that had been conducted, the man in the tinfoil suit elbowed his way through the crowd in the back of the room and approached the senators on the dais.

"Admit the truth!" the man shouted, interrupting the doctor mid-sentence. "We are all suffering from alien mind control." He jumped onto a chair, grabbed the doctor's microphone, and addressed the gallery. "The United States government is collaborating with aliens. Extraterrestrial technology started this illness because our leaders sold us out to the little green men."

The senators and audience members all began talking at once as Senator Plumkin grabbed his own microphone and shouted, "There will be order. The sergeant-at-arms will restore order in the gallery." Capitol Police officers rushed in, grabbing the tinfoil wearing man by the arms and lifting him from the chair as he continued to shout, "Stop the aliens! Save us from the extraterrestrial mind control!"

As the officers hustled the screaming man out the side door, Plumkin turned to the crowd and announced, "Anyone who disrupts these proceedings will be arrested. This is a Senate hearing not a side show."

Some reporters left the room, hoping to capture more antics from the man in the tinfoil suit. A brunette woman in a pant suit signaled her cameraman and began a live broadcast right from the Senate hearing. "I'm coming to you from the Hart Senate Building where senators are reeling from allegations our government is colluding with aliens," she carefully enunciated in a dramatic, yet hushed, tone.

Sitting in the second to last row of the audience section in the gallery, Harold Percy sank down lower in his seat, shaking his head. Last week, Alek had shared his theory about the Low Energy Nuclear Reactors being the cause of Southwest Syndrome. Much to his dismay, Percy could see the evidence. He hated to admit it, and he hated how this development had devastated his chief scientist, but all signs pointed to Project Z.

Percy had convinced Alek not to discuss his suspicions until they were absolutely sure and had crafted an appropriate response or, even better, a solution. Any hint that Project Z was contributing to Southwest Syndrome could seriously impact the lab's reputation, not to mention future funding. He needed to be prepared.

At least no one has mentioned a connection yet, he thought, running a hand over his close-cropped gray beard. We need to get in front of this thing and figure out how to stop it before the media and the public get ahold of the story.

Percy glanced over to the side of the room where a heavyset woman wearing a stained t-shirt reading "Fuck alien mind control" was handing out tinfoil hats to members of the audience. At the dais, Plumkin cleared his throat loudly, struggling to regain control of the buzzing crowd and resume the hearing. More TV reporters had started live broadcasts from the chamber. Any sense of order and decorum was lost.

"Let me repeat, this is a Senate hearing, not a side show!" Plumkin shouted.

Percy chuckled softly. One thing was certain, the Senate Committee Chair was wrong.

Chapter 16
The Taos Connection

AMANDA BERGER ARAGON USED TO like her job as chief security officer at Los Alamos National Laboratory. She enjoyed investigating possible threats posed by foreign intelligence entities, and she took this role quite seriously. Defending the lab from espionage and theft, protecting national security—these were noble causes in Aragon's eyes. Unfortunately, the individuals and incidents she had been asked to look into recently had nothing to do with foreign agents or sensitive classified material. Instead, Aragon was investigating her coworkers' personal problems, and she didn't like it one bit.

Among the cases she had been assigned were two suicides and a husband who had murdered his spouse. She was also following up on several suspected heroin addiction cases, something highly unusual for lab personnel. Reports of irrational behavior, various mental health issues, and an unusually high number of altercations between coworkers rounded out the list of her assignments. None of them were at all pleasant to investigate.

As Aragon drove to her office Monday morning, she passed two roadside stands selling tinfoil hats. She rolled her eyes as she drove by the stands, marveling at how fast people jumped on the latest TikTok-fueled trend. Even in a rather isolated town like Los Alamos, no one could escape the social media reports that announced tinfoil hats could block the effects of Southwest Syndrome. People were desperate for solutions and the fear of the illness was quickly becoming as dangerous as the sickness itself. Earlier that week, Aragon had found an Amazon box on her porch containing several tinfoil-lined ball caps. "Just wear one," her husband urged. "It can't hurt."

Although Aragon knew there was no way that wearing an aluminum foil hat could protect her from the irritability, depression, and exhaustion that had infected so many people, she obediently put the hat on when she left the house each morning, only to leave it in the car when she arrived at the lab. *I've never looked good in a ball cap*, she thought. *Plus, it's not a very professional look.*

Aragon flashed her badge as she drove onto the Los Alamos National Laboratory main campus and began searching for a parking spot. She would pass three more security checks and go through a metal detector before she made it to her office, which was considered a fairly low security protocol for a nuclear weapons lab. Aragon barely noticed the inconvenience of the security checks. It was a necessary part of working with highly classified information.

The lab itself was made up of numerous buildings, separated by parking lots and southwestern style landscaping of scrubby bushes and pine trees. Aragon's office was in the main administration building where scientists in khaki slacks, wrinkled button-down shirts, and sneakers strolled to their offices carrying steaming cups of coffee while chatting animatedly with each other about their recent research findings. Most of the time, it was a great place to work.

Lately, however, the lab had taken on the heaviness that was overwhelming much of the nation. People were on edge, arguing about trivial matters and sobbing behind closed doors. Aragon wished tinfoil hats could solve the problem. She wished her investigations led to a sense of closure. She wished for some kind of change.

Taking off her Patagonia parka, Aragon walked down the hall to her office. Much to her surprise, she had a visitor waiting on the bench outside her door. It was the Project Z researcher, Dr. Alek Spray.

"Dr. Spray, what brings you here so early in the morning?" Aragon only knew Dr. Spray in passing, although she was quite familiar with the groundbreaking work done on Project Z. She also knew how closely Dr. Spray worked with the lab director. Keeping Dr. Percy happy was important. A visit from Dr. Spray was certainly unusual, but unusual had become the new normal recently, so Aragon tried to take it in stride.

"I understand you've been looking into some of the recent unpleasant incidents at the lab... the murder, the suicides, the drug cases, the fights. I'm wondering if these things may tie into the phenomenon I'm investigating... the mysterious disorder, Southwest Syndrome, that is all over the news."

The two made their way into Aragon's office and, over a couple cups of weak office coffee, Alek described the odd frequency he and Gabi had measured and the way the amplitude of the waves decreased as they got closer to Colorado. He carefully avoided mentioning any possible connection to Project Z.

"Hmm," said Aragon, resting her chin on her hand. "So, you think the frequency might be causing the incidents I'm investigating? What you're describing... I know this seems like a reach but... could this weird frequency be kinda like the Taos Hum?"

"I've heard of the Hum—a mysterious sound or vibration that only a few people living in the Taos area seem to hear. No one knows what causes it. I've heard explanations ranging from underground UFO bases to secret government mind control and everything in between. It might be something stoned hippies in Taos made up to get more attention. What's the connection between the Taos Hum and Southwest Syndrome?"

"Here's the thing," Aragon said, leaning forward across her desk. "Most of the recent cases I've investigated involve people from the Taos area. It could be a coincidence... but it is kinda strange, don't you think?"

"I don't know," Alek replied. "Many of our lab employees are from the local area and Taos isn't far from here. It seems like a reach to say there's a connection to the Taos Hum."

Lost in thought, Alek glanced away, his eyes locking on a framed poster of Jackie Robinson, the famous baseball player, displayed on Aragon's wall. "Jackie Robinson—the first Black to play in Major League Baseball," Alek said, gesturing at the poster. "Are you a baseball fan?"

"No, not really. Not at all," Aragon replied. "Actually, one of the employees I interviewed recently gave me that poster. It was Sanders, the man who..."

"The man who killed his wife," Alek completed the sentence. "Why? What is the significance of that poster? Of Jackie Robinson at bat?"

"He said it was because of Robinson's number on his uniform... 42."

Alek rubbed his eyes. "Sorry, I keep getting headaches. Did you say 42?" he asked.

"Yeah, it's really strange. That number has come up in several interviews. A technician whose father worked on the Manhattan project told me one of the two atom bombs dropped on Japan had the explosive power of 42 million sticks of dynamite. Another guy told me that he was a marathon runner, and a marathon is 42 kilometers long. And then Sanders gave me that poster, right before the cops came to arrest him. So, I decided to hang it on the wall."

Aragon saw Alek write the number 42 on his notepad, underline the number, and scribble the word "coincidence" with several question marks.

"So, all these people... these lab employees who have been involved in unpleasant incidents recently... they are all from Taos?" Alek asked.

Aragon nodded. "Yep, all from Taos or very close to Taos. Could be a coincidence, but you have to admit that it's odd."

Alek stood, extending his hand to Aragon. "Thank you for letting me take up so much of your time this morning. I appreciate your insights. I'll definitely look into this Taos connection. It certainly seems odd and not very plausible, but lately, so does just about everything."

Chapter 17
A Reason to Celebrate

SAL GUTIERREZ FELT A RUSH of excitement as Nat Simon ushered him into her Arlington, Virginia laboratory. Finally, he would gain first-hand knowledge about the brainwave experiments Simon was conducting because this time he wouldn't just observe a test... he would be the actual test subject. Gutierrez was excited to try out the procedures he had been learning about over the past few weeks.

Simon led him into the lab that she had begun building shortly after completing her postdoc studies at the Weizmann Institute of Science in Rehovot, Israel. It was there she had started studying neurotechnology and the complex electrical circuitry of the brain. While at Weizmann, Simon presented several papers at international conferences, which led to an invitation to move to the United States and apply for a grant to study the emerging field of neurosystems engineering technology. She came to the states as an awkward outsider, a familiar role for her after her Russian parents moved her to Israel during middle school, but, although she was still an outsider, Natasha Simon was no longer awkward. In a few years, she had attained her U.S. citizenship and had established the lab.

Simon gestured to a small room off to the side housing a large piece of medical equipment that looked something like a cross between a CT scan or MRI machine and a freestanding hair dryer. "This is my pride and joy, the Brainaid," she said, gazing, almost lovingly, at the device.

"This specially shielded room contains a multimillion-dollar neuroimaging magnetoencephalography, or

MEG, device, thanks to a grant from the U.S. Defense Department," Simon continued. "It uses superconducting quantum unit interference devices to provide spatial and temporal measurements of the electrical circuits in the brain. This machine also contains incredibly sensitive magnetic field detectors, incidentally, operating at the super cold liquid helium temperature." Noticing the shadow passing across Gutierrez's face, she added, "Don't worry. You won't feel the cold. In fact, it won't be uncomfortable at all. Have a seat."

Gutierrez settled his lanky frame into the chair, and Simon began attaching electrodes to the back of his head. "Have you ever tried to meditate?" she asked.

Gutierrez shook his head. The self-made billionaire had immigrated to America illegally as a teenager and had overcome poverty to become one of the most successful entrepreneurs in the world. He had never made time for meditation or other relaxation and self-care pursuits. "I have read about meditation techniques, but never tried it," Gutierrez admitted.

Simon smiled. "So, you're a virgin. I think you will find this experience extremely satisfying."

Gutierrez tried to relax, but he couldn't help but wonder about the time Simon had served in the Israel Defense Forces. She was rumored to have been an expert in deception detection and brain monitoring, which no doubt helped lead to her current work in the lab.

Gutierrez tried to shake off these thoughts. Simon had assured him the procedure he was about to undergo was safe and painless. She has no reason to harm me, the billionaire reminded himself.

As she finished attaching the last electrode, Simon said, "I'm going to play a recording that will lead you through the basic eyes-closed guided meditation."

"Sounds easy enough," Gutierrez said.

"It is. Then, halfway through the session I will engage the electrical stimulator attached to the electrodes." She indicated the box where all of the wires from the electrodes were plugged in. "That will enhance the alpha frequency of your brain waves."

"Enhanced? Like a superhero?" Gutierrez chuckled.

"Not quite." She patted the large hair dryer-like device Gutierrez sat under. "The MEG will record your brain waves with and without the stimulation to determine how the electrical signals impact your brain function."

"Not negatively, I hope."

Simon patted his arm but didn't answer. Instead, she said, "The entire process will take a little less than an hour. Then, we'll take a look at the data and chat about how you feel. Are you ready to begin?"

Gutierrez settled back in the chair as Simon lowered the large helmet-like cover down over his head. "Close your eyes and listen to the recording. I won't tell you when the stimulation is engaged."

Simon dimmed the lights, and relaxing music and a calm voice filled the chamber surrounding Gutierrez's head. He sank deeper into the cushioned chair as the recording guided him into a meditative state.

"Sit comfortably and take a deep breath, in through the nose and out through the mouth. Notice the sensation of your breath. Follow the rising and falling of your breath. As you breathe out, focus on letting go of stress, allow your muscles to soften, allow your thoughts to come and go…"

"Okay, you can open your eyes now." Gutierrez blinked as Simon slowly brought up the lights and pushed the button to raise the mechanical helmet-like cover from his head. She gently began removing the electrodes. "How do you feel?" she asked.

"Did you decide not to conduct the test?" he asked.

"No, we completed it. It's been nearly an hour since you closed your eyes. How do you feel?"

Gutierrez rose from the chair and stretched his muscles. "Unbelievable. It feels like you turned on the recording just moments ago. I feel fantastic. I can't remember the last time I've felt rested and relaxed."

Simon handed Gutierrez an iPad displaying a line graph on the screen. "This is a graph showing your brain's alpha waves both with and without the frequency enhancement."

Gutierrez grabbed the iPad and studied the graph. He pointed to where the line jumped up dramatically. "What happened here?"

"That's when I began the brain stimulation. Do you see the boost? That's why you feel so good."

"It's incredible!" Gutierrez felt hyperaware, more alive, alert, and optimistic than he had felt in decades. "*Dios mio*, this is amazing. Such a transformation... and just 30 minutes of treatment..." Gutierrez grabbed Simon by the arms with excitement. "Nat, you'll be a billionaire."

"Perhaps," Simon replied calmly. "But the truth is, I need your help."

"Anything," Gutierrez said, running his hands through his thick black hair. "I feel like I could run a six-minute mile right now and climb a mountain. I want to travel, to dance, to make love."

Simon stepped back, overwhelmed by his exuberance. "Oh, don't worry, Nat. You're not my type," laughed Gutierrez. "But this machine... this Brainaid... it's incredible. Everyone will want one."

"That's why we need to team up, to make it possible," Simon said. "Imagine if we could put all of this stimulation equipment into a tiny device that could be worn like a hearing aid. The sensor, the power source, the excitation circuit, and the computer control... it all has to be packaged in a simple, wearable, battery-powered gadget."

"Well," Gutierrez raised an eyebrow, "you know I have access to plenty of rare earth metals to create the batteries to power the devices. We need to kick our research into high gear and, before you know it, our device will revolutionize the world."

"I knew you were meant to be my partner," said Simon. "Just one more thing before we get started—let's celebrate our future... and the future of our invention—the Brainaid—with some dinner."

"Absolutely. This calls for champagne and filet mignon. We'll drink a toast to Brainaid."

Chapter 18
Madness and Mini Vacations

"ARE YOU UP FOR A mini vacation?" Alek texted Gabi.

Gabi sent back a smiling emoji. "Of course. Where are we headed?"

"There's this bed and breakfast in Taos. I thought we could check it out."

Blinking dots on the screen indicated Gabi was typing her reply. "Somehow, I'm sure this is for your work, but I can't figure out the connection. But a vacation's a vacation. When do we leave?"

Three days later, Alek and Gabi were headed north again in his Toyota 4Runner, winding their way through the Sangre de Cristo Mountains, the windows rolled down and the satellite radio blasting oldies music. The High Road to Taos would take them through breathtaking scenery ranging from desert, to mountains, to forests, to farms and villages.

"So, is the real reason for this vacation related to the Taos Hum?" Gabi asked.

"How'd you guess?"

"I am a highly trained investigator for the FBI. Plus, I told you about the Taos Hum back when we took the first measurements. If I remember, you dismissed it as a bunch of baloney started by hippies."

"Well, I mean, UNM, Los Alamos and Sandia labs, plus other experts, have investigated the Taos Hum and nobody has figured out the source."

"Could it be related to the Schumann resonance you told me about? The Taos Hum could be a low frequency electromagnetic wave, similar to what we measured earlier. Plus, the Taos Hum was around long before Project Z."

"Some people think the Hum is caused by high-pressure gas lines or electrical power lines. Even the military and UFOs have been blamed. I'm interested in the Hum because Amanda Aragon—you know, the lab's security manager—well, she's been investigating some of the more unusual personnel incidents lately at the lab, and she's found that a number of the people involved are from Taos."

"You know, most of the people involved in the heroin trafficking ring I've been investigating are from the Taos area too. They are vicious, especially recently."

After driving for a bit in silence, Alek said, "I don't really know what the Hum is, but maybe learning more about it will help us find some answers. If Project Z is causing Southwest Syndrome, there must be a way to counteract the frequency. It's just a matter of understanding the physics behind all of it."

"Well, we certainly aren't the first people heading to Taos in search of enlightenment," Gabi replied with a laugh. "Maybe those hippies are on to something after all."

* * *

General Wu had started planning his vacation to the U.S., although, technically, it was a work-related trip. When the U.S. and China had agreed to ban space weapons development, both countries had also signed a treaty allowing for regular inspections of each other's facilities. Wu felt certain he needed to carry out an inspection at Los Alamos National Laboratory. Plus, a visit would give him a chance to learn more about the mysterious malady the Americans called Southwest Syndrome and see if the illness resembled *Lóng de Dànǎo,* the Dragon's Brain. Perhaps the Americans had already found the solution. Perhaps they had made a breakthrough but chose not to share it with their Chinese partners. *How typical of them,* Wu thought.

Over the past month, the general's struggle with insomnia, depression, and fits of anger had continued to grow, as did his alcohol consumption. He was eager to discuss his symptoms with his colleagues in New Mexico, but he was even more excited by the thought of seeing Sunli

Hidalgo again. The problem was that seeing Sunli meant also seeing her so-called husband.

Wu regretted introducing the two of them when they were working at the Advanced Energy Lab in Beijing. Technically, Wu had been holding Sunli captive while forcing her to work on the Dragon's CLAW. Fortunately, she appeared to have forgotten that unpleasantness and had treated him cordially while they completed their work on Project Z at Yucca Mountain. Unfortunately, she had not forgotten the man Wu had introduced her to in China: Peter Chang.

Wu had heard Chang and Sunli had married, but he was certain that she just needed to see him again and she would change her mind. He knew they belonged together. He had to convince Sunli.

Wu had hired a driver to take him from the Albuquerque airport to Los Alamos. Once, he would have chartered a private plane for a direct flight, but ever since he parted ways with the Mexican drug cartel, he had been forced to cut back on his expenses. Wu told himself he could make the best of the situation. He could rough it and spend the hour and a half drive in the back of the limo preparing to see Sunli. He hoped she would be pleasantly surprised to see him. It had been too long.

* * *

"Hey, you missed the turn," Gabi said as Alek sped past the exit for the road leading into Taos.

"Well, this bed and breakfast isn't technically in Taos," Alek admitted. "Technically, it's not even a bed and breakfast."

"Uh... what is it?"

"It's a yurt."

"A yurt?"

"It's sort of a round tent with wood lattice walls and a fabric covering. They're common in central Asia," Alek explained.

"Okay, I know what a yurt is. I'm not sure why we are staying in one. Where are we going, anyway?" Gabi asked as Alek continued to head north toward the Sangre de Cristo Mountains.

"We're going to the Haskalah Center. It's a spiritual community and retreat center. One of the leaders there has done a lot of research on the Taos Hum."

"And will this guru be able to help us figure out if there's a connection between the Taos Hum and what's been going on?"

"I hope so," replied Alek. "I know it's a long shot, but we have to start somewhere."

Alek pulled the 4Runner onto a rough dirt sideroad and they went bumping along toward a haphazard collection of buildings, including several adobe structures, a log cabin, and a large geodesic dome. In between the buildings was a large grassy area where a handful of people were doing Tai Chi.

Alek pulled his truck beside several other vehicles parked in a gravel covered area. "Let's go find ourselves a guru," he said.

As the two approached, a barefoot woman with dreadlocks detached herself from the Tai Chi circle and walked over.

"Namaste. How can I help you?" she asked.

"We're looking for Bernard Bhakta," said Alek. "He should be expecting us."

"Yes, let me show you to his office." The woman led them down a narrow path toward the geodesic dome. Colorful prayer flags, tall pine trees, and yellow rabbitbrush lined the pathway. Gabi stopped for a moment to take a deep breath of the cool mountain air and then scrambled to catch up with Alek and their guide.

"Here you go," said the woman, holding the door open. "Bernie," she hollered. "Bernie, you have visitors. He'll be right here," she said to them and left, apparently heading back to her Tai Chi practice.

A small, gray-haired, bearded man came shuffling around the corner. His face broke into a broad smile when he saw them.

"Dr. Spray and Ms. Stebbens, welcome to the Haskalah Center. Have a seat and let's chat."

Despite his advanced age, their host grabbed a large pillow from the side of the room, threw it down on the inlaid wood parquet floor, and nimbly sat on it cross-legged. Alek and Gabi also selected pillows and sat down more awkwardly.

"So, you are interested in our Hum? I was so pleased to hear a fellow physicist is taking our phenomenon seriously. So many have mocked it, but the Hum is a real thing, and its influence is increasing. I am eager to have your assistance deciphering it."

"So, you're a physicist?" Gabi asked.

"Retired physicist," Bhakta replied. "I once worked at Brookhaven National Laboratory in New York. I also ran a delicatessen, but that was back when I went by the last name Goldberg instead of Bhakta, and, of course, before I studied in Tibet."

"I guess that means we're not going to have pastrami on rye for dinner?" quipped Alek. "My mother raised me to appreciate a good pastrami sandwich—in fact, that was more important than memorizing the Torah portion for my bar mitzvah."

"You can't get good rye bread in New Mexico," Bhakta replied, "and a pastrami sandwich is not the same on a tortilla. Anyhow, let me tell you about my research on the Hum."

Bhakta explained that, for several years, Taos residents had been coming to the retreat center to get help coping with the effects of the bizarre Hum. Not everyone could hear it, but those who did complained of headaches, sleeplessness, and irritation.

"I've successfully treated the Hum sufferers by teaching them to meditate with a background signal of 10 hertz using alpha wave music. It was working marvelously until about a year ago."

Gabi looked meaningfully at Alek. A year ago was when they began operating the Project Z power plant near Taos. Alek looked away.

"I've brought some measuring equipment," said Alek. "Perhaps we can isolate the Hum and identify whether there is another signal—or anything else—present that could be amplifying the effect."

"Perfect," Bhakta declared. "I'd love to find out why meditation is no longer working and find a new way to help the sufferers. Let me find someone to show you to your yurt so you can get settled and begin your research. We will hold a community sitting meditation at 3:30 at the grass circle, and the Shabbat services are at seven followed by dinner. We're not having pastrami, but our chef makes a great green chile stew."

"Jewish Shabbat services and meditation?" asked Gabi.

"Oh, yes, we will also hold Native American prayers later in the evening. We embrace spiritual practices from nearly all religious heritages, and we welcome people of all backgrounds and traditions to live together and explore their common ground."

Gabi looked up at the sunlight shining through the star shaped window at the top of the geodesic dome. A ray illuminated Bhakta from behind, creating a glow in his flyaway white-gray hair. *Maybe*, she thought, *maybe we've actually found a guru.* Plus, she had never spent the night in a yurt.

Chapter 19
In Search of Enlightenment

GENERAL WU WAS FINALLY COMFORTABLY ensconced in the limo, recovering from the embarrassment of having to travel by commercial airlines all the way from Beijing to Albuquerque. He fondly remembered flying in Juan Velásquez's private plane, the Dassault Falcon. The Mexican drug lord's money had made life simpler. If only Alek Spray's interference hadn't led to the death of Velásquez, he would still be traveling in style.

Wu could have opted for a self-driving vehicle, but he preferred the old-fashioned luxury of having a driver. He wanted to sit in the rear of the car and enjoy the built-in bar. The limo was stocked with Wu's favorite beverage, Baijiu. He would need to have a steady supply of Baijiu to stay numb enough to face his American colleagues, especially Sunli Hidalgo, the woman he was certain he was destined to marry.

Los Alamos had no five-star hotels, so the general would be staying at the Four Seasons Resort Rancho Encantado in Santa Fe. In anticipation of his reunion with Sunli, he had chosen the so-called Sunset Suite, which was billed as offering panoramic mountain views. Spending $2,500 a night would be worth the investment if he could bring Sunli back for a romantic evening. If things went well, they would be too busy to notice the overpriced views.

As Wu's limo weaved through the narrow streets of Santa Fe, the general noticed people wearing bizarre silver hats that reflected the sunlight. "What are these contraptions on their heads?" he asked the driver.

"They're tinfoil hats. Supposed to stop the alien mind control that's making everyone sick."

"Sick?" asked Wu. "Sick how?"

"Depressed, angry, anxious," answered the driver. "Seems like lately everyone is in a bad mood."

Lóng de Dànǎo, the Dragon's Brain, thought Wu. He considered asking the driver to stop at a roadside stand so he could purchase a few tinfoil hats and then chided himself for indulging such a ridiculous idea. *If his employees are correct about the LENR devices causing some sort of signal that harmed people, tinfoil hats wouldn't be able to help.* As the limo pulled into the immaculate grounds of the resort, Wu forced himself to focus on his visit to New Mexico. He hadn't seen his colleagues since the Nobel Prize ceremony in Stockholm, and it had been impossible to find a way to talk to Sunli alone during that trip. This time would be different. It had to be.

Of course, the general couldn't just show up at an American nuclear weapons lab unannounced. He had arranged his visit and inspection in advance with Lab Director Percy and would be carefully monitored. Percy had informed Wu that Amanda Berger Aragon, the lab's chief security officer, would serve as his "minder" during the visit, but the general planned to escape from surveillance and pull Sunli aside to confess his feelings. He had worked closely with the Los Alamos scientists during the Project Z development, and he was certain he had earned their trust.

Percy had emailed yesterday about the scientists not being able to meet with him until the next day, so he planned to have the driver take him to the famed art galleries on Santa Fe's Canyon Road. With more than a hundred galleries, artist studios, and shops in a half mile area, he could find some new pieces for his Las Vegas casino. Vegas is nice, but Santa Fe also offers vacation possibilities, mused the general, particularly due to the proximity to Sunli. Perhaps he would be spending more time in Santa Fe. If only the local chefs weren't so obsessed with sneaking green chile into all their food.

* * *

Gabi rubbed her hands together, wishing she had brought some gloves on their mini vacation. The traditional Mongolian yurt featured a wood stove, which was old fashioned and unusual in this age of affordable electricity, and had been warm and cozy the previous evening, but the afternoon's high altitude winter air had an unusually strong bite. Gabi and Alek had spent nearly the entire day driving from place to place measuring the frequency and amplitude of the Schumann resonance magnetic field both in and around the city of Taos. Everywhere they went, their measurements showed 42 hertz with an incredibly high amplitude ranging from 375 to 624 microteslas. When Gabi asked Alek what that meant, he shook his head and muttered, "Nothing good."

As they headed back to the Haskalah Center, Alek flipped the radio to New Mexico's news leader, 77KOB. Reports of Southwest Syndrome topped the news.

"Things seem to be getting worse," said Alek. "People are acting erratically; crime is increasing; suicides are on the rise... and this is all my fault."

"How is it your fault?" Gabi asked. "You had no idea the LENR would create this strange frequency and impact people this way."

"No, but we wouldn't have the problem if I hadn't helped develop the technology in the first place. All I wanted to do is create something to help mankind; but look at the result... murder, divorce, suicide... not exactly the legacy I had planned." Alek focused his eyes on the road ahead. "Plus, there's another issue."

"What?"

"I've started researching the impact the LENR may have on climate change."

"Aren't the Project Z plants eliminating the use of fossil fuels and cutting down on pollution, so they're essentially eliminating the greenhouse effect?" Gabi asked. "That's a good thing, right?"

"Maybe. Climate change is complicated."

"What isn't?" Gabi murmured.

"In the past decade, we've seen a significant increase in weather instability. You know how the rising amount of carbon dioxide, methane, and other pollutants have caused an increase in the global average temperature?"

"Right," Gabi said.

"Here's the thing," Alek continued. "The Earth is a system. Everything is connected. Every change influences something else. We've seen drought, fires, flooding, rising sea levels, melting polar ice... all because of the changes mankind has caused."

"So, it seems like Project Z will solve all these problems by eliminating fossil fuels."

"That's what I thought too," Alek said. "Already we've measured a very slight reduction in the atmospheric carbon levels. But what if these changes add to the weather instability and make everything worse? What if the technology I developed is disrupting both the environment and people's brains?"

Gabi put her hand on Alek's shoulder as he drove along the winding mountain roads.

"Remember what you told me Percy said about technology? Technology is just a knife."

Alek nodded. "A knife can butter your bread or slit your throat. Technology isn't inherently evil—it's all in how it's used."

"And that's why we're here... trying to figure out how to use this knife responsibly. You can't lose focus on that. Project Z stands to revolutionize the world by ending poverty without boosting the use of fossil fuels. It is positive and transformative technology. We just have to figure out how to use it correctly. And we will."

Alek was silent. He didn't appear convinced.

Gabi was relieved when they finally arrived back at the Haskalah Center in time for dinner, which was served family style at long tables set up inside the geodesic dome. The Center members and visitors were a diverse group, representing a wide variety of ethnicities and dressed in an array of styles ranging from peasant dresses, to yoga pants, to kilts. The large room glowed with candlelight and buzzed with the sound of laughter and happy conversation.

"What are we having?" Alek asked Bernie as he and Gabi grabbed seats beside the guru.

"Posole," he replied, turning to shake hands with one of the other retreat-goers and bow to another. "We have traditional, kosher, and vegan posole," he added. "All three varieties have plenty of red chile. And there are home-made flour tortillas too, unless, of course, you're gluten free."

Gabi and Alek helped themselves to large bowls of the steaming New Mexican stew and piping hot tortillas. In between bites, Alek filled Bernie in regarding the tests they had run.

"Hmmm," replied the retreat center leader, resting his elbows on the table. "The Hum also has a frequency of 42 hertz, but it's never been measured at anything higher than 100 microteslas. Perhaps the increase in amplitude is the reason the Hummers have been suffering more."

"Hummers?" asked Gabi.

"Oh, that's what we call the people who hear the Hum," Bernie said. "Hummers or Hearers. They describe it as a whirring, or rumbling, or faint droning. Not everyone hears it, but many of the Hummers say it drives them crazy. They come here seeking relief."

"And the cause?" Gabi interjected. "What are your theories?"

"No one knows. It has been studied extensively. Could be high-pressure gas lines, electrical power lines, seismic activity. Similar phenomena have occurred in England, Australia, and even India, but no one can agree on the cause. Of course, a lot of people blame space aliens. Whatever the cause may be, I really thought I had the solution until recently."

"Meditation?" asked Alek. "It really worked?"

"Oh yes, it worked well," said the guru, shaking his head sadly. "But last year, our meditation practices became less effective for the Hummers. Something has changed."

Alek leaned forward and lowered his voice. "Last year, the Project Z Corporation built a power plant outside of Taos that uses Low Energy Nuclear Reactions to create energy. Please don't share this but... I'm investigating whether the Project Z plant is also putting out an unnatural electromagnetic frequency."

"An unnatural electromagnetic frequency that might be amplifying the signal the Hummers are already hearing," Bernie murmured. "Southwest Syndrome on steroids. That could explain things."

One of the retreat-goers interrupted to gather their dirty dishes. "Everyone helps here," Bernie told Alek and Gabi. "Thank you and namaste. I'll see you at the bonfire tonight," he said to the helper.

"Take a walk with me," the old man commanded. The trio stepped outside into the courtyard. The sun had set while they were eating, and the temperature had already dropped 20 degrees. The light of the full moon cast a blue glow on the rocky pathway as Bernie ambled ahead, seeming impervious to the cold.

After walking in silence for several minutes, the guru finally spoke.

"I have proven that meditating with a background signal of 10 hertz using alpha wave music can cure Hum sufferers... or at least could cure them up until last year. If they practice meditating consistently using the music, eventually they can train their brainwaves to slip into a meditative state without it. It's kind of like conditioning—like physical exercise... working out."

"That makes sense," Gabi said, shivering and zipping up her parka. "But is it weird to help people who are suffering without understanding the cause?"

Bernie stopped walking and looked up at the star-filled sky above him. "Why should the cause matter? The medieval rabbi and philosopher Maimonides once said, 'The physician should not treat the disease, but the patient who is suffering from it.'"

Alek ran his hand through his hair. "But what if we know the cause of this disorder?" Gabi slipped an arm around Alek, attempting to soothe him. Bernie appeared lost in thought.

The old man resumed walking down the path. Gabi and Alek followed. Suddenly, Bernie stopped and turned back to them. "Regardless of the cause, I believe training people to meditate will alleviate many of the effects of this new frequency, but some people, especially the Hummers, will require a more aggressive approach."

Bernie raised his hand to stop their questions. He wasn't finished. "Now, if your Project Z device is amplifying the Hum, you have two choices," he said. "You can stop using this technology, or we can find a way to offset its effects... a way to enhance the outcome of meditation."

"How?" asked Gabi.

"In answer to that, I will have to quote Maimonides again. He said, 'Teach your tongue to say, "I do not know," and you will progress.' I hope to see you both at the bonfire later this evening." Bernie bowed and disappeared into the darkness.

Alek sighed. "Now what?"

Gabi wrapped her arms around Alek and stood on tiptoe to kiss him. "Now, I have an idea. We have to go back to the yurt to get my phone. I want to show you an email I got last week from Sal."

Chapter 20
Now What?

BACK WHEN GABI HAD FIRST told Alek about her friendship with Salvador Gutierrez, Alek had been jealous. Although Gutierrez had the ability to help fund the LENR research, the handsome inventor struck Alek as a formidable rival for Gabi's affection. Relieved to learn Sal was not at all interested romantically in Gabi, Alek embraced Sal's partnership and the inventor had become a key part of making Project Z a reality. Now he was coming to the rescue again.

As Gabi and Alek bid Bernie Bhakta, the Haskalah Center, and their cozy yurt goodbye and headed back to Los Alamos, Alek urged Gabi to set up a meeting with Sal.

"He told you he's working with an Israeli chemist on a device that enhances meditation and trains brain waves, don't you think that's the ideal solution to the problems we're having with the LENR?"

"Of course. Why do you think I brought it up?" Gabi replied, a bit tensely. "Hmmm… maybe I need to try some meditation right now."

"Me too," said Alek. "Though I doubt it's really safe to meditate while driving."

"Well, we could switch the truck to self-driving mode, but we do need to be focused. Maybe we should try later. We could both set aside time to work on it. We can't afford to be arguing constantly because of the LENR frequency. We need to figure out how to train our brain waves to overcome the impact of 42 hertz."

"True," Alek agreed. "But I have a very important question."

Gabi turned, wondering what was on Alek's mind. He had never been very good at talking about their relationship or the future. Was this about to get serious?

"Yes?" she asked. "What is your important question?"

"How do we teach your pit bull, Max, to meditate?"

* * *

General Wu had his driver drop him off at the Bradbury Science Museum, near Los Alamos National Laboratory's 40-square-mile campus, where he was scheduled to meet Aragon. The lab security officer would be Wu's ever-present shadow during his visit, an irritating reality of being a foreign visitor at a national nuclear weapons lab. Wu was standing in front of the museum's replicas of Fat Man and Little Boy, the nuclear bombs U.S. had dropped on Japan during World War II, when he saw Amanda Aragon approaching. They had met during Wu's previous visit to New Mexico, and the general had struggled to hide his disapproval. He simply couldn't understand how the Americans could put a woman in charge of lab security. Wu sighed and dipped his head in a slight bow to greet Aragon. Together they headed to the badging office where Wu would be issued the security badge and radiation dosimeter that he would wear at all times while at the lab.

After providing the clerk at the badging office with all his required and extensive documentation, Wu answered a barrage of questions. "Are you carrying any recording equipment—audio, video, optical, or data—electronic equipment with a data-exchange port capable of being connected to automated information system equipment, cellular phones, radio-frequency transmitting equipment, computers and associated media, controlled substances, or any other items prohibited by law?" Of course, he answered "no" to all of these and soon was on his way to the Otowi Cafeteria to meet Percy. Naturally, Aragon remained by his side.

Wu winced as they entered the laboratory's main cafeteria on the second floor of the Otowi Building. The general found the smell of eggs and bacon repulsive. He yearned for his traditional Chinese breakfast of congee, a kind of rice porridge, and crullers, or *youtiao* in Chinese. Percy was already seated at a table on the far side of the room, enjoying a breakfast burrito with green chile and coffee. *New Mexicans and their green chile*, thought Wu, *how can they stomach the stuff with every meal?*

After Percy finished his breakfast and Wu forced down a cup of coffee, the two visited several unclassified research areas and discussed the expansion of the LENR technology. More Project Z power plants were opening every day across the United States. Already New Mexico, Arizona, Colorado, Nevada, and parts of Texas had become 100% reliant on the Low Energy Nuclear Reaction devices to generate energy.

Wu asked Percy about Southwest Syndrome, admitting they were experiencing similar phenomena in Beijing. Depression, anxiety, irritability, and loss of motivation ran rampant among his employees. He did not act surprised to hear of Alek's unusual frequency and amplitude measurements, but he appeared taken aback when he learned the frequency consistently measured at 42 hertz.

"In Chinese numerology, certain numbers are considered auspicious, and others are deemed inauspicious," Wu explained. "The number four is thought of as an unlucky number in Chinese because it is nearly homophonous to the word 'death.' Some buildings in East Asia omit floors and room numbers containing the number four, similar to the Western practice of some buildings not having a 13th floor because 13 is considered unlucky. In the Lucky Dragon, my casino in Las Vegas, I skipped the fourth floor."

"What about two?" asked Percy.

"Two is generally a lucky number," replied the general. "When you pair two with four, however, things get tricky. In Cantonese, two is a homophone with the characters for 'easy' so 42 could signify 'easy death.'"

Percy raised an eyebrow. "Sounds like a silly superstition to me." The lab director glanced at his phone. He had a text from Alek. "Hang on a sec, I need to take this," he said, stepping down a nearby hallway and leaving Wu and Aragon behind. A few minutes later, Percy returned and addressed the general. "Alek has asked that I call an emergency meeting and he asked that you join us. Let's head to the conference room. Amanda, please come along."

* * *

Alek, Gabi, Sunli, and Chang were waiting around the long table when Percy and Wu walked into the conference room with Aragon following. Alek had connected with Salvador Gutierrez in Washington, D.C., and Tom Lowe in California, by video conferencing on the wall monitor at the end of the room.

"What is all this about?" asked Percy. Alek knew his boss disliked not being in control of the situation. While he trusted Alek, he preferred to be the one to call the meetings.

"You guys know I've been investigating a possible connection between Project Z and Southwest Syndrome," Alek began.

"Yes, Alek, everyone has been brought up to speed on your theories," Percy said impatiently. "Get to the point."

Alek quickly filled the group in about what he and Gabi had learned from his latest frequency and amplitude measurements, the Taos Hum, and meditation. Sal then explained why Nat's invention offered the ideal solution to the detrimental effects of the 42 hertz frequency.

"Didn't a Sandia Labs physicist patent a similar device about 15 years ago?" Lowe asked from the screen.

"Yes, that was an early precursor to this invention," Sal replied. "There has been lots of research on using electrical stimulation and feedback to modify and entrain brain waves. Many scientists have theorized that the right approach could treat stress, depression, and PTSD. It could enhance relaxation and focus, and it could even improve sleep. Here's the difference with Nat's Brainaid: it will be the first tiny wearable device that works like a multimillion-dollar neuroimaging magnetoencephalography machine. The key lies in the miniaturization of the sensor, the stimulator, and the computer control to create a tiny battery-operated device that looks no bigger than one of those hearing assist gadgets. The Brainaid will include a computer chip that analyzes the brain waves and calculates the needed feedback stimulation, along with a battery-driven brain stimulator. What's really wild is that she's building the batteries to power these devices using the rare earth waste products from the Project Z power plants."

"When will it be ready to test?" asked Percy. "Could you mail me a few of these devices to experiment with?"

"I'll do better than that," replied Salvador. "We're currently building our first wearable Brainaid prototype. As soon as we complete our testing, Nat and I will get on a plane and bring the device to the lab. I can't wait for you guys to meet the mind behind this amazing machine."

Chapter 21
Natasha and the Brainaid

"I'M NOT SURE WHY, BUT I don't trust her," said Gabi. She and Alek had snuck away from the lab for a bit after spending the entire morning in briefings over the Brainaid. Natasha Simon had led the meetings with some assistance from Salvador. Sunli and Wu both were extremely excited to try out the invention. Percy and Alek were cautiously optimistic. Only Gabi had concerns.

"Maybe you're jealous," said Alek as they arrived at Los Alamos' only Starbucks on the city's Trinity Drive. In a town where every local business was named "Atomic This" or "Nuclear That," Alek and Gabi sometimes enjoyed the generic sameness of Starbucks. Once you were inside, you could be anywhere. Even the baristas looked the same in every city, large or small. Gender-neutral looks with multi-colored hair styles and numerous piercings were a requirement for serving coffee, apparently.

The two placed their orders and settled at a table in the corner to wait for their drinks.

Gabi inhaled deeply. "Just the smell of coffee is invigorating. I know it's 'basic' of me, but I do love this place."

Alek laughed and hopped up to retrieve their coffees. Gabi had chosen a double espresso, while Alek's order was a mocha. She liked to tease him about his sweet tooth, but no matter what Alek consumed, the lanky scientist never gained weight.

After a few quiet minutes sipping their drinks, Alek tackled the issue. "So, what don't you like about Natasha? She does come on a little strong."

"I appreciate strong women," said Gabi, methodically shredding her napkin as she thought about the morning. "Maybe it's the mix of Israeli and Russian cultures, but she seems... I guess the word is ruthless. Driven by the money. Committed to taking care of number one."

"Well, she was in the Israel Defense Forces. I'm sure she's trained to look out for herself, but she also seems brilliant, and I really think the Brainaid is the cure we need."

Alek swallowed the last of his coffee. "I guess we should head back. The plan is to spend the afternoon running experiments. Is there anything I can do to put your mind at ease?"

Gabi sighed, staring into her empty coffee cup. "I don't think so... I just have a weird feeling about Natasha Simon and her invention. I can't put my finger on it, but something about her gives me anxiety."

"Anxiety," laughed Alek. "Now that is something I'm very familiar with."

"Well, you shouldn't be anxious. You're a rocket scientist for God's sake."

"Yeah, with a badass FBI agent taking care of me," he said, smiling. "How could anything go wrong?"

* * *

"Now that you know how the Brainaid works, who wants to volunteer to try it?" Natasha opened the small metal box on the conference table and withdrew several tiny devices, each about the size of an old-fashioned hearing aid. Dressed in her brightly colored Hawaiian shirt with olive green cargo pants, combat boots, and a lab coat, the charismatic chemist commanded the attention of everyone in the room.

"I'll volunteer," said Sunli, stepping forward.

"Me too," added Wu eagerly.

Chang grabbed Sunli by the elbow. "Are you sure about this? We don't even know if there are any side effects."

"Please, it's perfectly safe. She explained everything this morning," said Sunli, pulling her hair back into a low ponytail and inserting the Brainaid in her ear.

"Ummm... *Nǐ néng bāngzhù wǒ ma?* Can you help me?" Wu asked Sunli. She walked over to him and placed his Brainaid gently into his ear.

"Anyone else?" Natasha asked.

"You're missing out. It's really relaxing," Sal said. "But I certainly understand that some of you want to observe the process before you try it out."

"The Brainaid only works on people who use it voluntarily," explained Natasha. "The key to brainwave entrainment is that the brain wants it to happen. It's like going to a gym to build up your muscles. You have to want to train your brain."

"What exactly does 'brainwave entrainment' mean?" Gabi asked. "I realize I'm the only one here who's not a scientist, but 'entrainment' is a new word for me."

"Brainwave entrainment, also called brainwave synchronization or neural entrainment, is when brainwave frequencies align with the rhythm of periodic external stimuli," Natasha explained impatiently.

"Uh, I didn't know that either," Alek interjected, smiling at Gabi.

"Entrainment occurs naturally," Sal said. "Flocks of birds synchronize the beating of their wings, a room full of pendulum clocks will all swing in the same rhythm, fireflies flash off and on in unison. Our goal is to use the phenomenon to improve people's brains."

Natasha nodded. "Basically, the idea is to use low frequency waves to enhance the brain by syncing up brain activity with the electronic signal. Regular use of brain entrainment can enhance meditation, improve sleep, reduce stress and depression, and boost cognition."

"So, basically, it could counteract the effects of Southwest Syndrome?" Alek asked.

"Seems like that's the plan," Natasha replied condescendingly. "Are we ready to begin?"

The Israeli chemist had Sunli and Wu sit in their chairs with their feet flat on the ground. "Okay, I'm going to lead you both through a process of guided meditation," she told them. "I want you to close your eyes and listen to my voice..."

An hour later, Nat wrapped up the meditation session. Wu and Sunli were radiant; both saying they had never felt better in their lives.

"Next, I want to show you our documentation of

brainwave scans before and after, and our measurements of how regular use of the Brainaid can enhance overall physical and mental health," Nat said.

"You don't have to convince me. I feel fantastic," said Sunli. "I think I'm going to go to the gym and work out before we meet for dinner tonight."

Chang looked at his wife as if she were a stranger. "You don't work out."

"Maybe now I do," Sunli replied.

"I'd love to see your documentation, Nat," said Percy. "I think President Thornton might be very interested in your studies, and I'm excited to find a way Los Alamos can collaborate with you to manufacture this revolutionary device to fight Southwest Syndrome."

Alek could almost see the wheels in the lab director's head turning. Percy was always looking for ways to ingratiate himself with political leaders and funnel more money to the lab.

"Gabi and I are going to head home to walk Gabi's dog before dinner. We'll see you guys at El Paragua in Española at eight," said Alek.

"I have some things I need to finish up in my office before dinner," said Chang.

"I think I'll stay here and learn more about the Brainaid," replied Sunli, apparently abandoning her exercise plans.

"Me too," Wu chimed in. "We need to discuss how China can contribute to the development of this technology."

Chang left the conference room with Alek and Gabi, looking back over his shoulder at his wife who was sitting at the conference table talking to Wu in Chinese.

"I don't know what it is about all this," Chang said as they walked down the hall. "For some reason I feel..."

"Anxious?" supplied Gabi.

"Yes, that's it. Anxious. For some reason, this whole Brainaid thing is giving me anxiety."

Gabi sighed. "Me too."

* * *

Percy's secretary had reserved a large table at El

Paragua for the evening's dinner. Located at the back of the restaurant, the group's dining area was secluded enough for the scientists to talk shop without worrying about listeners. Nevertheless, with the many margaritas and bottles of Dos Equis delivered to the table, the evening appeared to be geared more toward celebration than work.

Sunli, still glowing from the afternoon's meditation, sat between Wu and Chang, enjoying the way the two men competed for her attention. She had changed from her work clothes into a turtleneck dress that hugged her curves and complemented her hair, which she wore twisted into a chignon.

Gabi and Alek had also changed for dinner, but rather than dressing up, they had slipped on their jeans. Everyone else was still in work clothes, but Nat had freed her hair from its topknot, and it stood out in a chaotic tumble of red curls.

The popular restaurant was crowded, and the atmosphere was festive and loud as waiters hurried past carrying platters of steaming New Mexican specialties. A mariachi band roved from table to table playing traditional music.

"What do you guys recommend I order for dinner?" Nat asked, setting down her menu. "I get the impression you tend to come here a lot."

"I suggest anything with green chile," replied Percy, leaning forward to point out a couple of items on his menu.

"Every dish has green chile in it in this state," Wu muttered. He tried his margarita, made a face, and pulled out his pocket flask of Baijiu. Wu offered the flask to Sunli before taking a large swig. She declined but leaned closer and whispered something to him in Chinese, both of them laughing. Chang watched disapprovingly.

"You should get the carne adovada," Sal told Natasha. "It's almost as good as my mother's... almost. Top that off with hot sopapillas and honey and another round of margaritas and you're all set."

The orders were placed, chips and salsa devoured, and soon the food arrived, delighting everyone but Wu who prodded his enchiladas with his fork suspiciously and then pushed his plate aside. Sal showed Natasha how to tear off a corner of her sopapilla and add honey. Percy proposed a toast to the Brainaid and everyone, even Gabi and Chang, drank to the future of the invention. Glasses clinked as they congratulated one another on the beginning of a successful partnership.

Suddenly, a loud crash and the sound of raised voices came from the front of the restaurant. "Sir! Sir, come back here. You can't be in here with a gun," shouted one of the waiters. The scientists turned toward the outburst.

A thin, wide-eyed man in his late twenties, wearing ragged clothes and carrying a handgun, came running through the restaurant with two waiters careening after him. The man's face contorted in anguish as he shouted, "Make it stop! Make it stop!" In obvious pain, he clutched at his head with his free hand.

"Sir, you have to leave. You can't be in here," cried the waiter, stepping back as the man brandished the gun.

"You're one of them, one of the aliens, aren't you," screamed the man. "You're doing this to me. Make it stop!" Weeping hysterically, the interloper turned toward the large table of people in the back of the restaurant. "I can't stand it," the man screamed, his face contorted in agony. "You have to stop the noise, the pain, this pressure in my head. You're trying to control my mind."

The man locked eyes with Sunli then darted forward, grabbing her and wrapping an arm around her torso, holding the gun to her head. "Stop this alien mind control or I'll shoot the woman. Don't tempt me. I'm not afraid of seeing your green blood."

Still holding the gun on Sunli, the man turned to Percy. "They are here already," he said ominously. "You are next."

The lab director reached for his phone to dial 911, but Wu moved faster. The Chinese general grabbed his still-warm plate of enchiladas and hurled it into the attacker's face.

Reeling from the hot grease and cheese, the man released his hold on Sunli, who ran breathlessly to Wu's side. A single shot rang out and the attacker crumpled to the ground.

Nat stood on the opposite side of the table, her Glock still smoking.

"What?" said Nat, looking at the stunned scientists. "Of course I'm always armed."

PART THREE
Three Months Later

Chapter 22
And So It Begins

"AS THE NUMBER OF CASES continues to sky-rocket, the World Health Organization has declared the constellation of symptoms known as Southwest Syndrome to be a neurological pandemic. Doctors in China are reporting similar symptoms. The Chinese are calling the illness the Dragon's Brain. We go live to the White House now where our reporter, Raymond Alvarez, has come from a news briefing with President Thornton. Raymond, how is the president responding to the pandemic declaration and what should people at home do in response to this alarming issue?"

Alek flipped off the TV in his Washington, D.C. hotel room, not wanting to watch the news anchor nod sympathetically while the reporter stood on the White House lawn reliving the news conference. He already knew everything that would be in the news report.

Earlier that day, Alek and Natasha had met with President Thornton to present the research on the Brainaid. Thornton had been optimistic and eager to commit government funding for large-scale production and distribution of the device. Alek couldn't seem to share the president's enthusiasm. Maybe he was just lonely.

Alek's spacious room in the Capitol Hill Hilton offered more luxury than he was accustomed to, but somehow it was impossible to enjoy the accommodations. The king-sized hotel bed seemed as vast as an empty ocean. Alek realized it had been a long time since he had felt like this. It scarcely compared to his loneliness he experienced after the death of his daughter and the divorce that followed, but over the past year, he had begun to forget those dark times. Alek realized Gabi had filled a hole in the heart that he once considered unrepairable.

So much had changed since he first met Gabi. Alek thought back to the time when they traveled to Mexico seeking the Ramos brothers. He remembered strolling with her through the Spanish Old Quarter in Monterrey, zip lining through the jungle, and that first kiss. He recalled their first night together at the Little A'Le'Inn motel on the Extraterrestrial Highway. He remembered the time they spent together in the tiny trailer at Yucca Mountain, the long conversations where they shared things they had never told another soul.

Now, Alek couldn't imagine life without Gabi. Against the odds, they had become a couple. Not even the stress and irritation caused by Southwest Syndrome could break their connection. There was no one else Alek wanted by his side.

Alek wanted to protect Gabi. It was silly. She was an FBI agent, perfectly capable of taking care of herself, but even so, he hated to think of her being alone. It had been three months since that armed man had burst into El Paragua, but he still felt shaken. *If something had happened to Gabi...* The buzzing of an incoming text interrupted Alek's gloomy train of thought. Grateful for the interruption, he rolled over and grabbed his phone.

"Neurological pandemic?" read the text from Gabi.

"IDK," Alek replied, adding a shrug emoji. "I don't like it. It's not a neuropandemic. It's neuro*pollution* and Project Z is the cause."

"Thornton denies that?"

"He doesn't deny it in private, but he isn't about to go public with the truth or stop Project Z operations. The White House insists that Project Z is crucial to solving the climate crisis. In fact, Croft said the plan is to double the number of Project Z devices in the next two years."

Alek sighed and then continued texting. "Thornton isn't worried about the conspiracy theorists who are suggesting the Chinese are behind the whole thing. He's just letting people believe that. Honestly, I wonder if our government is planting some of the conspiracy theories to distract people from the truth. I can't stand to look at social media. Never thought I'd be part of a government coverup."

He smiled as his phone lit up with a closeup of Gabi's pit bull and the message, "Max misses you. I do too."

"Kiss his squishy face for me," Alek texted. "I'll be home soon to kiss you myself."

* * *

As Alek contemplated the room service menu, Sal and Natasha were nearby enjoying a glass of bourbon at the elegant Cosmos Club. But their mood was more serious than celebratory. The two were planning how to rapidly scale up production on the Brainaid.

"Here's the thing," Nat said, leaning forward with her elbows on the table, unaware that her unkempt red curls, unconventional clothing, and comparative youth were drawing the attention of the established members of the Club. "We have to find a way to avoid the FDA."

Sal sat back in his chair, arms crossed, and nodded. "I agree completely. Even if fast-tracked, the endless review committees, the esoteric arguments about brain theories, the extensive human subject testing... We could pursue an emergency authorization, but that could still slow things down. What if we avoid making any medical claims?"

"True," Nat agreed. "Once we make claims of medical effectiveness, the need for FDA testing would have to start before widespread applications could begin."

"Also, if we take a non-medical approach, we won't risk competition with pharmaceutical companies that manufacture anxiety drugs and sleep medications. Although widespread use of the Brainaid will cut down on the need for sleeping pills and similar treatments, we don't want the pharmaceutical lobbyists at our throats."

"Absolutely," said Nat. "It sounds like Thornton is willing to funnel government money into the production and distribution, so we won't have to worry about marketing. The question is, how will we meet the demand?"

"That's where the national labs come in," Sal replied. "Let's see how soon we can meet with Percy. He's always ready for the next big project and the next big source of funding."

* * *

Peter Chang paced back and forth in his Santa Fe home. He had planned to take Sunli to dinner that night at The Shed, but she had insisted on meditating before dinner. That was two hours ago.

"Ummm, hey, are you done yet?" Chang called out. "We missed our reservation."

Chang walked into the bedroom. The tastefully furnished room was dark. Sunli sat in a wingback chair, eyes closed, her Brainaid installed in one ear. She was smiling.

"I, um, wondered if you were ready to go to dinner?" Chang asked hesitantly.

His wife didn't react or even acknowledge his presence in any way. Chang leaned down in front of Sunli, but she appeared to be oblivious to his presence. Even though she was right there in the room, she wasn't really there.

"Uh, okay, I'm going to make myself a sandwich," Chang said awkwardly. Sunli did not respond.

Chang backed out of the room, quietly. He missed his wife.

* * *

On the other side of Santa Fe in his hotel suite, General Wu was also enjoying his Brainaid. He'd had no idea how much he would be using the device when Natasha offered him the chance to test it. Now, he could scarcely imagine life without his daily meditation sessions. Actually, he had started using the Brainaid several times a day.

Wu hadn't given much thought to the fact that the Brainaid was stimulating his brain to produce more serotonin, a naturally occurring chemical that improved mood. He didn't realize that the device emitted alpha waves, which had a calming effect on the body and lowered cortisol, the body's stress hormone. Nor did he realize the device was helping him sleep better by prompting his brain to produce a restful state that accelerated sleep onset and enabled longer periods of sleep. He did realize that the Brainaid counteracted the depression and irritability he had been feeling—the *Lóng de Dànǎo*. But the benefits of the Brainaid did more than stop the illness. For the first time in years, Wu felt at peace.

Reluctant to return to Beijing, Wu had stayed at the

Four Seasons in Santa Fe so he could meet with Sunli and compare notes on their experiences with the Brainaid. They had met several times to discuss the device and their reactions to it. Wu felt closer than ever to Sunli. She seemed to have forgotten he had once held her captive in Beijing while he forced her to work on the LENR technology. If that time wasn't forgotten, it appeared to be forgiven. Wu was certain that Sunli was beginning to realize that she belonged with him, not with Peter Chang.

The general felt certain that he was slowly laying the groundwork for Sunli to choose him over Chang. After all, it was the choice she should have made years ago. So far, things were going well. The future looked promising—at least it looked promising from Wu's perspective.

Crime was increasing, suicide had hit record highs, and the World Health Organization had declared a global neuropandemic. General Wu smiled. He had never been happier.

Chapter 23
I Want a New Drug

THE LAST FEW ORANGE-HUED rays of sunlight crept across the porch and through the window into the living room of Alek's quaint casita. Another long day had ended, and Alek was glad to be home. He was finally taking a break from the endless work of implementing the federal plan to produce Brainaids and distribute the free electronic wellness gadgets to all American adults.

Alek glanced at the television. As always, he had left it on CNN's 24-hour news coverage with the sound turned off.

The drone camera view, shot from high above, showed long lines of people waiting patiently at Albuquerque's University Stadium, the outdoor football stadium where the University of New Mexico Lobos played. Instead of being there to watch a ballgame, thousands of people had flocked to the stadium to pick up their Brainaids. The line of people snaked around the stadium. In some parts of the Southwest, people were reportedly camping out in line for weeks to receive their Brainaids.

So far, the federal government had distributed a little more than 14 million Brainaids free of charge to people in parts of Texas, New Mexico, Arizona, California, and Nevada. The national labs had stepped in to assist with production, with Sal and Natasha coordinating efforts across the United States. Much of the work had been carried out at Los Alamos, where the technology Nat had created was perfected and produced.

Despite America's willingness to share the Brainaid technology, the Chinese government continued to deny the existence of the condition that their citizens called *Lóng de Dànǎo*, choosing instead to ignore the growing crisis. Violent crime in China was increasing, and the Chinese government had stepped in to stop several protests and demonstrations tied to the bizarre neurological condition and the resulting unrest.

Meanwhile, in the U.S., crime statistics were finally dropping back to pre-pandemic levels and reports of suicide had decreased. Unfortunately, news of fights breaking out at the Brainaid distribution centers was common, as people tried to obtain multiple devices or fought for spots in line. Political pundits took to the airwaves to reassure viewers that the reports of violence among people waiting to get the devices simply reinforced the need for the Brainaid.

Researchers were getting closer to a decision about whether it was safe for children under the age of 18 to use the Brainaid. Teachers had held rallies calling for the government to issue the device to children, since the syndrome had created an extremely disruptive environment in schools. Safety concerns arose when a high school student who had used his father's Brainaid committed suicide. However, Brainaid advocates pointed to the rash of school shootings that had taken place since Southwest Syndrome began.

Despite the controversy, the devices clearly were working. Doctors and therapists were no longer besieged by complaints of irritability and anxiety and as tempers settled, everything else slowly improved. Alek and Gabi noticed one day that even Max had become calm again. They concluded the pit bull's bad behavior had been a reaction to Gabi's own stress.

The only problem with the Brainaid was that the rate of production couldn't keep pace with the demand. Wealthy people were buying the devices on the black market, eager to skip delays and avoid the humiliation of waiting in long lines. People bragged on social media about getting their Brainaids and encouraged the doubters to join them in their pursuit of good health. As millions took selfies with their Brainaids and posted them online with glowing reviews about how they had overcome Southwest Syndrome, others remained skeptical about the devices, posting wild theories about side effects on Facebook and questioning their safety. Conspiracy theories ranged from collusion with aliens to government mind control. Impassioned social media arguments erupted as every outlet was overtaken with discussions of the Brainaid.

Controversies had also arisen over the limited distribution of Brainaids in low income and minority areas. While some people openly rejected and condemned the technology, others longed to get their hands on it but couldn't. Politicians alternately praised and condemned the distribution process, and the morning television news programs were consumed with arguments about how to equally distribute the device.

Meanwhile, the number of Project Z plants was increasing, and, as additional power plants went online across the country, Alek was certain that the need for Brainaid units would continue to grow. Alek couldn't help thinking that they weren't doing anything to address the actual cause. He wanted to shut down the Project Z plants until they could find a better way to mitigate the frequency output. He had addressed these feelings several times with Percy—who refused to hear his theories and proposals. With the many billions already invested in Project Z, and the way old-fashioned energy sources were being replaced by proliferating LENR devices, a Project Z shutdown could have economic consequences. The thought of facing a recession, or even a depression, was unacceptable. Shutting down the Project Z plants could devastate the American economy. Neither President Thornton nor any other political leader was ready to take that chance.

"The Brainaid is the only workable solution," Percy had said.

Other than the relentless need to build and ship the Brainaid devices, life in the Los Alamos area had become peaceful again. Most everyone in town was affiliated with the lab and had quickly obtained a device without having to deal with long waits or government red tape.

One of the drawbacks of being a production site for the Brainaid was the endless parade of protesters. Fears of alien mind control had quickly transitioned to claims that the government was trying to regulate people's brains. The conspiracy theorists were out in full force. Calling themselves Anti-Aiders, the protesters tended to hang out at the entrance to the facility, holding signs and hurling insults. Amanda Aragon said her job had never been so busy nor so focused on people who didn't work at the lab.

The Anti-Aiders claimed the Brainaid devices allowed government officials to monitor their thoughts and pinpoint their locations. That made Alek laugh. Most of these people shared their thoughts and their latest conspiracy theories openly on social media, so there was no need for special equipment to monitor them. As for pinpointing their locations, their cell phones took care of that.

At first Alek found the Anti-Aiders entertaining— even more amusing than the tinfoil hat crowd—but now he was growing weary of the constant chaos. As he told Gabi one night, he was tired of living in "unprecedented" times.

* * *

Meanwhile, the distribution of the Brainaids was having a dramatic impact on the drug cases Gabi was investigating. Many former addicts were turning to the Brainaid instead of depending on illegal drugs. Although she was initially pleased by this trend, Gabi felt that most people were simply substituting one addiction for another.

"Would you prefer people choose heroin over sticking a tiny electronic device in their ears?" Alek asked one day. "I mean, outside of the fact that heroin addiction is good for your job security, it doesn't do much for society as a whole."

"I know that," she replied, swatting him with a couch pillow. "You know that's not what I meant."

"So, what's the danger of drug users transitioning to the Brainaid? What do you think will happen to them?"

"Well, some of the Cartel members I've been monitoring haven't left their houses since they started using the Brainaid. I mean, I know that's good... Who doesn't want drug dealers staying at home? But it's weird."

"So what?" Alek replied. "Seems like a good thing to me."

"I don't know," mused Gabi, sinking down on the couch between Alek and Max and stroking the dog's head thoughtfully. "You would think so, but here's the thing about addiction. Addicts build up a tolerance to their drug of choice, meaning they need more and more of the drug to get the same euphoria, the same positive sensation. They will commit violent acts to obtain more of the substance or will move up to something more dangerous to achieve the same level of high. What happens when a new generation of addicts becomes desperate for a new drug?"

"Hang on." Alek tapped something into his phone, pulling up a YouTube video and turning up the sound. It was the 1984 song "I Want a New Drug" by Huey Lewis and the News.

"Very funny," Gabi said as Alek jumped up, grabbing her hands and trying to get her to dance with him. Despite her best efforts, Gabi started to giggle and joined Alek as Max watched in confusion.

Alek pulled Gabi into a tight embrace as snow began falling outside the window. "You know Huey Lewis said this song was never about drugs, anyhow."

Gabi smiled. "You're right. This song is about love."

Chapter 24
The Plot Thickens

IN HIS OFFICE AT LOS Alamos Lab, Peter Chang leaned forward, studying the image on his computer monitor. Ever since he had first seen Natasha's presentation on the Brainaid, he had been studying brain entrainment and had built complex simulations of brain waves and the human brain.

Chang felt certain the Brainaid device held the promise of revolutionizing the treatment of all neurological problems. For the past three months, he had poured all his time into this research, compiling data, running calculations, and building three dimensional models. The deeper he explored the connections between neurology and physics, the more intrigued and encouraged Chang became. He spent long days at the lab, bringing home piles of articles and scientific reports to read each evening. He had convinced himself the work was imperative, sinking every moment into his research.

Chang refused to face the truth that his real reason was to distract himself from the feeling that he was slowly losing his wife.

Over the past few weeks, Sunli had spent more and more time meditating while using the Brainaid. She'd stopped going into the lab, assuring Alek that she was working from home. But Chang knew she spent her days and nights in the darkened bedroom with her Brainaid. On the rare occasions she left the house, she met with Wu at various local restaurants to discuss their "research." On the days they met, Chang never knew how long she would be gone.

Sunli's mother grew worried when Sunli stopped coming to visit and then quit returning her calls. She gave up trying to reach her daughter and started calling Chang each day. "*Wǒ nǚ'ér zěnmeliǎo?* What is wrong with my daughter?" she asked.

Chang simply responded, "She is working," and Mrs. Hidalgo encouraged him to make sure Sunli ate.

Always obedient and respectful of his mother-in-law, Chang brought Sunli plates of food. He set them beside her on the end table in the bedroom and then removed them uneaten. He tried not to notice how tightly his wife's skin stretched over her prominent cheekbones or the dark hollows under her eyes. On the rare occasions that she spoke to Chang, Sunli exclaimed that she had never felt better, and she encouraged him to spend more time using the Brainaid.

Frustrated, Chang cornered Alek in his office. "Something is seriously wrong here. Sunli has stopped eating. She barely interacts with me. She has stopped talking to her mother. All her time is spent using the Brainaid or meeting with Wu. She is acting strange and secretive. I feel like I don't even know her anymore."

Alek gestured for Chang to have a seat. "What about you?" Alek asked. "How often do you use the Brainaid?"

"At first I used it twice a day, then once a day, now once a week," the scientist replied. "I don't feel like I need it the way I used to. I'm no longer experiencing symptoms of malaise or irritability. In fact, I think I have used the device to align my brainwaves to cope with the LENR signal. Eventually, I may not need it at all."

"It's the same for me and Gabi," said Alek. "Basically, we are using it every couple of weeks and then meditating in between. But Gabi thinks some people are getting addicted to the Brainaid. Maybe it's something about their brain chemistry or the physical structure of their brains?"

"It's possible," Chang replied. "I'm developing a computer code that will allow us to create a new model and run some simulations. I know we think we solved a problem, but the technology we created may be leaving us with an even bigger problem on our hands."

* * *

Wu's limo pulled up in front of Sunli and Chang's

Santa Fe home and she slipped into the back seat. The Chinese general commanded his driver to head to NM-502 West. Light snow swirled around the car as they drove.

"Where are we going?" Sunli asked Wu in Chinese.

"Let's go to Bandelier National Monument," he replied in English for his driver's benefit, then quickly returned to Mandarin.

"I fear people are watching us. The Ministry of State Security has eyes and ears throughout New Mexico, but I doubt they will follow us to Bandelier on this bitterly cold day." The Bandelier Monument was made up of 50 square miles on the Pajarito Plateau in the Jemez Mountains. It had once been the home of Ancestral Puebloan people who built cave dwellings in the volcanic cliffs.

Wu was wearing a long-wool coat over his suit. He gestured to a fur coat on the seat beside him. "For if you get chilly," he told Sunli.

The two rode in silence. Snow dusted piñon trees whipped past the car windows as they sped along the empty highway. *This is not a good day for sightseeing*, thought Sunli as the minutes ticked by, and the limo curved past soaring ponderosa pines and rocky red cliffs.

Finally, she turned to Wu. "Why do you think the MSS is watching you? What do they want?"

The general leaned closer to Sunli as though concerned the driver would hear him, even though he was speaking in Mandarin. "They expected me to return to Beijing and, as you can see, I haven't. I believe they suspect me of working with the Americans, but there's only one particular American who has captured my interest so far, and this individual isn't American by birth." The older man smiled suggestively at Sunli. "Tell me about the tests you've been conducting. Have you made any more progress on enhanced cognition and collective brain power?"

Sunli nodded. "My husband is researching possible Brainaid applications. It seems he wants to find a way to use the technology for other applications. He thinks it's the ideal solution for several neurological issues. He believes he can use the Brainaid to create an enhanced restorative sleep phase that cures dementia and use it as sort of a brain defibrillator that can reverse coma. He's doing extensive computer simulations and modeling. I have been making copies of all his data and documentation. Of course, he has no idea I've been borrowing his research. I'm afraid that he wouldn't exactly approve of our plans."

The general locked eyes with Sunli. "Are you concerned about maintaining your husband's approval?"

"Not at all," replied Sunli with a flirtatious tilt of her head.

* * *

Wu glanced over his shoulder. A black Chevy Suburban was tailgating them on the undivided highway. The limo driver waved at the Suburban to go around. The SUV driver didn't respond.

"Speed up," Wu commanded his driver.

"Sir, it's not safe to go much faster," replied the driver. "Especially in the snow on these curvy roads."

Wu looked over his shoulder again. He couldn't make out the face of the other driver through the falling snow and the tinted windshield. The two cars continued to speed through the snow as the road snaked its way through the cliffs into the Jemez Mountains.

Wu turned back to Sunli who was explaining how they could build on Chang's research. "Already we both have successfully used the device to enhance our brain function, and if we can use the entrainment techniques to synchronize brain waves among a group of like-minded individuals..."

Sunli glanced out the car window at the large snowflakes flying fast and thick. She returned her gaze to Wu. "General, this research is so exciting. I haven't felt this this alive since we were working in Yucca Mountain on Project Z. It's been so long since I've had a sense of purpose—a goal to achieve."

Wu nodded distractedly as the limo driver turned onto the road entering the national monument. As they pulled up in front of the guardhouse at the entrance, the driver pointed at the annual pass displayed on his windshield. The park ranger waved them through, and Wu grunted with satisfaction to see the Suburban forced to stop and purchase an entrance pass.

The limo driver proceeded into the monument grounds, winding past the visitors' center and several parking and picnic areas. Wu glanced back and saw the SUV about 50 feet behind them. He scanned the area, struggling to figure out what to do next.

"Pull over here," he barked at the driver, heaving the fur coat at Sunli. "Just in case the driver of that car has some... interest... in us, let's get out of the way." The driver pulled to a stop, and Wu and Sunli quickly got out. Wu looked over his shoulder, grabbing her hand. "Hurry. I think we are in danger," he hissed.

* * *

The two scrambled through the snow on the rough trail, working their way toward the small cave openings carved into the cliffs looming above them. Sunli regretted choosing elegant Italian leather heels for the outing. The icy cold quickly permeated her shoes and snow worked its way inside her pant legs. She wrapped her burgundy cashmere scarf around her neck and pulled the fur coat tighter, trying to keep pace with the Chinese general, who was spry despite his age. Wu led the way up the steep trail that climbed from the canyon floor to the ruins of the ancient Pueblo dwelling constructed nearly 1,000 years ago.

"Who are we running from?" Sunli puffed, trying to catch her breath and avoid twisting an ankle on the rocky, snow-covered terrain.

"*Wǒ bù kěndìng*. I'm not sure yet," Wu answered tersely. They had reached the side of the cliff. A wooden ladder leaned against the rocky cliff leading to the caves above. Wu gestured to the ladder. "Here, go in front of me. Take off those shoes; they'll slow you down."

Sunli bent down, slipped off her heels, and shoved them into the pockets of the coat. She began to climb the ladder, wincing as the splintery old wood cut her feet. A jagged piece of wood from the ladder caught on her cashmere scarf, tugging against her neck. Frustrated, she unwound the scarf, trying to pull it free.

"*Gǎnkuài*. Hurry up," Wu commanded. Sunli pulled at the scarf again. Suddenly, it slipped from her grasp and spiraled to the ground. "*Kuài diǎn. Cōngmáng.* Come on. Hurry," hissed Wu.

As they climbed, sounds of shouting from the parking lot echoed through the canyon. Sunli struggled to understand what was being said as she climbed the seemingly endless ladder. Was it even in English? It sounded like people arguing. Was the limo driver fighting with the Suburban driver? The falling snow muffled the sounds like a blanket. Everything sounded so far away. Was that a gunshot? She couldn't be sure. Sunli shivered as the cold wind whipped past her. She wondered how she had ended up fleeing from unknown attackers in a snowstorm.

Finally, they reached the end of the ladder. Wu grabbed her hand, dragging her into a dark cave carved into the volcanic tuff. Sunli shivered, slipping her shoes back on her cold bare feet. Outside the opening to the cave, the snow was still falling steadily as the sun dropped in the late afternoon sky, sending tendrils of red into the deepening blue. Wu flipped on his phone flashlight as they ventured further into the dwelling. Sunli looked up at the soot darkened roof of the cavern. This had been the home of the Ancestral Pueblo people, the ancient culture that dug these structures deep into the cliffs. The cave resonated with a sense of other-worldly mystery. Inside the cave, the sounds from outside vanished. Sunli couldn't even hear the howling of the wind.

Wu took off his coat and spread it on the ground, gesturing for Sunli to sit down. In a hushed voice he said, "Now we have to wait. He will not see us. He will give up and leave." Wu pulled his Brainaid out of his pocket. "You have yours, right? Excellent. At least we can make good use of our time."

Sunli nodded distractedly. She was thinking about her burgundy scarf lying at the base of the ladder, like a bright beacon shining in the snow.

Chapter 25
Facing the Cold Truth

"SOMETIMES I WANT TO GRAB you and shake some sense into you," Percy said. Instead of violence, however, the lab director suggested camaraderie. "Why don't we head over to the Friggin Bar for a beer?"

Gabi was in D.C. and, although Alek was watching her dog, he had already run home to walk and feed Max earlier that afternoon. As hard as he tried, Alek couldn't come up with a decent excuse to avoid having an after-work drink with his boss.

Walking to the parking lot, Alek flipped up the collar of his parka against the brisk wind sweeping in from the north. He was grateful for the heated seats in his electric 4Runner and even more grateful for the overall ample energy supply during this brutal cold snap. Alek remembered when a polar vortex had plunged the country into the single digits and overtaxed the electricity and natural gas supplies. Despite rolling blackouts to conserve electricity, millions of Americans found themselves without power or heat. The worst of the problems occurred in the southern parts of Texas, where no one was accustomed to the cold temperatures. Alek remembered how people struggled to deal with broken pipes, flooding, overcrowded shelters, and cases of carbon monoxide poisoning caused by using cars in garages, gas stoves, and unvented space heaters to stay warm. The aftermath of the electrical shortages had haunted the country long after the weather had improved.

Now, thanks to Project Z, there were no fears of electrical shortages. People had access to more affordable energy than they could ever use. As he drove the short distance from the lab to the bar, Alek considered the role he had played in providing that reliable source of unlimited clean, cheap energy. He should feel proud of his contribution. Still, he couldn't stop worrying that, in addition to creating the neurological pandemic, the Project Z devices were contributing to weather instability.

He never should have brought up that concern to the lab director. All he'd done was make Percy mad.

The minute Alek walked into the bar, his glasses fogged up from the contrasting temperatures. Sliding into the booth across from Percy, Alek pulled off his glasses. It was easier to apologize to someone he couldn't see anyhow.

"Look, I'm sorry," Alek said, wiping his glasses on his shirt tail. "I'm not about to sabotage Project Z. I'm just worried."

Percy took a drink of his Dos Equis. He had ordered one for Alek as well. "I know, Alek, but you have to let this stuff go. Project Z is not impacting temperatures or weather patterns. It's not. The LENR devices may be slowing down the pace of global warming ever, ever so slightly, which is desirable, but even if we eliminate all greenhouse gasses, it will be decades before we see any significant impact on climate change."

"Decades? How do you know that?"

"How does anyone know anything about climate change?" scoffed Percy. "Pick a so-called expert and quote them. That's how it works."

Alek began tearing the label off his bottle of Dos Equis. "But what if we have created something that has disrupted the balance of nature? Chaotic multivariable phenomena can change conditions abruptly. What if the technology we created is plunging us into the deep freeze?"

Percy snorted. "What if that Swedish girl who won the Nobel Prize was right and we're facing mass extinction due to rising temperatures? That's why it's so crucial we turn to Project Z now and eliminate fossil fuels."

"Look, all sarcasm aside, the weather has been pretty bizarre lately," Alek protested.

"I know. It has been unusually cold this winter... but that's all this is. An unusual cold spell. It's happened before and it will happen again. At least now we have access to affordable energy to keep people warm and safe."

Alek nodded. "Okay. I'm still concerned, but I promise I'll drop it. What about the issues surrounding the Brainaids? Do you think they're addictive?"

"That's a more complicated question," said Percy thoughtfully. "A few people seem to be having an... odd reaction to the Brainaid. Not really an adverse reaction... just odd."

"Like Sunli?" Alek asked.

"Yes, like Sunli," the lab director agreed.

Alek nodded. "She certainly seems to have withdrawn since she began using it. I haven't seen her at the lab in weeks, and I know Chang is concerned."

Percy leaned forward, looking serious. "Here's the thing, Alek, Sunli is a grown woman. The only thing you need to monitor is her work, not her relationships. If Sunli and Chang are having problems, they have to deal with that. None of what has happened is remotely your fault."

Alek sighed. "It's just that... I can't help thinking about Candale and Digali. If they hadn't gone to China to help me develop Project Z, they would still be alive today."

Percy reached over and gave Alek an awkward pat on the shoulder. The younger man smiled. He viewed Percy as a father figure, which was one of the reasons why he hated bringing up problems that made the lab director angry. Still, there were issues he felt had to be discussed.

"Alek, I know you miss them. They weren't just colleagues, they were our friends, but you must remember that you had nothing to do with their deaths. The Chinese were responsible. There was nothing you could have done."

Percy stood, signaling the visit was over. "Look, Alek, I know you feel the need to save the world. Just remember, you're doing your part."

* * *

The sun was sinking in the sky, bathing the snow-dusted roads with hints of periwinkle, when Alek pulled into the gravel driveway in front of his casita to find Peter

Chang parked there, waiting.

As soon as Alek stopped, his friend jumped out of his car and pulled open the passenger door of the 4Runner. "Alek, I need your help."

"Of course. What is it? What's going on?"

"It's Sunli," Chang replied, tension evident in his strained voice. "She left with Wu this afternoon and hasn't returned... and it's been snowing. I tracked her on my phone app, and for the past hour she's been at Bandelier National Monument. I'm just... worried something's gone wrong."

"You have a tracker on her phone?"

"It's a family-safety app. We both put it on our phones when we first got married," Chang said. "It wasn't that long ago that we always wanted to know where each other was," he added bitterly.

"And they drove into the park and then stopped moving?" asked Alek.

"Yes, that's what the app shows. I want to try to find her, but—" Chang's voice broke off, choked with emotion. "I'm not sure what I will find if I go after her. Will you come with me?"

"Of course," Alek replied. "I'll drive. Let me take Gabi's dog out to pee real fast before we leave."

Alek ran into the house, wondering what he was getting himself into—especially after Percy's advice to leave Sunli and Chang alone to work things out. Grabbing the dog's leash, Alek clipped it onto Max's collar. Maybe pit bulls weren't hunting or tracking dogs, but it seemed like a good idea to bring the dog along.

A few minutes later, they were speeding toward Bandelier on Highway 4. Darkness was falling rapidly, but the snow had stopped, and the full moon was rising. In the blue moonlight, the fallen snow glittered like diamonds. The road was empty, and Chang stayed quiet, lost in thought.

Alek wondered if he should turn on the radio. He glanced at Chang's solemn expression and left it off. They drove along the curving road into the dark canyon. Alek was grateful for the moonlight reflecting off the snow.

Finally, Alek decided to break the awkward silence.

"So, you've been looking into different applications of the Brainaid?"

"Yes! It's very promising."

Alek relaxed, glad that he had hit on a conversation topic that might distract Chang from his worries. Enthusiastically, Chang began describing his research into using the Brainaid to reverse coma in vegetative patients. His findings were impressive, and Alek found himself getting excited by the possibilities. Before they knew it, they were pulling into the entrance to the park.

No one was in the dark guardhouse at the park entrance. Chang got out and swung open the heavy metal gate that stretched across the road. He returned to the 4Runner and they proceeded slowly into the park, winding past the closed visitors' center and empty parking and picnic areas. Chang stared at the map on his phone, checking Sunli's location and muttering, "Keep going, keep going." Max sat in the back seat looking out the window, occasionally growling quietly, deep in the back of his throat.

The truck's headlights glinted off something ahead of them. "What's that?" Alek asked, slowing down and squinting in the darkness.

"It's a car. It's Wu's limo!" shouted Chang. "Pull up behind them and stop."

Sure enough, it was Wu's limo, parked in the lot by the entrance to a trail, but something was wrong. The driver's door was standing open, the car's interior dome light shining onto the snow.

Alek and Chang got out of the 4Runner, and Alek let Max out. They approached cautiously. It didn't look like anyone was in the car. The dinging signal from the open door echoed across the empty parking lot.

Chang swung the limo door closed. The dinging stopped.

"What the hell," said Alek. Max growled. Alek looked at the ground, studying the footprints around the limo. It appeared that multiple people had been there. The snow was disrupted. Had there been some sort of struggle? A fight?

Chang grabbed Max's leash. "Find Sunli," he commanded. The dog sniffed at the snow and growled again, deep and low. He looked toward the trailhead where footsteps in the snow led away into the dark. Chang followed the dog's gaze.

"This way!" shouted Chang. "Come on."

The two men sprinted down the trail with Max tugging at the leash ahead of them. Suddenly Chang pointed to something lying in the snow, a splash of bright burgundy against the white backdrop.

"It's Sunli's scarf," he said.

Chang picked up the wet, ripped cashmere scarf that just that morning had been draped around his wife's neck. A few feet ahead, he spotted the ladder. Handing the dog's leash to Alek, Chang climbed toward the cliff dwellings above. Alek backed up so he could get a glimpse inside the dark opening to the cave. Holding his breath, he watched his colleague climb the rickety wooden ladder, uncertain of what lay at the top.

* * *

Chang reached the top of the ladder. Flipping on his phone flashlight to light up the darkness, he walked into the cavern.

Wu and Sunli were sitting on the floor of the cave, side by side, a fur coat draped over them. Their heads leaning against each other, both had their eyes closed, mouths curved in a look of serene bliss. Each of them was wearing a Brainaid device.

Chang erupted in a stream of furious Mandarin.

Pulled abruptly back to consciousness, Wu and Sunli blinked, struggling to recall where they were and make sense of the screaming man in front of them.

"*Wǒ yǐwéi nǐ shòushāngle.* I thought you were hurt. I thought you were kidnapped. All this time you were with him."

"Wait," said Sunli, awkwardly getting up from the cave floor. "Let me explain."

"There's nothing to explain," Chang replied coldly. "This is not a marriage. You've made your choice."

Chapter 26
The Lucky Dragon

AT LAST, SOME OF THE snow covering the streets of Los Alamos had begun melting. Saturday morning brought clear skies, piercing sunshine, and little wind, but it was still extremely cold. Alek sat on his porch, shivering, with Max beside him. Both were too excited about Gabi's arrival to give up and go inside to get warm.

Finally, she pulled up.

After exuberant greetings, they headed inside, welcomed by the sweet caramelly smell of brewing coffee. With Navajo rugs hanging on the adobe walls, a thick Sherpa blanket draped across the leather sofa, and a crackling fire in the rounded kiva fireplace, the casita was an oasis. Gabi was tucked between Alek and Max on the sofa, Max resting his large head in her lap.

But Alek was impatient. "Okay, tell me everything you know and then I'll fix us an omelet. I have fresh Hatch green chile. What did you find out when you went to Bandelier?"

"Mmm. I'm hungry," said Gabi, smiling. "Wu's limo driver was one of my FBI operatives. I assigned him because I've never trusted Wu, and I felt we were better off keeping an eye on him. But now, my agent has disappeared."

Alek walked to the kitchen and pulled the eggs out of the refrigerator. Setting a frying pan on the colorful Mexican tile countertop, he turned on the stove.

Gabi continued her story. "I drove up to Bandelier to see if I could find out what happened. I talked to the park ranger who was working at the guard house when Wu and Sunli went up there."

"What did he say?"

"This guy, Harold something... I don't remember... Harold the forest ranger... he said the limo entered the park at about 4:30 that afternoon followed by a man in a black Suburban. Harold said the guy driving the Suburban was white, but when he pulled up to the guard house, he was talking on his cell phone in another language... maybe Chinese."

"Chinese?" Alek said. "Was Harold the forest ranger sure?"

"No, he said it sounded kinda like Chinese—an Asian language. I'm not sure this guy is a reliable witness. The park closed at 5 p.m., and it was snowing so Harold decided to leave early. He left the exit gate unlocked so the visitors could leave."

"Seems irresponsible. Did he see the Suburban exit?"

"No, he was probably gone before the Suburban left, so we don't know if the limo driver left with the Suburban guy. There's a video camera at the park entrance, but the ranger said it hasn't worked in years."

"Hmm," said Alek. "When we arrived, the limo was parked at the trailhead with the door open. No one was there."

"So, what do you think?" he asked Gabi over his shoulder as he scrambled the eggs. "Was it the MSS?"

"That's what I suspect," she answered. "We know Wu had been working with China's Ministry of State Security, but that relationship appears to have soured. My guess is that Wu is tired of sharing with the MSS."

Gabi got up from the sofa, pulled out a stool at the kitchen bar, and watched as Alek finished cooking. He handed her a plate. She took a big bite of the green chile and cheddar omelet and sighed with pleasure. "Delicious. Were you a chef in your former life?"

Alek laughed. "Better watch out, Max is drooling on your knee."

Alek poured them both more coffee. He grabbed his plate and joined Gabi at the bar. "So, what happens now?" he asked.

"We need to figure out where Wu and Sunli went."

"After Chang and I found them, Wu and Sunli got into the limo and took off. Sunli barely looked at me as they left," Alek said.

"Yeah, Chang is beside himself. He refuses to even talk about what happened. Meanwhile, Sunli was spotted leaving Santa Fe with Wu the next day. He had apparently hired a new driver."

"Another one of yours?" Alek asked hopefully.

Gabi shook her head. "I wish. If he were, I'd have an eye on Wu now."

"I have a pretty good idea where Wu could have gone," Alek replied thoughtfully. "His hotel and casino in Las Vegas. It's called the Lucky Dragon, though I'm skeptical about Wu's luck."

"I think his luck is about to run out," Gabi laughed, adding, "I've already alerted the Las Vegas field office to keep an eye open for him and Sunli. I advised our operatives not to approach either of them, but to monitor who they associate with and what they are doing. It will be interesting to see how their plans unfold."

* * *

General Liu Wu purchased the Lucky Dragon Hotel and Casino in the 1980s when Las Vegas real estate was relatively cheap. Over the years, the hotel on the north end of the strip had served as an excellent way to launder money, and Wu had enjoyed many vacations in his penthouse above the casino. Now the hotel and casino offered more than an escape from reality. It would be the place where he and Sunli built their own empire, thanks to the Brainaid. Sunli's theories about expanding the capabilities of the Brainaid held great promise. The device clearly offered more than the cure to *Lóng de Dànǎo*. Regardless of how the beautiful scientist modified the Brainaid, Wu already viewed the venture as successful. After all, it had finally brought Sunli to her senses and into his life.

Sunli had her own suite of rooms, but Wu was certain that eventually she would decide to share his bed. Already they spent many hours together planning their next steps in Wu's comfortable penthouse apartment. The general marveled every time he saw Sunli seated on his luxurious white leather couch beside the teak curio cabinet that held his imperial Ming vase. Once the vase had been Wu's prize possession, but he had nearly gained the one thing that he valued above anything else—Sunli.

Wu was grateful to have multiple reasons to meet with Sunli daily. Together, they had plenty of work to do, modifying the Brainaid to enhance cognition and tap into collective brain power. Already they were building a coalition of followers who loyally subjected themselves to experiment after experiment. They recruited research subjects who were more than willing to serve as guinea pigs for Sunli's Brainaid modification tests.

* * *

Sunli had taken few possessions with her when they left Santa Fe, choosing instead to use Wu's credit card to shop at the high-end boutiques on the strip. She had traded her tailored business suits for silk slip dresses that clung to her slim figure. She favored deep jewel tones like burgundy and teal green and completed the look with high heels and a simple strand of pearls. Sunli enjoyed regular manicures, pedicures, facials, and other spa services, all thanks to Wu's generous funds.

In between shopping, dining at Las Vegas' most elegant restaurants, and enjoying spa and beauty treatments, Sunli worked on modifying the Brainaid using the research and computer codes that Chang had developed and she had surreptitiously duplicated before leaving New Mexico. She had to admire Chang's brilliance—his work had opened up so many possibilities for the Brainaid.

After a few weeks of testing, Sunli had discovered how to use the device's transcranial stimulation to boost the performance of specific sectors of the brain. So far, the trials had demonstrated the ability to improve white matter connectivity, which multiplied brain function exponentially. The modified Brainaid showed the ability to enhance creativity, bolster spatial and quantitative learning, and even improve language acquisition. While Sunli had access to a steady stream of volunteers to test her theories, she also experimented on herself and now referred to herself as an "enhanced" human.

One evening, while she sipped her ginger martini and

Wu enjoyed his customary Baijiu at the Shanghai Lounge in the Lucky Dragon casino, Sunli shared her scientific findings with the general.

"The Brainaid modifications have increased white matter connectivity so dramatically that the test subjects are beginning to outpace computers at solving complex problems."

Wu scoffed. "How is that possible in the age of Artificial Intelligence?"

"AI has its uses, but it lacks some of the gifts of humanity. By enhancing an individual's cognitive power, I can give them the computer's logical ability and problem-solving power along with a human being's creativity, intuition, and empathy."

"So, there's no need for AI then?" Wu asked, signaling the waitress for another drink.

Sunli leaned forward, her eyes gleaming with excitement. "The next step is to use AI to connect the enhanced humans. We can maximize collective cognition by uniting people with enhanced brain power to achieve an exponential increase in the ability to solve complex problems."

Wu grimaced. "I'm still not sure what role AI plays."

"I've programmed the Brainaid AI to be part traffic cop and part mentor. Using AI to monitor individual and group behavior and provide feedback to each of the participants, while at the same time assessing brain function patterns, will allow me to create a sort of human-powered supercomputer. The AI will manage and oversee the collective of enhanced humans to successfully meet certain goals."

"What kind of goals?"

"The potential is unlimited!" she replied. "Basically, I'm creating a sort of human-powered supercomputer that's better than any computer we've ever built before."

"Huh," Wu said.

"Don't you see what an amazing breakthrough this is? It's far beyond anything I've ever accomplished. More important than the LENR. I don't think you understand the power this gives us. The power to do anything... have anything... we want."

Wu yawned. "Can you use this collective cognition

thing to make money?"

"Absolutely," Sunli said, the rising pitch in her voice betraying her desire to capture Wu's interest. "Just think how this will help us in the stock market."

"I already use algorithmic stock trading," Wu said. "My securities guys have enabled computers to use formulas and mathematical models to make trading decisions faster than any human can. This doesn't sound any better."

"I don't know why you can't see that it's the human-powered collective cognition that makes it better," Sunli said, trying to control the irritation in her voice. "We can boost human intuition, flexibility, and insight, and combine that with machine learning algorithms that can employ automation to react swiftly to market opportunities. Trust me. I'll show you. You'll see."

Setting her empty martini glass on the table, Sunli stood and with a flip of her hair strode quickly from the room so that Wu wouldn't see the tears building in her eyes.

Chapter 27
What Started with a Fish

NATASHA SIMON SHOULD HAVE BEEN happy. Using the national labs for support, she and Sal Gutierrez had successfully coordinated the production and distribution of hundreds of thousands of Brainaids. Complaints of Southwest Syndrome were decreasing every day.

Unfortunately, as the bizarre neurological disorder had begun to disappear, cases of Brainaid addiction had become more prevalent. So instead of feeling a sense of accomplishment, Natasha was worried, and now she knew Gabi shared her concerns.

Gabi's work investigating drug cases throughout New Mexico had given her a clear understanding of the dangers of addiction. Watching certain Brainaid users abandon jobs, friends, family, even food to pursue the pleasure of the Brainaid seemed far too reminiscent of people addicted to drugs. But Percy, Chang, Lowe, and even to a large extent Alek, all dismissed Gabi's worries. Feeling frustrated, she had reached out to Natasha. A few days later, the two met at Natasha's lab in Arlington, Virginia.

"First of all, remember, I'm not a scientist," Gabi said, looking around in awe at the high-tech devices displayed throughout the room. "I'm trying to figure out what makes the Brainaid addictive for some people and if there are any dangers we need to try to mitigate before things get worse."

Natasha perched cross-legged on a lab table, tapping a sneaker-clad foot impatiently. "Let's start from the beginning. I'll make things extremely clear." The Israeli chemist didn't intend to be condescending, but the attitude was evident. Natasha had little time or patience for those who couldn't immediately understand or appreciate her work.

"It all started with a fish," Natasha said, jumping up and beginning to pace between the lab tables.

"A fish?" Gabi asked.

"Yes. It began in 43 AD. The Roman emperor Claudius had a court physician named Scribonius Largus. This doctor got the idea to use an electric fish to treat headaches. And it worked. Since that time, numerous scientists have experimented with electrical stimulation to treat various maladies. Most of these experiments involved connecting wires to people's scalps and turning on the switch. Also, most of the experiments failed."

Natasha sat back down, twisting her wiry red curls into a haphazard topknot as she continued her explanation. "I decided a more interesting approach would be to use alternating current in phase with the brain waves to simultaneously measure brain frequency and use feedback control in a simple device to entrain and modulate the brain in a controlled manner. That's how the Brainaid was born."

"Sounds a lot better than smashing a fish on your forehead," Gabi said with a laugh.

"Smells better too," Natasha agreed. "Here's the thing, some people's brains are wired in such a way that the active synchronization of cortical oscillatory activity the Brainaid produces is simply too enticing. Users become dependent on the electrical stimulation and lose interest in other aspects of life."

Gabi nodded. "That makes sense. It certainly correlates with the definition of addiction. Addicts have intense focus on using a substance to the point where their ability to function in day-to-day life becomes impaired."

"Yes," Natasha agreed. "People with a substance use disorder also often experience distorted thinking and behavior caused by changes in the brain's structure and function. It could be possible the Brainaid is having that sort of effect."

"And what about tolerance? When someone has a substance use disorder, they usually build up a tolerance to the substance, meaning they need larger amounts to feel the effects. Do you think that will happen with the Brainaid?"

Natasha shrugged. "Honestly, I have no idea. It's not like we did years of testing before handing these things out."

"For God's sake, we are screwing up people's brains," Gabi said. "It sounds like you suspected all along that it would be addictive. Don't you care?"

"Of course I care. I hate this. But I'm just a scientist. I don't have the slightest idea what to do."

"Me neither," replied Gabi. "But I have an idea about someone who might, and I want you to meet him. I want you to come to Taos with me."

Gabi looked down as her phone buzzed with an incoming text. She read it, typed a short message, and sat down heavily, staring into space.

"What is it?" Natasha asked.

"One of our FBI agents had gone missing. They finally found him."

"That's good news, isn't it?"

"Well, it would be, but he's dead."

* * *

Sunli had transformed one of the conference rooms at the Lucky Dragon into her operations center. Twenty glowing computer monitors lined the walls, displaying updated market data and reports. Bathed in the dim blue light of the computer screens, a handful of enhanced humans, all wearing Brainaids, typed away on laptops hooked to a giant bank of servers in the center of the room. Using collective cognition to calculate nondeterministic algorithms, examine data sets, and generate hypotheses for high frequency trades, Sunli's Brainaid-enhanced volunteers were using collective cognition to play the stock market.

And it was working.

Sunli had realized that, while the movement of markets appeared to be random, advanced human intelligence could synthesize vast amounts of information, detect patterns, and make predictions. Working together to make millions of calculations every minute, the enhanced human team knew exactly what to purchase and what and when to sell. In this way, Sunli's collective was matching the pace of the machine learning algorithms that dominated stock trading. But the collective had an advantage—its humanity. Enhanced intuition, creativity, and insight gave the collective an edge over other computerized stock trading methods. It was the best of both worlds.

Sunli knew that it was merely a matter of time before the Department of Justice and the Securities and Exchange Commission began investigating them for possible market manipulation, but in the meantime, they were making lots of money. Even more importantly, she was learning more every day about the power of collective cognition and the abilities of people enhanced with the Brainaid. The possibilities were truly endless, incalculable wealth and power appeared to be at her fingertips.

She gazed proudly at her team, the volunteers wordlessly typing away on their laptops, many with their eyes closed. The longer that the enhanced humans used their modified Brainaids, the more their addiction and dependence grew. They spent all day, every day, plugged into their Brainaids and connected to the central computer. They would be rewarded for their loyalty. Soon, there would be plenty of money to go around.

Sunli left the operations center and walked out to the hotel courtyard where Wu crouched, hand feeding the fish in the Koi pond. The fish crowded near him, their slick orange and white scales catching the sunlight as they competed for morsels of food. Wu closed his hand over the pellets, forcing the Koi to slam their bodies into his hand in an attempt to knock the food free. Finally, he relented and let them eat from his palm.

Sunli walked over to the general. "My plan is successful," she said, placing a hand on Wu's shoulder. "By the end of the day, we will have made hundreds of thousands of dollars."

Wu shrugged, rising and brushing his hands off on his trousers. "Paltry sum. I thought you were going to impress me."

Sunli sniffed and looked away. "The amount doesn't

matter," she finally replied. "Don't you see that? This experiment reveals the tip of the iceberg of what we can do."

Sunli watched the sparkling fish as they dispersed through the Koi pond. "Why would you, a Chinese general, install such a common feature of Japanese gardens on the grounds of your hotel?" she asked.

"Tourists don't know the difference. As long as it's vaguely Asian, it fits the Lucky Dragon theme. Plus, I like my fish."

"You know, the technology behind the Brainaid started with a fish," Sunli said.

"A fish? Like these fish?" The general raised an eyebrow skeptically, while casting an admiring gaze at the exquisite beauty standing beside the Koi pond. His eyes skimmed across her body, draped in an emerald-green silk dress that dipped low in the front, framing the curve of her breasts.

"Yes, a fish." Sunli smiled. "In ancient Rome, the court physician to Emperor Claudius used an electric fish to treat headaches, and ever since then, man has sought a way to harness the power of electricity to treat the human brain."

Sunli grabbed Wu's hands. "Natasha Simon may have created the Brainaid, but I am the first to perfect it and create the ultimate human being. This is one of the greatest scientific breakthroughs mankind has ever achieved. Surely you have to see that. And to think it all started with a fish."

Chapter 28
Smoke and Music

"THEY RECOVERED HIS BODY FROM the Los Alamos Reservoir," said Gabi as she propped her Doc Martens on the dashboard of Alek's 4Runner. They were headed back to the Haskalah Center to see Bernie Bhakta. Natasha, Sal, and Chang were following in a rented Jeep. Percy had declined the offer to join their excursion, claiming he had too much to do at the lab.

"So, Harold the forest ranger was the last one who saw the agent, when he drove Wu and Sunli into Bandelier National Monument? And when Chang and I found the limo a few hours later, the agent was gone. A week later they find his body in the lake?"

"Apparently," said Gabi, shaking her head sadly. "We suspect China's Ministry of State Security has operatives that were following Wu. They must have seized our guy, thinking they could get information on Wu out of him. And when they couldn't…" Gabi shrugged, trying to appear tough, but Alek noticed the way her lip quivered, and her eyes grew watery as she held the emotions in.

"You've confirmed that Wu and Sunli are in Vegas?" Alek asked, trying to change the subject.

"Yes, that's where they are—holed up at the Lucky Dragon. They appear to be building a large group of followers. Rumor has it they claim to be using the Brainaids to create 'enhanced humans.'"

"Whatever that means. Oh, that's our turn." Alek swung the wheel and drove under the colorful prayer tags flying above the dirt road leading to the Haskalah Center. Snow covered the ground in front of the geodesic dome. Alek parked the 4Runner as Chang pulled up beside them in the Jeep. There was no one waiting outside to greet them, so they grabbed their bags and headed into the dome.

Inside the dimly lit room, about 20 people were arranged in a ring sitting on large pillows on the parquet floor. Smoke curled up from a large brass bowl in the center of the circle as the sweet, balsamic scent of lavender wafted through the air. Low rhythmic music vibrated in sync with the sound of steady breathing. Flickering candles and the purple-tinted hues of the late afternoon sun filtering through the window at the top of the dome filled the room with rippling shadows that seemed to move in time with the pulse of the music.

After the rush to get there, the conversation about the dead FBI agent, the worries of the past month, Alek suddenly felt calmer. Standing at the edge of the gathering, he took a deep breath, letting his scattered thoughts go. Gabi slipped her hand into Alek's and leaned her head on his shoulder, giving a small sigh of relief.

Immediately upon entering the room, Natasha and Sal dropped their bags and joined the meditation circle, but Chang, ever resistant to the very idea of relaxation, began pacing on the far side of the room. Bernard Bhakta, the guru they had come to see, lowered the volume of the music, and spoke.

"Tonight, as we close our time together, with every breath we take, we vow to walk with grateful hearts and ease the burdens of others. Let us never forget our promise to go forward spreading peace and love."

Bernie stood and bowed slightly in several directions, acknowledging the participants. "Namaste. I will see you all at seven o'clock for dinner. We're having homemade tamales so don't be late."

With that, the room erupted into many quiet conversations as the participants stacked their pillows, gathered their belongings, and meandered toward the door. Bernie didn't waste a moment spotting Alek and Gabi. He ran over nimbly to welcome them with a hug.

Alek quickly introduced his colleagues. Natasha and Sal peppered Bernie with questions about the music, the incense, and the practice of meditation, while Chang fidgeted anxiously. Noticing Chang's discomfort, Bernie

193

quickly texted an assistant to show them to their rooms.

"We'll talk more over dinner," he reassured Sal and Natasha. "Try a walk outside and get some deep cleansing breaths," he told Chang.

Gabi and Alek had asked to stay in the same yurt they had occupied during their previous visit. The others were assigned private rooms in one of the adobe buildings near the geodesic dome. The yurt hadn't changed since their last visit, though Alek noticed the addition of a fluffy featherbed on the futon and several soft comforters to combat the cold weather. Thanks to the old-fashioned wood stove, it was toasty warm.

"Nama-stay right here," said Gabi, grabbing Alek's arm and pulling him down onto the futon beside her. "We have an hour and a half till dinner, and I have a pretty good idea how we can pass the time."

* * *

When Gabi and Alek arrived at dinner, they found Natasha, Sal, and Chang seated at one of the long, family style tables listening to Bernie talk. A mound of discarded cornhusks on the table suggested they had already eaten their share of tamales, so Gabi and Alek grabbed themselves each a plate of the traditional Mexican meal of masa-wrapped meats and cheeses cooked in cornhusks and served with rice, beans, and green chile on the side.

When they returned with their food, Bernie was explaining how he had used the Brainaid to cure those who came to him suffering from the Taos Hum. Natasha, Sal, and Chang listened intently.

"As I'm sure you know, meditation is based on the principle of sympathetic resonance. Resonance is the vibration rate of an object, and sympathetic resonance is when one vibrating object causes another to vibrate in harmony with it or match its rate of vibration."

"Yes," said Natasha enthusiastically. "We are accustomed to being in the beta brain rhythm when we are consciously alert. When we alter our brain rhythm to alpha, we are slowing our brainwaves down and putting ourselves in the ideal brain state for optimal performance and learning."

Bernie nodded. "Alpha waves increase the release of melatonin, beta-endorphin, norepinephrine, and dopamine. These brain chemicals are linked to increased mental clarity and generate an ideal environment for learning. There are many benefits to entraining one's brain waves to enter an alpha state.

"In the past, even those who suffered from external frequencies such as the Taos Hum could use meditation to enter an alpha state and experience relief from the Hum frequency," Bernie continued. "But when the Project Z plants were built, the Low Energy Nuclear Reaction powering the plants created a frequency of 42 hertz that amplified the effects of the Hum. This new frequency couldn't be countered through simple meditation. That's where the Brainaid came in."

Natasha nodded. "Yes, the Brainaid offers neural feedback that enhances the entrainment process—making it faster and more efficient than meditation alone," she said. "I'm not surprised my device offers the only solution for people plagued by the combination of the LENR frequency and the Taos Hum."

Bernie smiled. "Here's the part that will surprise you. None of my Hummers—that's what we call people who experience the Hum... Hummers or Hearers—anyhow, none of them need the Brainaid anymore."

"How is that?" Natasha asked sharply.

"With each of the Hummers, I begin the entrainment process using the Brainaid in tandem with alpha wave music and aromatherapy," Bernie explained.

"That's what you were doing during the meditation circle this afternoon," Gabi said. "I love the lavender incense."

"Lavender on its own can induce a relaxed state, but, by introducing the Brainaid and the music and aromatherapy at the same time, we can teach the brain to remember certain patterns. Once those patterns are established, we can eliminate the use of the device and rely strictly on natural sources to enter an alpha wave state. I think this is key because I fear that the extensive use of the Brainaid poses a danger of addiction."

Chang reached out and grabbed Bernie's arm. "Can

you cure Brainaid addiction?"

"Possibly," answered Bernie. "But the best way to avoid issues of addiction is to never allow it to begin in the first place."

"That's certainly true," mused Gabi. "I've spent years combating the drug cartels in New Mexico. Addiction is difficult to end."

Chang's eyes burned with intensity. "So perhaps you could use these techniques to reverse Brainaid addiction?"

Sal interrupted. "The Brainaid isn't dangerous except when it is misused or misapplied by certain people. I don't think we should demonize it."

"No, of course not," Chang agreed. "In fact, I've been researching numerous applications for the device. I even think it could be used to reverse coma in some patients."

Bernie stood. "The Brainaid is an amazing device with multiple therapeutic benefits. I do believe it is the only way for most people to learn the entrainment techniques necessary to render the LENR frequency harmless. The issue is every new invention creates a new set of problems." Nat and Sal exchanged pointed glances. Alek kept his eyes on the ground.

Bernie then shook hands with each of them. "Let's meet again tomorrow to discuss this. I must assist with dinner clean-up before this evening's shamanic drum ceremony. Do join us if you wish."

The gray-headed guru smiled broadly, his eyes twinkling. "Just remember, I leave you with one warning... always beware the danger of too much of a good thing."

Alek watched Bernie walking away, trying to remember why that phrase sounded so familiar. He felt certain someone else had given him a similar warning once. He caught Gabi's eye across the table. The candlelight reflected off her soft blonde curls, highlighting the curve of her cheek, flushed in the warm room. Of all the good things that had happened recently in his life, Alek was certain that meeting Gabi was the best one.

Could you really have too much of a good thing?

Chapter 29
Sealed with a Kiss

THE NEXT MORNING SAL STOPPED Gabi and Alek as they headed down the path toward the dome. Dressed in jeans, hiking boots, and a Patagonia parka, the tall, dark-haired entrepreneur appeared to be on a mission.

"Hey, I have an idea. Nat and Chang are already in there talking to Bernie about the Brainaid. They will have endless questions and I bet they can bug Bernie for days. So, here's my idea. What if, while they geek out over meditation, aromatherapy, and brain waves, we hit the slopes?"

"Go skiing?" asked Gabi. "I didn't know you skied."

"Well, actually I never have," Sal replied. "But Taos Ski Valley is supposed to be one of the best ski resorts in the Southwest, and since we're here, I thought, why not."

"True," said Alek. "I wish I had thought of that. I would have brought my gear."

"It's fine. We can rent or buy stuff. And I'll buy the lift tickets. The whole thing will be my treat."

"That isn't necessary," Alek interjected.

"I want to, Alek. You both have done so much for me, and Project Z has made me rich beyond my wildest dreams. I know the lab won't allow you to profit from your inventions, so, let me treat. What good is money if you can't spend some on your friends?"

"You know, Sal, Taos isn't the easiest spot for a first-time skier," said Gabi kindly.

"I know. I researched it. I'm going to enroll in ski school. I'll be their star pupil—especially if the instructor is cute."

Laughing, Gabi replied, "I'm excited! I haven't gone skiing in ages and there's so much snow now. It's actually remarkable this late in the season."

"Spring skiing is the best," Alek agreed. "Although this year's snowfall is unusual." Shaking off his concerns about the climate, he focused on the proposed excursion. "Let's reserve some rooms at the St. Bernard Hotel. We can ski this afternoon and tomorrow and then head back Wednesday to pick up Nat and Chang."

"They will have solved all the world's problems by then," Sal said. "I'll go tell them our plans and then we can get packed and on the road."

* * *

Wu reclined on the white leather couch in his penthouse apartment. He loved watching Sunli while she worked. Her excitement was palpable. She practically glowed, perched on a bamboo chair across from him, as she explained her latest plan.

"A single neuron in the human brain can respond only to what the neurons connected to it are doing, but all those neurons working together can write novels, compose music, and cure cancer. Imagine if we boost that cognitive power one hundredfold." Dressed in beige silk pajamas, her long black hair secured in a low ponytail, Sunli looked more like a high-end courtesan than a brilliant scientist.

Sunli continued her explanation, seemingly more to herself than to the general. As she spoke, she made notes on her iPad. "A human has 100 billion neurons, but the Brainaid can achieve entrainment of a single human brain and then connect it to dozens of entrained brains. Together, through collective cognition, these humans can outthink any computer." Wu nodded absently and reached for the television's remote control.

Sunli rose from her seat, grabbed the general's shoulders, and focused her intense dark eyes on him. "I feel as though you are underestimating my invention. You aren't recognizing it's capabilities."

Wu shrugged. "You made some money in the stock market, maybe a little more than my algorithmic trading, but nothing life changing."

The general began flipping through television channels, while Sunli turned away lost in thought. She began walking toward the door, then wheeled around suddenly.

"Here's what I propose," Sunli exclaimed. "Using our collective of Brainaid enhanced humans, we can penetrate the computer security protecting the Federal Reserve."

Wu shook his head dismissively. "That system was created to prevent the manipulation of trillions of dollars. Others have tried and failed over the years."

"We won't fail. We can create thousands of subtle financial manipulations that are not detected, transferring funds to various small, crime-ridden countries that have no operating legal systems. Our collective is the secret to making this work—enhanced humans acting together... exquisite timing, buying treasuries low, running up the price slowly, dumping gradually at high prices, and transferring the earnings. The Fed prints money. No one will be able to detect a distributed and cleverly coordinated operation. Hundreds of augmented brains operating as a collective are the key!"

Wu was starting to pay attention. "You can do that? Your collective cognition has that kind of power?"

"It's like an anthill," Sunli explained. "Colonies of ants, bee hives, schools of fish, flocks of birds, and fireflies flashing synchronously... They're all examples of highly coordinated behaviors that emerge from collective intelligence. We have that power, and we can use it. We can transfer the funds out of the Fed and then... then we'll use the casino to trade millions of dollars for chips that can be exchanged to create untraceable cash."

"A brilliant invention!" Wu cried out. "I must admit I am surprised to see you abandoning your ideals and condoning criminal action, but now I do recognize the value of this breakthrough you've made."

Sunli's cheeks flushed. Her eyes gleamed. She appeared to be drunk on her success. "Life is a game, and I plan on winning," she exclaimed. "Let's play high stakes Baccarat."

"Of course," Wu murmured, reaching out his hands to draw her closer. "The house always wins—especially in our game."

And with that, Wu finally achieved the goal he had

been working toward for more than a year. Sunli, giddy over her plan, her success, and her power, leaned in and gave the general a long-awaited kiss.

* * *

Taos Ski Valley was a short drive up the mountains from the Haskalah Center. Alek wove the 4Runner through a canyon of tall pine trees. The snow piled alongside the roadside increased steadily as they ascended toward the peaks.

In little time, the three skiers arrived at the quaint ski village and checked into the Hotel St. Bernard. Established in 1960, the European-style ski lodge was located at the base of the mountain, allowing guests to ski right from their rooms to the slopes.

Walking into the lobby, they saw several tourists gathered around a large stone fireplace enjoying a late breakfast. The rustic, homey atmosphere felt soothing and familiar. Alek hadn't skied at Taos in years, and he wondered why he had waited so long.

After finding their rooms and getting settled, Alek, Gabi, and Sal met on the hotel deck to enjoy a cup of coffee while drinking in the breathtaking view of the mountain towering above them. Intense sunshine warmed their shoulders, counteracting the extremely brisk temperature as they watched the skiers coming down the final run.

"I feel like we've been transported to the French Alps," Sal said with a happy sigh.

"Have you ever been to the French Alps?" asked Alek.

"Ummm no. But this is how I imagine it. Anyhow, I've already signed up for ski school," Sal said impatiently. "Finish your coffee and we can head to the ski shop and rent our gear."

Inside the ski shop, a colorful array of high-tech winter gear awaited. Sal immediately rushed over to a display of gloves and bounded back with three pairs. "Check these out—they're heated using the rare earth batteries that Nat and I have been manufacturing. They'll keep you warm all day!"

As they selected long underwear, waterproof pants,

warm parkas, ski boots, goggles, poles, and, of course, skis, Gabi marveled at how busy the shop was on a weekday. Record snow had fallen every day that month, and all the customers in the store were talking about the two feet of fresh, dry, light powder that a storm left the night before. Both veteran skiers and newcomers chattered about the ideal conditions. Although some complained about the bitterly cold temperature, most of the would-be skiers appeared eager to get to the mountain that sparkled and shone under the bright sunshine. Preoccupied by eavesdropping on other skiers' conversations about the record snowfall, Alek took his time browsing through the vast selection of parkas.

Frustrated by the delay, Sal chose a bright yellow jacket and thrust it at him, saying, "Just get that and let's go."

Sal paid the bill and the three went back to their rooms to change into the new clothes. Gabi was ready first and found herself forced to wait for the two men. Sitting near the circular fireplace beneath heavy dark wooden beams, Gabi listened to nearby conversations. Visitors from all over the world came to Taos for the challenging skiing. Gabi overheard a family talking in German and even picked up a few sentences in Chinese. Two ski patrollers walked out of the hotel dining room talking about avalanche conditions. Gabi felt grateful they were there to monitor and maintain the ski area.

Finally, the two men arrived, and the next stop was the Taos Ski School, where Sal looked out of place among crowds of children. He overcame his discomfort after meeting his instructor, an athletic blonde man in his twenties named Stefan, and was soon learning to snowplow while Gabi and Alek cheered him on.

"Go on, you two. *¡Fuera de aquí!* Get out of here and do some skiing," Sal shouted over his shoulder.

"Hey, before we go, there's this tracking app that Chang mentioned that we should all install on our phones so we can keep track of each other," Alek suggested. "That way we'll be able to check on where everyone is when we are separated and plan when we can get together for dinner and drinks."

As they downloaded the app and entered each other's information, Gabi gave Sal a hug. "Now, be a good student," she teased him.

"I'll keep a close eye on him for you," the ski instructor said as Sal smiled and winked.

Alek and Gabi shouldered their skis for the short walk to the chair lifts. "So, where do you want to start?" Alek asked.

Gabi pointed to the slopes of Kachina Peak, the resort's highest point at 12,481 feet, and the site of the ski area's most challenging expert runs.

"Let's start at the top," she said.

"Sure you don't want to warm up with Al's Run?" Alek asked, referring to the black diamond run along the front face of the mountains. Known for its challenging moguls, Al's Run was a legendary facet of every Taos ski story, especially since the famous slope angled dramatically downward in full view of the chair lift. Often described as a gigantic egg carton standing on its edge, the intimidating nature of Al's Run led Taos Ski Valley founder Ernie Blake to put up a sign that read, "Don't Panic! You're Looking at Only 1/30th of Taos Ski Valley. We Have Many Easy Runs Too!"

"We'll do that one later today, I promise. Unless you're scared," she giggled, kissing him playfully on the nose.

"Scared?" scoffed Alek. "I am a physicist. I laugh at danger while calculating my trajectory down the ski slope. Let's go."

Chapter 30
A Question of Desire

BERNIE BHAKTA GESTURED TO THE long counter lined with glass canisters of herbs, mortar and pestles, distilling equipment, candles, vials, beakers, and droppers. "Welcome to my mad scientist's laboratory," he told Chang and Natasha. "Pull up a chair and I'll describe what I do here."

Dust motes swirled in the dim sunlight filtering through the small, round windows carved into the adobe building that Bernie called his laboratory. The dusty, dark room shimmered with a sense of mystery. Natasha immediately felt a longing to learn more, and Bernie quickly obliged.

"Smell is our most primitive sense. It impacts our brains, our moods, our overall health," explained the former physicist. "About 10 years ago, I started studying research on aromatherapy and the way it changes the electrical rhythms of the brain. My goal was to find a way to enhance the alpha waves, which are dominant in meditation, to create changes in the central nervous system."

"What did you learn?" asked Chang.

"Inhaling lavender and its main constituents, linalool and linalyl acetate, produce a calming effect that reduces stress and moves users into a state of relaxed alertness."

Bernie grabbed a canister and held it out to his guests. "Here, smell this. Take a deep whiff now." Natasha bent over the canister of silvery dried leaves and flowers. "Mmmm, that's delicious," she said.

"It's lavender. Researchers at the Tokyo University of Pharmacy in Japan found that breathing distilled lavender oil can reduce the measure of adrenocorticotropic hormone in the blood plasma. Other herbs can decrease anxiety, fatigue, depression, and hostility. Until recently, I had found that the right combination of meditation and aromatherapy could help anyone to achieve an alpha state of mind."

"Even the Hummers?" Natasha interjected.

"Even the Hummers," Bernie replied. "But as you know, all that changed when the Taos Project Z Power Plant began to operate. The combination of the higher 42 hertz frequency and the Taos Hum was too much for my methods. That's where the Brainaid came in."

Chang nodded. "So, it helped but then you faced the issue of addiction. What did you do to combat that?"

"Like I said earlier, by combining the Brainaid with aromatherapy, alpha wave music, and meditation, I could move the brain into a state of entrainment and then slowly wean the user off the Brainaid. There's no reason why Brainaid addicts can't be cured in a similar way."

"What if someone is deeply addicted?" asked Chang. "Is there hope for them?"

"That, my friend, depends on only one thing."

"What is that?" Chang asked eagerly.

"Their desire to be cured."

* * *

Holding their poles in one hand, Gabi and Alek bent slightly as the chairlift came up behind them. Seated comfortably in the metal seat, they leaned back to take in the breathtaking views as the Kachina Peak Chairlift whisked them to the summit.

The highest triple chair lift in North America had been installed by helicopter in 2014 at an estimated cost of $3 million. Since then, it had taken countless skiers to the double black diamond expert runs once only accessible by foot.

Under the bright blue sky, the triple lift covered 1,100 vertical feet in about five minutes, offering riders an excellent vantage point to see Wheeler Peak, the Taos Plateau, and all the way to the Spanish Peaks in Colorado. Smooth stretches of snow dotted with tall pine and piñon trees and thick stands of spruce unfolded below as they zipped up the mountain.

Alek looked down at the many ski runs traversing the mountain in a haphazard pattern of steep, snowy, tree-lined chutes. The sun reflecting off the snow was dazzling. Alek squinted through his ski goggles at the peaks surrounding them on all sides.

"I've never seen so much snow in April. What if this is another unintended consequence of the LENR?"

"Why would it be? I wish it weren't so cold," Gabi replied. "Even with the sun shining, it's frigid, but the skiers don't seem to be complaining. There are people here from all over the world. Waiting in the lobby, I heard people talking in German and Chinese."

"Hmmm. I overheard two guys speaking Chinese in the ski store. The weird thing was when they noticed me, they switched to English. Also, they were both white."

"That's odd," said Gabi, looking momentarily concerned. "Oh, we're almost there."

The lift swept them past the tree line as the summit appeared in the distance, marked by a wooden post with tattered prayer flags flying in the wind. As the chair began to slow, the two raised the safety bar, stood up, and gently pushed themselves down the slope.

Spotting a large red and white sign that warned, "Caution. Extreme terrain. No intermediates or low-level skiers," Gabi grabbed Alek's elbow and said, "Sure, you're up to this?"

"Ha! I'll beat you to the base," Alek exclaimed, pushing off down the run.

Alek felt the cold air on his face as he sped down the mountain. Gliding through the knee-deep powder, he felt weightless. He was floating. He swooped across the snow, making rhythmic turns, and delighting in the thrill of hurtling downward at nearly 40 miles per hour. After traveling a little farther down the run, Alek turned his skis parallel and dug into the snow to stop and wait for Gabi, his heart pounding with adrenaline. A few moments later, she was at his side.

"Woohoo," shouted Gabi, pulling off her goggles, breathless with exhilaration. "You're pretty good at this."

"I'm good at lots of things," said Alek and pulled her in for a snow swept kiss.

* * *

Sunli walked through the Lucky Dragon conference room monitoring the work of her team—dozens of enhanced humans working together to transfer money out of the Federal Reserve Bank. The scheme was unprecedented, untraceable, and unbelievably successful. The silent room was a hive of obedient Brainaid addicts, all willing to do exactly as she commanded. She shivered with pleasure watching them work.

General Wu stepped into the open doorway. "Sunli, *qǐng guòlái zhèlǐ.*" With a reluctant glance over her shoulder at her room of loyal prodigies, Sunli joined the Chinese general in the hall.

"*Tā shì shénme?* I'm working," she protested petulantly.

"Darling, I must advise you of certain developments and some key precautions I have put in place." Wu grabbed Sunli's hand, drawing her toward the hotel elevator. He didn't speak again until they were safely ensconced in their penthouse suite.

"Remember the man in the Suburban who followed us at Bandelier National Monument?" Sunli nodded. "Well, I have reason to believe that people are still looking for us and so I've enlisted the service of some bodyguards to keep you safe."

"Who are these people?" asked Sunli. "What do they want from us?"

The general sat down slowly on the elegant sofa. For the first time in months, his face revealed his age and the weight of years spent manipulating the Chinese government to further his personal aims.

Wu sat silently for a moment and then spoke quietly and deliberately. "As you know, I have worked closely with the People's Liberation Army and the Ministry of State Security. But when I came to New Mexico to investigate Southwest Syndrome, the Dragon's Brain, I stopped communicating with the MSS. I cut those ties."

He leaned forward, grasping both of Sunli's hands, suddenly a haggard old man desperately seeking a solution. "You know the MSS is deeply embedded in Los Alamos. I am certain they heard about the Brainaid and our work with collective cognition. They will do whatever it takes to acquire this technology, which means you are in danger. I must protect you. These are dangerous men."

Sunli threw back her curtain of shiny black hair and laughed.

"My love, you underestimate me. I am not the same person who you and the MSS held captive in Beijing. I am far stronger and more capable than you can even dream."

Wu nodded. "Yes, I do believe that, but humor me on this. We must keep you and your talents hidden. I will do everything in my power to keep you safe."

Sunli drew her fingers lightly across the general's cheek and kissed his lined forehead.

"Relax, my dear. Spend some time with your Brainaid. Everything will be fine."

Chapter 31
What Took You So Long?

AFTERNOON SHADOWS CREPT ACROSS THE slopes as Gabi and Alek returned to the chair lift for one last run down Kachina Peak. They waited in comfortable silence, then settled in the chair as they rose above the trees.

Alek glanced over his shoulder. "You see those guys two chairs behind us?" Gabi turned her head slightly so she could see the two men, dressed in black. Both wore balaclavas covering their faces.

"I think they may be the men I heard speaking Chinese in the ski store. I spotted them a few hours ago too when we were going down Al's Run."

"How can you tell?" asked Gabi. "You can't even see their faces."

Alek shrugged. "I don't know. I have a weird feeling. It's like they're following us."

"Don't be paranoid. Maybe they're expert skiers like us who want to check out the best runs," Gabi replied, turning her head again slightly to glance at the two men.

"I wish I hadn't let Sal talk me into this bright yellow parka," said Alek. "I feel way too conspicuous, too easy to spot."

They dismounted the chair lift, noticing that the wind had picked up. Clouds raced across the sky and snow swirled through the air. "Hmm. The weather is turning. This will have to be our last run," Gabi said.

She noticed the two men getting off the chair lift along with a handful of skiers. They seemed to be waiting. Perhaps Alek wasn't being paranoid.

"Let's hike a bit," Gabi said.

"Why?"

"It's too crowded here."

"We can ski the Wild West Glade to get away from all these people," Alek said. Gabi nodded, excited at the idea of trying out the isolated, heavily forested expert run that she had only read about. It would be a great way to end the day and to confirm whether Alek's suspicion about the two men was correct or not.

The two shouldered their skis and began hiking along the ridgeline. Wind-whipped ice crystals stung their skin as they walked.

Gabi stopped and grabbed Alek's elbow. "Hey, those guys you pointed out on the chair lift are following us."

"Now who's paranoid?" Alek asked.

Gabi wondered if she was being paranoid, or not paranoid enough.

Breathing heavily from the high altitude, they reached the chute and clicked their boots into their ski bindings. Alek glanced back again. "Here they come."

"Let's just ski," said Gabi. "This is a tough run. We need to concentrate."

The two headed down the steep tree-lined path, swooping through the deep powder. The run was deserted. The only other people in sight were the two men in black.

Gabi slowed down so she could ski closer to Alek. The men were getting nearer. One of them shouted something, but the wind carried his words away. Gabi couldn't tell if he was talking to them or his companion. She gestured to Alek, and they pulled to a stop next to a thick glade of pine trees.

Gabi squinted, watching the two men traverse the shadow-dappled snow. One of the men was holding something. Was that a gun in his hand? The man raised his arm. A gunshot, muffled by the wind and snow, echoed down the mountain. "Take off your skis," Gabi hissed at Alek. "Leave them here."

"What the hell is going on?" whispered Alek. "Who are they and why are they after us?"

"There's no time to ask questions," Gabi responded. "Remember, my agent was found dead."

Clicking out of their bindings, the two struggled

through the deep snow into the forest. Alek and Gabi could hear the men shouting but couldn't see them. As they wove their way deeper into the trees, a second gunshot rang out.

"Stop!" shouted Alek, grabbing Gabi's arm and looking down at the snow-covered hill beneath them. A spiderweb of shooting cracks was spreading through the snowpack before them. "Quick, we have to get to those rocks."

Alek and Gabi ran toward a rocky overhang a few feet away, ducking beneath the rocks in a narrow cavern as the snow on the mountain shattered like a pane of glass. The snow roared downhill, a moving wall of white, hurtling past them carrying trees and rocks along in an icy tidal wave. It seemed as if the entire mountain was catapulting toward the base with an ear-splitting rumble and a whoosh of air pressure. Snow poured down, packing the entrance to the rocky crevasse where Gabi and Alek had taken shelter, blocking out all the light.

Then... silence.

Gabi grabbed Alek's hand in the darkness. "Was that...?"

"Yes," he replied. "An avalanche."

* * *

Sunli slipped her arm into Wu's as they walked into the VIP room in the Lucky Dragon casino. The general had traded his uniform for a tuxedo that perfectly complemented Sunli's shimmering silver floor-length gown. Game play at the large round tables stopped when they entered. As the casino owners, they were nearly royalty. Several players rose to shake Wu's hand or bow respectfully to their hosts.

Then the deferential silence gave way to the murmur of voices, cards flipping, chips clicking, and ice cubes tinkling in glasses as winning hands were dealt. The deep red walls and gilded Asian decor provided the ideal setting for the green felt tables and the elegant men and women gathered around them, smoking Chinese Double Happiness cigarettes and drinking glass after glass of Hennessy Ellipse Cognac or Baijiu. Red-shirted dealers shuffled the cards as the most serious high-rollers, most of whom were middle-aged Chinese visitors, focused intently on their fast-moving games.

Two large men in business suits, Wu's recently hired bodyguards, positioned themselves on either side of the room, monitoring the doors, their eyes in constant motion. The general congratulated himself on the decision to hire them. *Even if there is no real threat of danger, the investment is worth it for my piece of mind*, the general thought. He finally had won Sunli's affection. He would do anything to protect her.

Sunli draped herself across one of the tables, running a handful of chips through her fingers. "I love Baccarat," she said to Wu. "Unlike life, Baccarat is based purely on luck."

"I scored an eight when I met you," Wu replied. Sunli smiled, knowing that the word eight, which is pronounced "ba" in Chinese, translated to "wealth" and "success." Eight was also the second highest score a Baccarat player could receive.

"Some might say I'm a nine," she countered.

The general strolled through the room, congratulating the winners. As a casino owner, he once would have been dismayed to see the VIPs doing so well, but nowadays, he wasn't looking to win every hand. The Baccarat tables offered the ideal way to launder the money that Sunli and her Brainaid collective had moved from the Federal Reserve that day.

Sunli greeted the gamblers, laying her hand on one player's thigh, blowing on the back of another's cards to ward off bad numbers. Her thick curtain of shiny black hair fell forward as she leaned over to whisper words of encouragement in another VIP's ear.

The general sighed. In the past, he would have been jealous, but watching Sunli manipulate the players was like watching an artist at work. He had never met a woman so beautiful and brilliant. Finally, he had won his prize.

Wu brushed away the thought that Sunli was technically still married. There really was no choice—Peter Chang had to die.

Wu caught Sunli's eye as she glanced up. He held out a hand and she glided to his side. "Things seem to be going well here," she whispered. "Perhaps we should head upstairs and try our luck at something else."

"I thought you would never ask," said the general.

* * *

Gabi and Alek huddled together in the darkness. Snow filled the entrance to the small cavern, wedging them in with barely room to move.

"The ski patrol will find us soon," Alek said, struggling to sound confident and reassuring. "We just have to sit tight for a little bit."

Gabi pulled her cell phone out of her zippered parka pocket. "No signal. Figures."

"It never occurred to me to rent an avalanche beacon," said Alek.

"It never occurred to me that two lunatics would chase us and shoot at us," Gabi replied.

"If we could reach Sal, that tracking app could pin-point our location right before the avalanche," said Alek.

"He's probably still in ski school. Or having drinks with the instructor," Gabi said.

They fell silent, shivering in the darkness. Finally, Gabi spoke. "It has to be the MSS. Wu had been working with them, but recent intelligence suggests that he broke with them when he and Sunli ran off to Vegas. I don't understand why they would come after us."

"Well, it's no secret that Sunli had been conducting research at the lab with us. Think they just wanted to chat?"

"Somehow, I doubt that. Most people I know don't start a conversation by pulling out a gun." Gabi sighed. "I suppose we should be quiet. There's only so much air in here and the more we talk, the more we use up. We need to conserve our oxygen."

Alek nodded. "Yeah, that's true but... there's some-thing I need to say."

Alek couldn't see a thing. They were sealed in the cave with no way to know how much snow was piled on top of them. Pinned in side by side in the darkness, he felt almost as if they'd been buried alive. He also felt the heavy weight of the need to say what was pressing on his heart.

"Here's the thing. Ten years ago, when Maggie died and Julie left me, I made a vow that I would never get close to anyone again... that I would never allow myself to hurt someone... that I didn't deserve to fall in love... to have a family. I didn't deserve any happiness after what I had done."

"Alek, that's not..." Gabi interrupted.

"Just hear me out," he replied. "It's not like you can go anywhere." Gabi gave a snuffley laugh.

Alek thought back to the day long ago when he was supposed to be watching his two-year-old daughter. Instead of paying attention to her, he was focused on early calculations for the creation of Project Z. Maggie had wandered outside and fallen into the swimming pool. By the time Alek found her, it was too late. After the accident, Alek and Julie's marriage never recovered. Finally, they split up and Alek moved to Los Alamos where he poured all his time and energy into his work. He promised himself that he would be alone for the rest of his life.

Alek reached out and took Gabi's hand in the darkness as he continued. "So, when I met you, I tried to fight our connection but... deep down I knew I'd finally found someone who truly gets me. As cheesy as it sounds, you are my soulmate, Gabriella Stebbens."

Gabi sniffed, wiping away a tear in the darkness. "Alek Spray, you're my soulmate too."

"So, if... I mean... when... we get out of this cave... well, I want to marry you. I want us to start a family. I want to see you holding our baby in your arms. Look, I'd get down on one knee, but there isn't room in here. Will you marry me?"

In the darkness, Gabi reached up and placed her gloved hand over Alek's mouth.

"Shhh... I think I hear something. Is that a dog barking?"

The two strained their ears, trying to hear what was going on above them. Through the thick, packed layers of snow, they heard a muffled bark.

"Hey!" Alek shouted. "Hey, we're in here." He scrabbled at the snow packing the entrance, trying to dig through it with his hands. "Hey! Hey! Help!"

More muffled noises came from above and then the sound of scraping. Alek strained to thrust his arm through the snow covering the mouth of the cave. Finally, he managed to wriggle his arm through a tiny crack in the cement-like snowpack.

"I see something yellow," someone shouted.

"That's them. The guy was wearing a yellow parka," another voice replied. "Dig!"

Suddenly, Gabi and Alek blinked as light penetrated the darkness and powerful hands lifted them to safety. As their eyes adjusted to bright emergency lights shining down on them, they saw two ski patrollers and a golden retriever—an avalanche rescue dog.

"What took you so long?" shouted Alek, laughing with relief.

Chapter 32
Digging Out

BACK AT THE ST. BERNARD Hotel, Alek and Gabi thawed out in front of the fireplace, drinking hot buttered rum from large mugs, and trying to piece together what had happened. Chang's tracking app they had installed on their phones had apparently saved their lives.

"It didn't take long for news of the avalanche to spread through the resort," Sal said. "I remembered we had the app, so I contacted the ski patrol. They used the last location on the app's tracking readout to find you."

One of the hotel's resident dogs wandered up to them and licked Gabi's hand.

"It's called the St. Bernard Hotel, but this looks like a labrador," she said, patting the dog on its smooth black head.

"Yeah, I thought St. Bernard dogs carrying casks of brandy were supposed to rescue us," laughed Alek. "We had to wait till we got all the way down the mountain to get a drink."

The three friends fell silent, reflecting on the events of the day.

While the resort officials had refused to draw any conclusions about what caused the avalanche, Alek suspected the gunshots had triggered it. Who were the two men who had been chasing them and why were they shooting at them? After the avalanche and rescue, they were nowhere to be found.

"Do you think those men were killed in the avalanche?" Sal asked. "Buried under a mountain of snow? Do you think they were even there?"

"Are you saying we imagined them?" snapped Gabi.

"No, no of course not," Sal replied quickly. "It's just

strange."

"I'm going to sleep," said Gabi. "You two solve all the mysteries and let me know in the morning." Setting her empty cup on a nearby table, she headed off down the hallway. Alek watched her walk away.

"I've known Gabi a long time. Something's not right with her," Sal mused. "Do you think it was something one of us said?"

"Oh yeah, absolutely," replied Alek. "I definitely said the wrong thing." Alek fell silent, staring into space.

"What on earth did you say to her?" Sal asked.

Alek continued looking off into the distance. "I asked her to marry me."

* * *

A few weeks later, Percy ushered Alek into his office, giving the younger man a fatherly pat on the shoulder. "Sit down. Let's visit for a minute. You haven't seemed yourself lately. What's going on?"

Alek shrugged. "Nothing. Everything's fine. I'm excited about Chang and Bernie's work on setting up Brainaid addiction clinics. They plan to use aromatherapy and alpha wave music to wean people off the devices. Of course, not everyone is interested in overcoming the addiction..."

"And have you heard anything about the men who were shooting at you? Is the FBI still looking into it?"

Alek shrugged again. "They suspect the MSS, but they haven't been able to confirm anything. Plus, I haven't heard from Gabi lately. She's been out of town a lot."

"Hmmm," said Percy a little too sympathetically. "You know, I've been married 25 years, if you want any, you know, advice."

Alek stifled a laugh. Percy's definition of a happy marriage was seeing his wife once a month for a nice dinner in Santa Fe. The rest of the time, one of them was usually out of town or working on an important project. They had never had children and led largely separate lives.

"I, um, I really appreciate the offer, but everything's fine. I mean, I'm still concerned about Sunli's disappearance and, y'know, those guys did try to kill us in Taos, but everything's... fine."

"Okay. That sounds... fine." Percy swiveled in his desk chair, grabbing his laptop and immersing himself in email. "If anything changes..."

"There is one thing I'd like to talk about—the climate implications of the LENR. I really think we should be researching it."

Percy waved his hand dismissively without looking up from his computer. Apparently, his momentary attempt at empathy had ended. "Alek, I told you, it's nothing. There's no way the Project Z plants could have a negative impact on the environment. I need you to give Chang a hand with his project. He could use the help."

"Sure. Thanks for the... um... talk." Alek wandered down the hall to Chang's office.

Chang was sitting behind his desk watching a livestream of CNN on his computer monitor. He gestured to a chair, held a finger to his lips, and then pointed to the monitor. Listening to the news broadcast, Alek took a seat.

"The HEAL Act is headed to the Senate," a news anchor said. "The U.S. House of Representatives approved the bill today in record time after heated debate on Capitol Hill. The Help End Addiction Loss, or HEAL, Act will allocate $3 billion to setting up Brainaid addiction clinics throughout the nation and providing Americans with one-time $1,400 incentives for trading in their Brainaid devices. The devices will be refurbished and reallocated to treat new sufferers of Southwest Syndrome.

"In other news, the FBI reports no progress on the investigation into the illegal transfer of an undisclosed amount of money out of the Federal Reserve Bank. Officials say the theft represents one of the most sophisticated heists they have ever..."

Chang clicked a button, ending the livestream. "Did you hear that? All we need is Senate approval and we can begin opening our clinics."

"Yeah, that's great," replied Alek unenthusiastically. "I mean, I guess it's great. Seems like every solution we create leads to a new set of problems. Kinda makes you wonder what's next."

"Well, aren't you rainbows and sunshine," Chang

laughed. "Go get to work. Stop raining on my parade."

Alek rose, deciding not to mention that Percy had sent him to help Chang. "Hey, well, I hope the HEAL Act can, uh, heal everyone. Sorry to be so gloomy."

As he was walking back to his office, he heard his office phone ring. Cursing the lab's security policy that forbade the use of cell phones, he ran down the hall.

"Hello?"

"Hey."

Alek felt excitement at hearing Gabi's voice. She sounded far away and breathless, like she had been running or climbing stairs. "I'm at the airport in New York. I'm coming to town tonight. Can I see you?"

"Uh, of course," Alek said. "New York?"

"Yeah, it's a long story. I land in Albuquerque at 4:30 so I'll see you at your office at about 6?"

"Sure. Are you bringing Max with you?"

"No, he's still at the dog sitters. Okay, see you soon." She hung up abruptly and Alek headed back to his office, wondering what to expect.

* * *

Alek spent the afternoon trying to work, but mostly passed his time by staring into space. He picked up the phone, set it down, started typing a report, then walked to the breakroom to get a snack. The hours crawled by. Finally, his phone rang, and it was Gabi.

"Hey, I'm in the parking lot."

"I'll be right out," Alek replied.

When she saw him walking toward her, Gabi slipped out of her car and hugged him, burying her head in his shoulder.

"Are you hungry?" Alek asked.

"No, not really," she replied without meeting his eyes.

"I know this cool place we should check out. It's not somewhere for dinner, but we could get a snack."

Gabi left her car parked in the lot and hopped into the 4Runner. Alek placed his hand on her thigh. "It's good to have you here." Gabi nodded but didn't reply.

A few minutes later, they pulled up in front of a run-down building that clearly had once been a gas station. A tattered awning covered the spot where the pumps used to be. "Dutch's Doughnuts" read the hand-lettered sign over the door.

"Doughnuts?" asked Gabi.

"You'll see," Alek said.

Inside, the small room was packed with people—people sitting at tables, people leaning against walls, people standing in corners, people eating doughnuts, and people dancing near the front of the room. On a makeshift stage, a couple of guitarists and a singer in her mid-twenties were performing country music for the doughnut shop full of onlookers.

Gabi stood dumbfounded, looking around the crowded room as toes tapped and listeners swayed to the music. The audience included everyone from grandparents to toddlers, all enthusiastically enjoying the music. The atmosphere was a far cry from a typical smoke-filled honky-tonk filled with beer-swilling patrons, but, somehow, it worked.

"Live music in a doughnut shop?" said Gabi, raising an eyebrow.

"Yeah, they get some great musicians here, and the doughnuts are pretty good too. For the past year, they've done this at least once a week."

Alek gestured to an empty table. "I'll get us some doughnuts and coffee," he said. "Still like jelly-filled?" Gabi nodded. Moments later, Alek returned with steaming cups of black coffee and sugar covered pastries.

Gabi surrendered herself to the music. In contrast to their odd surroundings, the performers were excellent. "In my alternative life, this is what I did for a career," she said.

"There's still time," Alek replied, laughing. "A few weeks ago, I drove past an old building in Vaughn, New Mexico that had a sign on the window that said, 'Female Vocalist Wanted.' It could be your big break."

"You've never heard me sing," Gabi murmured.

"You've never seen me dance or I'd ask you," said Alek, pointing to the handful of couples dancing near the stage.

"It's okay. My two-step is kinda rusty." Gabi licked some jelly off her fingers. "Look, Alek, we need to talk."

"Ummm. I was afraid of that," he said. Alek looked around. No one in the room was paying attention to anything but the music. "What's going on?"

Gabi traced the silver sparkles embedded in the linoleum tabletop with one finger. "Y'know when we met, I wasn't looking for a relationship, but somehow... somehow something happened between us."

"Yeah, and it's been good."

"It has been, but I'm starting to feel like you're looking for something more permanent."

"Like when I asked you to marry me?"

"Mmmhmm. That." Gabi stared down at the table. "Alek, I can't get married and raise children. You need to find someone who can give you what you want."

Alek struggled to speak. The lump in his throat threatened to choke him. "Gabi, you are what I want."

Gabi shook her head. "No, you don't understand. I can't be. You need someone else."

"You're right about one thing. I don't understand." He reached across the table and grabbed her hands. "Gabi, I love you. I thought you loved me."

A tear rolled slowly down her cheek as she replied, "It's not that I don't love you. It's just that..." Her voice caught. "It's just that... this isn't going to work. Look, I'm in the middle of a big case. I'm going to be gone for a while. I wanted to let you know."

The song came to an end and the room erupted in applause. Gabi stood up. "Can you take me back to my car? I need to get going."

Alek felt like he was in shock. He was numb. Could he even move? What was happening? Somehow, he managed to walk toward the door. "Sure, let's get going," he mumbled, concentrating on the effort it took to place one foot in front of the other.

Alek looked over his shoulder at the young woman singing on stage. She had launched into a soulful ballad about saying goodbye. Alek shook his head and turned to watch Gabi walking ahead of him across the parking lot. Nothing made sense.

Chapter 33
Time to Go

AS THE BELLS RANG THROUGHOUT the Capitol signaling the opening of a day's session, Peter Chang and Bernie Bhakta slipped into their seats in the visitors' gallery to watch the Senate debate over the HEAL Act. The gallery, on the second floor of the rectangular, two-story room, looked out over the Senate floor where the lawmakers sat at individual desks arranged in a semicircle. Most of the desks were full that day, clearly indicating the importance of the legislation they were about to discuss.

Chang fidgeted as they sat through the opening prayer, Pledge of Allegiance, opening speeches from the majority and minority leaders, and then the introduction of bills and resolutions.

"Let's get to the point," he whispered to Bernie.

"Settle down," the older man replied.

The proposed legislation had already passed the House and had been through committee. Finally, the reading clerk began going through the act piece by piece and the debate began. Senator Plumkin was the first to speak, arguing against the one-time $1,400 incentive proposed for all adults trading in their Brainaid devices. Speaking slowly with his disarming Southern drawl, the congenial but ruthless Republican from Mississippi commanded the attention of the other senators and the news media gathered to cover the vote.

"I certainly do not disagree that the Help End Addiction Loss, or HEAL, Act is needed to create Brainaid addiction clinics. I do, however, oppose the idea of giving monetary trade-in incentives. What's next? Heroin addicts demanding we pay them for turning in their heroin? This is a dangerous and slippery slope."

As Plumkin droned on, Chang leaned over and whispered to Bernie, "Without the cash incentive, I'm afraid a lot of people won't be willing to trade in their Brainaids." Bernie nodded without taking his eyes off the Senate floor. Senator Ruth Marshall, a Democrat from New Hampshire, spoke next.

"Given the unprecedented and isolated nature of this issue, I do believe the financial incentives are the best way to motivate citizens to act in a timely fashion before the addiction crisis grows. The name of the legislation is Help End Addiction Loss because America has already suffered great losses." The silver-haired senator looked pointedly at Plumkin. "While we have successfully ended Southwest Syndrome, we must take steps to ensure the solution isn't worse than the original problem. Quick and thoughtful action is needed to prevent a predicament from becoming a crisis."

Bernie whispered to Chang, "Here's the thing. President Thornton needs the overall boost in his approval ratings that this cash incentive will give him. He has already pressured the senators who were against it to change their minds. Today's vote is just a formality."

About an hour later, Bernie's prediction became a reality as the Senate voted in favor of the unamended bill. Chang breathed a sigh of relief.

"Let's get out of here," Bernie told Chang. "We have clinic leaders to train and addiction treatments to schedule. It's time to go."

* * *

Gabi drove to the airport, her mind in turmoil. Her thoughts felt like a hamster on a wheel, endlessly looping in circles and going nowhere. Only one thing was certain—she needed to get out of town. Fortunately, her supervisor had agreed to assign her to the new case. It was a definite change of pace, since she had been focused on drug cartels in Northern New Mexico for several years. But Gabi had history with the suspects and background knowledge on the issues in this case that no other FBI agent possessed. Gabi was headed to Las Vegas to investigate the activities of Dr. Sunli Hidalgo and General Liu Wu.

Gabi took I-25 to the airport, the Albuquerque International Sunport for those who preferred the more pretentious title for the largest airport in New Mexico. The busy interstate traffic offered a welcome distraction from her swirling thoughts. After finding a spot in the long-term parking lot, she strode through the terminal. Gabi spent a lot of time in airports, but the Albuquerque Sunport was unusual due to its southwestern art and cultural decor. For years, the airport had even had its own meditation room for travelers, proof that at least something in New Mexico was ahead of its time.

Gabi was too consumed by her thoughts to admire the artwork in the concourse. She glanced at her phone as if somehow it could supply the answers she sought. For a moment, her thumb hovered over Alek's name in her contact list. No, it was over. It had to be. She couldn't text him. She had to let him go.

Finally at the gate, Gabi sat down in one of the uncomfortable southwestern chairs and shoved her phone into her pocket. It was time to move on. Gabi had always been a loner, an outsider. She had grown up in Española, New Mexico, known as the lowrider capital of the world. The primarily Hispanic city of about 10,000 had a reputation for violent crime and poverty. The city's crime rate often soared more than four times the U.S. average, and the rate of drug overdose deaths always exceeded the rest of the nation.

Tucked into a valley next to the Sangre de Cristo Mountains, Española offered the only affordable place for many people who worked in nearby Santa Fe. Hotel housekeepers, retail and construction workers, and custodial employees all made the daily commute to and from Santa Fe. Needless to say, the blue-eyed, blonde-haired high school track star didn't fit in.

Gabi's father didn't help the situation. Everyone in town made jokes about the Swedish physicist, whose strong accent and aloof mannerisms set him apart from the locals. Anderson Stebbens never noticed. Other than his wife and daughter, Stebbens had little interest in people. He had moved to Los Alamos after studying with magnetohydrodynamics pioneer Alven Hannes in Stockholm. At the lab, he researched geomagnetic MHD insta-bilities. He fell in love with a young woman from Española who worked as an administrative assistant there. Nora Aragón adored the absent-minded foreign scientist and convinced him to buy a home close to her family in Española. This worked out well when Gabi was born since her grandmother could babysit while both parents went to work. Gabi's *abuelita* taught her to speak fluent Spanish and consoled her when her Hispanic classmates teased her about her blonde ringlets and sparkling aquamarine eyes.

Frustrated and friendless, Gabi poured her energy into school and running track. She finally made a friend during sophomore year in high school when Salvador Gutierrez's family moved to Española. As a child of undoc-umented immigrants, Sal kept to himself until he met Gabi. They became each other's best friends and only con-fidants—an island of two in a sea of judgmental, insecure teenagers. Gabi knew she probably wouldn't have made it through high school without Sal's friendship. When her father passed away from a sudden heart attack during senior year of high school, Gabi was devastated and ready to give up on her education, but Sal convinced her not to drop out of school. They sat together at graduation, and Sal reassured her that her father would have been proud.

Unlike many high school friendships that end at grad-uation, Gabi and Sal had stayed in touch as adults. Over the years, they had dated off and on, but Gabi wasn't at all surprised when Sal finally came out to her. They were both satisfied with the friendship and support they could give each other and understood that there would never be more.

Since Gabi grew up seeing the damage that illegal drug use had caused in her community, she decided to pursue a degree in criminal justice at the University of New Mexico and apply for a position with the FBI. Gabi had succeeded as an FBI agent, but, when it came to per-sonal relationships, she remained the awkward 13-year-old girl sitting alone in the school cafeteria while her classmates laughed and gossiped. Always the outsider. Always alone.

And then there was Alek. Being with Alek felt like coming home.

No, she couldn't think about him. Alek deserved better. He had grieved the loss of his family... had overcome his guilt about his daughter's death and had dealt with the aftermath of his divorce. Alek was ready to start over and he needed a partner who could give him what he wanted. Gabi blinked back the tears welling up in her eyes as the boarding call for her flight came over the loudspeaker. It was time to go.

* * *

The administration building at Los Alamos National Laboratory was dark and cold. Only one office light remained on, only one scientist was still hunched in front of his computer long after everyone else had left. Alek sat at his desk studying the results of his climate research—research he had carried out against Percy's wishes. Research that scared the hell out of him.

Climate statistics showed the earth had been in a natural long term cooling cycle from 1940 until 1980. In the '80s, scientists began measuring how carbon dioxide and other air pollutants and greenhouse gases had begun to collect in the atmosphere, creating a steady increase in the planet's temperatures. Environmentalists raised the alarm about human activities that contributed to global warming such as burning fossil fuels, deforestation, ranching and farming. Calls for decreasing dependence on fossil fuel, cutting $CO2$ emissions, and moving to renewable energy sources dominated the news and shaped national and international policy. Scientists were desperate for a solution. Then Alek created Project Z.

The ultimate source of clean, affordable energy had begun alleviating concerns about global warming. Pollution had already started clearing in the locations that converted to reliance on Project Z power plants. Environmentalists were celebrating the Project Z breakthrough. But Alek feared they were celebrating too soon.

Project Z had created problems. It was more than the 42 hertz frequency and Southwest Syndrome. Alek's research suggested that the introduction of the LENR power plants, and the elimination of fossil fuels had accelerated the pace of climate change and was now sending temperatures in the opposite direction. Using a simulation process similar to the one Chang created to troubleshoot the LENR trigger, Alek built an atmospheric prediction model to calculate the pace of climate change. He collected and entered temperature data and statistics on unusual geological activity, such as volcanic eruptions, increased cloud cover, and violent storms. The results were disturbing.

Since the installation of the Project Z plants across the American Southwest and China, the climate had entered a cooling phase. Alek suspected that the Project Z sites had disrupted the natural atmospheric feedback loop.

Alek slipped off his glasses and rubbed his eyes. Maybe he was overreacting. He had spent the past two weeks obsessed with this research, barely sleeping, giving himself no time to think about anything else. At some level, he knew the desire to avoid dealing with his feelings about Gabi drove him, but this was important. Percy refused to acknowledge his concerns.

Alek knew he was far from an expert in climatology, but when he looked at his computer model, he saw alarming trends. He had to bring his concerns to someone who would take them seriously. He couldn't ignore this, even if that's what Percy preferred. In the meantime, however, he would have to go home to the empty casita, the couch where Gabi once napped, the porch where they shared stories from the past and dreams about the future, the bedroom... Gabi's absence loomed huge over every aspect of his life and, no matter how long he stayed at work each night, Alek eventually had to go home.

He saved the findings on an encrypted thumb drive and stored his printouts in a folder labeled for classified material. Alek had decided it was time to take his research to Washington. He had put off acting on his findings as long as he could out of respect for Percy's wishes, but enough was enough.

It was time to go.

Chapter 34
Two Men Walk into a Bar

THE SHANGHAI LOUNGE IN THE Lucky Dragon Hotel and Casino captured every Chinese decor cliche. There were red and black tablecloths, gold dragon wall sculptures, hanging paper lanterns, and black lacquer chairs. Neon Chinese characters and Chinese zodiac charts adorned the walls, and attractive Asian waitresses were employed to set the mood.

That afternoon, the dimly lit room was deserted except for a busboy folding napkins in the back. Sunli and Wu sat in a booth in the corner huddled together over her iPad, carefully reviewing the profits from their latest money transfer scheme. Wu had a plan to take their earnings to the next level, and Sunli was eager to make it work.

"We need to expand by enlisting the triads," Wu said. He was well-acquainted with the leaders of several of the triads, the largest Chinese organized criminal organizations in the world. Wu saw the illicit crime networks as the perfect way to invest the money their Brainaid-fueled coalition of enhanced humans had stolen. Then, the triads would use their connections to grow the money through illegal narcotics trade, manipulation of cryptocurrencies, gambling and prostitution rings, and blackmail.

"The leader of a triad is called the dragon head," Wu said. "You see, it's meant to be."

Sunli smiled. Wu didn't have to convince her. She had no concerns about doing business with the Chinese mafia. In fact, she felt excited to explore the opportunity. Sunli wanted to pursue anything that increased her wealth and power. She barely remembered the weak woman who had cried and cowered when held captive in Beijing. Thanks to the Brainaid, she had become an enhanced human and had embraced her ability to control her fate. More importantly, now she could control the fate of others. She curled her fist open and closed, studying her blood red fingernails. She held the future in her hands.

"Remember El Verdugo?" Sunli asked, laughing. The Mexican cartel leader known as The Executioner had taken her prisoner and forced her to work for Wu and the Chinese Ministry of State Security on the development of the Dragon's CLAW weapon. Both El Verdugo and General Wu had wanted the weapon for their own. Sunli had used the very weapon she had developed for them to shoot a beam that incinerated the drug lord's brain.

"El Verdugo would be in awe of us," Sunli said, rising from the booth and draping herself seductively across the table. "I am El Verdugo now."

"Well, you are much better looking, and far more deadly," Wu responded admiringly. "We will achieve riches that El Verdugo could only imagine. *Zuì hǎo de hái zài hòutou*. The best is yet to come."

* * *

Alek slid into the booth across from Sal and Natasha at the hotel bar in The River Inn in Georgetown. Sal handed him a Dos Equis and raised his own bottle in a toast.

"To the HEAL Act," Sal said. "May it provide the funding and incentives we need to end Brainaid addiction."

Natasha sniffed. "I'll drink to the funding, but I will not drink to demonizing my invention." She took a long swallow of her vodka martini. Alek felt fairly certain it wasn't her first cocktail of the evening and wouldn't be her last."

"Of course not," replied Sal, throwing his arm around Natasha's shoulders. "The Brainaid is an incredible device, it's just that some people misuse it."

"Technology is just a knife," Alek mumbled to himself.

"What?"

"Nothing," said Alek, quickly changing the subject. "Percy sure is excited about the funding. He has managed to funnel millions to the lab to design systems to monitor the success of the Brainaid addiction clinics. I think long-term the research will be valuable, but I hate that his first thought is always about how the lab can make a buck."

"So, what brings you to the District?" asked Natasha. "Are you working on a new project?"

"Well, I came to D.C. to meet with Dale Croft, President Thornton's science adviser. I'm worried about the impact that the Project Z plants may be having on the climate. I honestly feel that instead of solving the climate crisis, our use of the LENR technology is increasing change. Worst case scenario: we could be headed for another ice age."

Natasha laughed. "How did the bow-tied bastard react to that?"

"He laughed like you did," said Alek. "He suggested I go talk to some guy at the National Geospatial-Intelligence Agency. I think they make maps." Alek slumped down in the booth, dejected. "Croft was trying to get rid of me. No one will take me seriously. I have the data... I've run the models and simulations... This is a real concern."

Sal nodded, forcing himself to look serious and worried. "It's just that all we have heard about for the past decade is the danger of global *warming*. You have to admit that global *cooling* sounds a little ludicrous."

"Yeah," Natasha chimed in. "Project Z has eliminated greenhouse gasses. That should be a good thing. It should be the solution to climate change."

"You'd think so, but my research shows that the reduction in carbon dioxide has created even greater instability in the earth's atmosphere. My predictions are that this will lead to an overall drop in temperature and more climate chaos. Trust me, it looks bad."

"Hmph," said Natasha. "Have you talked to a climatologist? This seems like a reach."

Alek rubbed his forehead. "I don't know why anyone can't take this seriously. Have you studied chaos theory? The butterfly effect? Climate is subject to many nonlinear variables and a small change can lead to dramatic results."

Natasha laughed again, running a hand through her tangled mass of wiry red curls. "In other words, shit happens."

"It sure does," said Alek, peeling the label off his beer

bottle without looking up.

Salvador leaned forward. "Alek, I don't care about the weather. What's going on with you and Gabi? Have you guys talked?"

Alek tried to respond but the words stuck in his throat. He shook his head and continued tearing the label off the bottle.

"So... you asked her to marry you and then...?"

"And then we broke up." Alek pulled off his glasses and rubbed his eyes. "Look, I don't want to talk about it. I told her I wanted to get married and start a family and she said she couldn't... and then... she left."

"Ah, I think I finally understand," Sal said. "I've known Gabi since high school. Did she ever tell you about her health problems?"

"Health problems?"

"During freshman year in college at UNM, Gabi started having a lot of pain. She was finally diagnosed with ovarian cysts and endometriosis. She had to have surgery to remove one of her ovaries."

"And?" Alek threw up his hands in frustration. "What's your point?"

"My point is that Gabi may not be able to have children. When you said you wanted to start a family, I bet she got spooked."

Alek stared at Sal, trying to absorb this new information. He glanced at Natasha, who shrugged and said, "Well, it makes sense. You know, women can conceive with only one ovary, but it depends on the condition of the fallopian tubes and the extent of the endometriosis. It could definitely be a concern."

"I had never seen Gabi in love until she met you, Alek," said Sal. "I know how she adores you. She didn't want to disappoint you by not being able to give you the family you want."

"But that's ridiculous. I love her. If she loves me, that's all I care about!" Alek stood up, knocking over his beer bottle. Natasha grabbed a napkin and began mopping up the spill.

"Where are you going?" asked Salvador.

"I have to go call her. I need to talk to her right now."

"You don't know?"

"Know what?"

"Gabi's gone undercover. She didn't give me any details, but she said she's working on a new case. She did mention that Wu and Sunli have recruited a bunch of volunteers and are experimenting with using the Brainaids to enhance human cognition. I think she suspects they're up to no good."

"Wu—up to no good?" scoffed Natasha. "Shocking. From what I've heard about our friend the general, it would be more surprising if he *weren't* up to no good."

"Anyhow," Sal continued, "you can't contact Gabi. She indicated she'll be out of touch for quite a while but said not to worry."

Sal watched the complex emotions passing across Alek's face. In a matter of minutes, he had nearly gained everything and then lost it again. His shoulders slumped as he sat back down, defeated.

Natasha signaled the waitress. "How 'bout another drink?"

Chapter 35
Ice Ice Baby

ALEK RENTED A CAR TO travel from D.C. to the National Geospatial-Intelligence Agency, or NGA, head-quarters on the Fort Belvoir Army Base in Springfield, Virginia. He spent the 20-minute drive debating whether the trip would be a complete waste of time. Croft had suggested that he contact a researcher there who specialized in climate change. After emailing Dr. Farid Khadem and getting an enthusiastic reply almost immediately, Alek had decided to take a chance and follow up on the science advisor's recommendation, but he seriously wondered if Croft was trying to find a way to pacify him. As he approached Fort Belvoir, Alek hoped Dr. Khadem wouldn't dismiss him as easily as Croft had.

Pulling into the drive leading to the NGA, Alek marveled at the size of the facility. The crescent-shaped steel, concrete, and glass structure rose eight stories high. Trapezoid-shaped windows covered every surface. It looked more like a giant spaceship, hundreds of acres long, than an office building housing a little-known government agency. Alek wondered if he had underestimated the significance of the NGA.

After checking in at the visitor's center, an aide led Alek into the main office building, where he stopped in awe at sight of the soaring glass ceilinged atrium. "It's 500 feet long and 120 feet wide," said the young woman escorting him. "The atrium is large enough to house the Statue of Liberty. We have a dry cleaner, a beauty salon, a credit union, a state-of-the-art fitness center, and a dining facility all inside," she added. Alek looked around, speechless. High-tech lighting and bright green and blue wall panels added to the other-worldly ambiance. Shaking his head, he wondered, *What is this place?*

"It's the third largest government building in the Washington, D.C. area with more than two million square feet of office space," continued his tour guide, as if she had read his mind. "More than 8,500 people work here and we have a second facility in St. Louis." Now Alek was certain that he had underestimated the NGA.

"Oh, here is Dr. Khadem," said the aide. "I will leave you with him. Be sure to check out at the visitor's center and turn in your badge when you leave." Alek turned to see a black-haired man approaching.

"Welcome, I'm so glad you reached out, Dr. Spray," Khadem said, directing Alek toward a bank of elevators. "I've carefully considered our recent phone conversations and I've reviewed the data you sent. I want to show you our climate data visualization lab. I think you will be interested in our recent findings."

They exited the elevator and began heading down a long hall. Khadem walked quickly and talked even faster. Alek scrambled to keep up.

"As you may know, the NGA focuses on global imagery, geospatial datasets, and mapping to serve the nation's intelligence agencies. Now, as for our research on climate change, we use information on the effects of climate change for civilian outreach efforts, such as rescue operations and rebuilding after natural disasters and humanitarian crises and for strengthening national security efforts. Our job is to focus on the security threat of climate change."

"Climate change presents a national security threat?" asked Alek.

"Of course," Khadem replied. "The 21st century has seen the hottest global average temperature since record keeping began in 1880, and these rising global temperatures have had a dramatic impact on the environment. Recent data, however, has shown a drop in temperatures, particularly in China and the southwestern U.S."

Khadem ushered him into a large dimly lit room. Panoramic high-definition screens covered the walls displaying up-to-the-minute environmental data along with advanced modeling and simulation visualizations. "We are dealing with a congruence of environmental phenomena that are drastically influencing temperatures. As I'm sure you know, climate change is caused by the increase in the amount of carbon in the atmosphere. What you may not know is that the increased carbon has caused a rapid rise in atmospheric water vapor, creating chaotic weather patterns."

Pointing to a graph on one of the large screens, Khadem continued. "We've seen catastrophic floods, destructive storms, and punishing droughts. Then about three years ago, we experienced unusual volcanic activity in the Pacific. Scientists call these eruptions a 1-in-1,000-year event."

"What are your theories regarding the volcanic impact?" Alek asked, studying the graph.

"The unusually high volcanic activity throughout the world has increased the amount of particles of ash and dust and gasses spewed into the atmosphere. These tiny particles can stay in the stratosphere for months, collecting water vapor and blocking sunlight. This heavy cloud cover has led to a significant amount of environmental cooling."

"So, Project Z has nothing to do with the drop in temperatures," Alek exclaimed. "What a relief!"

"Not so fast," Khadem replied. "Based on our research, Project Z alone has not had a significant impact on global climate. But, combined with the volcanic events and the rising climate instabilities, the electromagnetic output from the LENR machines has had an environmental impact. With the abnormally high level of aerosol water vapor in the atmosphere and the volcanic activity in the Pacific increasing, the addition of the LENR frequency is catalyzing this abnormal concentration of particulates and modified water vapor. It seems to be—what's that old expression—the straw that broke the camel's back."

"Wow," said Alek. "After all the abuse mankind has dealt the planet, Project Z could be the reason it finally snaps."

"Basically, yes," Khadem said. "The LENR frequency has changed the photo optical catalytic properties of the dust and modified water vapor aerosols. These aerosols are catalyzed by the enormous electromagnetic output. On top of that, the dust enhanced clouds have an inverse greenhouse property. They reflect sunlight but allow the infrared radiation from the planet to escape."

Alek sat down heavily in one of the rolling chairs in the room.

"But wait there's more, as they say in cheesy advertisements," Khadem said. "The implementation of Project Z plants has decreased greenhouse gasses and slowed global warming, which, up until recently I would have applauded as a good thing. Regrettably, all these factors added together have sent the climate in the opposite direction. The planet is getting colder, and a big part of the cause is Project Z."

Khadem turned from the computer screen to face Alek, his dark eyes reflecting the depth of his concern. "This data clearly reveals an emerging threat pattern that my colleagues and I find unprecedented and extremely disturbing."

Alek felt a wave of relief. Studying the graphs and satellite views, infrared maps, and detailed temperature readouts on the screens, he realized he wasn't crazy. He had actually come to the right place. But along with the triumphant revelation that his suspicions were correct, came a new surge of worry.

"Extremely disturbing?" he asked the NGA scientist. "Have you run simulations predicting the outcome?"

"Naturally," replied Khadem. "The way global temperatures are dropping, it appears that if we don't take steps to stop this, we could be headed into another ice age."

* * *

Gabi walked down the Las Vegas Strip, tugging her crocheted sweater tighter to ward off the unusually chilly air. Summer in Las Vegas tended to be blistering, even after the sun went down, but this year was different. She stopped to watch the Bellagio fountains, transfixed by the brightly lit jets of water catapulting high into the sky in sync with the music. A group of drunken tourists hurried past her, complaining loudly about the weather. She needed to stop delaying. She needed to stick to the plan.

Gabi pulled out her phone and texted Sunli.

"Are you in Vegas? I'm in town and I'd love to see you."

Gabi watched the moving dots on her phone indicating Sunli was replying. Would it really be this easy? Impatiently, Gabi shifted from one foot to another and looked around. A few feet away from her, an out-of-place looking man in a business suit seemed to be more interested in watching her than the fountains. Gabi turned and began walking again as finally she received Sunli's reply.

"Yes! Let's get together. Could you meet tomorrow at the Shanghai Lounge in the Lucky Dragon?"

"Absolutely!"

"Great. Come by about 7. I've missed you."

Gabi stood still, looking at the phone, feeling the spray from the water jets hurtling above and shivering from the cold. She texted back. "Yes, Sunli. I've missed you too. Can't wait to catch up."

* * *

As the last few clinic patients left the large Albuquerque Civic Center banquet room, Peter Chang walked up to Bernie Bhakta holding out a hand to congratulate him on the session's success. Ignoring the attempt at a handshake, Bernie pulled Chang in for an enthusiastic hug.

"We did it! The first aromatherapy meditation clinic," the gray-haired guru exclaimed, releasing Chang and clapping him on the back. "Thank you so much for your help, son. Soon, Brainaid addiction won't be a problem at all."

Chang began gathering the floor pillows they used in the session. "The next step is to roll out our 'train-the-trainer' workshops," he said. "With the HEAL Act funding, we should be able to train close to 100 clinic leaders over the next few months."

Bernie nodded. "Absolutely. Your computer simulations gave us the plan to scale up our outreach. Once we fully launch this effort, we'll give everyone in the country the tools to overcome Southwest Syndrome and achieve productive brain entrainment without debilitating addiction."

"Well, almost everyone," Chang said, sitting down

heavily on one of the pillows. "What's the point of all my work if I can't help my wife?"

Bernie sat cross-legged beside the younger man. "The Jewish philosopher Maimonides said, 'In the realm of nature there is nothing purposeless, trivial, or unnecessary.' You have to maintain the faith that your work fighting the addiction will ultimately help Sunli."

Chang looked away, hoping Bernie wouldn't notice the tears in his eyes. "*Fàng shǒu hé jiǎ zhuāng nǐ yǐ jīng wàng jì le shì yǒu qū bié de,*" he mumbled to himself.

"In English?" asked Bernie.

"There is a difference between letting go and pretending you have forgotten," Chang replied, rising and returning to the task of stacking the pillows. "Sunli was the love of my life, but her heart has turned to ice and nothing I can do can melt it."

Bernie handed him the last pillow. "Then you should focus on those people you can help, son. Maimonides said the highest form of charity is when you help others to help themselves."

* * *

General Liu Wu sat alone in the penthouse, sipping a glass of baijiu. Sunli had gone to what she called the "control center," where her team of enhanced humans were manipulating computer data to move funds seamlessly between accounts leaving behind no records of the thefts. The retired general sighed deeply. He had won his prize. The beautiful mysterious Sunli Hidalgo now shared his life. She even shared his bed, but somehow in the process of winning her over, he had also lost control.

Wu wasn't sure what had happened. Sunli had eagerly embraced the idea of working with the triads and had quadrupled the initial earnings in a few days. As her success grew, she seemed to have less and less time for him, though she still had plenty of hours in the day for shopping at expensive boutiques watched carefully by the bodyguards he insisted accompany her. She was happy to join him at the Baccarat tables in the casino. She willingly held his arm as they walked through the hotel lobby, and she never missed an opportunity to praise him during lavish dinners with the team. At nearly 70 years old, the general prided himself on his ability to win over such a gorgeous young woman. Sunli's blend of Mexican and Chinese heritage created an unparalleled beauty, and her newfound confidence and power added to that appeal. Wu felt they were well-matched in the bedroom, and he couldn't remember the last time he had enjoyed such enthusiastic lovemaking, yet, even as they bonded physically, they seemed to be drifting further apart.

Somedays, the general found himself wondering if he was losing his edge. Was it okay to let Sunli take the lead? Had he spent long enough maintaining his tight grip of control?

Wu found himself worrying that Sunli didn't share his concerns about the Chinese Ministry of State Security. The MSS were formidable foes and he had betrayed them. Sunli had laughed at his worries, but he found himself frequently looking over his shoulder, debating whether the strangers he glimpsed around the casino could pose a threat.

Wu turned to gaze at his prized imperial Ming vase. The large blue and white vase sat safely on its shelf in the teak curio cabinet, protected from harm. He could not extend the same margin of safety to Sunli. The general shivered, an icy chill running through his body. It wasn't his job to protect her. He no longer held the power. Perhaps he was still suffering from *Lóng de Dànǎo*. Sighing again, he reached for his Brainaid.

Chapter 36
A Beautiful Friendship

THE NEXT EVENING, GABI DRESSED in black slacks, a turtleneck, and a sweater. She tried buttoning the sweater to conceal the Glock tucked by her side, but finally chose not to bring the gun and instead locked it in the hotel safe. One thing she could hide successfully was the miniature recording device taped between her breasts. It would capture her conversations and transmit them directly to FBI headquarters in D.C. Gathering her hair back into a ponytail, Gabi decided to walk to the Lucky Dragon to calm her nerves and work out some of the jitters she felt about facing Wu and Sunli.

Gabi's plan was to convince her former colleagues that she had embraced the Brainaid and wanted to join them in becoming an enhanced human. If she could become an accepted part of their organization, she could collect evidence that the two were involved in criminal activity. She needed enough proof to tie them to an actual crime. She suspected they were behind the Federal Reserve transfers and the increase in organized crime in China, but she needed evidence.

The sun was sinking behind the massive casinos as throngs of people roamed up and down the Vegas strip. Swerving through the crowds, she walked briskly toward the Lucky Dragon. Gabi ran the facts of the case round and round in her head. She felt convinced that Sunli had to be the mastermind behind these illegal operations. The key to proving it was gaining Sunli's trust. They had been friends once, well, sort of. They had bonded in Beijing, when fighting the Mexican drug lord, and then in Nevada at the first Project Z test. Sunli had always been reserved, but she had been friendly in a cool and distant way. Still, they had a shared past to build on.

Gabi hoped she could convince Sunli that she sincerely wanted to join her team of Brainaid enthusiasts. She shivered with disgust thinking about the concept of enhanced humans. Nevertheless, she had to feign interest. She couldn't allow Sunli to suspect her true intentions. If Sunli doubted her, this plan wouldn't work.

Gabi realized she had arrived at the Lucky Dragon. She regretted walking so fast. Taking a deep breath, she crossed the courtyard in front of the casino and entered the building, making an immediate right into the Shanghai Lounge.

Sunli was leaning against the black lacquer bar in the back of the dark room. At least, Gabi thought it was Sunli. This woman was thinner and dressed in much more suggestive clothing and higher heels than Sunli had ever worn. The low-cut crimson silk dress clung to her figure and her face seemed older, harsher. Although she was meticulously groomed, with clearly no expense spared on beauty treatments, she also looked as though decades had passed rather than mere months since they had last seen one another. While Sunli had often seemed distant and aloof, obsessed with her research, she had never looked powerful and hard like this woman. As Gabi walked closer, she realized it really was Sunli.

"Gabi, how delightful!" Sunli held out her arms and embraced Gabi. "I'm excited to catch up with you. How are things? Can I get you a drink?"

The two settled in a booth, and Gabi quickly filled Sunli in on her breakup with Alek, her disillusionment with the FBI, and her disgust with the way the U.S. government was trying to eliminate the use of the Brainaids a few months after handing them out like candy. Soon they were drinking and laughing like old friends, joking about how boring Chang was, Percy's obsession with money, and Alek's annoying habit of watching CNN incessantly. Gabi confessed that Alek had insisted she turn in her Brainaid and now she missed it and longed for the relaxation and release the device had provided. Sunli promised to get her a new one.

"Where are you staying? You should stay here," said

Sunli. "I will get you a special suite."

"I'm at the Marriott, off the strip. It's ugly and boring," said Gabi. "But I can't let you do that."

"Of course you can," Sunli replied. "You have no idea how much I need a girlfriend."

Gabi giggled and raised her highball glass in a toast. "To friendship! God knows I need a friend. I'd been spending all my time with Alek, and when I dumped him, I was alone. But what about you? Don't you have Wu?"

"Ah, the general," said Sunli with a smile. "Liu is an ideal partner, but he won't go with me to get a manicure. Like I said, I need a girlfriend."

Gabi laughed, pretending to be tipsier than she actually was. This was going so well, so much smoother than she had expected, which made her nervous. "If you need a girlfriend, then I'm your gal!" she exclaimed.

"Good. Let's get you moved over here and set up with a new Brainaid. Tomorrow we'll have a spa day and after you've relaxed a bit, I'll fill you in on my new business ventures. I think you'll realize you don't need to worry about leaving Alek and the FBI behind. The best is yet to be."

* * *

After hours in the NGA visualization center, Farid Khadem and Alek grabbed lunch in the onsite cafeteria and then headed to Khadem's office. The room was lush and modern with wall-to-wall computer monitors. Khadem handed Alek a binder labeled *Eyes Only*. "This is classified NGA information, but you have a Top-Secret clearance through the DOE, and I think it's highly relevant to your concerns, so I'm going to go against protocol and share it with you."

Alek flipped the binder open and saw pages of maps and diagrams of a well-known underground military complex in Russia called Mount Yamantau, built deep below the Ural Mountains, a lingering remnant of the cold war.

"Yamantau? It's been there for decades. What's your point?" Alek asked.

"My point is that we have been monitoring activity there, and we believe the Russians are also concerned about the sudden climate changes. In the past few weeks, our satellites have picked up increased activity at the complex."

"What does an underground Russian military base have to do with the possibility of a new ice age?"

"Everything. Yamantau could house at least 300,000 people comfortably for a long time. It's a massive underground city where people could survive the harsh weather conditions above ground."

Alek looked at the binder again. "So, the activity at Yamantau suggests the Russians are studying the recent environmental issues and are worried?"

"Yes, and we have seen construction increase on similar bunkers throughout China. America seems to be ignoring this crisis. Of course, we have a long history of downplaying climate problems in the U.S."

"So, this is really happening, it's not my imagination?"

"Most of my colleagues are skeptical," Khadem said with a sigh. "Of course, many scientific experts and U.S. political leaders dismissed the threat of global warming for years. I think this is serious. The impact our so-called scientific advancements are having on the natural world is evident, and we are in trouble. My greatest concern is that there's no turning back."

Alek ran a hand through his dark brown hair. "And, if this new ice age were to actually take place, we would need to find a safe underground facility where we could survive it?"

"Possibly, but it seems more sensible to find ways to stop the issue before it becomes too extreme. While building underground cities sounds ridiculous, at least the Russians and the Chinese appear to be aware of the problem," said Khadem. "There are steps we can be taking, but first we must acknowledge that something is actually going on."

"The Project Z plants were supposed to help the environment," said Alek. He looked around the luxurious high-tech office, thinking about the state-of-the-art government facility he was sitting in, the thousands of scientists at the national labs, the years of research they had devoted to creating a safer, cleaner energy source. Everything had backfired. They had built the knife and now the knife would slit their throats.

Alek handed back the binder. Setting it on his desk, Khadem gestured to the reports and statistics displayed on the large computer monitors throughout the room. "For so long, our goal simply was to stop the pace of global warming caused by greenhouse gasses produced by human activities. Who would have guessed that our problems would increase in complexity in such a short period of time?"

Alek reached out to shake Khadem's hand. "Well, that's why they call this sort of thing a 'wicked problem.' As scientists, we need to lead the effort to find the solution. It's what we do best."

"Agreed," Khadem said as he walked Alek to the building exit.

"Thank you for your time," said Alek. "It's been most... enlightening. I'm sure we will see each other soon."

Khadem smiled. "To quote *Casablanca*, 'This looks like the beginning of a beautiful friendship.' That is, if we don't freeze to death first."

Leaving the massive glass and steel building, Alek hurried to his rental car. He needed to get back to Los Alamos. Lost in his thoughts, he never noticed the black Suburban following behind him as he headed down the highway toward D.C.

* * *

Percy was sitting behind his desk at Los Alamos National Laboratory when Alek burst through the door. "We have to talk about this," Alek said. "I've been consulting with the NGA, and I have proof that we are headed for an unprecedented climate catastrophe."

Percy walked around the desk and put his hand on the younger man's shoulder. "Okay, calm down and I'll listen." He led Alek over to the loveseat in the corner of the office and pulled a bottle of water out of the small refrigerator beside his desk. "Take a breath and have a drink of water. Just relax."

"We can't relax." Alek sprung up and began pacing around the large office. "We have to do something. We should start by shutting down the Project Z power plants."

"Alek, you know we can't do that. The power plants aren't even under our control."

"Well then, we need to talk to someone who can. I tried Croft. He wouldn't listen but he did send me to the NGA. A guy there, Dr. Farid Khadem, has all the research, plus documentation that the Russians and Chinese are already preparing by building facilities for people to survive underground."

"To survive underground? Why would we need to do that?" asked Percy, continuing to look at Alek like he was a wild animal that had wandered into his office and needed to be treated with great care.

"I already told you." Alek slammed his fist down onto Percy's desk in frustration. "A new ice age is coming, and we have the power to prevent it. Pick up the phone and call Thornton or at least Plumkin. We need the Senate Select Committee on Intelligence to look into this as soon as possible."

Percy nodded. "Look, I know how committed President Thornton is to the Project Z initiative. I doubt that anything could dissuade him from continuing the program. Even Southwest Syndrome hasn't derailed the steady progress on building more Project Z plants across the U.S."

Alek sank into a chair, putting his head in his hands. The fight had gone out of him.

Percy pulled up a seat beside him. "Alek, I trust you. I have always respected your judgment. Maybe it really is time to take a risk and speak up about this, but first I need to get all the facts straight."

Alek sat up straighter. Was Percy actually willing to bring the issue to government leaders' attention?

"Here's what we'll do," said Percy. "I want to bring in Peter Chang and Bernie Bhakta and maybe also Tom Lowe from Lawrence Livermore. Can we set up a video conference with this guy at the NGA?"

Alek nodded, relieved that Percy was finally coming around.

"Good. We'll need to get all our ducks in a row before we talk to Thornton and the Senate Intelligence Committee. Let's reach out to Sal too. I'm not about to become the boy who cried wolf."

Alek laughed. "Ducks, wolves... boss, I think you're mixing your metaphors."

"Maybe I am." Percy cracked a smile. "Then again, maybe we'll need all the animals. The last time there was an unprecedented world-ending climate crisis, I think someone built an ark."

* * *

When Sunli told Gabi to dress up for dinner, the undercover FBI agent shared that she hadn't packed anything suitable; so her host promised to send up an outfit. Gabi wasn't surprised when the front desk clerk delivered a package containing a dress and shoes for the evening, but she was shocked at how little fabric the dress actually contained.

Gabi rarely dressed up. She would occasionally slip on something formal for dinner with Salvador at the Cosmos Club but dressing up in New Mexico meant putting on clean jeans. She hoped she had told Sunli her correct sizes. Since the breakup, she hadn't had much of an appetite and had lost some weight.

Gabi slipped the midnight-blue beaded dress over her head and evaluated her appearance in the luxurious bathroom's floor length mirror. The off-the-shoulder bodice plunged deep, revealing more cleavage than she felt comfortable with, and the asymmetrical fringed hem bared her leg up to her hip. Even so, Gabi had to admit the overall effect was stunning. It didn't look like her in the mirror. Not one bit.

Concealing the recording device in the close-fitting dress proved to be a bit of a challenge, but after a few minutes of fiddling, Gabi managed to tuck the microphone where it wouldn't be seen. *At least not by anyone keeping a reasonable distance*, she thought with a cynical laugh. Sweeping her hair into an updo with curling tendrils escaping around her ears, Gabi opened the makeup case Sunli had provided. Fifteen minutes later, with deep red lipstick and sparkling eyeshadow, she looked even less like herself. Gabi laughed, remembering the red lipstick and low-cut sweaters she wore when waiting tables at the

Friggin Bar back when she first met Alek. Then she sighed, thinking about Alek, wondering what he would say if he could see her now.

Gabi fastened on the strappy sandals, grateful for the pedicure she and Sunli had gotten earlier in the day. Walking in such high heels would be a challenge. She hoped most of the evening would be spent sitting down. As Gabi took a final look in the mirror, she heard a knock on the door. It was Sunli.

"Perfect!" exclaimed Sunli. "Just one thing missing. Come with me."

The two took the elevator to the penthouse, where Sunli unlocked the door with her electronic keycard.

Gabi gasped as they entered the penthouse. The opulence of Wu and Sunli's suite far eclipsed her own. Sunli led her to the bureau in the bedroom and pulled open a long drawer filled entirely with jewels.

"Are those... real?"

"Of course," Sunli replied. "The general and I have recently come into quite a bit of money. I told you that you should join us. You'll never have to worry about needing a job."

Sunli pulled a pair of diamond and sapphire drop earrings from the drawer and held them up to Gabi. "Yes, these will be ideal," she said.

Gabi walked to the mirror and inserted the earrings into her pierced ears. They sparkled brilliantly, highlighting the blue in her eyes. As the two left the bedroom, Gabi spotted a rack of laptops in the corner of the living room. "What's all this?" she asked, gesturing to the computers. "Is this your office or where you live?"

"Oh, we do our office work downstairs," said Sunli. "We store the records here. It's important to have a digital backup of everything we do. Now let's go down to dinner and meet the general and our new colleagues. I believe you will enjoy spending an evening surrounded by enhanced humans."

Chapter 37
What Ifs

AFTER SEVERAL VIDEO CALLS WITH the newly formed Percy Study Climate Team, Alek, Percy, and Khadem were headed to a hearing with the Senate Select Committee on Intelligence. Percy and Alek met Khadem in the hallway leading to one of the most tightly secured areas on Capitol Hill, the electromagnetically shielded room in the Sensitive Compartmented Information Facility, known as the SCIF, on the second floor of the Hart Senate Office Building. Both Percy and Alek had testified before the Senate committee many times before, but Alek still felt his heart racing as they arrived. A lot depended on whether the senators took his concerns seriously. There was no guarantee that they would.

As they approached the Senate chamber, an armed guard used a facial recognition imager to scan and verify each of them. He inspected their credentials, confiscated their cell phones, and instructed them to sign a form promising not to reveal anything. Then the three men walked through the heavy door into the small room furnished with a table and chairs for the witnesses. In the circle of seats behind the witness table, the full array of 15 senators filled the seats. These were the people tasked with overseeing the various federal agencies that made up the United States intelligence community. They had their fingers on the pulse of all national security concerns.

The head of the committee, Senator Larry Plumkin, the Mississippi Republican, called the meeting to order and welcomed the witnesses in his southern drawl. As usual, Percy was the first slated to speak.

"Thank you, Mr. Chairman and the rest of the members of the Senate Intelligence Committee. It is a privilege to be here to address recent concerns regarding global climate change. Extensive tracking by the National Geospatial-Intelligence Agency has revealed a pattern of cooling temperatures that we believe represents a true climate crisis. After consulting with the NGA, we at Los Alamos National Laboratory found it imperative to bring this issue to your immediate attention."

As Percy droned on, Alek reviewed what he knew about testifying at this kind of hearing. The strategy was to communicate on the level of an intelligent audience member who may not have a technical background or depth of knowledge in the area in question. In the past, he would have Gabi read over his remarks before each hearing to make sure nonexperts could understand the material. She would help him adapt his testimony and practice answering tough questions. Without her support, he felt nervous and unprepared.

Next, Khadem testified about the NGA research regarding the dramatic drop in temperatures, the coincidental volcanic activity's environmental impact, and the possible role of the Project Z plants in contributing to the unprecedented cool down.

Plumkin cleared his throat. "You're saying that volcanoes are making the planet colder? That doesn't make sense."

"Volcanic eruptions shoot aerosols and particulates into the stratosphere," Khadem explained. "Those aerosols combine with water vapor and block sunlight high in the upper atmosphere. It's a natural phenomenon that has always existed."

"If it has always existed, why should we give a damn?" asked Plumkin, with a dismissive wave of his hand.

Unrattled by the senator's comment, Khadem continued calmly. "It's what we call a series of unfortunate events. The increase in carbon—what we call climate change or global warming—boosted the amount of water vapor in the atmosphere. At the same time, unusual volcanic activity spewed particulates and aerosols that combined with the water vapor."

"What does that have to do with Project Z?" Plumkin asked.

Khadem gestured to Alek. "As you know," Alek said, "the LENR plants generate an unusual electromagnetic frequency—the frequency responsible for Southwest Syndrome."

"That hasn't been proven," Plumkin muttered under his breath, but Alek heard him and responded, "Although the government hasn't acknowledged Project Z as the cause of Southwest Syndrome, it has been scientifically proven to be the case."

"This isn't a hearing about Southwest Syndrome," Plumkin spluttered. "Get to the point."

"The point is that this electromagnetic frequency has changed the photo optical properties of these newly modified dust and water aerosols causing them to additionally block the sunlight in the upper atmosphere. At the same time, we have begun to reverse global warming thanks to the elimination of fossil fuels and the increased use of Project Z power plants. These combined factors have created a tipping point. The planet is getting cooler at an alarming rate."

"We worked hard to push through this so-called Project Z clean power initiative," said Plumkin. "Now you're telling me it's contributing to a new climate crisis? What happened to global warming? Just a few years ago, everyone was up in arms about eliminating greenhouse gasses. The glaciers were melting; heat waves, droughts, and flooding were increasing. Everything we have done was focused on decreasing emissions and cooling the planet. Now you say it's too goddamn cold?"

"Isn't this a normal climate cycle?" asked another senator. "Project Z didn't cause the volcanoes to erupt. So, without their increased activity, you wouldn't be here complaining to us."

"Maybe the cooling you've tracked is an example of the environment fixing itself," another senator said.

Several hours passed as the senators downplayed the findings and rehashed everything they had ever learned about global warming and Project Z. Alek ran his fingers through his hair, tired and frustrated by the barrage of questions. Yes, he had testified in favor of Project Z a few years ago. No, he had not anticipated this problem. Yes, he still believed in the need for clean, affordable, unlimited energy. No, he did not think this issue would go away. Yes, he felt the problem was serious.

Alek remembered when he was young, his Jewish mother once warned him that no good deed goes unpunished. Clearly, his mother was right. As he struggled to respond to the senators' questions, he thought about how he had achieved his dream of creating the ultimate energy source. But what came next? The neuropandemic, the consequences of Brainaid addiction, the global climate cooling crisis.

Alek found himself wondering, *What would have happened if I had abandoned the Project Z project? What if I had never built the knife?*

* * *

Natasha had to look twice at the text message. Why was Peter Chang texting her at 10:30 at night? More importantly, why did the message read, "I'm at your front door. Can I come in?"

Reluctantly, Natasha grabbed a bathrobe. She had been planning to head to bed and was less than happy about the interruption, but since he was already here, she might as well open the door. Cinching her robe tightly, she unlocked the door.

Chang barreled into the apartment without a greeting. His eyes were red-rimmed and sunken. He looked as if he hadn't slept in weeks.

"Peter, hi. Would you like a drink?"

Chang began pacing back and forth in Natasha's living room. Her Dupont Circle apartment was high end and modern, but not large, so Chang couldn't pace far. It was like watching a tiger in a cage.

"So, I just got off the plane from Albuquerque. I came here directly from the airport," he said. "I've been thinking about the Brainaid and Sunli." Chang continued pacing, talking more to himself than to Natasha. "I've been thinking that if your device has altered her brainwaves, if it has programmed her, made her different, turned her into a so-called 'enhanced human,' why couldn't it deprogram her?"

"Deprogram?" Natasha asked.

"Undo whatever damage your toxic little device has caused," Chang spit out angrily.

"Now wait one minute." Natasha put her hand out, halting Chang's pacing. Her cheeks flared red as she raised her voice. "I'm pretty sure your wife has altered my device and used it irresponsibly. She is to blame for any damage it has caused. You can't show up at my apartment unannounced and start attacking me and my work. Sunli Hidalgo *Chang* is the issue, not the Brainaid, so be careful what you say."

Chang's eyes blazed as the two stood staring at each other. Then, the Chinese scientist's face crumpled, and he collapsed, sobbing on the couch.

Shocked, Natasha sat down beside him, awkwardly putting an arm around his shoulder, patting and rubbing his back as he cried. She was unaccustomed to dealing with emotional outbursts.

"Ummm, can I make you a cup of tea?"

Chang sniffed, trying to get control of himself. "Yes, that would be nice," he replied in a choked voice.

Natasha walked to the kitchen and began opening and closing cabinets as Chang wiped his nose on his sleeve. "I don't have any tea. How about vodka?" she asked.

"Yes... thank you," Chang replied huskily.

The two sat silently sipping their Stolichnaya Elit. Finally, Chang spoke. "Do you know that there is a Dutch company based in Hong Kong that makes premium vodka? It's called Royal Dragon Vodka. Their most expensive vodka is called The Eye of the Dragon. It comes in a diamond-studded bottle."

"Well, we're going to have to get some of that," Natasha said, handing Chang a box of Kleenex. "Look, maybe I could build a new device that could alter Sunli's brainwaves, but we'd have to find a way to get it close to her and expose her gradually. I'm not sure how we could do that."

Chang looked up, his eyes glimmering with hope. "She and Wu are in Las Vegas."

"And?"

"And we could sneak into their hotel and plant it

somewhere? Or maybe kidnap her and treat her until she comes to her senses? I don't know, but I know that I have to do something. I can't give up."

Natasha gave Chang another awkward pat on the arm. "Okay, I'll look into it. I'm not promising that I can do anything, but I will try. Honestly, I'm impressed by your love for her. I've never felt that sort of thing."

Chang didn't lift his eyes from his vodka glass. "It's my fault. I drove her away. I told her to get out, that our marriage was over. I let her stay with Wu instead of fighting to get her back."

Once again, Natasha put her arm around Chang. This time, it was a little less awkward.

"You did nothing wrong, Peter. Sunli made a choice."

Chang sniffed and drank the last of his vodka. "Let me get you a blanket and a pillow," Natasha said. "You can lie down on the couch here and get some sleep. Tomorrow we can go to the lab and run some experiments. It may not be possible but... what if it is?"

Chapter 38
Friends and Enemies

THE NEXT MORNING WHEN CHANG left to run to Kramers, a popular Dupont Circle cafe and bookstore, to pick up something for breakfast, Natasha called Sal then Bernie. Sal was intrigued by the idea of building a device to "reset" Sunli's brainwaves, but Bernie was worried about Chang.

"He still loves Sunli so much that he can't abandon the idea of winning her back," mused Bernie over the phone. "Maimonides wrote that the risk of a wrong decision is preferable to the terror of indecision. Chang wants to do something. He needs to feel that he has made every possible effort before he moves on."

"I suppose that makes sense," Natasha said, pacing back and forth in her apartment as she talked on the phone. "Still, I think the issues with Sunli stem from more than just the Brainaid. I can't say that I understand what Peter sees in that woman. When I first met her, I sensed an odd emptiness, almost as though she was searching for something to fill a hole in her life."

"Well, if she has finally found what she was seeking, somehow, I doubt she will welcome the chance to be 'reset.'"

Natasha examined her reflection critically in the mirror, trying to remember when she last got a haircut. She had been too busy working to pay attention to her looks. "Brainwave entrainment won't succeed without a willing participant," said Natasha. "Nevertheless, I feel we have to help Peter try something, even if it's just to give him a sense of closure."

"Yes indeed," said Bernie. "We need to support our friend and colleague. I do not doubt your scientific prowess, but I do doubt Sunli's ability to change. If you will indulge me, one more quote from Maimonides seems quite relevant. He wrote, 'We each decide whether to make ourselves learned or ignorant, compassionate or cruel, generous or miserly. No one forces us. No one decides for us, no one drags us along one path or the other. We are responsible for what we are.'"

* * *

Working as an FBI agent often means playing a role, thought Gabi. Lately, she was certainly using her acting skills to elicit information from Sunli, Wu, and their team of enhanced humans. Ever since the formal dinner, the general had paid more attention to Gabi. She had no doubt that what had attracted him was the skimpy blue dress. With that in mind, she had asked Sunli for guidance revamping her wardrobe. "I want my clothes to reflect the new me," she said. "Bold and not afraid to flaunt my assets, if you know what I mean." Soon her hotel room closet was full of slinky, low-cut dresses and high heels, items she would never wear in her normal life.

Gabi longed to slip on a pair of well-worn jeans, but instead she reached for a turquoise silk dress with spaghetti straps and a high side slit that bared her thigh. *Time to shave the legs again*, she thought with a sigh.

Despite the inconvenience, the wardrobe change was worth it. Wu began following Gabi around like a puppy. She found it easy to manipulate the general and trick him into revealing information. Gabi told Wu that it seemed Sunli didn't appreciate his sharp mind, asking, "Why is she ignoring your brilliance and devotion?" Soon Wu began to share details about the criminal activities that monopolized most of Sunli's time. One afternoon, as they strolled through the Lucky Dragon courtyard admiring the Koi pond, Gabi steered the conversation toward their involvement with the triads. Wu was more than happy to explain.

"We have been funneling more and more of the money we've moved from the Federal Reserve to the triads. Sunli works with several of them, but I believe she does the most business with the 14K," the general said.

"I've heard that this group is responsible for large-scale drug trafficking around the world, heroin and opium. Is that right?" Gabi asked, trying to appear naive.

Wu knelt beside the pond, flinging a handful of pellets to the greedy fish. "Yes, drugs are their main source of income, but they are also involved in illegal gambling, loan sharking, money laundering, contract murder, arms trafficking, prostitution, human trafficking, extortion, counterfeiting, and, to a lesser extent, home invasion robberies."

"Sounds like a wholesome group," Gabi said, grabbing some fish pellets from Wu and bending down to feed them. She tried not to notice the general's eyes roaming across her backside as she leaned over the pond.

"We are investing in them, and they are paying dividends. It is a very profitable arrangement."

"Who wouldn't want a profitable arrangement?" Gabi murmured suggestively.

Wu reached across Gabi and slipped the strap from her shoulder, pulling her close. Gabi placed her hand on his chest in resistance, but he gripped her arm harder as she squirmed, trying to wriggle away. Angrily, Wu forced her down on the hard bricks beside the pond.

"No," Gabi cried as he slid the top of her dress down, revealing the wire of the recording device.

"*Zhè shì shénme*?" the general screamed. "What is this?" He barked rapid orders to the bodyguards lingering nearby as Gabi sprang to her feet and began to run. One of the bodyguards tackled her, throwing her to the ground.

Her head smacked against the pavement as she fell.

The two large Asian men that the general had summoned hauled Gabi to her feet. Blood seeped from a wound at the edge of her hairline where her forehead had met the ground.

"Take her to her room and lock her in," Wu commanded. "We will deal with her later. Stand guard outside her door."

* * *

Gabi examined her face in the mirror. The wound on her forehead had finally stopped bleeding. It looked as if it would heal without stitches but might leave a scar. Her cheek was scratched, as were her arms and legs from the fall on the rough pavement. The dress was torn and dirty. She slipped it off, throwing it on the floor, and headed to the bathroom. Maybe a hot shower would help her bruised body. Her ego was equally wounded. How could she have allowed this to happen? She was an experienced agent. She knew better than to let the general take control.

Gabi stood under the showerhead as the warm water sluiced over her body. Gingerly she shampooed and rinsed her blonde ringlets, being careful not to apply any pressure to her injured forehead. She needed to rest a bit and gather her thoughts.

A loud, insistent knock thudded against the bathroom door.

"Who is it? I'm in the shower," Gabi yelled, shutting off the water and wrapping herself in a bath towel. She heard a gruff reply from one of the guards.

"We are taking your suitcase, general's orders. We will leave you some clothing items and your Brainaid."

Gabi heard the outside door click shut as she dried herself off. Sure enough, they had taken her suitcase, leaving behind a few of the dresses and some lingerie. Not exactly the clothing most people would pick for spending time on house arrest, she thought. The guards had also taken the hotel room phone, her cell phone, and even the television set. The only electronic device left behind was the Brainaid.

Gabi grabbed it with two fingers as if it were contaminated, walked to the bathroom, dropped the Brainaid in the toilet, and flushed. It seemed the best way to avoid the temptation. Sunli and Wu might be holding her prisoner, but she vowed never to allow them to capture her brain.

Chapter 39
Opportunity or Crisis

ALEK, KHADEM, AND PERCY LEFT the Hart Senate Office Building. Their second, and final, day of testimony was complete.

"I'm not certain they took us seriously," said Khadem.

"Well, what we need, both at the NGA and at the lab, is research funding. This was a good first step," said Percy.

As the three began walking toward the parking garage, Alek tripped over a curb.

"You okay?" Percy asked.

"Just thinking," Alek replied, recovering his footing while they walked briskly along Constitution Avenue. "This isn't about funding, Percy. This really is a crisis."

Percy shrugged. "Crisis, opportunity... it's the same thing. Oh, hang on." He reached into his pocket to grab his ringing phone.

"Oh, uh huh... She did...? You did...?" Percy's face grew serious as he listened to the caller. The three stopped walking. "I understand," he said. "Keep me posted if you hear anything else."

Percy hung up and Khadem and Alek waited for an explanation, but the lab director was silent, deep in thought.

"Hey, what's going on?" Alek finally asked.

Percy shook his head. "That was the director of the FBI. It seems Gabi went to Las Vegas a couple weeks ago to try to infiltrate the crime syndicate that Wu and Sunli are suspected of building. The FBI was monitoring her whereabouts and receiving daily transmissions but yesterday the signal vanished." He put a hand on Alek's shoulder. "They suspect that Gabi has been captured or... or worse."

* * *

Chang and Natasha leaned over the tiny device on the counter in Nat's high-tech Arlington, Virginia lab. Sal leaned back in his chair, watching. He found himself intrigued by the drama of scientific discovery, but not knowledgeable enough to make much of a contribution, other than fetch coffee and provide moral support.

The silence in the room was deafening as the two scientists focused on their task. Sal couldn't stand it any longer. "How's it going?" he asked.

Without looking up, Natasha replied, "When an electric field is applied to drive ions into the head or soma of a neuron, it creates an increased electric field across the neuronal membrane. The generated voltage caused by changing the ion distribution primes the neuron and makes the neuron excitable and it fires rapidly when triggered."

Chang picked up the explanation. "In contrast, if you apply a field with opposite polarity to the neuron, you extract the ions from the neuron and the neuron is less likely to fire. You can get enhanced firing from the positive anode potential near the soma. With the opposite polarity, you get attenuated firing. The physics shows that neurons can be excited or attenuated with an electric field."

Sal nodded approvingly and tried to arrange his face in a manner that appeared educated but encouraging. "That is exactly what I would have anticipated you would discern from your experiments. Indeed, it is."

Natasha burst out laughing. "You are so full of shit, Sal. You don't really have any idea what we're talking about."

Sal tried to keep a straight face. "It's elementary, my dear Natasha. The neural feedback is positively excitable... and, and some other scientific crap," he added, convulsing with laughter. "No, I have no idea what you're talking about."

Even Chang was smiling. "What we're doing is a combination of neuroscience and physics. Neuroengineering if you will," he said. "We have to reengineer the Brainaid to change the frequency at which Sunli's brain is oscillating. If we can get one part of the brain to function at a specific frequency, then the other parts of the brain will couple and oscillate in a synchronized manner. In other words, we want to re-entrain her brain."

"I think we've got it working," said Natasha. "Now the issue is determining how close to Sunli the device will need to be in order for the signal to have an effect. Unfortunately, the Brainaid is not designed to operate at a distance. So, how can we get close enough to make it work?"

Sal leaned forward. "What if you switched this modified Brainaid with the one Sunli typically uses? She wouldn't know the difference. All the devices look the same."

"That's a great idea," said Chang. "But we'd have to find a way to sneak into the hotel and switch out the devices without anyone knowing. First, we have to go to Vegas, I guess."

The door to the lab slammed open and the three looked up to see Alek standing wild-eyed in the entryway.

"We have to go to Vegas," he exclaimed.

* * *

An hour later, the four sat in the lab, drinking Dos Equis and making plans.

"Hey, Sal, grab me another beer," Natasha said.

Sal leaned over to grab a bottle out of the small refrigerator under the counter. "Nat, are those, umm, eyeballs in there?"

"Probably," she replied with a dismissive shrug. "We do a lot of different experiments here."

"Wow, *que asco*, that's gross," Sal said at the same time Chang murmured, "Wow, that's cool."

Alek took a drink of beer and leaned forward to get a better look at the map displayed on the computer monitor on the counter. "Okay so, this is the Lucky Dragon Hotel and Casino and the FBI last tracked Gabi in the building's courtyard. Then, the signal went dead."

Alek scribbled something down on a notepad. "Based on geolocating, they believe her room was on the southeast corner of the twelfth floor of the building."

Chang shook his head. "If it's truly a Chinese hotel, the

twelfth floor will actually be called the thirteenth because a Chinese hotel owner would insist the fourth floor be skipped."

"Why?" asked Natasha.

"Because the number four is bad luck in Chinese. Just like some American hotels skip the thirteenth floor."

"That proves it," said Natasha.

"What?" asked Alek.

"Both Americans and Chinese are weird."

Chang ignored Natasha's snide comment. "Explain something for me," he said. "If Gabi was working under-cover for the FBI... and they were monitoring her whereabouts... and they suspect she has been captured, why wouldn't they mount some kind of rescue operation? I mean, it would make sense."

"I know," Alek said, rubbing his temples. "That was the first thing I asked Percy. His buddy at the FBI said they don't want to move in now 'cause it could blow their whole investigation of Wu's crime syndicate. They've invested too much time, and they almost have enough info to obtain a warrant for his arrest. The FBI guy said they figure that if Gabi's still alive, they probably aren't plan-ning to kill her, so she's safe. And if she's dead... what's the point of going in?"

"Hmmm. That's cold but logical," Natasha murmured.

Sal leaned forward. "There's something else you need to explain, Alek. Didn't you and Gabi break up?"

Alek scraped at the label on his beer bottle, unable to make eye contact with his friends. "Well, yes, she broke up with me, but then when you told me about her fear of being unable to have children, I felt responsible. I'm just hoping..." Alek swallowed hard, his voice breaking. "I'm hoping that she'll take me back."

Natasha put a hand on his shoulder, wondering why she kept ending up in situations that required her to show empathy. It wasn't part of her skillset. Fortunately, it was part of Salvador's. He pulled Alek in for a hug.

Alek choked back a sob. "It's just that I love her. I want her to be okay."

"We'll figure something out, I promise," said Sal. "We'll get her out."

"So, getting back on track," said Alek with a sniff, "we'll have to get into the hotel and casino so we can locate Sunli and determine where they are keeping Gabi. I know she's still alive, I know it. I'm sure they're holding her somewhere in the hotel."

Chang nodded eagerly. "Then we can sneak into Sunli's room and exchange the modified Brainaid for the one she uses every day."

Sal shook his head. "We can't wander around the hotel or casino without Wu or Sunli spotting us and getting suspicious. They would recognize us immediately. We have to send in someone they don't know who understands what we're doing."

The group fell silently and then, suddenly, all four spoke at once.

"Bernie Bhakta!"

"Naturally," Natasha said with a smile. "Who else?"

Chapter 40
What Happens in Vegas

AT HARRY REID INTERNATIONAL AIRPORT in Las Vegas, Bernard Bhakta emerged from the plane wearing white socks, black sandals, long khaki shorts, and a Hawaiian shirt. A camera hung from his neck. His flyaway gray hair was slicked back from his large forehead. The Taos guru had transformed into Bernie Goldberg, one of the many annoying Las Vegas tourists who came to play the nickel slots, leer at the dancing girls, and eat at the buffets.

"Wow!" Natasha exclaimed. "I almost walked right past you."

"That's the goal," Bernie said with a smile, reaching out to shake hands with each of them. "Well, we're all here in Sin City. I have a feeling we're going to win big."

Natasha grabbed Bernie's collar and gave his outfit an appraising look as though trying to determine whether to be insulted or not, since Hawaiian shirts were part of her typical style. Sensing the tension, Alek joked, "Just look at you two—you could be father and daughter."

Natasha relaxed, laughing, and hugged the gray-haired man. "Hi, Dad," she said. "You look fabulous."

"*Guapísimo*," Sal said as the odd-looking group began walking toward the baggage claim.

"Thank you for doing this," said Alek.

"Yes, thank you," echoed Chang.

"Helping others is the highest form of *tzedakah*," Bernie said.

"Doesn't *tzedakah* mean charity?" asked Alek as they walked toward the baggage claim.

"You're Jewish by birth, aren't you?" asked Bernie. Alek nodded. "While many people think of the Hebrew word *tzedakah* as meaning charity, the word actually means 'justice,' specifically, doing the right things by helping people or causes in need. Maimonides urged his followers to help others become self-sufficient. I'm here to help you two help yourselves," he added, pointing to Alek and Chang.

"And we're here to help you help them," Sal said, pointing to himself and Natasha. "Let's get your bags and head to the Mandalay Bay. It's on the other end of the strip from the Lucky Dragon. Once we check in and get settled, we can make a plan."

"The die is cast and I'm ready to dance with lady luck and shake hands with the one-armed bandit," laughed Bernie. "Seriously, I'm here to help. Tell me what to do."

* * *

After settling in at the Mandalay Bay, where the tropical paradise theme soothed the travelers' harried nerves and the scent of bay rum wafted through the lobby, the group reconvened near the wave pool. Despite the unusually cool summer weather, numerous families had gathered in the swimming area and the sound of crashing waves and laughing children swept across the simulated beach. Grabbing a personal cabana, they ordered mai tais and watched the tourists float along the lazy river. Alek envied the ignorance of the hotel guests on their doughnut-shaped rafts. None of them realized the chill in the air represented an unprecedented global climate crisis. None of them were wondering whether the woman they loved was alive or dead.

"Alek, *escucha*. Pay attention," Sal said, pulling the physicist back to the moment. "We have to figure out what to do after Bernie determines where Gabi's being held and pinpoints Sunli's location. I'm sure we can get that far, but then what?"

"Oh, that won't be a problem," Alek replied as he chugged the last of his mai tai. "In fact, someone is bringing me a package that will provide a useful distraction," he said.

Bernie gave Alek a serious look. "Son, what's in this package?"

"A Low Energy Nuclear Reaction weapon. We're going to set off an EMP."

* * *

Alek had first encountered the power of an EMP a few years earlier when he was trying to determine if Will and Joe Ramos had stolen intelligence from the lab. He'd tracked the brothers to their home in Altavaca, New Mexico. While he was trying to decide how to approach the two men, they detonated a Low Energy Nuclear Reaction, or LENR, device, using technology that would later become the key to building Project Z.

Alek would never forget how the LENR detonation created a powerful pulse that wiped out all nearby electronic circuitry. In a fraction of a second, the EMP silently disrupted his car's electrical systems. The engine had stalled, the radio had quit playing, and the lights had flipped off. He'd turned the key, trying the car's ignition, but nothing happened. The LENR explosion had also vaporized the Ramos brothers' home, but Alek didn't think they'd need quite as powerful a device to create a distraction at the Lucky Dragon. At least, he hoped not.

If the LENR worked as planned, they could detonate it in the casino basement and generate an EMP that would cut all power in the area for up to 10 minutes. The hotel and casino would be plunged into darkness, cell phones, walkie talkies, and other radio communication devices would stop working, and the employees would scramble to figure out what was going on. Alek figured the distraction would give them enough time to rescue Gabi and switch out Sunli's Brainaid without being noticed. He figured it was a foolproof plan.

It was a foolproof plan except for the problem of getting an LENR device to Vegas. And, of course, the issue of having an LENR device at all. Five years ago, bilateral arms talks with China had led to a total ban on all development of weapons technology. The United States had agreed to abide by the treaty, but secretly at Los Alamos Lab, weapons development continued. "After all, we have to be prepared," Harold Percy, the lab director, said. "I'm sure the Chinese are working on similar weapons. Plus, there's the issue of terrorism—remember the Ramos brothers deployed a similar device. We need to be ready with our own, just in case."

Detonating an LENR device wasn't the first thought Alek had when Percy told him Gabi was in trouble. His initial plan was far more logical, relying on the FBI to ensure their agent's safety. But when Percy informed him that the FBI wasn't willing to do anything to jeopardize their ongoing investigation, Alek decided to take matters into his own hands. If Gabi was dead, well, there was nothing they could do and if she was being held prisoner... well, she would have to sit tight for a while. Alek wasn't willing to wait for FBI officials to make up their minds to rescue Gabi. He'd do it himself.

Alek Spray wasn't a risk taker by nature. He had grown up avoiding conflict and, after the accidental death of his daughter and his divorce, he had withdrawn even further, focusing all his time and energy on work. For years, Alek had no interest in personal relationships. He didn't put himself out there and he didn't get hurt. Then, Gabi came along, and everything changed.

Gabi was the one Alek was willing to risk everything for. He had let her go once and he regretted it. That wouldn't happen again.

Alek had begun brainstorming. How could he get into the Lucky Dragon to rescue Gabi? Surely Sunli and Wu had her locked up and guarded. To free her, he would have to find a way to distract her captors. That's when Alek came up with the idea an EMP. The resulting blackout and confusion would give him the distraction he needed to free Gabi and switch out Sunli's Brainaid with the modified device.

Then, Alek faced his biggest hurdle in making his plan a reality—convincing Percy to help.

After making the initial plan with Sal, Natasha, and Chang to head to Vegas, Alek had returned to the River Inn in Georgetown to meet Percy at the bar to explain his dilemma. He could have predicted his boss' response.

"Absolutely not. Are you out of your damn mind?" the lab director asked. "We shouldn't even have the LENR weapon. We built it in violation of an international treaty.

We could both lose our jobs. We could lose our security clearances. We could go to prison."

"That's why we have to keep it secret," replied Alek. "I need you to help me figure out a way to get the device out of the lab and transport it to Vegas. Tomorrow I'm flying out there with Natasha, Sal, and Chang. We're meeting Bernie Bhakta there 'cause he's the only one of us Wu and Sunli can't identify. He'll run surveillance and figure out where they're keeping Gabi."

"What does this have to do with me?" asked Percy. "Seems you've got your harebrained plan all figured out."

"Like I said, you have to drive the LENR weapon to Vegas. You need to find a way to disguise it and load it up in a truck or van or something."

"Let me repeat: are you out of your damn mind?"

Alek reached across the bar and grabbed Percy's hand. "Please. It's Gabi. I... I love her."

"Hmph. Love. Never really believed in that." The older man snorted, but Alek could see him softening.

"I'll think about it," Percy said grudgingly. "After all, what good is having your own LENR weapon if you can't use it," he added with a smile.

"I promise, no one will ever know about your involvement," said Alek. "What happens in Vegas, stays in Vegas, y'know."

Chapter 41
You Can Do This

GABI AWOKE TO THE SOUND of drilling. She opened her eyes to see Wu's bodyguards installing a new lock on her hotel room door. Wrapping herself in the bedsheet, she walked over to the men.

"Hey, what's going on here?" she asked.

"The general's tired of us always having to guard your door," grunted one of the men. "He asked us to install a special electronic device so that you could be locked in from the outside."

Gabi moved a little closer.

"Are you sure that's entirely necessary?" she asked. "I mean, you don't have to keep me locked up—"

"*Bùyào tīng tā dehuà mǔgǒu zài shuōhuǎng.* Don't listen to her. The bitch is lying," the other man interjected. "Come on. Let's finish up."

Gabi shrugged and walked toward the bathroom, feigning indifference.

"Don't bother shouting for help," replied one of the men as she retreated. "There's no one else staying on this floor. No one will hear you no matter how much you scream."

Gabi sat in the bathroom listening to the two men working until the hotel room fell silent and she was certain they had finished and left. Then she ran to the door and desperately tried the knob. It didn't budge. Even the hotel room windows didn't open. There was still no way out and still nothing she could do.

Gabi threw herself down on the bed, her injured head throbbing, and began crying softly. She truly was trapped.

* * *

Percy flipped on the light in the dusty basement laboratory hidden in the bowels of a rarely used building at Los Alamos National Laboratory. In the corner of the room sat the weapon that his team had secretly constructed—the Dragon's CLAW.

When the U.S. signed the arms ban with China, Percy had instructed his team to continue clandestine work on the weapon. The lab director knew from experience that someday his government would call for the device regardless of the arms treaty. He would be ready to deliver the ultra-deadly pulsed-beam weapon and would be recognized and rewarded for his foresight. As a boy, Percy had been an Eagle Scout. He was always prepared.

Alek wanted to detonate the device to create an electromagnetic pulse to disrupt the electronic systems in the Lucky Dragon Hotel and Casino. The machine's Dense Plasma Focus would use an e-beam trigger to produce a high current beam and generate the EMP with minimal energy release. To succeed, however, he'd have to get the device close to the casino's utility and security control room in the basement of the building. It had to be near enough that the relatively weak pulse would temporarily wipe out the power in the Lucky Dragon. A larger detonation could take out the city's entire electric grid.

The device wasn't large, but it wasn't exactly small either, about six feet long, four feet tall, and three feet wide. How could Percy get it to Vegas without drawing attention? How could Alek sneak it into the basement of the hotel? There was no way this could work.

Percy shrugged. He had always seen Alek as the son he never had. Would a father let his son down in this situation? Was it worth this big of a risk? More importantly, if he refused to help Alek, would his lead physicist simply take matters into his own hands and somehow implicate Percy? Was it safer to help Alek to ensure everything was done right? The lab director always preferred to be fully in control of matters, especially when his job was at risk.

He signed and headed back to his office. As he walked through the door, the encrypted landline phone on his desk rang loudly, making him jump. He looked at the phone number. His wife. She always picked the most inconvenient times to call.

Rose Percy's high-resolution image popped up on the flat screen computer monitor. Rose was standing in front of the Sandia Resort & Casino near Albuquerque, where she and her friends were enjoying a "girls' weekend."

"Hi, honey," he answered with a deep sigh.

"What are you doing?" Rose chirped.

"I'm at work. You know... working," muttered Percy. "What's up?"

"Well, we had a great day. We went shopping at ABQ Uptown then went to the Green Reed Spa to relax before dinner. Got manicures, facials, the whole bit."

Percy winced, thinking about the cost. "That's nice," he said.

Rose continued as though she hadn't noticed his lack of interest. "Tonight, there's a concert. Some country group. I don't know. Margaret picked it. I hope they're good. I think it's called Rascally Flat, something along those lines. Have you heard of them?"

Percy didn't answer. He was busy looking at what was happening behind Rose as she stood outside the Sandia Resort, boring her husband with the mundane details of her day. Percy watched as a handful of roadies wheeled cases into the casino, huge black cases on castors that contained musical instruments and audio, lighting, and production gear for the concert. The cases were about... about six feet long, four feet tall, and three feet wide.

"Honey, I've got to go," Percy said quickly. "There's something I have to take care of."

He hung up before Rose could even say goodbye. What had seemed like an impossible task moments before had suddenly become a possibility. Maybe they could do this after all.

* * *

"I'll have a gin and tonic," said Bernie. "Bombay Sapphire gin." He hoisted himself onto a stool in front of the long black lacquer bar in the Shanghai Lounge at the Lucky Dragon. He smiled at the attractive Asian woman taking his order. She didn't smile back. Leaving a tip, despite her unpleasant attitude, and grabbing his drink,

Bernie swiveled around to study the other patrons. The lounge was crowded although it was still early in the evening, the time before the serious gambling began. Most of the guests wore elegant clothing and carried themselves with the confidence that comes from easy access to money and ample time for leisure. Bernie looked out of place and yet, because it was Vegas, no one even noticed. In Vegas, there were no rules.

He watched as a small woman in impossibly high heels entered the lounge, her long, glossy hair swinging. Both men and women turned their heads to watch as she glided past. Her striking appearance, extravagant jewelry, and overall air of authority could only mean one thing. This was Dr. Sunli Hidalgo, one of the two women he was looking for.

Sunli strode to the bar and whispered something in the ear of the bartender, who smiled and handed her a glass of wine, returning the whisper along with the drink. The two women threw back their heads, laughing at the exchange. Bernie was close enough to see that the laughter failed to reach Sunli's eyes. Bernie Goldberg wouldn't have noticed, but Bernie Bhakta spotted it instantly. Sunli's aura needed healing. Something wasn't right.

Bernie studied Sunli. Her mixed heritage had bestowed on her an unusual beauty, but he also sensed a lack of harmony within her, a feeling of internal conflict. Somehow, she was at odds with herself. She was waging a personal battle and, so far, both sides were losing. Despite her casual confidence and poise, Sunli was struggling, but, except for Bernie, no one in the Shanghai Lounge could tell.

He watched as Sunli glanced warily over her shoulder toward the doorway leading to the casino where two olive-skinned men in black suits leaned against the wall. Her eyes narrowed when she saw them. Handing her now-empty wineglass back to the bartender, she strode briskly to the front door and left the room. The two men lingered for a moment and then followed. Bernie wondered who they were.

Shaking himself to cast off the spell Sunli had left lingering, Bernie decided to head to the hotel restaurant. He needed to figure out where Sunli and Wu were keeping Gabi, so his plan was to find out if the hotel staff were regularly delivering meals to a particular room. Sunli was a formidable enemy. Rescuing Gabi would be more difficult than he had thought.

Bernie took a calming breath and focused on adjusting his own aura. *You can do this*, he told himself.

Chapter 42
The Dragon's CLAW

PERCY FOUND A MUSIC SUPPLY company online where he could purchase gear and equipment cases. He ordered a large, wheeled container for the weapon and a smaller case that he would fill with sound gear as a decoy. That way, if someone wanted to look inside the cases, they would be able to open the one on top.

Next, he paid cash for a used pickup truck at a mom-and-pop car lot in Española. To make the truck look more official, he decided to have a magnet sign made for the side of the truck showing the band name. What should he name his imaginary band?

And who could he get to drive the truck from Albuquerque to Las Vegas? Percy didn't want to spend nine hours driving, but he also didn't want to take his eyes off his clandestine cargo. The older truck he had purchased lacked the sophisticated self-driving system found in newer vehicles, so that wasn't an option. Even if it had been, Percy didn't like the idea of dozing off while an automated car drove a stolen secret weapon across the Southwest. After a great deal of thought, he decided to have one of the lab's security officers do the driving while he rode shotgun. The security officers were accustomed to handling sensitive matters with discretion, and an unexpected week's vacation in Vegas would be ample reward.

As he executed the plan, Percy realized how much fun he was having. It had been so long since he had felt the challenge and excitement of solving a problem, the adrenaline of knowing he faced a deadline with people counting on him, the rush of devising a way to achieve his goals. The lab director smiled. This was like writing the plot of his own action movie and then getting to star in it. As long as there was a happy ending, of course.

The LENR weapon fit perfectly into the larger case. Two lab guards hoisted it into the bed of the pickup truck, stacking the smaller case full of sound gear on top. Percy had even ordered t-shirts printed with the band name. The security officer would wear one but, as always, the lab director wore a suit. If anyone asked, he planned to say he was the band's executive producer and was ensuring the roadie got the equipment to the right place.

Less than 72 hours ago, Percy had thought this caper was impossible. Now he was making it happen. He hoped he had made the right choice. *Well, too late now*, he mused, hopping in the cab of the truck and giving the officer the go ahead. As they sped off toward Vegas, Percy watched Los Alamos National Laboratory grow smaller in the rearview mirror.

* * *

Natasha Simon hated waiting. Nevertheless, there was nothing to do but wait for the delivery of the device that Alek adamantly ensured was integral to their plan. Relaxation wasn't her talent, even with careful usage of her own Brainaid device. As evening fell, she knocked on Chang's hotel room door.

"Let's go for a walk. I have to get out of here."

Chang had been reading research on coma recovery and was grateful for the interruption. The past few days of waiting had given him the opportunity to spend more time researching his theories about using the Brainaid to correct traumatic brain injury.

The heaviness of the subject as well as his thoughts about Sunli were weighing on him. He was ready for a break.

The Russian-born Israeli chemist and the Chinese physicist strode down the sidewalk together, blending in with the people roaming up and down the Las Vegas Strip. For a while they walked in companionable silence, winding their way in and out of casinos—the Luxor, the Excalibur, the ARIA, the Cosmopolitan—stopping occasionally to watch the tourists or make a sarcastic remark.

They passed packs of college boys carrying giant frozen daiquiris in plastic cups shaped liked the Eiffel Tower, a guitar, or The STRAT Tower; homeless people displaying cardboard signs with sayings like, "Why lie—need money for beer;" bachelorette groups teetering down the strip in clingy dresses and high heels; Japanese couples with babies in strollers; dancing girls wearing elaborate headdresses and tail feathers; and all the other characters that comprised the Vegas ecosystem. About the time they reached Caesars Palace, both Chang and Natasha had started to relax.

"You should try an outfit like that," said Natasha, pointing at a man wearing a toga in front of the casino.

"Indeed," Chang replied. "After all, when in Rome..."

"The Lucky Dragon is past the Wynn," remarked Natasha. "I'm not sure I want to walk that far." She steered them toward the escalator leading to a bridge that crossed the street. "Let's go to Harrah's. Have you ever been to the Piano Bar?"

"This is my first time in Vegas," Chang replied.

As they entered Harrah's and turned to the left, they saw the orange, red, and purple neon lights outlining the Piano Bar, a location famous for its dueling piano performances. That night, however, a crowd had gathered for karaoke. Chang and Natasha ordered beers and took a seat.

An overweight couple was onstage belting out "Islands in the Stream" with a great deal of enthusiasm. Chang winced. "They certainly aren't Dolly and Kenny," Natasha said.

"So, you know American music?" he asked.

"Of course. There's this thing called the internet." She smiled. "Now, growing up in China, you might not have heard about the internet. Some people call it the world wide web."

Chang laughed. "I went to college at Princeton. That's where I met Alek. Not only do I know American music, but I can also dance to it."

"Care to show me?" Natasha asked.

"That will take a few more beers."

The two fell silent again, pretending to watch the

singers. Chang contemplated his companion. Natasha was mysterious, born in Russia, raised in Israel, successful in the U.S., and always confident and strong. He wished he had similar energy. She was aggressive, almost pushy, but he liked that. She said the kind of things he only thought about saying.

Natasha downed her beer and signaled to the waitress to bring another round. "I don't know that we can drink enough to get you dancing, but what if we get up and sing?"

"I don't sing," Chang said. "Sunli would be appalled if she saw me standing up in front of a crowd of drunken tourists singing in a karaoke bar."

"That's exactly why we should do it," Natasha said, laughing. "Look, I know our goal is to help Sunli, but honestly, I think you should get over her. You can do better. It's time to move on."

"Oh yeah, you think I can do better?" Chang reached over and brushed a strand of Natasha's curly red hair out of her eyes.

"Seriously. You're brilliant, successful, good looking, and you're letting her destroy your life."

"You think I'm good looking?"

"That is not the point," Natasha said, taking a drink of her beer. "The point is that you can do better. You can't let her destroy your life."

Chang nodded, contemplating the strange turn of events that had led him to a karaoke bar in Las Vegas.

"Okay, I'll sing if you sing with me," he said.

"What are we singing?"

"'I'm Still Standing' by Elton John."

Fifteen minutes later, the two took the stage, and Chang discovered he could sing in front of a crowd of drunken tourists. Maybe he was ready to move on.

* * *

Bernie dropped a washcloth into the toilet bowl and flushed it, watching calmly as the water level rose slowly and spilled over the rim. He picked up the phone and called the front desk.

"This is Bernie Goldberg in Room 381. I'm having an

issue with the bathroom plumbing... Yes, of course, please do send someone up to look at it, but, honestly, it's been a little wonky since I got here... Is there any way I could move to a different room?" Bernie listened to the response, smiling. "Excellent. I'll be right down to make the arrangements."

The desk clerk already had an electronic keycard prepared for Bernie when he reached the front desk. "Oh, thank you," the gray-haired man said, examining the number. "Room 516. Is there possibly anything available on the 13th floor? It's kind of a habit of mine. I prefer staying on the 13th floor whenever possible, but a lot of hotels actually don't have a 13th floor. Superstitious Americans, you know? Anyhow, I forgot to ask for that when I first checked in, but I'd sure prefer something on that floor."

"Yes, we have a 13th floor," said the woman working the front desk. She typed a series of commands into the computer and then frowned. "Oh, I'm sorry. It appears that the entire 13th floor has been reserved indefinitely. I'm not sure why. It's entirely empty. Maybe they're planning some remodeling there. None of the rooms are available right now."

"Oh, that's a disappointment," sighed Bernie. "But I appreciate the effort. Room 516 will work for me. Do you think you could send up someone to help me move my bags?"

Taking his new keycard, Bernie wandered toward the only restaurant in the hotel, the Lemongrass Cafe. Early dinner guests were scattered throughout the dining room. Bernie approached the woman at the hostess stand.

"Excuse me. I placed a room service order and now, because of a plumbing problem, I'm having to change rooms."

"That's no problem, sir," replied the hostess. "What's your name and room number? I'll get your order changed."

Bernie pulled out his keycard and looked at the number written on the paper envelope. "The new room is 516, but when I placed the order..." he wrinkled his forehead in confusion. "Gosh, I can't even remember. Getting old is such a drag. I know it was on the 13th floor."

The young woman put a hand on his arm in an attempt to soothe him. "It's okay, don't worry. My grandfather gets confused a lot too. How about if I just go in the back and see if they have prepared anything for a room on the 13th floor?"

"Thank you so much, sweetie," Bernie replied, embracing his role as the doddering old man. "I'll sit down here for a bit while you check on that."

After a few moments, the hostess returned smiling. "We do have a tray of food that was about to be sent up to room 1342. Could that be your order?"

Bernie smacked his forehead. "That's it. 1342. How did I forget that? If you could send that to 516 instead, I would be most grateful."

Leaving the restaurant, Bernie marveled at how easily he had manipulated the hotel staff into revealing the information he was seeking. Now he knew for sure that Gabi was being kept in Room 1342. He also knew that tonight she wouldn't get dinner. He hoped she could forgive him.

* * *

"Thanks for the lift," Percy told the security officer, handing him a wad of $100 bills. "Take a few days and enjoy yourself, then grab a flight back to New Mexico. And, as far as this trip, if anyone asks, it never happened."

"What never happened, sir?" the officer replied with a raised eyebrow.

"Exactly," Percy replied, shaking his hand. Dismissing the officer, the lab director crossed the Mandalay Bay parking garage and headed toward the lobby to find Alek and get the show on the road.

He walked briskly, wondering how he'd gotten himself into this. Then again, he hadn't had this much fun in years.

Alek, Chang, Natasha, and Sal were waiting in the lobby. They decided to go upstairs to Sal's suite so they could talk without being overheard. The billionaire inventor had chosen some of the resort's finest suites for their stay in Vegas. Naturally, all were reserved under a pseudonym to avoid any possibility of being tracked. Alek wasn't accustomed to the luxury. His room on the 50th floor of the hotel was larger than his former Los Alamos apartment and had amazing views, but Sal's suite eclipsed it. The two-story Presidential Suite featured a pool table and an exercise room in addition to four bedrooms. As the sun set and the lights of Las Vegas began twinkling, the group settled in the elegant living room to discuss their next steps.

"We have the weapon now, and Bernie has determined that Gabi is being kept in Room 1342, which is actually on the 12th story of the hotel," Alek said.

"Wouldn't 1342 be on the 13th story?" asked Percy.

"No, 'cause the Chinese are weird," Natasha said, raising an eyebrow at Chang who responded with a grin.

Alek gave them both a look. "Anyhow, if we can move the weapon close to the hotel control and utility room and then detonate it, the resulting EMP will temporarily knock out all the power to the hotel and casino. It will create a distraction and render all the electronic door locks inoperable, so we can release Gabi and get into Sunli's room. The EMP is the only thing that will give us the chance to rescue Gabi and switch out Sunli's Brainaid. We have to work fast while the electricity is out."

"And how are we going to get a small nuclear weapon into a hotel?" Natasha asked, throwing her hands in the air in frustration.

"That's easy," said Percy. "The weapon is in a musical gear case loaded in the back of a truck labeled with a band name and driven by roadies who have come to deliver the equipment for an upcoming performance. They park in the lowest level of the hotel parking garage, which is close to the utilities and control room for the hotel and casino. That way, when the weapon is detonated, the EMP will take out all electrical systems in the Lucky Dragon for about 10 minutes."

Sal rose and walked to the nearby bar to pour himself another glass of scotch. "And how do we detonate the weapon without harming ourselves?"

Percy laughed. "It's called a remote control."

Sal chuckled. "Who are the roadies?"

"You are," replied Percy. "You and Chang. I even got

you t-shirts with the name of the band."

The lab director grabbed the bag he had brought with him and started handing out t-shirts. Alek held a shirt up so he could get a good look at its black and red design.

"I like the band name: The Dragon's CLAW."

Chapter 43
The Calm Before

THE NEXT EVENING, AS THE sun ducked behind the horizon, Sal attached the large magnet sign to the side of the pickup truck. The beauty of the magnet was that they could remove it quickly, rendering the truck generic and unmemorable. When in place, the red and black design on the sign added credibility and perfectly matched the logo on Sal's t-shirt and ball cap, proudly proclaiming the band name: The Dragon's CLAW. Sal had decided that if anyone asked, he'd say the group played alternative rock music with an Asian twist. He hoped no one wanted him to pull up one of their songs on Spotify or YouTube.

As Sal got behind the wheel, Chang arrived, wearing an identical t-shirt and ballcap. "We should have gotten jackets with the band name instead of t-shirts," Chang said. "It's really cold out."

"Yeah," Sal agreed. "I've never seen it this cold in Vegas. If we were in New Mexico, I'd think we were expecting snow."

Chang hopped into the passenger seat of the pickup. "Nat, Percy, and Alek will meet us at the Lucky Dragon," he said.

"Here goes nothing," Sal said, shifting the truck into drive and heading out of the parking garage onto the Las Vegas Strip. The sun had set, leaving streaks of orange and pink illuminating the heavy clouds building in the rapidly darkening sky. Chang and Sal neared the Lucky Dragon and pulled into the parking garage.

Chang stifled an exasperated gasp. Instead of an automatic ticketing machine at the entry to the garage, the Lucky Dragon garage had a manned booth. They might have to answer some questions. An older man wearing a turban and a pair of small glasses was sitting in the booth as Sal and Chang pulled up.

Looking over his glasses at the pickup, the man slid the booth window closed. He slipped a sign in front of the window that read, "Be Back Shortly" and walked to the other side of the booth where he began making a sandwich.

"You have got to be kidding," Sal grumbled.

Sal and Chang sat in the truck while the man completed assembling his turkey sandwich and ate it with small deliberate bites. A line of cars began forming behind the pickup truck.

"They're all here to see the show and we're holding them up," said Chang.

"The show?" Sal asked.

"Yeah. The Dragon's CLAW. They're the hottest band in town," he responded with a smile.

The parking attendant returned to his spot in front of the window and then removed his glasses and began slowly cleaning them while Sal and Chang watched. Finally, he reached for the "Be Back Shortly" sign, moved it aside, and opened the window.

"Can I help you?" he asked.

"Yes, we're here to drop off the equipment for tonight's musical performance. Y'know the group, The Dragon's CLAW."

"I only listen to heavy metal," the man replied, handing them their ticket. "Don't park in compact or reserved spaces," he admonished.

"We definitely won't," Sal replied with a sigh of relief.

Sal drove to the lowest level of the parking garage and pulled up next to the curb closest to the entrance to the area that served as the control and operations center for the hotel and casino. Carefully unloading the cases, he and Chang wheeled them through the door.

Inside the control center, two men sat monitoring a bank of computers displaying video feeds from across the facility. One of them put down the doughnut he was inhaling and rose when he saw Sal and Chang coming in with the cases. "What are you doing with those?" he said gruffly. "You can't leave them here."

"It's the sound equipment for the band performing tonight," Chang said. "Apparently, General Wu is having a party. Can I leave the gear here for a few minutes while I figure out where it needs to go? I need to get a hold of my boss."

"I guess," said the man with a shrug. "Park 'em next to the wall so I can walk through here. No one told me there was gonna be a show."

Chang pushed the cases to the side of the room next to the massive rack of computer servers controlling the facility. This was the brain center of the hotel and casino. Every utility, security, and communication of the building was managed here. Sal raised an eyebrow. Talk about good luck.

"So, we'll be right back," Chang said. "Keep an eye on that equipment for me." The man nodded grudgingly and then turned back to the video feeds and his doughnut.

Sal and Chang hurried out of the control room back to the pickup. "Okay, let's take the truck to the rendezvous spot. Then we can check in with the rest of the team," Chang said quietly.

Sal nodded and looked over his shoulder back at the entrance to the casino control center. "So, Alek's going to detonate a miniature nuclear weapon inside the building?"

"Not exactly," Chang replied. "The nuclear reaction is very energetic so only a fraction of a teaspoon of fuel will release the energy equivalent of a stick of dynamite, but in the form of an EMP. The device itself will implode and collapse into a heap of rubble. It's far enough from the control room operators that no one will be hurt."

"So, it will knock out the power?" Sal asked.

"Yes, it will shut down all the electricity and all the electronic controls and software in the facility, including the electronic locks on all the doors. Nothing will work until the entire system is rebooted, which should take about 10 minutes."

Sal handed the parking garage ticket and $10 to the man in the turban at the exit. He considered complaining that they shouldn't have to pay to park since they had only been there a few minutes, but he decided not to do anything to make them more memorable. Once again, the man in the booth was in no hurry. Finally, he raised the wooden arm, releasing them from the parking garage.

"Hmmm, 10 minutes without power," Sal said thoughtfully as they drove out of the facility. "I sure hope that's enough time."

As they drove down the street to the rendezvous spot one block from the casino, the two men looked through the windshield in confusion.

"What the hell is this?" Chang asked.

"I didn't think this happened much in Vegas," replied Sal. "It's starting to snow."

* * *

General Wu watched Sunli walk through the Baccarat room. He admired the way her black dress matched her glossy hair, which she had twisted into an elegant chignon. The general noticed that he was not the only person in the casino looking, and he fought a surge of jealousy. Even as a child, Wu had always hated having to share.

Wu stepped away from the Baccarat table. He was off his game tonight, unable to concentrate. He needed some peace and solitude. Every day, Sunli seemed a little more distant. She spent much of her time plugged into her Brainaid, communicating with her enhanced human team using their collective consciousness through the central computer system. The rest of the day, she circulated through the casino mingling with the high rollers. She had very little time for Wu. Still, he assured himself that she was his. She had left Chang and joined him at the Lucky Dragon. She had made a choice.

Nevertheless, Wu could tell he had become less and less of a priority. Sometimes he felt that Sunli viewed him as merely a means to an end.

The general had expected Sunli to be pleased when he'd exposed Gabi as a spy, but instead she seemed angry. Maybe she was disappointed that her friend turned out to be disloyal, but it seemed almost as though she was disappointed in him.

Stop this pathetic line of thought, Wu told himself. He had commanded countless soldiers. He had power, wealth, and influence. Sunli clearly adored him, she just had a lot of responsibilities.

Wu walked to the Shanghai Lounge and grabbed a bottle of Baijiu from behind the bar. He would relax in the suite and enjoy a drink and a nap perhaps. Then when he was feeling better, he could return to Sunli's side.

Taking the elevator to the penthouse, Wu let himself in with his electronic key card. Flicking on the lights, he grabbed a glass from the kitchen and headed for the high-backed recliner in the corner of the spacious living room. Settling into the chair with a sigh, he poured himself a glass of Baijiu and plugged in his Brainaid. *I'll rest my eyes for a moment,* Wu thought. In minutes, he was sound asleep.

* * *

From his seat in front of the bar, Bernie watched Wu wander into the lounge and leave carrying a bottle. The general looked dejected. Bernie wondered what was going on. A few minutes later, the two men he had seen earlier in the week walked into the room, their eyes scanning the scene, looking for something or someone. The men made Bernie nervous. They radiated anxious energy and danger, as though chaos and violence were a normal part of their lives. Walking with a measured pace, the two circled the lounge and then exited. Clearly, they hadn't found what they were looking for.

Bernie sipped his drink and checked his phone for messages. If everything was going as planned right now, Sal and Chang should be meeting Percy on the side street bordering the casino. They would remove the band name magnet sign and change the license plates on the truck, so they would be ready for a quick getaway. Meanwhile, Alek and Natasha would enter the casino and Alek would use the remote control to deploy the weapon, plunging the hotel and casino into darkness.

When the power went out, Alek would head to the room on the 13th floor where Gabi was being held prisoner, while Natasha went to the penthouse to trade Sunli's

Brainaid for the altered version she had made. Bernie was in charge of watching Sunli and Wu, and if necessary, distracting them so they didn't try to return to their suite of rooms while Natasha was switching out the device.

The big question was whether Sunli kept her Brainaid in her room and if Natasha could find it. Bernie had a few days studying Sunli and he had seen no indication that she carried the device with her, but there was no way to know if it was actually in her room. Natasha said she felt certain Sunli kept her Brainaid tucked in the drawer of the nightstand beside her bed. "You know, next to her vibrator," Natasha said, ignoring the way the four men blushed at her comment.

"How do you know she keeps her vibrator in the nightstand drawer?" asked Alek.

"I know. I'm a strong, independent woman, like Sunli," Natasha said, looking directly at Peter Chang. "That's where I keep mine."

All the doors in the hotel had electronic locks that the EMP would temporarily disable. Natasha would have no trouble entering the penthouse, and Alek would be able to open the door to the room where Gabi was being held captive. Gabi, Alek, and Natasha would meet the others at the truck in the rendezvous spot and then leave the area separately with plans to reunite later at the Mandalay Bay.

Bernie glanced down at his phone. Chang had texted, letting him know the device was in place and asking for an update on his surveillance of Sunli and Wu.

"Still in the lounge. The dragon lady hasn't come in yet," Bernie replied.

"Don't call her that," texted Chang.

"Wu came in and left about five minutes ago. Keep an eye out."

"Probably in the Baccarat room," Chang texted back.

Bernie drained the last of his gin and tonic and swirled the ice around in his glass. He gestured to the bartender for another drink. Everything was going as planned, they had discussed every detail, but Bernie felt worried. For some reason, nothing felt right.

Chapter 44
The Storm

ALEK AND NAT KEPT THEIR heads down as they walked into the casino, striding purposely across the garishly colorful carpet and slipping into a row of $1 slot machines tucked in the back of the main room near the emergency exit stairs. Alek looked around, taking in the glaring neon lights of the slot machines, each with its own jingle or sound effects. Murmured conversation and laughter floated through the room. Music drifted out of the Shanghai Lounge and bells rang in the distance as someone hit a jackpot.

Making eye contact with Nat, Alek reached into his pocket and punched the button on the remote control, triggering the miniature nuclear weapon in the basement of the casino and launching the EMP.

The vast room plunged into darkness. The music, bells, slot machine sound effects, and people's laughter fell silent. Someone screamed.

Alek and Natasha bolted for the stairwell and began pounding up the stairs. With even the emergency generators out, the stairs were completely dark, so they switched on their flashlights as they ran up the stairs. A few frightened guests passed them on the way down. "Do you know what's happening?" an elderly, overweight man asked them.

"We work for the hotel. We're going to check things out," Natasha replied.

Alek exited the stairwell on the 13th floor as Natasha continued up the stairs toward the penthouse.

"Stay calm," Alek told himself, extinguishing his flashlight. *Easier said than done*, he thought, sliding slowly along the wall in the pitch-black hallway. From somewhere deep in the building, he could hear the distant sound of people shouting, their angry, frightened voices cutting through the darkness. Then a series of gunshots. A scream. That wasn't part of the plan. What was happening?

No one should be on the 13th floor, except for Gabi. Alek hoped the guards were too busy dealing with the consequences of the blackout to send anyone to check on the woman he intended to save. This was not what he had anticipated when he earned a PhD in physics. Nothing in his life had prepared him for a task like this.

Alek wasn't sure he was ready to face Gabi. He had no idea what to say to her. The last time they had spoken, she made it clear that she no longer wanted to be part of his life. *That isn't the point. The point is to save her*, Alek told himself. They'd deal with the details once she was safe.

Room 1342. He reached for the door handle. As expected, the EMP had disabled the electronic lock. Alek took a deep breath and opened the door.

Gabi was sitting on the bed. When she saw him in the dim light, she jumped up with a gasp.

"Sorry, I'm late. Traffic was a bitch," said Alek with a shy smile. Gabi threw herself into his arms.

* * *

"Everyone please stay calm," Sunli said as she walked into the Shanghai Lounge using a candle to light her way. "We are experiencing a minor technical issue, but I anticipate the electricity will be restored shortly. Please stay seated and we will have everything back to normal in a few minutes."

"My phone won't work," barked an older woman sitting near Bernie. "Does anyone's phone work?"

"All our phones are completely dead," one man replied. "What's going on?"

"I'm sure it's something minor, some kind of electrical interference," murmured Sunli, attempting to reassure the customers. Her voice sounded strained, and her forehead wrinkled with worry as her eyes darted across the dark room. Bernie wondered where Wu was. He was supposed to keep an eye on both of them, but if he left the lounge, he wouldn't be able to watch Sunli. Bernie moved closer to the door leading from the lounge into the casino, peering out into the depths of the dark casino. Then he heard a shout from behind him.

"Hey, take your hands off me." It was Sunli's voice, and she sounded angry. Bernie moved closer to the bar in the back of the room. In the candlelight, he could see one of the two black-suited men he had spotted following Sunli earlier. The man had grabbed Sunli by the arm.

"She said to leave her alone," said the bartender.

"Who's going to make me?" the man replied gruffly without releasing his tight grip on Sunli.

"I am," said the bartender pulling out a gun from behind the counter. Suddenly, shots rang out and the bartender crumpled. Several people screamed as the second of the black-suited men emerged from the darkness, holding a gun.

"I'd prefer that no one else get hurt," he said quietly. "Just take your seats and wait for the lights to come back on."

Bernie watched as the bartender's blood pooled on the black lacquer counter and began to drip slowly down the edge onto the floor. The older woman sitting at the bar began to cry.

"We will be leaving now. It would be wise of you not to follow us," the black-suited man said, brandishing his gun as his companion steered Sunli roughly toward the door.

Like the other bar patrons, Bernie watched the two men leave with Sunli. Then he headed for the rendezvous spot—he had to find Chang.

* * *

Natasha had thought she was in good physical condition but running up 25 flights of stairs had left her winded. She emerged on the top floor of the Lucky Dragon gasping for breath. She stood for a moment in the dark hallway outside the penthouse. Her heart was racing. *Calm down*, she told herself. *All you have to do is switch out the Brainaids and then you can leave.*

Quietly, Natasha turned the door handle. With the

electronic lock disabled, it swung open in her grasp. She tiptoed into the suite, straining her eyes in the darkness but reluctant to use her flashlight. The master bedroom was to her left.

She entered the bedroom and headed directly to the nightstand, feeling her way across the room in the dark. She opened the nightstand drawer and found it empty. Not even the Gideon Bible inside.

Frustrated, Natasha felt her way around the king-sized bed to the other nightstand. Blind in the darkness, she slid the drawer open and began feeling around. Immediately her fingers closed on something. It was the Brainaid.

Natasha smiled. This was too easy. Taking the altered Brainaid from her pocket, she slipped it into the nightstand and placed Sunli's original device in her pocket where the other Brainaid had been. *So simple*, she thought triumphantly. Then, she heard a sound from the living room of the penthouse.

* * *

"I can't even begin to explain how happy I am to see you," Gabi said after she had finally stopped hugging Alek.

Alek felt himself smiling. "I can see that. Now, we need to get out of here. Uh, do you mind me asking why you are wearing an evening dress?"

Gabi glanced down at the midnight-blue beaded dress she was wearing, the same dress she had worn earlier that week before she became a prisoner. It felt like a lifetime ago.

"Wu and Sunli's henchmen took my clothes," she said, laughing. "This is what they left me."

"Well, you look great. Let's get out of here. Do you have some shoes?"

"They took everything but high heels. I'd rather be barefoot. What I wouldn't give for a pair of sneakers and some jeans."

As the two headed into the hallway, Gabi said, "We need to go to the penthouse first. Wu and Sunli are storing all the records of their money transfers on servers up there."

"In Wu's suite? Are you sure that's necessary? I'd rather get you out of here and go back later for that stuff."

"No, we need to have it to prove their involvement with the crime syndicate. Without the records, it could be my word against theirs."

Glancing at his watch, Alek grabbed Gabi's hand. They entered the stairwell and began climbing the stairs to the penthouse. "We don't have much time," he said. "We needed to cut all the power to the building and disable the electronic locks so..."

Gabi gasped. "You didn't!"

"Oh, we did. We set off an LENR in the basement of the casino creating an EMP that knocked out all the electrical systems and power. But the effect is limited, and the casino control system operators should be able to restore everything soon, so we need to hurry."

"I get it," murmured Gabi. "Let's go."

* * *

Bernie ran out of the casino and jogged through the whirling snow to the side street where Sal and Chang were waiting in the pickup. Struggling to catch his breath and shivering from the cold, he explained what had happened in the Shanghai Lounge.

"What do you mean two men took her?" Chang shouted, grabbing Bernie by both arms.

"They were armed, wearing black suits and carrying guns," the gray-haired man said.

"Why didn't you follow them?"

"I'm a retired physicist who teaches yoga and meditation. This action-thriller stuff isn't really my thing."

"I know," said Chang, looking a little guilty. "Did you see which way they went?"

"They took her out the door. That's all I know. She didn't want to go with them."

"And Wu? Have you seen him?"

"No," admitted Bernie. "He left the lounge about an hour ago, looking sad."

Chang checked the time on his watch. "They should be getting close to rebooting the control systems and restoring the electricity. We need to find Sunli."

"Okay, let's go," Bernie replied, placing a hand on Chang's shoulder. "Hey, I'm sorry. We'll find her."

"I know," Chang said. "Percy has been in touch with the FBI."

"Percy?" asked Bernie. "Shouldn't he be here now. Where's Percy?"

The Chinese physicist pointed up to the dark, snowy sky. High above them a black helicopter circled.

"Percy?" Bernie asked again.

Chang nodded. "And the FBI."

Chapter 45
The Big Action Scene

ALEK AND GABI CLIMBED THE dark, empty stairwell to the penthouse. His footsteps echoed eerily, while her bare feet padded soundlessly as they hurried up the stairs. To avoid tripping, Gabi held the long evening dress gathered in one hand as they ascended the stairs as fast as possible.

Finally, they reached the penthouse. Thankfully, the electronic lock was still disabled. Alek turned the knob and the door swung open revealing the dark suite.

"The servers are in the left-hand corner of the living room," Gabi whispered. "Sunli said they store all the records of their illegal transactions there." The two tiptoed across the living room to the rack of MacBooks in the corner of the room.

"Should we unhook them and take them with us?" asked Alek.

"I think we can get them all if we each carry three," she replied, beginning to unplug the laptops from the system. Suddenly, they heard a noise behind them. They froze.

"*Nǐ zài zhèlǐ zuò shénme?* What are you doing here?" shouted General Wu.

* * *

The Chinese general had been dozing in his armchair when he heard a noise in the darkened room. He blinked as his eyes adjusted. Who was in his hotel suite? Why was it so dark?

Peering across the room, he saw Gabi and Alek hovering in front of the server rack. *How did she get out of her room? How did Alek Spray get in here? What's going on?*

Quietly, he rose from his chair. They were disconnecting the laptops with all the records of their wire transfers. They had to be stopped.

Wu wondered what had happened to his security guards. Gabi Stebbens had been locked securely in her hotel room. There was no way for her to escape, but somehow, she had. Somehow Alek Spray had freed her. It seemed impossible, but here they were in his living room.

Creeping across the room in the darkness, Wu considered his options. There was a loaded gun in the end table drawer but that was on the other side of the living room. Still, it was his best chance and neither of the intruders appeared to be armed. If he could get the gun before they noticed... Then the general bumped his knee into the side of the couch, grunted at the sharp pain, and saw Gabi and Alek freeze.

""*Nǐ zài zhèlǐ zuò shénme?* What are you doing here?" Wu shouted, debating whether he should lunge for his gun or try to fight the two barehanded. Then Gabi launched toward him with fury in her eyes. Panicked, Wu looked around for a weapon. Beside him in the teak curio cabinet, he saw his prized Ming vase, his most beloved possession. It was his only chance.

Raising the $5 million porcelain vase high, Wu smashed it over Gabi's head. She crumpled to the ground as the general bounded to the end table, grabbed the gun, fixing the laser sight on Alek's forehead. "It's over, Spray," Wu said coldly. "I won't be sad to see you go."

He racked the slide on the Glock and put his finger on the trigger, but before he could fire the gun, he heard a loud popping noise and felt a sting in his chest.

The general looked down at the crimson stain blossoming across his white shirt. He collapsed on the floor.

* * *

Natasha was standing in the bedroom door holding her gun. "I told you. I'm always armed," she said as the electricity turned back on in the hotel, flooding the room with light.

She walked over to Wu and crouched beside him. "He's dead."

"She's unconscious," said Alek as he lifted Gabi from the floor. Shards of the broken porcelain vase spread across the marble floor, mingling with the blood pooled around Wu.

Alek weighed their options. "We've gotta get out of here before Wu's security officers come looking for him. With the power restored, we don't have much time."

Natasha grabbed her phone. "Phones are working again too," she said. "Let's see where the others are." She texted Chang and then stared at her phone at the reply.

"Can we get Gabi to the rooftop?" she said with urgency. "There's a helicopter landing there right now."

"A helicopter?" asked Alek incredulously. "And who is in this helicopter?"

Natasha looked down at her phone and shrugged. "Apparently Percy and the FBI."

* * *

"Goddamn it, you have to land on the roof now!" shouted Percy.

"I'm trying," said the pilot. "I've never seen a storm like this in Vegas. The snow and the crosswinds are making it impossible to put this bird down."

"Well, do something. My people need help." Percy peered out the window into the swirling snow.

"Cross your fingers or say a prayer 'cause I'm going to try."

As the black helicopter hovered closer to the roof of the Lucky Dragon, the rotors whipped the snow, eliminating all remaining visibility. They were flying blind. Then miraculously, they were down.

Through the falling snow, Percy spotted Natasha and Alek emerge from a doorway with Gabi draped between them. Her head lolled to the side as they half carried, half dragged her across the snow. Alek leaned over and said something to Natasha, and then lifted Gabi into his arms. Natasha ran back into the hotel as Alek approached the helicopter.

"Quick, get her in here. What happened?" shouted Percy. "Where is Natasha going?"

"She went to get Wu's laptops. They have all the

records of the wire transfers," Alek said, setting Gabi down carefully in one of the helicopter seats. "Here she comes. Hang on."

Running back out into the snow, Alek grabbed some of the laptops from Natasha. As the strong winds buffeted them, the two struggled to make their way across the roof. Alek nearly slipped on the wet snow but recovered.

Then three of Wu's security guards burst out of the door from the hotel onto the roof, their guns drawn. The first shot was fired right before Nat and Alek reached the helicopter. They handed the laptops to Percy as more shots were fired at them. Natasha fired back.

"Get in here!" shouted Alek, grabbing Natasha. "Shut the door. Come on, let's go."

"Taking off in this weather is tricky," mumbled the pilot as a bullet hit the side of the helicopter. "But I think we'll take our chances with the snow."

The helicopter rose into the snow-filled night, rising above the Lucky Dragon and the lights of the Las Vegas Strip. Alek wiped some blood off Gabi's cheek as Percy placed his hand on the younger man's shoulder. "It's over, Alek," the lab director said. "The FBI is sending in a ground team as we speak. All we have to do is get Gabi to the hospital and everything will be fine."

Alek nodded somberly and took Gabi's hand in his own as they sped off through the storm.

Chapter 46
Redemption

LYING UNCONSCIOUS IN THE HOSPITAL bed, Gabi looked small, pale, and helpless, surrounded by tubes, lights, and beeping medical equipment. Alek was sitting in the stiff-backed chair beside her, unshaven and exhausted, as Percy walked into the room.

"Still no change?" he asked.

"No, the doctors say that all we can do is wait to see if she comes out of the coma. There's nothing we can do."

"Have you gotten any sleep, son?"

"I've dozed. I'm not leaving her," said Alek. "What if she wakes up when I'm gone?"

The lab director shook his head sadly. "I'm not a doctor but I would think she would have woken by now. It's been three days."

"Did the FBI locate Sunli?" Alek asked.

"No sign of her, but they took all of Wu and Sunli's collective consciousness crime team into custody. Apparently the EMP knocked out the connection between their Brainaids and the central computer, so most of the so-called enhanced humans were in a daze when the agents arrived."

"Does the FBI have any leads on the men Bernie saw taking Sunli?"

"They suspect undercover operatives from China's Ministry of State Security. Probably the same people who shot at you in Taos and caused the avalanche," Percy said.

"Speaking of snow, how's the weather?"

"It's still coming down some. The TV weather guys are stroking out with excitement. They never thought they'd get to cover a significant snowfall in Vegas." Percy sat down on the hospital room's other uncomfortable chair. "You may be right about the ice age. There's nothing normal about this storm."

The men looked up as they heard a knock on the door. Chang, Natasha, Sal, and Bernie slipped into the room.

"No change?" asked Natasha. Alek shook his head. The tough, unemotional Russian-born Israeli chemist walked over to Alek and hugged him awkwardly. Then Bernie moved in with a warm bear hug.

"Hey, Alek. I have an idea," Chang said.

"You should listen to this," Sal chimed in. "I think it will work."

The Chinese scientist continued. "I've been researching the possibility of using the Brainaid to reverse coma. Do you remember me telling you about that back in Los Alamos?"

"If it weren't for the Brainaid, we wouldn't have any of these problems," said Alek bitterly.

Natasha took a deep breath. "It's not the technology, it's the way people use it. Technology can be used for good or evil, but we must continue to pursue scientific breakthroughs. After all..."

"I know, I know," Alek interrupted. "Technology is a knife. A knife can slit your throat or butter your bread. Our job is to build the knife."

Chang stepped forward. "I really think the Brainaid can help. Please, let me try."

Alek took one of Gabi's limp hands in his own. "Her mother and grandmother don't even know she's here in the hospital. They don't even know she's hurt."

"Let Chang try the Brainaid. If it doesn't work, then we can contact them," said Percy. "Technology may have created this problem, but perhaps it's also the solution. After all, we built the knife, now let's put it to good use."

Alek nodded.

Chang pulled a small box out of his pocket. "This is a modified Brainaid. I've programmed it for forecasting and controlling neurological disturbances under a multi-level control," Chang said. "The cognitive enhancement module will monitor her brainwaves and then subtract the current frequency from the target frequency. When the difference between the current frequency and the target frequency is greater than a predetermined amount, the Brainaid will send a signal that will modify the current frequency toward the target frequency. We will probably need to repeat the measuring, determining, and sending steps until the target brain state is achieved. The Brainaid provides feedback that will allow me to make real-time adjustments to cognitive enhancement and cancelation of undesirable signals as I control the frequency, amplitude, waveform, and location of the signals sent to the brain."

"So how long do you think it will take to revive her?" Alek asked.

"The goal is to take an extremely gradual approach to bringing her out of the coma," said Natasha. "Even in the best-case scenario, it will take several days. Our first step will be entraining her weak brain waves. Then we will begin increasing the amplitude and slowly boosting the frequency a little each day until the frequency is two hertz. Then we will readjust the signal and raise the frequency to five hertz. We will need you guys to measure her vital signs around the clock so we can monitor her physical response to the stimulus. If everything goes as planned, we will know if we are making progress almost immediately, and, if this is going to work, she'll regain consciousness in about a week."

"I picked up some sandwiches on the way over," said Bernie. "Pastrami on rye. Why don't we go to the waiting room and have a snack while Chang and Natasha get the Brainaid set up."

Moments later in the waiting room, Alek paced back and forth, while the others sat nearby eating sandwiches. Sal offered him half a sandwich, but Alek waved him away.

"I'll eat later," he said.

"Alek," said Bernie, setting down his sandwich, "what's your take on this weird weather?"

"Well, based on studies by the National Geospatial-Intelligence Agency, the transition away from fossil fuels to Project Z combined with other natural phenomena and decades of greenhouse gas emissions have sparked a slide into lower temperatures," Alek said.

"So, no more worries about global warming?" Bernie asked.

"Does it look like it?" Alek replied, gesturing to the snow on the ground outside the window.

"Hmph. Good point."

Chang and Natasha walked into the waiting room. Alek ran across the room to greet them. "How is she? Are you ready to start the entrainment?"

"She's unchanged," Chang replied. "We'll begin in a moment but remember it will take several days before we see any response."

"I just want her back," said Alek.

"I know," Chang murmured. He frowned, apparently thinking of Sunli. "I understand what it's like to lose someone and yearn for them to return to you. Believe me, I know."

* * *

Three days passed without any improvement. Chang and Natasha used their phones to monitor Gabi's brainwaves, adjusting the frequency incrementally every day.

Alek rarely left Gabi's bedside. The others came and went, checking on both Alek and Gabi. Neither looked particularly well.

On the fourth day, Bernie arrived with some lavender incense and burned it next to Gabi's bed until the nurse scolded him and explained that he couldn't light things on fire inside a hospital room.

"But aromatherapy can reinforce the brain entrainment process," argued Bernie

The nurse nodded calmly and said, "You still can't light incense in a hospital room, no matter what the studies say. What if you got her some lavender oil?"

"That's a good idea," Bernie said eagerly. Patting Alek on the arm, he said, "I'll be back with some lavender oil. That will do the trick." As the guru rushed from the room in search of more suitable aromatherapy, Sal walked in and pulled up a chair next to Alek.

"I don't know what worries me more," Alek said quietly. "One minute I'm thinking, 'What if she never wakes up.' The next minute I'm thinking, 'What if she wakes up and says she never actually loved me.'"

"She loves you. She loves you so much she was willing

to sacrifice her happiness for yours. In my book, that's the ultimate true love."

Alek shook his head. "I don't know about that. No one should have to give up their own happiness for someone else's. If only she had talked to me about her feelings... Gabi *is* my happiness. At least, she was..." Alek grabbed Gabi's cold hands and laid his cheek against hers.

Bernie, Chang, Natasha, and Percy walked into the room. Chang and Natasha bustled around checking the monitors, while Bernie started assembling the essential oil diffuser he had purchased in the hospital gift shop to disperse lavender oil into the air. Percy sat down and started scrolling through his phone messages.

Suddenly, Alek shouted, "Guys!" and everyone froze.

"What is it?" asked Chang. "Should we buzz the nurse?"

"Her eyelids fluttered," said Alek. He stroked her forehead. "Gabi, I need you to come back to me. Remember all the adventures we had together? We need to have some more. We'll go on a road trip and get some Allsup's burritos. We can stay in a yurt and go skiing. Let's head to the Mexican jungle and go zip lining, or maybe we can go for a drive under the full moon late at night and explore Area 51. We can even go to the Little A'Le'Inn motel on the Extraterrestrial Highway. Gabi, please, just come back."

Slowly the pale woman in the bed opened her eyes, blinking, and murmured, "Alek, don't be ridiculous. I can't do all those things right now. I've been sick."

Smiling through his tears, Alek embraced her. The others gathered around.

"Why do I feel like I'm in the final scene of *The Wizard of Oz*?" asked Gabi. "Where is Auntie Em?"

"You're not in Kansas anymore, or even in the Lucky Dragon for that matter," laughed Alek. "Gabi, I love you."

"I'll get the nurse," said Chang.

"Let's give them a minute," said Natasha, ushering the men out of the room.

Alek touched Gabi's blonde curls. "You were unconscious for nearly two weeks. I thought I lost you."

Gabi struggled to sit up in her hospital bed. "Alek, there's something I have to tell you... I lied."

"You lied? You lied about what?"

Brushing away a tear, Gabi said, "I lied about not loving you... about not wanting to marry you. I didn't want to tell you that I might not be able to have children. I wanted you to find happiness—so I lied."

"Gabi Stebbens, you are the only thing I need to find happiness," said Alek. "Will you be my wife?"

Epilogue

BLOWING SNOW AND ICE PELLETS buffeted the windows of Alek's casita. Max growled at the wind.

"Settle down, boy. It's okay," said Alek, patting the brown and white spotted dog's broad head. "You look so fierce, but you're such a chicken," he added. The pit bull mix whined in response and looked out the window. "I know. I miss her too. She'll be here soon."

Alek looked out the window at the swirling snow. Every day it seemed to be getting a little colder and darker. Alek didn't want to think about Khadem's predictions. He finally had Gabi home. She was healthy, able to work again, and best of all, they were together. He wanted to plan for their wedding instead of planning for how to survive life in a perpetual deep freeze. Alek felt confident that, by combining the lab's expertise with the knowledge of the nation's climatologists, they could find a solution to this new climate problem. Right now, however, he had other priorities.

Alek grabbed some logs from the basket on the hearth, started a fire in the small kiva fireplace, and turned on some music. Then he returned to the kitchen to put the finishing touches on the green chile casserole he was fixing for dinner. The tangy smell of the chile wafted through the house. *Maybe we should try aromatherapy with green chile instead of lavender*, thought Alek. It would certainly be soothing for anyone who loved New Mexico the way he did.

Alek looked around the cozy little adobe abode. He had carefully chosen the Navajo rugs, the weathered leather sofa, the kilim pillows, but it was Gabi who made the house a home. When she moved in, she brought far more than belongings. This was where he and Gabi would make their life together. Tucked away in the Jemez Mountains of New Mexico among the pine trees, the casita was close enough to the lab for convenience but far away enough to feel like an escape. Though Gabi had decided to keep her apartments in Albuquerque and D.C. for when she had to leave town for work assignments, Los Alamos was where she chose to spend most of her time. Her presence had transformed the casita. With Max curled on the Sherpa blanket on the couch and the smell of dinner cooking, it certainly felt like home.

Max whined again and ran to the large window. Gabi had finally arrived.

Both Alek and the dog watched her pull her electric jeep into the gravel driveway in front of the house and stomp through the snow to the front door. Alek opened the door to welcome her in with a hug and a kiss as she slipped out of her snow boots and heavy coat. Max wiggled all over in excitement, and Gabi reached down to pat him without extracting herself from Alek's arms.

"What took you so long?" asked Alek. "Don't tell me, traffic was a bitch?"

"Actually, I had to make a stop. I had an appointment," Gabi said, pulling off her knit hat and shaking out her blonde curls. "Remember that thing we thought would never happen?"

Alek shrugged. "Lots of things we thought would never happen have happened in the past few years. We created an unlimited source of clean, affordable energy. We inadvertently started a neuropandemic. We invented a revolutionary device that treated the neuropandemic. We discovered the solution to the addiction problems caused by the revolutionary device we created. We defeated a crime syndicate run by so-called enhanced humans."

Alek sat down on the couch pulling Gabi down next to him. Max snuggled up and laid his big head on Alek's lap. "When you say, 'Remember that thing we thought would never happen,' I think, look at everything that's happened. Clearly anything is possible."

"You're absolutely right," said Gabi with a smile. "I'm pregnant."

Author's Note and Acknowledgements

The Dragon's Brain is the third book I have published. The first was a memoir of my time spent as the chief scientist of President Ronald Reagan's Strategic Defense Initiative, published in 2017. I based this non-fiction book, *Death Rays and Delusions*, on my notes from 1983 to 1986, chronicling Reagan's attempt (in his words) to "make nuclear weapons impotent and obsolete." During my two-year Pentagon assignment, I was supposed to conduct technical analysis and advise decision-makers. Instead, I discovered that my real job was public relations, explaining a complex, mostly psychological, economic, and slightly technical program to a worldwide skeptical audience.

After completing *Death Rays and Delusions*, I realized that much of what I'd written sounded more like fiction than fact. So, in 2020, I decided to try my hand at writing a techno-thriller loosely based on my real-life experiences. Thus, *The Dragon's C.L.A.W.* was born.

When writing fiction, I enjoy the freedom to invent slightly plausible science and technology that could never pass the test of any technical review. Letting my imagination go free without restraints is fun, but I think it also leads to new ideas and sparks creativity. So many real scientific concepts and achievements first existed merely as science fiction. Science fiction writing has inspired many real scientists to dream of new possibilities, moving fiction to fact.

My fiction-writing career wouldn't be possible without the invaluable support of my daughter Jill Gibson, who helped with character development, plot, and dialogue; my publisher Geoff Habiger, who in addition to publishing the book served as a skillful content editor and science advisor; and my wife Jane Yonas, who is always my first reader and most patient, insightful critic. Thanks also go out to Derek Weathersbee for designing a fabulous cover for *The Dragon's Brain* and creating the Project Z website, https://projectzbooks.com/. Last, but certainly not least, I am grateful to all my colleagues, friends, and fellow scientists who have served as early readers, have provided tips and suggestions, and have supported my new adventure by buying my books. Who would have thought I could start a new career (okay—a new hobby if you consider my earnings) in my eighties!

In writing *The Dragon's Brain*, I was captivated by the unfolding discoveries, character transitions, and global conflicts that emerged both in the novel and in the world around me. I think we will all agree that the past few years have been... interesting. I am always amazed at the eerie way current events often mirror the fictional world of my books. As with *The Dragon's C.L.A.W.*, *The Dragon's Brain* ended with many unanswered questions. And, as you may have already guessed, the next installment in the Project Z series is now underway.

In closing, I want to thank you for reading—a novel is nothing without readers. Finally, my unending gratitude goes out to all the real scientists who are solving the wicked problems and keeping the world safe. Keep building that knife.

About the Author

Dr. Gerold Yonas served as the acting deputy director and chief scientist during the implementation of the Strategic Defense Initiative, also known as Ronald Reagan's Star Wars Program. He has consulted for numerous national security organizations including the Defense Science Board, DARPA, the Air Force, the Army, the U.S. Department of Energy, and the Senate Select Committee on Intelligence. He is a Fellow of the American Physical Society and a Fellow of the American Institute of Aeronautics and Astronautics and has received many honors, including the U.S. Air Force Medal for Meritorious Civilian Service and the Secretary of Defense Medal for Outstanding Public Service.

Yonas has published extensively in the fields of intense particle beams, inertial confinement fusion, strategic defense technologies, technology transfer, and "wicked engineering." After his time leading the Strategic Defense Initiative, Yonas went to work for Titan Corporation in San Diego, where he managed a group of small research companies. Three years later, he returned to Sandia National Laboratories to lead the pulsed power fusion program and several weapons related programs in the role of vice president of Systems, Science and Technology. At Sandia, Yonas went on to create the Advanced Concepts Group and explore new opportunities including brain research.

Following his retirement from Sandia, he joined the Mind Research Network as the director of neurosystems engineering where he explored the link between neuroscience and systems engineering. He also developed a graduate course in this field and taught as an adjunct professor in the Department of Electrical and Computer Engineering at the University of New Mexico. Yonas holds

Yonas

a Ph.D. in engineering science and physics from the California Institute of Technology and a bachelor's in engineering physics from Cornell University, where he also received a varsity lightweight crew letter. He is married to his high school sweetheart, Jane, and is the father of two daughters, Jill and Jodi, and the grandfather of five children—Libby, Jenna, Jonathan, Emily, and Ben. Yonas makes his home in Albuquerque, New Mexico.